WHO IS THE PET AN

Everyone has a soft spot for some kind of pet, whether actual or virtual. But when is a pet not a pet? What sorts of pets will become part of our households in the future? Here's your chance to meet an extraordinary future menagerie, some of whom may bring you joy and some of whom may scare you away from "pets" forever:

"Objects of Desire"—The skewlis was the in-pet right now and Kirby really wanted one—but sometimes getting what you think you desire can turn out to be very different from what you expect. . . .

"Not Exactly a Dog"—Stan had seen the poddlings when they arrived. He knew what they were really like. But how could he convince the rest of the world?

"ThenAgain"—Some people were meant to be losers, and Simon was certain that he was one of them—at least until he received a very special legacy from his grandmother. . . .

ALIEN PETS

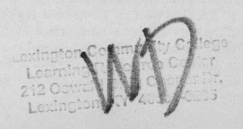

ALIEN PETS

EDITED BY

Denise Little

DAW BOOKS, INC.
DONALD A. WOLLHEIM, FOUNDER
375 Hudson Street, New York, NY 10014

www.dawbooks.com

ELIZABETH R. WOLLHEIM
SHEILA E. GILBERT
PUBLISHERS

DAW TRADEMARK REGISTERED
U.S. PAT. OFF. AND FOREIGN COUNTRIES
—MARCA REGISTRADA
HECHO EN U.S.A.

PRINTED IN THE U.S.A.

40349002

ACKNOWLEDGMENTS

Introduction © 1998 by Denise Little.
Objects of Desire © 1998 by Nina Kiriki Hoffman.
What Fluffy Knew © 1998 by Kristine Kathryn Rusch.
Diamonds © 1998 by Michelle West.
Not Exactly a Dog © 1998 by Bruce Holland Rogers.
Winner Takes Trouble © 1998 by Jane Lindskold.
ThenAgain © 1998 by Gary A. Braunbeck.
Bongoid © 1998 by David Bischoff.
As the Robot Rubs © 1998 by Dean Wesley Smith.
Dog Is My Copilot © 1998 by Karen Haber.
A Boy and His Alien © 1998 by John Helfers.
The Pet Rocks Mystery © 1998 by Jack Williamson.
In the Storm, in the Stars © 1998 by Paul Dellinger.
Every Home Should Have One © 1998 by Tim Waggoner.
Elmer © 1998 by Peter Crowther.
Watchcat © 1998 by John DeChancie.

CONTENTS

INTRODUCTION

Denise Little

IT'S a rare person who hasn't craved a pet at some point in life. Whether you wanted a cat or a dog, a fish or a parrot, a snake or a ferret, a hamster or a tarantula, odds are you wanted something—a creature to share your life that wasn't exactly human. A bundle of alien intelligence and emotion waiting for you every day when you got home.

And it's amazing what humans throughout history have gone through to satisfy that urge. Hunters and explorers from the dawn of time have brought back living gems, souvenirs from the untamed places, and made them part of the family—pets who serve, guard, amuse, and accompany us as we go through our days.

The relationship isn't just a one-way street, either. For all the control we think we exert over our pets, we are not always in charge. I'm owned by two cats. I know exactly who is running things at my house, and it isn't me. The pets in question are currently sitting on my keyboard, objecting to the writing of this introduction. I could, they tell me, be spending my time much more constructively by, for example, petting them. That's their opinion, and they're sticking to it.

Our pets put other worlds within our reach. They make us look at our lives from their point of view, make us see ourselves as they see us. They offer us a window into the realms they come from—a magical touch of the wild places they once, way back in the gene pool, called home. They release us in some important way from the narrow boundaries of our existence. And as our boundaries expand, so, too, have the varieties of pets we keep.

It only takes a very small leap of imagination to wonder what joys await us in the future when we roam the galaxy, or even now, if the galaxy decides to roam to us. What amazing and alien creatures will be curled up in our laps then, running our lives, making us laugh or cry, and letting us know if the quality of our company isn't up to their standards?

In this volume, fifteen superb writers have turned their attention to that very question. In a glittering collection of stories about alien pets, these fine writers spin tales of the wonderful, the terrifying, the fabulous possibilities of all kinds of creature companions. So turn the pages of this book and open your hearts and homes—there's something waiting there just for you. . . .

OBJECTS OF DESIRE

Nina Kiriki Hoffman

Nina Kiriki Hoffman has been pursuing a writing career for fifteen years and has sold more than 150 stories, two short story collections, two novels, *The Thread that Binds the Bones*, winner of the Bram Stoker award for best first novel, and *The Silent Strength of Stones*, one novella, *Unmasking*, and one collaborative young adult novel with Tad Williams, *Child of an Ancient City*. Currently she almost makes a living writing scary books for kids.

EVERYONE was getting skewlis. I wanted one so much it hurt.

I didn't know about trends. I hated that when three of my friends got black high-top shoes with light-up lightning bolts on them, I wanted my own pair *sooo* much. I mean, why should I care? It was like some chip in my head switched on and said WANT. It kept digging at me until I whined at Mom.

She used to just give me whatever I wanted, but since her job diminishment, she couldn't afford to do that anymore.

Sometimes she talked to me about worldview, global

perspective, how we were small in something giant and we had to work with all the other things to get along okay, and when I listened hard enough, I could shut the WANT chip off.

Sometimes she just said, "Kirby, shut up about it now," but the chip kept sending the WANT message. It was hard to ignore.

So anyway, people at school started showing up with skewlis. Sort of a cross between a weasel and a cat: skewlis had round heads with cute pointy ears and big eyes, slinky arms and legs that wrapped around your arm, and long bodies that bent when your elbow bent. They came in designer colors and patterns like Blue Razzberry and Circuitboard and Seawave. Smart enough to fetch, open cupboards and drawers, learn cute tricks, and accomplish small tasks. Motivated by specially engineered snacks that kept them willing and docile. Guaranteed by the F.P.A. to not be usable as weapons.

Pretty soon most of my friends and a lot of other kids were walking around with skewlis heads on one shoulder or the other, skewlis bodies doubling the width of one arm. People looked like mutants. Honto cool mutants.

The best skewlis brands had tons of max-excellent options. You could computer-blend a color scheme and the company would build you a skewlis to match. You could pick traits like "makes musical noises" or "will act as alarm clock." My friend Pati got one that would hold her bookscreen for her while she read, and press the text-scroll icon when she nodded.

I didn't want a skewlis at first. They were just too weird and creepy.

But after almost everybody I knew got one, I started feeling odd without that extra head on one shoulder, that widening of one arm, that pair of jewel eyes watching everything. I felt deformed.

So when Grandma got me a skewlis for my birthday, I was glad.

My fourteenth birthday party was nothing like my

thirteenth birthday party had been. Between this year and last year, Mom lost her big job and had to take little ones, so I couldn't have a huge party and invite tons of friends over.

Mom, Grandma, and I sat around the kitchen table. Mom had managed to get enough meat for us to have my favorite, beef stew, and Grandma had baked me a small square cake and covered it with strawberry frosting. Which was a great switch from basic rations. No matter what color or shape they make base, it all tastes pretty much like cardboard.

After we ate dinner and the cake and said how great it tasted, I opened my two presents: a new pen with temperature-sensitive skin that changed colors, and a silver shirt with a hologram of my favorite band on the front. Both of these presents were things I really liked. I throttled the little voice inside that whined because I didn't get more. I said a lot of thank-yous and hugged my presents and figured that was it.

Then Grandma brought the carry-cage out from under the table. A faint smell of lemons and incense came from the cage.

She set the carry-cage in front of me.

For a second I couldn't breathe. I knew we couldn't afford what I really wanted. Maybe she had gotten me a kitten. That would be okay. If Mom said it was, anyway. I would need to get extra after-school jobs so I could buy catfood.

I leaned forward and opened the door of the ribbon-wound carry-cage.

The skewlis emerged slowly. At first I thought it was gray, and I felt a flicker of disappointment. At school, people fussed most about skewlis with bright colors: turquoise, cotton-candy pink, acid green with baby-blue stripes. This one looked dull in comparison.

Then light glanced off it, and I saw that it was a soft lavender color. Its huge eyes glowed orange-red. Its front feet looked just like little black hands. It came out onto the table among the tempconfetti and torn gift wrapping, then sat back and stared up at me.

I stared back, wondering what it was thinking. What did any pet think confronted with a new owner? *I have to spend the rest of my life with you whether I like it or not? Amuse me? Oh, no?*

It lifted one small black hand and held it palm outward toward me. Confused, I lifted my own hand in answer and slowly brought it forward.

The skewlis touched its palm to mine. Its hand felt hard and small and hot. My hand tingled around its touch. It made a chirring noise, jumped over my hand, and clamped its arms around my upper arm, bringing its head up beside mine. Its lemony smell grew stronger for a second, then faded. The tip of a pink tongue flicked from its mouth. Its orange eyes stared at my face from unnervingly close.

It seemed to weigh almost nothing. The grip of its arms and legs around my arm felt weird for a moment, but then I stopped noticing. I turned to Grandma. "Thank you," I whispered. "Thank you."

"Oh, good," she said. "I hoped you would like it." She hesitated, then said, "It's not one of the famous brands."

Grandma was a veteran bargain hunter. She specialized in factory seconds, reconditioned obsolescence, open box returns, and "that stain is so small no one else will ever notice it, but they knocked five dollars off anyway." I used to think she was funny and irritating about that stuff, but lately I'd been trying to learn how she did it.

The best skewlis on the market had small seven-pointed stars branded onto their hind legs. There were two other acceptable brands, but after that, you got into the gray area of copycat skewlis. Rip-off companies put together inferior versions. I'd heard about near-skewlis fakes and their problems.

I didn't want to think about that on my birthday, when my grandmother had just given me the perfect present.

My skewlis had a brand I'd never seen before, a little blue spiral almost hidden by the silver-lavender fur on its hind leg.

"It's all right," I said.

"It doesn't have any of those fancy features," she continued, looking worried.

"It's great, Grandma," I said. "It's perfect. Thank you." With the skewlis so close to me now, I could see a very faint tiger-stripe pattern in blue over the silvery lavender of its coat. My skewlis looked like a ghost-version of others I had seen, and I thought it was really honto neat.

"What will you call him, Kirby?" Mom asked me. Her voice had a familiar edge to it. Grandma had done something important without asking her again. Mom was mad. But it was my birthday, and she didn't want to be the bad guy.

I stroked my finger over the top of the skewlis's head. It closed its eyes and chirred. "Her name is Vespa," I said in a small voice.

Vespa opened her eyes to stare into mine. Her chirrs grew louder. I didn't remember any of my friends' skewlis making noises like this, but it sure made me feel warm and strange.

"Vespa?" Mom said. "You're naming her after a scooter?"

"Huh? I don't know what you mean. It's just her name."

"Oh," she said. She smiled and shook her head.

I looked at Grandma. "Is there a manual? How do I take care of her? What do I feed her?" I thought about the special food my friends fed their skewlis: small soft brown cubes. I wondered how expensive it was. Probably really expensive, the way most designer stuff was. Had Grandma bought some? Was Vespa hungry now?

Grandma licked her lips, looking away from Mom's accusing stare. "There's no manual," she said. "The man I got her from told me she'll eat what humans eat, and she just needs a little box with sand in the bottom to do her duties in. Always give her access to fresh water, and bathe her about once a week with water and baby shampoo. He said . . . he said she'll teach you what she needs." She reached under the table and brought up a small sack of cat litter and a high-sided plastic tray. "For starters," she said.

"Thanks!"

Vespa rubbed her head against the side of my head. Her fur was exquisitely soft. She smelled so good. Lemon, stick incense, fresh bread.

There wasn't much left of dinner, it had all been so good. I pressed cake crumbs together and held them up in my hand. Vespa reached out, grabbed a handful, and sniffed them, then ate them. She chirped.

"You can keep the carry-cage," Grandma said.

"Thank you, Grandma. It's a terrific present. Thank you." I glanced at Mom. "I'll get more babysitting jobs. I'll make enough money to feed her," I said. "She's so little, I bet it won't take much."

Mom's frown softened. "Oh, Kirby, it's not that."

Whatever it was, I didn't want to hear about it now. I just wanted to be happy for a little while. "Thanks, everybody, for the best presents and a great meal," I said.

I didn't even have to rack the dishes that night. I took my new things up to my room.

I only thought for a little while about the mountain of presents I had gotten last year when we could afford a big party, when Mom had loved getting me anything I wanted. A lot of those presents were broken and gone now, and a few I had sold so I could get some honto rad school clothes this year instead of the basics that Mom could afford.

I still had my lightning-bolt shoes from last year. Nobody in my class except me wore them anymore, but I still liked them, even though the batteries in the bolts were almost dead and the lightning only flickered when it rained.

It had been kind of weird not following everybody else from one trend to the next since Mom's downgrade. I watched how much I wanted something when all the other kids got it, and I watched how much I didn't want it two or three weeks later when they had moved on to something else. I felt like I was getting this figured out.

Until I got *total* skewlis envy, no matter how hard I tried to pretend I thought they were creepy and weird.

But so what? Grandma had done it! She'd managed to get a skewlis for me, who knew how! I didn't have to fight my longing anymore.

I glanced at Vespa. Her furry cheek was close to mine. She scanned my bedroom with fire-orange eyes. Warmth spread through me.

What if everybody had already moved on from skewlis to something else? What if, when I got to school tomorrow morning, I was the only one with a skewlis?

Vespa turned and stared into my eyes. I remembered how much I had wanted a skewlis, even though I knew there was no way. This time I didn't want my wanting to fade. I had Vespa. I needed to keep on wanting her, for both our sakes.

She reached out a tiny black hand and patted my cheek. Her fingers were warm. She grasped my earlobe, stared at it and muttered small sounds more like bird-chirps than purrs. My throat tightened for a moment. I felt amazingly happy.

I filled a cup with water in the bathroom and showed it to Vespa. She jumped down off my shoulder and drank three cups full. I also set up the litter box and showed it to her. She stared at it for a long moment, then looked at me sideways. I wasn't sure what to think. What if she had never used a litter box before? Was she even housebroken?

Oh, well, deal with that tomorrow, if I had to.

Vespa jumped up onto my right arm. I patted my left shoulder, and after a moment she crept across my shoulders and locked onto my left arm. I cleaned my teeth and washed my face right-handed, with her still clinging to me. I wondered how we would sleep, or how I'd even change into the mega T-shirt I slept in.

But she responded when I patted the bed: jumped down off my arm and curled up, watching me change into my T-shirt. I went into the closet to hang up my clothes, though, and the instant I was out of her sight she made loud beeping/clicking noises that sounded sort of like a burglar alarm. I ducked back into the room and stared at her.

"Che, che," she scolded, reaching one hand out to me and frowning with her eyebrows. She looked like the ruler of the world.

Did all skewlis act like this? I wished I had documentation. Or that I could go downstairs and log on and look for information. But I didn't want to walk in on Mom and Grandma fighting.

I could ask people at school tomorrow.

I slid under the covers and waved the light out. A second later it lit again. Vespa held her hand out to it. She stared at the light for a moment, then looked at me. Her eyes looked spooky with the light coming from the side; small green moons floated in their centers.

Then she bounded up the bed until she was on the pillow next to my head. She held up her arm and waved the "lights-out" signal, and my room darkened.

I listened to her breathing, smelled her lemon-and-fresh-bread scent. I felt keyed up. I couldn't remember how smart my friends' skewlis had been. Could a skewlis figure out complicated cause-and-effect from just seeing it once? Maybe Vespa had learned that light switch trick somewhere else.

She purred.

I'd heard skewlis make all kinds of noises. I'd never heard one purr before. Before I could consider that, though, I got sleepy. The purring sounded so fine and reassuring. Like, "All's right with the world."

* * *

I opened my eyes the next morning and felt Vespa's
hands on my forehead. She let go a second later, so I
wondered if I had dreamed it.

When I went into the closet to get my school clothes,
she followed me in. She clasped her arms and legs
around my leg, scolding at me. I wondered if I was going
to like close attention in such big doses.

Vespa shared my breakfast bars with me, and took a
sip of juice concentrate.

What was I going to do about the litter box situation at
school? Maybe somebody would explain it to me.

In the halls before school started, skewlis were still
everywhere. My friend Pati rushed up to me and compli-
mented me on Vespa. I looked at her baby-blue-eyed,
pink-and-green-checked skewlis (named Ramtha) and
realized I liked Vespa's coloring much better. Not that I
said anything about it. Other friends gathered around and
stared at Vespa, checked her brand, nodded to me as if I'd
managed to squeak into their club.

I noticed five or six kids in the hall with black buttons
big as hands on their jackets. Colored letters, kana, and
sanskrit flashed across the buttons, not making words,
just pulling at my eyes.

"Oooo," said Pati, and raced off to inspect one of the
buttons.

I noticed the kids with buttons didn't have skewlis.
Well. *The Next Hot Thing is here,* I thought.

Vespa patted my forehead. I didn't remember other
skewlis doing that to anybody.

But it was strange. The WANT chip had switched on
in my brain as soon as Pati ran away to look at buttons,
even though I thought I had killed that chip by getting
Vespa. I mean, I really thought I had killed that damned
chip. What could be better than Vespa?

Stupid black buttons that didn't even make words?

I saw Rico smile as two girls asked him about his
flashing button.

Vespa patted my forehead.

And the WANT chip switched off.

It was just school, and I hadn't done all my homework yet because I had celebrated my birthday by not making myself do the subjects I hated. I ignored the bright new buttons and plowed past everybody to get to study hall.

After school Pati and Arco and I walked through the downtown maximall, windowshopping. Pati and Arco went into Everything Matters to look for belts. I didn't go inside. I love that store so much. I always see stuff I want, want, want and can't afford. It's easier for me to just stay out of it and not know what I'm missing. So I wandered over and looked at the food court instead, which was also not a good idea. Vespa and I had shared three lunch bars, and I wasn't hungry at all. But I saw a creampuff with chocolate on top. WANT.

Vespa patted my forehead.

Unwant.

Even though I could almost taste that creamy filling, the nice flaky, buttery pastry texture, the cold, hard bittersweet chocolate shell . . .

Vespa patted my forehead again, and I stopped craving.

Dazed, I wandered into Everything Matters. Glass earrings with little eyeballs in them. Pendants made of splattersteel, jingling and throwing off light. Shoe gewgaws with colored gems all over them. The latest in cutaway gloves. Dice chains, fake eyebrow and nose piercings, and a whole row of wide leather belts with small copper and steel shapes grommeted to them.

WANT.

Pat, pat. Unwant.

"Look," Pati cried, showing me a belt. Gold weave with green gems.

"Pretty," I said as she twisted it around her waist. Her skewlis clung to her arm, but didn't seem to be paying attention.

"No, really," Pati said. "Do you think it's me?"

"It's *so* you," Arco said. "Ja? What about this?" She

held up a scarf with concentric black and red circles on it, then twisted it around her orange-streaked blonde hair. "Moi?" Her butter-yellow, tiger-striped skewlis seemed passive, too.

"Def," Pati said.

Last time I had come in here with Pati and Arco and a couple of other girls, I had been so jealous of their credit ratings I couldn't think straight.

I narrowed my eyes and studied Arco. "Not," I said. "*So* not."

"Honto?" Arco said.

"Too down," I said. It did darken her whole look. "You're an up girl."

"Huh," said Arco. She put the scarf back.

She and Pati experimented with other things in the store. I watched, feeling Vespa's hand on my forehead every once in a while, almost before I knew I was getting sick with wanting again. The want kept going away. I felt a little dizzy and strangely good.

I went outside and over to the window of the leather store. There was a baby-blue suede jacket I had been craving for two weeks. I stared at it and felt nothing, even though Vespa didn't touch my forehead.

I had to sit down.

What was my skewlis doing to me?

I glanced at her. Her head turned as she watched people go by. She seemed fascinated by everything.

I watched, too. Lots of people had skewlis grafted to their arms. Most of the skewlis looked tranced or dazed or asleep. None of them patted their people's foreheads. They just looked like . . . accessories.

"What are you?" I whispered to Vespa.

Her orange eyes stared into mine for a long moment.

Then Pati and Arco came out of the store, loaded down with plastic shimmer bags full of stuff. "Let's get pastry!" Arco said, and we went to the food court.

Pati treated me. She'd been doing that since Mom's

diminishment. She never said anything about it. She was a good friend.

I gave Vespa a chunk of my brownie.

"Ack!" Pati said. "You're not supposed to do that!"

"Huh?"

"You're never, ever supposed to give them human food," she said. "It kills them."

Vespa ate her piece of brownie in three small neat bites, then licked her delicate black fingers and looked at Pati.

I said, "I didn't get any documentation. Grandma said she was supposed to eat human food. That's all I've fed her, and she hasn't died yet."

Arco shook her head. "That's *so* wrong. First thing in the manual is a great big warning to never feed them anything but their cubes." She broke off a piece of her raspberry doughnut and offered it to her skewlis, who gasped and shook its head. "Yours is weird," Arco said.

I stroked my hand down Vespa's back.

I knew she was weird.

I just didn't know how or why.

"I mean," Pati said. "Not that she isn't neat, or anything." Her face said one thing while her mouth said another.

"I like her a lot," I said.

Both my friends looked glum and uncomfortable.

Oh, no, I thought. Not now.

They had stuck by me when Mom diminished. Pati even loaned me stuff that wasn't the latest, but was the next latest, so I wasn't too far behind and people weren't ashamed to be with me. Was my in-ness going to disappear just because my friends thought my pet was strange?

Vespa touched my forehead and I relaxed. Why want? Why fight? It would be all right.

"Eww," said Arco. "It keeps doing that."

"I like it," I said. Though I wasn't sure I did.

Arco's eyes narrowed a fraction. I felt her going away from me. It made me feel dizzy. Like she was on a motorcycle, looking back over her shoulder, and I was standing in the road. I would never catch up again.

I checked Pati to see if she was going away, too. She smiled. "Maybe she's the new, improved kind."

I tapped the table with my free hand and Vespa dropped off my arm. She sat on the table in front of me and looked up into my eyes.

"Eww," said Arco. "You let her on the table? That you eat off of?"

"Huh?" There was so much I didn't know about skewlis care. I thought back to the scene in the cafeteria at lunchtime. People still wore their skewlis. In fact, the skewlis acted kind of like clothes, even in gym class. People ate with them on, did track with them on, played tennis and baseball. . . .

I looked around. People at neighboring tables had skewlis. But the skewlis stayed on their arms even as they talked, gestured, used chopsticks or forks or spoons. What was the difference whether the skewlis was on your arm or on the table? I couldn't figure out Arco's distaste. And then I realized.

Nobody else took their skewlis off where you could see it.

I tapped my left shoulder, and Vespa climbed up to lock herself on my left arm.

"She's . . ." Arco said. Her face pinched into a thoughtful frown. "She thinks too much." She shuddered, her yellow skewlis riding it out with flat, uncomprehending eyes.

Vespa blinked and looked down.

The rest of the afternoon she acted like all the other skewlis I could see.

Dumb.

When we got home, though, we could be alone. Mom and Grandma were still out. I sat down in the kitchen, where no trace of last night's party remained. I tapped the table, and, after a glance at me, Vespa dropped down.

Grandma and her bargain-sniffing ability. Huh.

"You're not really a skewlis, are you?" I asked.

Vespa wandered across the table, glancing at the salt and pepper shakers. She touched the napkin holder, then paced around the edge of the table and ended up in front of me, exchanging gazes.

Finally she shook her head.

"Not really a skewlis," I said again. "What are you?"

She sat. She patted the table in front of her with one little black hand. Confused, I stared for a minute. Then I put my hand palm up on the table.

She put her hand palm to palm with mine, and I felt a strange tingling again.

Then it was like she talked to me, but not with words, exactly.

You're my test, she told me.

"Your test?"

My . . . experiment. My . . . guinea pig.

I felt totally creeped out then. My skin crawled. The hairs on my arms stood up. Every mad scientist movie I'd ever seen started playing in my head at the same time. "It's alive. ALIVE!"

Vespa tapped my palm. I shuddered and shook my head, then stared at her. She was just some weird little animal, not a mad scientist. Just some kind of computer glitch, probably, a rip-off skewlis whose dealer prep had misfired.

It was hard to believe that when she looked so . . . smart. Perfect. Not wrong.

It had to be something else. But what?

Maybe she was someone's experiment, too.

She set her palm to mine again, and I stilled. *You're driven so by want,* she said.

Well, yeah, I thought. Duh.

All of you.

Everyone? It wasn't just me tortured and sliced open by wanting all these things that I usually couldn't get? I thought about Pati racing over to look at someone's shiny button that morning. I bet she knew by now where you could buy those things. She would have her own soon. Then maybe she'd stop wanting.

I was *so* sure. Of course she wouldn't. There would be the Next Hot Thing.

I licked my upper lip. "Okay," I said. "Let me get this straight. You're experimenting on me?" Silly. Idiotic. Scary, even.

She nodded.

"Like, how?" Not that I believed this for a second.

What happens to you when you don't have to want?

Sometimes I made myself sick, wanting things so much.

Today I had walked through Everything Matters, and I'd managed not to want anything in there.

With Vespa patting my forehead, anyway.

Everything in Everything Matters was sooo cool, sooo essential. Yet I didn't actually need any of it.

"What happens to me when I don't have to want?" I wondered out loud.

I don't know yet. Maybe . . .

Before she finished that thought, she snatched her hand out of mine. But I'd seen a swirl of strange pictures and thoughts. Earth from space. The bridge of a spaceship, or close enough, anyway, with lots of small blob-shaped people talking to each other and studying TV programs coming from Earth. An intense fear that these *wanting* people would want so much they would force themselves into space, searching for some elusive thing that wouldn't satisfy them long.

They would boil into space, these Earth people, scorching everything before them and leaving smoke and ash behind.

Unless.

Unless they could be taught not to want so fiercely.

Who would they be if that one thing changed?

Why not find out?

"Stay here," I said, jumping up. I ran upstairs to my

room and locked the door. Then I wrapped myself in a blanket and curled up in a corner to brood.

Kind of disgusting to think I was just some dumb rat in someone's maze. With, like, electrodes attached to my brain, zap, teach you not to have *that* impulse, zap, run this way, that way, zap, oops! Ha ha ha, let's get another rat.

Maybe this was just another thing that had happened because of Mom's diminishment. Only people with no money got bargain basement skewlis, which turned out to be alien mad scientists instead.

But Vespa was so much neater than all the other skewlis.

Sure. And she was playing with my mind. Stinging me in my want.

When I didn't really want to want things so much anyway.

Could she make it stop hurting?

But Arco thought it was weird that she patted my head. If she kept doing it, maybe I'd lose all my friends.

Maybe I wouldn't care, because I wouldn't *want* friends.

Ewwwww.

Maybe I'd turn into some kind of robot! Or a walking vegetable. Or just a giant chicken. Buck buck. Or a cow. Chew, chew, chew, moo.

Maybe I'd be happy.

Maybe I'd change into someone else completely.

Would that be so bad?

I thought for a while longer, then wrote myself a note.

DO YOU WANT TO GET OUT OF BED IN THE MORNING? IF YOU DON'T, STOP THE EXPERIMENT.

I taped it to the ceiling over my bed, then went downstairs.

Vespa was still sitting on the kitchen table, hugging

herself. She looked really worried. Not something I'd ever seen a skewlis do before.

I sat down in front of her, took a deep breath, let it out. "Here's what I want," I said. Then laughed. I started over. "What if this turns me into some kind of walking zombie? I don't want to be a walking zombie! I don't want to be dumber than I already am. I don't want to be a . . . a ghost or an empty person. Do you understand that?"

She nodded.

"I'd kind of like to find out what happens with this experiment too," I said. "But what if it turns out to be a diminishment? I'm scared."

She looked away for a moment, then turned back and nodded.

"If it's just turning me into some stupid goomer, I want you to stop and make it go backward! Can you do that?"

She closed her eyes and hunched her shoulders. She made some little thinking noises. She shifted from side to side.

Then she opened her eyes. She tapped the tabletop with her hand. I put my hand on the table, and she touched my palm.

I can't guarantee I can return you to a prechange state.

My mind startled up. Oh, no. Forget it. Tell her to leave right now. She can find another rat.

It might already be too late for that.

But—huh? I didn't feel changed at all yet. I checked. I was still totally Kirby. As far as I could tell.

I will promise to stop whenever you ask me to, Vespa thought, *and do my best to put wants back inside. You'll still be a little different.*

I took some deep breaths and let them out slowly. This was about the rest of my life. Even if we stopped tomorrow.

After a minute, I said, "Let's do it."

* * *

So it's been about a week.

So far what I notice is that it's easier to think. I'm not looking around all the time, distracting myself with thoughts about what I can't have.

I can still rent videos and choose clothes. I still hate green basic rations. I can still think about all the feelings I connect with wanting stuff and not being able to have it. I don't know. It's weird.

Everything happens in tiny pieces. I don't know if I'll know when to stop.

Maybe I won't care.

WHAT FLUFFY KNEW

Kristine Kathryn Rusch

Kristine Kathryn Rusch has worked as an editor at such places at Pulphouse Publishing and most recently *The Magazine of Fantasy & Science Fiction,* though she is currently a full-time writer. Current novels include *Hitler's Angel* and *The Fey: The Resistance* (Bantam, 1998). Her short fiction has recently appeared in *Once Upon a Crime, First Contact,* and *Black Cats and Broken Mirrors.* A winner of the World Fantasy Award, she lives in Oregon with her husband, author and editor Dean Wesley Smith.

FLUFFY knew she was a princess. Her person told her so. And Fluffy herself could see it, in her white, white fur, her long elegant whiskers, and her dainty paws. Fluffy had a soft bed that smelled of cedar. She had as much food as she wanted. People came to her house, and when she presented herself, they all spoke in awe of her beauty and petted her gingerly, as if they couldn't believe they were allowed to touch her sacred body. She bumped them gently to let them know that petting was preferred in her kingdom, and they usually responded with a laugh and a good ear rub.

Life was good. It didn't even matter that her people occasionally took in other cats. There had been other cats in her life as long as she was alive. She knew, however, that they weren't as great as she was. No other cat was as beautiful or as soft or as well loved. Other cats lived with her, and she tolerated them. She would have put up a large fuss, but her people had found a new palace, one with many rooms, and she rarely saw the other cats, except at feeding times.

Her routine was perfect in its simplicity. She spent her mornings in the kitchen waiting for someone to brush her, her afternoons sprawled on the couch in the warm sunshine, and her evenings on the nearest lap. Sometimes she watched the water droplets in the bathtub after her people took showers.

Nights were her special time. She prowled and explored, took food her people sometimes left near the sink, and occasionally slept on their soft bed. She was in her cedar bed at dawn just to make sure no one else used it, and then she was up, beginning her routine all over again.

Yes. It was a very good life.

Until *they* came.

"Please give the boys a thorough examination. I'll pay you extra. I know your time is limited when you do your house calls, and I appreciate the fact that so few vets do such a thing, but this has me bothered."

"Mrs. Winters, what's happened is tragic, but not uncommon. These adorable creatures are miniature lions. We think they're civilized, but they're not. And occasionally they remind us, often in particularly unpleasant ways."

They seemed to know who the weak ones were. Later, Fluffy found herself wondering: If she had known what *they* were going to do, would she have crushed *them* on that first day? Would she had stopped *them? They* were, after all, little bigger than a flea. But even fleas were hard to kill, weren't they? She had had fleas as a kitten, before she was elevated to her proper position, and she remembered the sudden sharp pain of the bite, the uncontrollable urge to scratch, the impossibility of catching a flea between your teeth. So perhaps she wouldn't have been able to do anything even if she had been paying attention. Even if she tried to stop the problem on the day it had started.

They went for her littermate, Streaker, and his little friend, Rook. Streaker's royal blood was diluted by his street tough father, a swaggering Tom that Fluffy barely remembered from her kittenhood. Her own father was a sweet white cat, a little on the fat side, just as her mother was. A "Pedigreed Pair," her former people used to say. The litter, they said to the people who would become her people, was ruined by the black-and-white kitten. A Tom had gotten to their precious girl at the right time. So they had to give the kittens away, unable to prove the purity of their bloodline.

Her people didn't care. They liked the black-and-white kitten with the impish streak, and they named him Streaker because he liked to run from one end of the house to the other for no apparent reason. He refused to show her the proper respect, slapping at her when she got in his way, or demanding that she give up her food. His little friend Rook, a long-haired tabby, showed many of the same behaviors. Rook was a stray her people had rescued, and to them he was kind. To her, he was as insensitive as her brother.

But she could avoid them—and often did. Streaker and Rook spent most of their time together, sleeping, eating, playing. She spent most of her time with her human companions, as it should be.

So the afternoon *they* appeared, she thought nothing of it.

* * *

"Yes, but they've never done anything like this before. I'm beginning to wonder if something's wrong—"

"Trust me, Mrs. Winters. We get complaints like this all the time when house cats show their animal natures. There's nothing wrong."

It was summer. Her favorite window was open, the one overlooking the garden and the birds. She could smell flowers, which sometimes made her sneeze; other cats, which always made her curious; and birds, which usually made her want to be slightly energetic, in a wholly disgusting way. She, as her people always told her, was a princess, and didn't have to kill her own food. The boys, as her people called Streaker and Rook, didn't quite understand that, but the other two cats, Starlight and Cupcake, did. They preferred to sleep and eat, just as she did, and fortunately for her, weren't as good at attracting caresses and pets.

She had been asleep in the sun below her favorite window when *they* arrived. Rook and Streaker were sprawled in the door, playing their nasty little game: Trap Fluffy. If she hissed at them, they would jump on her and pull at her fur. If she pretended not to notice, they would leave her alone and eventually grow tired of the game. She had decided not to notice, and the hot sun had put her to sleep.

A slight whirring sound woke her up. She sat up, stretched, and saw a tiny machine, rather like the ones her people watched on the box in the living room, a round machine that had doors and windows too tiny for any cat to use.

The fur rose on the back of her neck and she felt a hiss start in the back of her throat. But something warned her not to hiss. She didn't want to call attention to herself. Instead, she slipped beneath the couch, and watched.

The little door opened, and tiny human shaped creatures emerged. They were no bigger than ants. They spoke a strange language, stranger than the one her people used. It was much harder to understand. The creatures had other creatures held by silver threads—leashes as thin as spiderwebs and nearly as invisible. Fluffy watched as the bigger creatures unhooked the leashes, snapped their fingers, and pointed toward the door.

The smaller creatures flew across the room, like tiny flies on a mission. The larger creatures went back through the door. Fluffy heard a whirring sound, and the tiny machine was gone.

She adjusted her position under the couch, and saw the small creatures fly into Rook's left ear. Another group of them flew into Streaker's right ear.

And then the terror began.

"What about the alien virus?"

"Mrs. Winters—"

"Don't use that tone with me, Doctor. I've been doing some reading—"

"Tabloids."

"They mentioned it on CNN. They said that ever since those tiny spaceships landed—"

"There's no proof that those are spaceships, Mrs. Winters."

"—animals have been acting strangely. You told me yourself last month, when you gave Cupcake her shots that all sorts of strange things were happening to the animals in town."

"I was talking about illnesses."

"Well, so am I. Rook and Streaker haven't been acting normally, and I'm really worried about the other cats. . . ."

Rook let out a yelp like a cat in severe pain, and Streaker shook his head as if something were biting him. Then they ran in opposite directions, and Fluffy didn't see them for the rest of the day.

Of course, she had to go back to sleep. The spot under

the couch, despite the dirt, was much more comfortable than she had expected.

She didn't see the attack on the dog.

It was, or so her people said later in very excited tones, extremely strange. Their neighbor had brought his dog over when he came to get a package one of her admirers—the one who drove the loud brown truck— had left. Rook and Streaker bit the dog's legs and made him bleed before her people could pull them off. Her people apologized, but the neighbor got upset. Fluffy never did understand that part. It was just a dog, after all. She was more concerned about the smelly blood all over the kitchen floor.

Rook and Streaker licked it up, and smacked their lips as if they'd had a particular taste treat. Her male person had said it was fortunate the boys were up to date on their shots or the entire experience would have been a costly one.

The other cats chalked it up to Dog Phobia, but Fluffy didn't. She saw the look in their eyes. She had been their target many times, and she had never seen them look so sad after an attack. Usually they were gleeful. Instead, they smacked their lips and scratched their ears, and when they finally fell asleep, they whined.

A lot.

She made sure they were nowhere near her as she prowled and snacked later that night.

"One article, in the local paper, said a university researcher thought that the aliens were experimenting on mammals as test cases before they started experimenting on humans."

"Mrs. Winters, really."

"I know it sounds silly, but after what the boys did, I'm looking for any explanation. Please, Doctor. Take just a few moments. Examine them."

*   *   *

For the first three days, they tried to get outside, but her people were too fast for them. The boys were getting older and were well fed and didn't move as fast as they used to. Their people stopped them at the door, every time, usually with a foot blocking their way. And then they turned their attention on the other cats.

Cupcake, the obese Persian who wanted Fluffy's spot as princess of the house, found a hiding spot behind the dryer. Fluffy stayed close to her people because she knew the boys wouldn't attack her in public. But Starlight, the black-and-gold stray, wasn't so lucky.

The boys cornered Starlight behind the toilet, and had ripped out her throat before their people could stop it. Their male person took the boys and threw them in cat carriers. Their female person tried to save Starlight. She bundled her in a towel and took her to the Emergency Vet, a place Fluffy had—fortunately—never seen.

The boys spent the night in cages in the garage. Their people promised a Mobile Vet visit in the morning. Cupcake slept well for the first time in a week.

Fluffy woke once and shivered. The boys were wailing as if they had seen the end of the world.

"All right, Mrs. Winters. I'll examine them. But before I do, let me be blunt. Starlight was a very old, malnourished stray. She wasn't part of your cat family."

"Yes, she was."

"Not to the cats. And it might not have mattered even if they had known her well. Cats live in prides and have hierarchies. And one rule that exists from lions to barn cats is that the alpha male destroys the weak so that the rest have enough to eat."

"They have enough to eat."

"It doesn't matter. It's in the genetic code."

"We've taken in strays before and they've never—you know. Killed the cat."

"Maybe the other strays weren't as sick."

"You don't think you'll find anything, do you?"
"No."

Fluffy hated puzzles, and she really didn't like the boys. They harassed her and didn't give her the respect that royalty deserved. But she didn't like to hear anyone cry either. And her person was right: they hadn't killed Starlight. Those creatures inside them had.

She had to get those creatures out of the boys. And she had to do it without infecting herself or Cupcake.

The creatures had gone in the ear. The Mobile Vet had cold wet stuff that went in the ear. She had seen him use it on Starlight just last week. Maybe that would be enough to get the creatures out.

But how to tell her person and the Mobile Vet what she knew? They would think, if she wound around their legs, that she wanted pets. And even thought they thought themselves superior, they never had mastered Fluffy's language, not like she had mastered theirs. The problem was she couldn't speak it; she hadn't seen the use for it until now.

Her person had brought Streaker in from the garage. He had dried blood on his muzzle and his eyes were wide and dark. He looked like a cat in pain to Fluffy.

Her person put Streaker's cat carrier on the kitchen counter, and started to open the gate. Fluffy had to act now. She took a flying leap—something she hadn't done since she was a kitten—and landed on the Vet's medical bag.

He made a small sound, and her person spoke her name in that sharp reprimanding tone. Fluffy ignored her. Instead she scratched on the top of the bag until a corner of it pulled back. She put a paw under it, and clung as the vet tried to lift her off.

Instead, he helped her open the bag.

There were rows of needles inside, and lots of little vials. She tried not to watch when he worked on the other cats, and she could barely remember what he had done to Starlight's ear.

He hadn't used a needle. He had used a bottle. A small white bottle that liquid dripped out of.

She only had a moment. She batted a bottle aside, and it rolled along the floor. Then she wriggled out of the vet's grasp and jumped on the counter.

Her person reprimanded her again. Fluffy stopped in front of Streaker's cage and scratched her ear. He frowned at her. She scratched her other ear, and her person shoved her on the floor.

She landed with an unceremonious thump, and she had to pause to lick herself. No princess ever allowed herself to be shoved like that, not even in the name of justice.

From above, she heard the sound of a back foot thumping against a plastic cage.

Streaker had understood.

"They're too big to be ear mites."

"Then what are they?"

"I don't know. But I'm going to take them to the lab with me and investigate. I'll leave this vial with you. If you see any more of them, scoop them up and bring them to me. Don't let them near the cats."

"Should we do the other cats?"

"Probably. Yes. Get them. We'd best make sure this is taken care of. Something this big in your ear would be painful. We don't want it to happen again."

For her troubles, she was grabbed, held by the scruff of the neck, and had cold liquid shoved down her ear, with instructions to have the same procedure repeated until the liquid was gone. Both the vet and her person were pleased to see that no creatures came out of her ears.

And then they went off to find Cupcake.

Streaker looked at her from his cage. She looked back.

His eyes closed slowly. She had never seen a cat seem so exhausted—and so relieved.

"Doctor?"

"Mmm?"

"Are those bugs what made my boys kill Starlight?"

"I can't answer that for sure, Mrs. Winters. I don't know what these bugs are or what they do."

"But the boys, will they hurt my other cats?"

"Cats aren't like dogs, Mrs. Winters. Once dogs get a taste for blood, they usually must be kept outside or destroyed. Cats—the thing that your cats did—is natural. They hurt things one minute and cuddle with their owner the next. Will your cats be the same loving creatures you've always known? Of course. Will they hurt Cupcake and Fluffy? Not unless they get so sick that they're a threat to the pride. I would say that you separate your cats in the future when one of them gets ill. That'll ensure something like this will never happen again."

"So I can let them have the run of the house, and they won't hurt anyone again?"

"If you follow my instructions."

"I will. Oh, Doctor. How will I ever forgive them for Starlight?"

"Realize they're not human, and that human laws don't apply. What they did was right in the feline world."

"That doesn't work for me."

"Then blame it on the bugs."

Three days later, Fluffy was asleep in the sun beneath her favorite window. The boys were cuddled on the couch, still exhausted from their ordeal.

A whir woke Fluffy up. She rolled over and saw the tiny machine on the windowsill. The little door opened and the bigger creatures came out. They held tiny whistles in their hands.

The high-pitched sound woke up the boys. They glanced at Fluffy. She glanced at them. Then she reached up with one paw, and knocked the machines—and the bigger creatures—off the sill.

The boys jumped down beside her, and the hunt began.

It was Rook who discovered that if you bit one of the creatures halfway between its head and its feet and then threw it against the wall, it didn't move again. Streaker discovered that a paw through the door crushed the little machines.

But Fluffy was the one who figured out how to knock down the machines in mid-flight; Fluffy who figured out how to dodge the tiny rays of light that hurt more than a needle's prick; Fluffy who figured out how to flush the machines down the toilet so that they would be gone for good.

Because Fluffy knew that if the creatures and their tiny machines succeeded in taking over Rook and Streaker, they might take over her. And if they took over her, and discovered how wonderful her life was, it wouldn't be long before they sent for more little machines and sent bugs into the ears of her people. And once they had control of her people, they had control of the entire world.

And Fluffy couldn't let that happen. In this world, she was a princess. And she would remain a princess—even if it meant dirtying her paws to do so.

The creatures hadn't known what they were up against.

But Fluffy knew.

And Fluffy won.

Just like she knew she would.

DIAMONDS

Michelle West

Michelle West is the author of *The Sacred Hunter* duology, *The Broken Crown*, and *The Uncrowned King*, all published by DAW Books. She reviews books for the on-line column *First Contacts*, and less frequently for *The Magazine of Fantasy & Science Fiction*. Other short fiction by her appears in *Black Cats and Broken Mirrors*, *Elf Magic*, and *Olympus*.

HE was eight years old when he learned where real diamonds came from. Until then, he'd always thought they were dug up out of the ground same as any other rock; cut and polished until they shone and caught the sunlight or lamplight as they dangled.

But rocks weren't alive, not quite; they didn't sing with light; they didn't glow in the shadows as if they had their own little heartbeats. And he knew that his family's diamonds *did*. They were special.

Allister's Jewelry had always had the best diamonds in the entire country—which was big enough to be the whole world, especially as Andrew wasn't very good at geography. All of his parent's clients always said so.

Each gem, no matter the size or weight, was perfect; flawlessly cut and polished, and expertly set into gold or platinum. His mother and father were very proud of the business they'd built over the years.

He was the youngest of three children. His brother, Norman, was well into his second year living at the place where people become doctors, and his sister, Cynthia, was at University because she was going to be a lawyer. His parents were proud of them both.

There was even a wood-framed picture above the mantle in which his mother and father stood smiling down upon Norman and Cynthia when they were much younger. Old-fashioned thing, that picture, that frame; something his mother had liked because it reminded her of paintings. So few people did those nowadays; resources were scarcer at school and computers just *did* things that paper and brushes couldn't. One of those things was to spit out pictures, like this one. Norman's hair was fine-spun and golden, Cynthia's dark as raven wings. They had perfect teeth, happy smiles, and curled up little school awards in their hands. They were very proud to be Allisters.

Mother always said they would have to have a new picture taken of the "whole" family one day, but it never happened—his parents were always too busy, and Norman and Cynthia were now away doing important, adult, things. So the Allister family, frozen in frame above fireplace, beamed warmly into the future without Andrew.

Andrew was an accident. Norman told him that when he was four years old, and Andrew never forgot it, even though Norman apologized for it later. It had to be true, didn't it? Andrew wasn't very smart, he was short and almost fat, and he didn't have many friends. It wasn't just his absence from the picture that proved it.

It was winter before the spring; the snow came lightly, and quickly turned to brown slush anywhere it met foot or tire. The skies were crisp and clear; sunlight cast its sharp relief through empty branches. Night fell less heavily now.

And in the glaring light of day, it was easy to see that Andrew had been pushed down the walk after school. His new wool coat had lost a button—two, really, but he'd managed to find one—and was salted and stained with mud. His mother was going to be angry; he could hear her now.

"Andrew, Allisters *do not* fight with other children in the school yard! How many times must I say this?"

As if he could just tell Billy to leave him alone. His jaw grew white with frustration, dark with bruising. Very quietly, he pushed his way into the house.

His mother was nowhere in sight. It was the first bit of luck that he'd had all day. His socked feet were very careful as they trod across the tiled floor. If he could just get to his room, he'd be safe. He would tell his mother, through a closed door, that he was studying. Then he'd be left alone until dinner. He liked to be alone.

Tile gave way to the challenge of wood, which proved almost impossible to navigate; after all, the floors in *this* house creaked even when no one was walking on them. He moved like a man in slow motion, raising and lowering his feet with deliberate care; a moon walk across the surface of the impenetrable Allister house.

He made the stairs, which were carpeted. He made the upper hall, and still no one came to greet him. The room, his safety, was just four doors down. At the end. Beside the bathroom. He had taken his fifth step down the powder blue carpet when he had to reach out to steady himself, leaving evidence of mud on the wallpaper. Horrified, he tried to brush it off.

His mother began to speak. He stiffened, bit his lip, and began to turn, when he realized that the anger in her voice was not aimed at him. It came from behind the almost closed door of his mother's sitting room.

"It's just gotten so slow, that's all."

"I know, Mary," his father said. He sounded tired. Why wasn't he at work?

"We can't afford that at a time like this. Why has it stopped?"

"I don't know. I just don't know."

"Did you try to get in touch with him?"

"Him? Good lord, no. He's long gone, and he doesn't owe us anything. I don't think he'd be happy about the way things have turned out."

Silence now. "Well, at least we're still getting something. I hate to have to go farther." Her voice was stiff and businesslike; it was the one that Andrew hated most. The floor creaked as her feet fell heavily against it. It stopped, and Andrew waited for something to happen.

That was when he first heard it; its voice was soft and high, and the sound it uttered like lowing filtered through a delicate horn. It was an awful sound; so awful that he swung the sitting room's door full open and was bounding across the threshold before he could stop and think.

His mother and father both swung 'round to face him, but he had no eyes for them yet: All he could see was the cage on the floor. It was a small dog's cage, with bright, stainless steel bars—the best, as befit the Allisters. And behind those bars, backed against the farthest wall, something gray and furry was curled and shuddering. Its face was not like any that Andrew had ever seen; it was long but not like a dog's, and its eyes were half its face, rounded and open.

The sound stopped as Andrew reached the cage and the creature shrank farther back. Large lids closed over the eyes like hoods, and from the corner of one, liquid trailed down. It was bright and thick, and it sparkled with sunlight as it traveled through matted fur.

Andrew's jaw fell as the tear came to rest against the cage floor. It rolled a bit, rocked, and then stayed still.

Hard now. Cold, with no sun to touch it. He knew what it was without asking. He had seen its like hundreds, maybe thousands, of times in the workshop of his parents.

Wide-eyed, he stared at the trapped animal, and after a moment, it opened its eyes to stare back. Andrew saw his warped reflection in the darkness, and reached out until the cage bars stopped his fingers.

He got in trouble, of course. A lot of trouble. But in the end, and after a sharp slap given graciously by his mother, he was allowed to leave the room alive. He had had to promise, of course, but he did so easily—who would he want to tell?

Seeing as he knew about the little beast, his parents told him more: that they had had it now for almost as long as Norman had been alive. They had bought it from an odd old Visitor in the east end of the city—when the east end had looked much, much less reputable—and had discovered early on that it cried diamonds. Not diamonds in the traditional sense of the word—not things that came from South Africa's famed mines, or from the ground beneath the drills and carefully chosen fuses of geologists—but *Allister* diamonds; things with fire and substance and a structure that defied explanation. People paid money for them.

The Visitor who'd sold them the creature had been in a sorry state, and perhaps belonged in the east end; he'd been nervous and twitchy when disposing of the creature. Quarantine was an issue—but so was oddity. They had originally purchased it because they felt they could sell it to a zoo—or better—for a vast sum more than they'd paid. Didn't work out that way. The Visitor had disappeared; he was wanted; they were stuck with a creature that couldn't be sold without connecting them to whatever their imaginations came up with as his crimes.

And then it started to cry. The crying literally changed their lives.

In those days, at the beginning, it had cried often. Andrew's father was a jeweler, and he was overjoyed at those tears. He called them Stellar Diamonds, and then just Allister Diamonds, and together, he and his wife had set to work creating settings for the most perfect diamonds that either had ever seen. Those diamonds brought curiosity seekers, and jewelers the world over came with glasses and compound testers and detectives and whatever else you could think of. They were the Allister secret.

His mother and father bought their own shop, and two years later bought another, larger one in the city's heart. They bought a house, and moved, this time into the best area in midtown because there was less crime. They had had their children, sent them to the best schools, and looked forward to good futures for all of them.

Except that, in the last few years, the tears almost never came. It was harder and harder to get the little thing to cry; it was hard enough to get its attention.

"In the spring it's better," his mother added. "We can take a few sprigs and ragweed blooms from the valley. When we bring them here and show them to it, that often works." Her tone said she doubted it would, this year. She let her face fall into her perfect hands. "I don't know what to do, Andrew. If you have any ideas, anything at all, we'd be happy to hear them. Norman's in medical school. It's—we need the money for him."

Andrew's mother had never asked *him* for help before. He didn't know how to feel about it as he made his way to his room after dinner; even food had offered no solace and none of its usual comfort. He made his way to bed and sat in the darkness, staring at the little specks of almost-light against his closed lids. Outside, in the long stretch of carpeted hall, the wooden floorboards creaked; his parents were coming to bed.

The whisper of their words was an unintelligible rush

of sound, like seashells that trapped the ocean's roar. Worried. And maybe he could help them—if he could think of something that could make the gray thing cry. His parents would be happy then. His parents would be proud and grateful. His mother would hug him, and she'd take a special picture, and he'd have his place as an Allister so that everyone who visited could see it.

He turned over and felt the blankets brush his forehead as he curled up against the sheets and dragged his pillow under the covers as well. He used to cry a lot, when he was just a kid. But he'd grown out of it, and hardly anything made him cry anymore—not even Billy Brantford.

The next day, Andrew emptied out his penny bank and carefully counted out quarters, dimes, and nickels. Just in case, he rolled up pennies in two sets of fifty. It took him a while, because the ends of the roll kept falling out before he could catch them, but he persevered. He would try the first of his ideas.

School was an agony for him that day; he was chastised more than usual for not paying attention, and Mr. McClaren had asked him questions three times, just to make a point. He became determined to behave well so that he didn't earn a detention—it was important that he leave the school grounds the minute the bells rang.

He bought flowers. Not one flower; not even one single type. His mother had said that flowers made it cry at the beginning—so it only made sense that *a lot* of flowers would make it cry a lot. He waited patiently while roses, lilies, carnations, large daisies, and peonies were wrapped carefully in plain brown paper. The florist insisted that all of these colors just didn't match, but he took them proudly in his arms anyway, secure in the knowledge that she didn't understand his plan. Chin brushing a wild profusion of colors, he left.

When he got home, it was almost all he could do

to take his boots off before nearly flying through the kitchen and up the stairs. The flowers still looked new and fresh, but they'd wilt and die soon; they always did.

His mother was home, his father nowhere in sight.

"Andrew," she said, turning sharply as the banging door announced his presence in her sitting room, "We *do not* run in this house." Then, as her disheveled son stood panting in front of her, she added, "What on earth are you carrying?"

He froze then, the magic of certainty leaving him.

"F-flowers."

"Flowers? Why?"

"Well, you said . . . you said flowers made it cry."

"I said—" She opened her mouth in an 'o' of surprise that quickly soured into annoyance. "Do you think just *any* flowers will do? How stupid do you think your father and I are? If those flowers—who on earth sold you such a motley bunch?—would make the thing cry, we'd have the room full!"

Brown paper crackled limply in his hands as the flowers began to fall. He did nothing to stop them, and only looked down at his feet; his shoes were covered in petals and greens.

The phone rang, and his mother left him to answer it. He watched her walk into her sleeping room; saw the door swing shut behind her back. His mother's laughter rose and caught his ear, where the softness of her words could not. He wondered if she was laughing at him, or if she was being "polite" with one of the neighbors. Defeated, he picked up the flowers; his hands were shaking with half-formed anger. Quietly he walked to the cage where the gray thing lay, head curled on folded legs, eyes wide and unblinking.

It raised its head and craned a thick, furry neck forward. Andrew would have thought it impossible, but its eyes widened still more, until they took up half of its face. It was looking at the flowers.

Maybe, just maybe, his mother was wrong. He knelt, knees crushing pile, and carefully peeled away brown paper, freeing his bouquet. The furry little head stretched farther, and the nose began to wiggle. Approaching it as if it were a wild thing, Andrew opened the cage door a crack and tried to jam the flowers in. They didn't fit, and he hesitated a moment before opening the door fully.

The little thing didn't even move. Instead, as the flowers drew closer to its face, it opened its mouth and began to gently gum the petals. Shoulders sagging, Andrew closed the door, but even this was quiet. He stood, and his shadow must have disturbed the creature, for it looked up at him until its neck and its nose were in the same long line. A little, pink tongue crept out before it turned back to the flowers that lay in the cage. Very gently it laid its head on a peony and closed its eyes.

It would be just his luck, Andrew thought as he mounted the stairs that led to his parents' room. Instead of making the stupid thing cry, he had discovered, over the course of two weeks, that it seemed to be, well, happy when he visited. It wouldn't cry at all for him, and after the first two days, Andrew gave up trying. The little thing—fat, sluggish, and helpless—reminded him too much of himself. And he didn't want to be Billy Brantford to anything, especially not a dumb, helpless animal.

One that cries diamonds, a small voice said in his ear. *Mom says we'll starve without them.* He ignored it.

He carried a small bowl of oatmeal, bran, and other inedible "food" in one hand, and a glass of milk in the other. He had to be careful not to lose his grip on either of these as he took the stairs slowly and cautiously.

He opened the door to his mother's sitting room, and saw the cage immediately. It was closed, of course, but the little gray lump was behind its shiny bars, wide eyes unblinking as they stared at Andrew.

"Hi," Andrew said.

The creature stared.

"Never mind. I, um, I brought some food." He walked over to the cage and sat down heavily in front of it. "Does your hair fall out in the spring?"

The door swung gently on its well-oiled hinges. Andrew placed the bowl down at the edge of the cage. Only when he was sure nothing would spill did he add the milk and drag a spoon from his pocket.

It snuffled like a pig, it really did. And it ate like a pig as well, which was why Andrew left it in the cage until it had finished. "You're disgusting, you know that?"

On top of it all, it burped as it finished, a great, loud burp that anyone in the house couldn't help but hear. Then it pushed the dish away with its ample nose and looked out at Andrew once again.

Andrew sighed and reached into the cage for it. Picking it up, he carried it out of his mother's room and down to the den. He looked guiltily up at the grandfather clock in the hall, and breathed a sigh of relief when he saw the time. Neither of his parents would be home for at least an hour. Together, he and the nameless creature sat down to watch the 3V in the quiet, darkened room.

Or at least Andrew did; after a little while, the lump fell asleep in his lap, waking only long enough to shove its nose into the palm of Andrew's hand when Andrew forgot to keep stroking its fur.

Winter loitered, turning the bare bark of naked trees into little icicle arms. The air was cold, and Andrew was sick twice, although not so badly that he was allowed to stay away from school. School itself was endless and repetitive, with only a quiet Christmas celebration to break the monotony. Norman and Cynthia came home from school, but Andrew's mother and father never quite seemed to be happy; they were worried.

Norman tried to find out why, but his parents wouldn't tell him, and even if Andrew hadn't been sworn to secrecy, he wouldn't have told either. He didn't want to share his secret with anyone.

They went away as they always did, and the Allister family continued to trudge through snow and slush and the gradual warming of days. Only the little gray lump seemed content and almost happy with Andrew's afternoon visits. It even began to perk up during certain cartoons—a sure sign, in Andrew's mind, that it was intelligent.

"Mom," he asked, on a January morning that was much like any other, "do you think I could keep the lump in my room?"

"Why?" She was reading something that looked official, and she obviously didn't want to be disturbed.

"Well, it kind of smells bad sometimes, and I thought you'd rather it was in my room." He tried not to fidget with the cereal box; it only annoyed her. "I mean, I don't mind the smell."

She looked up from her work, and the creases in her forehead smoothed out slightly. "That's very thoughtful of you, dear." Her fingers rolled her pen against her thumb for a moment. "Are you sure you don't mind?"

He nodded.

"Well then, I'll see to it this evening. Thank you, Andrew." She tried to smile, but it didn't really reach her eyes, and she gave up on it a few minutes later.

The gray lump became a living, breathing teddy bear in Andrew Allister's bed. It was sort of fat, and Andrew discovered that it liked to sleep on the pillow. Well, in the center of the pillow. It took them three days to sort out who was boss—and Andrew asked his mother for another pillow the following day.

He read stories to the lump, and he discovered that the lump liked only certain ones: fairy tales; wild stories with endless fields and flowerings of wood magic. It didn't mind that Andrew stuttered, and it didn't appear to mind when Andrew didn't really know the right word and made one up instead. It would curl up in Andrew's lap and open its eyes so wide Andrew thought they would swallow its face.

It was happy, and in a way, in the quiet of his room, so was Andrew. He didn't even mind not being alone anymore, although he still didn't talk to many of the other children in school.

Winter passed, and the little lump didn't cry at all for his parents. He could tell that they were worried; they argued a lot in their room when they thought Andrew wasn't listening. His father stayed away from the house—he was working, according to his mother—and his mother stayed in her study. But he knew that things weren't well; the mailman would come, and his mother began to dread opening the mailbox. She would mutter something about bills, or schooling, and would grow even more strained.

Andrew asked it to cry once or twice, and it stood—well, sort of stood—on its hind legs and shoved its nose into Andrew's face. It didn't understand, and Andrew didn't know how to make it, so he gave up. If he couldn't make the lump cry, he couldn't—but he felt a little sorry for his parents.

Spring began to crawl into the town; spring and its endless run of rain and mud. Little green buds appeared on the trees and shot up through the dirt, and everywhere along the road people in dungarees knelt in the dirt, turning it with spades and thinking of the summer and fall. Andrew didn't understand it, and neither did his mother; that sort of work was meant for machines and sims. Especially in a neighborhood where people could afford them. But people liked dirt, he guessed. He'd seen too much of it, too close to his face, to want to join them.

The little lump still slept in Andrew's room, which was why Andrew noticed the changes in it. First, its hair started to fall out. Not neatly, like a dog's, but rather in thick clumps and patches that looked like small bramble bundles. It was full of energy now, and it would jump up at the cage when Andrew entered the room, eager to be let out to play.

At first.

But as the weeks turned into the end of the first month, it grew very quiet. It stopped eating, and stopped watching 3V. Instead, it would turn its face up to Andrew's and whimper mournfully.

"What's the matter, lump?"

The lump never answered, not with words. Instead, it would look up with unblinking eyes, and utter some animal sound in the back of its throat.

In the middle of April, Andrew and his parents went for a drive. He didn't ask them where they were going; both of them were too tense to be disturbed with his stupid questions. Instead, he dutifully got into the back seat of the car and let his father take him to their destination.

The city fell away like curtains from a window, leaving a view of the new green of trees along the highway. Here and there he could see the yellow-green of bushes that would eventually yield raspberries, and along the ditches, he could see the first of the ragweed rear its head. He opened the window so the roar of the wind's voice could properly fill his ears.

The highway became a packed dirt road, still wet from the previous night's rain, and the road led at last to a valley. Andrew's father stopped the car; the engine took a little while to die into near silence.

Silence? No. The air was alive with the sounds of insects and birds calling out their territory. The wind caught grass that was already too tall, and turned it into the sound of the sea—or at least the sound that Andrew thought the sea must make; he had never been to the ocean.

"Now," Andrew's mother said, as she too left the car, "come and help us."

He was pleased that they wanted his help, and listened as carefully as he could.

"We need to gather some small branches—like those—with little, new leaves. If you see any flowers, gather those as well. We only need a few, though, and we'd like to get back as soon as possible."

He nodded and left the car, wading into fields of unruly nature, his eyes looking for those things his mother had described. When he came back to the car, his hands were scraped and dirty, but they were full as well. She smiled tersely at him, called his father, and got into the car. They drove home in silence.

His parents were careful to leave their muddied shoes behind in the vestibule; Andrew mimed their actions. Together, they went up the stairs, his father first, his mother next, and Andrew trailing behind.

"This has to work," he heard his mother whisper to her husband's moving back. "It's spring."

His father had no answer, but his large hands gripped the railing tightly for a moment. They were both worried, both afraid. It made Andrew nervous, because his parents almost never were.

Instead of going to their own room, they went to Andrew's. The light switch brought lamplight into the shadows, and his mother walked over to the window to pull the curtains wide. In silence, they walked to the locked cage and knelt before it, holding their offerings in open hands for the lump to see.

It looked at them, backing into the far wall of the cage.

Andrew bit his lip.

"Well?" His mother asked quietly. Her voice did not have the usual softness of whisper.

His father opened the cage door and shoved the branches toward the lump. Then he pulled his hands back and shut the door again. He waited. The lump snuffled forward and nosed through the leaves. It stopped a moment at one of the flowers, and then began to low in a deep, sad voice.

Andrew's mother relaxed. Her shoulders seemed to tremble for a moment before she stood. His father caught her hand and held it tightly.

But the little lump didn't cry that day. Instead, it lowed sadly and tried to catch Andrew's eyes. Andrew was very frightened.

That night, the lump curled tightly into Andrew's arms. It didn't want the pillow; it didn't want the 3V; it didn't want stories. It whimpered, even in its sleep. Andrew threw out the weeds and branches, hoping to make the little lump feel better, but this didn't help at all. He held it, and stroked its fur, and stayed awake most of the night whispering into its little ears.

The next morning, early enough that the sun had barely touched the horizon, he heard them arguing. It was quiet enough at first, but it grew loud, and louder still. The little lump was awake and quivering in Andrew's arms, as if it had heard the whole thing from the beginning. It kept meeting Andrew's eyes and then hiding its face in Andrew's underarms. It was shivering.

Andrew placed it firmly down on the pillow and got out of bed. He got dressed quickly, and did his best to be quiet; it did no good to disturb his parents when they were angry at each other. But this morning the lump didn't want to be put aside; it cuddled up to his legs and stared at the wall from behind them. Andrew sighed and, after a moment, picked it up.

Then he left his room, swinging the door quietly forward until he could just get out.

"—but we don't have any choice!" This was his father's voice, loud and angry as only his father could get. "What are we going to do? What do you suggest?"

There was silence for a moment, and then his mother spoke. "We have to be careful, that's all. We don't want to hurt it too badly."

"We don't want to hurt it at all—but I don't see what else we can do. We can't frighten it anymore, you know that doesn't work. We can't even make it cry in spring— and that was always the best season for it. Look—"

He heard something slamming down, and jumped away from the door in a panic. After a moment, he returned to it, but he was very nervous.

"I know what they are. I just—"

"We don't have a choice, Mary. We have to do this. Norman's almost finished; Cynthia has a year to go. If we lose the business, sure we'll be fine—but what kind of live have we given our children?" Footsteps, but not close to the door. "Look, how much different is this from slaughtering cows? We eat beef all the time. And I know you—if it was a choice between killing a cow and watching our children starve, do you think killing a cow would be so hard?

"And we aren't going to kill it. We only need a few of its tears right now, that's all."

She sighed; even through the door, Andrew heard her. "I know," her voice was low and cracked, "And you're right. I won't hesitate here either—it's necessary. But—" She took a deep breath, "Will you explain it to Andrew?"

"He'll understand it when he's older."

But he understood it now.

He wasn't very smart, and he wasn't very quick— but he wasn't completely stupid either. He froze for a minute, but only a minute, as his parents continued to talk. Then, the lump tightly tucked under his shaking arms, he ran down the stairs.

He put the lump down for a moment, slid into his shoes, tied them and double-knotted them, and then picked it up again. Without another backward glance, he ran out of the back doors to the Allister house, and began to head down the road to the bus.

The lump quivered and looked up at him, but he didn't stop to comfort it—he was too close to his house, and at any minute now his parents might notice that he was missing.

Only when he got onto the bus, and ran the small debit card his parents had given him for school through the meter, did he wonder where he was going to go. He didn't have any friends in the city, or not any that he could count on, and he didn't think that he could get to where Norman or Cynthia were living. He didn't have any relatives here either, but that was probably better. Most likely they would just make him go home.

He walked awkwardly down the aisle of the bus, trying to ignore the people who stared at the bundle he held in his arms. He went right to the very back, and chose a seat close to the window. Then he stared out for a long time as houses drifted by, to be replaced by large, empty industrial buildings. They'd fill up soon, he was sure; the first of the cars were already arriving.

He rode to the very end of the bus loop, and got off. There, where what was left of conservation land met the very edge of the city, he began to walk into the rising sun.

He wasn't much good at walking, and his feet were already sore by the time the sun was mid-sky. But it wasn't very hot, and he didn't have to run, and the little lump was cooing contentedly in his arms. With every step he took, it seemed to get lighter and happier somehow, and he chose his direction by the thrum of its voice in the back of its throat.

Birds flew by, chittering in annoyance when he came too close to their new nests; insects crawled across the highway, made clear by the strip of yellow in the road's center. Clouds came and went, but remarkable few; it was a nice day to be running away from home.

He didn't know where he was going, and his feet got sorer. He wanted to take his shoes off, but the double knots were stuck that way, and he gave up fidgeting with them when the little lump began to butt against his rib cage. Sighing, he picked it up and continued to trudge down the road. It got later. He got hungry. His stomach made more noise than the lump.

He began to wonder where he was going to go, and how he was going to live. It made him nervous, but there was one good thing to be said for it: He wouldn't have to go to school again. The lump cooed happily, and it trembled in his arms. He had never seen it so happy—and he knew, without question, that it was happy.

It made him feel good, even though his legs hurt and his arms were now sore with the lump's weight. He couldn't remember a time when he'd made anyone happy before. Well, maybe the lump wasn't a person, but so what? It was a friend.

So caught up was he in his thoughts that he almost failed to notice how far the sun had sunk. But when it turned pink and orange, he knew it was time to rest. The road beneath his feet was packed dirt and gravel; it dwindled in the distance into forested land and weeds.

"I can't keep walking," he told the lump, "I have to rest. Okay?"

Its eyes were wide as it stared into Andrew's face. It seemed to say, just a few steps more, and Andrew sighed and continued to walk.

The valley opened before him, all new, just as it had been the day before. His heart stopped as he saw the treads in the mud where the car had braked. He looked down at the little gray lump, and in a flash, he understood.

Understood why his parents had come to the valley, and why they had brought things from it to place in the lump's cage. Understood why the lump had been so happy, and had led him—if being carried like that could be leading—to the valley.

"Home?" he whispered.

It cooed, its eyes dark and wide and full.

"This is like where you lived before, isn't it?"

Very gently, it reached up to nuzzle Andrew's face. His arms were trembling and his legs couldn't take him another step. "Are you going to leave me?"

It continued to nuzzle his face, and Andrew knew that the answer was yes. And he knew that all he had to do was put it down, and it would run away, into the green of the valley. He didn't want to. For a moment, he wanted to keep it, just as it had been in the winter, a secret friend.

But only for a moment. He couldn't take it away from here now, not even if he wanted to.

"All right," he said, his voice shaky. "Down you go, then."

Something seemed to happen to it as its feet touched the ground. The faintest of lights, colored in hues that only a rainbow could hold, began to swirl around the patchy gray fur, lending it color. Its nose was still thick, and its face still chubby and soft, but somehow that didn't matter. The lump was really beautiful. Not a lump at all. It wuffled a bit at Andrew's feet, as if it didn't believe that the ground was truly beneath it, and the bars truly gone.

Andrew gave it a little nudge with his toe. "Go on, get out of here."

And off it went, capering down the valley's side with a whoop of joy that might—just might—have been like a human voice. He heard the receding noise of branches snapping as it ambled through the undergrowth, clumsy after so long in captivity.

Left alone, Andrew began to cry. Not loudly, and not, at first, noticeably, but the tears streaked down his face, filling his eyes with the colors of sunset mixed with green. He didn't know what to do next; he couldn't go home now, and he had nowhere else to go. Maybe, just maybe, he could stay in the valley with the lump, learning how to live here in peace and quiet.

His tears, wet and warm, continued to trail down his cheeks, and he closed his eyes, wanting to be rid of the last of them.

Only when he opened them did he see truly, see clearly: The valley floor was twinkling with the colors of the dying day. Incredulous, he stumbled forward and knelt. His hand closed on something hard and cold, and when he opened it, he saw a diamond. There, at his knee, another. And beyond it, winking out a welcome, yet another.

He heard the whooping joy of the little gray lump—it was far away, and he couldn't see where it came from—but he knew, suddenly, that the entire floor of the valley would be covered with crystal tears.

And Andrew cried for the second time that day—but his tears, like the little gray lump's, were tears of joy. They weren't hard, and they weren't cold, but in their own way, they were just as beautiful.

His parents came, hours later. He had waited, knowing that they would figure it out eventually. He thought they would be angry, but he thought that the sight of his bulging pockets, his filled hands, and the inside of his shirt would make it up to them.

The car pulled in, and his father got out, holding a flashlight. His mother also stepped out of the car, clutching her coat tight around her shoulders. It was cold here—but that cold didn't touch Andrew.

"Andrew! Andrew!"

He stepped out, into the flashlight's range, a chubby, dirty young boy.

The light passed him by once, twice, three times. It stopped on the fourth swing, and he heard an exclamation. "Here, Mary!" his father's voice boomed. "We've found him!"

As quietly as possible, Andrew approached the car. He started to stammer out an explanation, when his mother opened her arms and caught him in a fierce hug.

Stunned, he noticed that she, too, had been crying. It

seemed that it was the day for it. "Where have you been?"

"Here," he answered, a little confused. "I came here."

"You—you brought . . . it."

He nodded. "I heard you. I had to—I let it go."

Her expression rippled uncertainly, and he caught fear and resignation in the lines of her face before she looked down at him again. She swallowed. He swallowed. His father came up behind him and put a hand on his shoulder. Even his father's hand was shaking.

"We understand," his father said, at last. He was angry, but not just with Andrew; still, Andrew was certain he would be in trouble when he got home. "Come on, Andrew. Let's go home. I guess you must be exhausted."

Andrew nodded quietly. "And hungry."

"Did you come all the way out here on foot?"

"After the bus ends."

"Well." That was all. Just well.

Andrew wanted to tell his parents then, but he didn't know how. So he uncurled his hands beneath his father's flashlight. Like a blaze of fire in a winter landscape, the diamonds sprang to life. His father nearly dropped his flashlight before swinging it up to Andrew's uncertain face. His mother's gasp lingered in the air.

"It was happy," Andrew whispered, as he gave the tears to his parents and began to cry again, "It was so happy just to be free."

And his parents, maybe moved by the tears themselves, looked over the head of their youngest son to each other. Andrew couldn't see the questions, and the bitter guilt, that passed between them, but he knew that something was washed clean by the tears that they, too, began to cry.

They went home together, as if it were the first time they had ever been together. They carried tears within and without, and in the night, if the little gray creature watched, they didn't know.

And two days later, his mother very carefully took

the picture of the Allister family down from its place above the fireplace, and had another one made, adding to it with more care than he would have ever thought possible a person he'd given up on seeing there: Andrew Allister.

NOT EXACTLY A DOG

Bruce Holland Rogers

Bruce Holland Rogers is no stranger to anthologies, having appeared in *Feline and Famous* and *Cat Crimes Takes a Vacation*. When he's not plotting feline felonies, he's writing excellent fantasy stories for such collections as *Enchanted Forests*, *The Fortune Teller*, and *Monster Brigade 3000*. Winner of the 1996 Nebula Award for best science fiction novelette, his fiction is at once evocative and unforgettable.

1. What Most People Want

I'LL tell you what my customers want.

Some want novelty. For them I imported the fire lice, filled up half the store with them. I don't have many left. By the time every kid in Luna is using them for night-lights, I won't be selling them. Novelty customers will want something else.

A few customers want danger. See that pressure tank? Got a Yill inside. Go ahead, have a look. Putting a chlorine breather like that in your living room is like eating fugu fish every day. If the seal breaks, your oxygen kills him, but his chlorine gets you.

Then there's fragility, the pleasure of owning a pet that's notoriously difficult to keep alive. A paperwing, say. Or the Yill, for that matter.

Beauty. There's this couple who can't afford to buy yet. They come in once a week just to stare at my sungazer.

Fascination: buying a hive of trigger wasps to watch them build.

But I'll tell you what most people want.

Most people want a dog.

2. A Primer in Corporate Responsibility

He had gone to sleep in his own bed but woke up in a plastic armchair, naked. He tried to shift, but his skin was glued to the armrests, the back, the seat.

White walls. A holo-room. On the floor, wall to wall white rabbits.

A trans-dermal taped to his forearm flashed red, delivering a drug.

"Mr. Nathan Ing," said a voice behind him. "Vice President of Consumer Products, Pleiades Corporation. You seem alert now. Good."

Ing tried to turn around.

"I'm not in the room with you," said the voice.

"Where am I? What the hell is this?"

"A review of the facts, Mr. Ing." The front wall shifted, took on color and shape: Blue oceans. Clouds. "This is Kay Zed Two, a planet chartered by your company." The wall shifted into a foggy green plain, dotted white. "One of the southern continents." The perspective shortened. The white dots resolved into small, round-headed animals, grazing. "Colonists found two species of herbivores." Another shift. Two white-furred, animals stood side by side. They looked similar, except that one had eyes on either side of its head, like a rabbit, and the other had both eyes looking forward, like a cat. "The colonists called them moss skippers and moss hoppers."

"What the hell is this?" His feet were free. He kicked. The rabbits shied away.

"Our time is limited, Mr. Ing. Listen."

Ing had good security. Snatching him out of his own bed would have taken some fancy tech. And bribes. "Who are you?"

"The skippers were skittish," the voice continued. The image of the rabbit-eyed animal vanished. "But the moss hoppers were easy to catch. They seemed fearless, as well they might. There weren't any predators on their continent. Colonists started keeping hoppers as pets. The company proposed exporting them over the objections of the colony's academy. The animals, although they seemed harmless, could still prove dangerous. It was your decision to make. Market studies showed that round heads, big eyes, soft fur, and intelligence made for an irresistible pet. The biochemistry was tricky, which meant steady profits from the sale of moss pellets."

"Who the hell are you?"

The image shifted again. Two children in jumpsuits grinned and waved, drifting in freefall. "Sasha and Piotr, my grandchildren."

Now the same two children stood among several adults. The moss hopper perching on the girl's shoulder yawned, exposing flat teeth. "Sasha and Piotr's parents own a significant share of an orbital station. A big, successful, very *crowded* station. I bought them one of your pets. It was absurdly expensive, but my grandchildren meant a great deal to me." The wall went white.

"Meant? *Meant?* What are you saying?"

"Consider: Two species of herbivores occupying the same niche. No predators. You'd expect overgrazing, periodic famines. In an ecosystem like that, one species should out-compete the other and drive it to extinction. But things weren't as they seemed. You should have waited until you had the facts, Mr. Ing."

"I'm just one man in a big organization!"

"What triggers the moss hopper's transformation from grazer to predator? A biochemical signal from the moss skippers? Hunger? The first hints of famine? No. Moss hoppers are cued visually. When they find themselves in a great crowd of other animals—people on an orbital station, say, or rabbits in a holo-room—they enter a dormant state. Their flat teeth grow long and sharp. Their claws harden. Their jaws elongate. When they wake up, they hunt."

Ing saw it then, in the corner of the room. One ball of white fur that wasn't a rabbit lay curled up, sleeping. Only just now it twitched. Just now it uncurled, stretched and yawned, exposing rows of pointed teeth. "You can't do this!"

"They attack smaller prey first. Rabbits or children. But the rabbits in this room are holo-projections."

The rabbits vanished. The moss hopper finished stretching and fixed its gaze on the chair in the center of the room.

"What do you want?" Ing shouted. "I'll give you whatever you want!"

The voice said, "I know you will, Mr. Ing."

3. Tease

You've had another bad day. The client was impossibly demanding. You snapped at him. The boss dressed you down in front of everyone. How long until you're fired? You couldn't hail a levicab and had to ride street level. The cab driver was rude. Now you've come home to a mail screen full of bills, all of them chirping overdue notices while your fencher sits up on its hind tentacles and begs for dinner.

On days like this, you're bottom man on the totem pole.

Bottom *man.* But there's someone lower than you.

The fencher follows you into the kitchen. You open the

canister, take out a chowie cube and hold it just beyond the fencher's reach. It strains, elongates, vents a little puff of frustration from its blowhole. Those big black eyes plead with you. You laugh. *Tough.*

Tonight, though, something happens that you didn't know could happen. White fibers shoot from beneath the fencher's eyes, into yours. You start to raise your hand to break these filaments, then can't.

Your arm goes numb. The chowie falls. After the fencher eats, you lie down without knowing you wanted to. The fencher climbs onto your back, wraps its tentacles around your shoulders.

You feel yourself stand. The fencher steers you around the house, practicing. You're on your feet all night. At some point, still walking, you doze. You wake up to see your face in the mirror grimacing, smiling, frowning, looking surprised.

In the morning, the fencher hides inside your jacket and takes you for a walk in the park. You feel your face smiling as people pass.

When you're hungry, the fencher takes you home to the refrigerator. It walks you to the toilet, where you bend close to the water. You both drink.

Are you only imagining that you hear its thoughts?

Good boy, you think it's thinking when you hand it a chowie.

And the rest of the time: *No, I'm not going to let you wander around on your own. You were bad before. Bad! Bad!*

4. Don't You Just Love Your Poddling?

The object came down with a thump in the back yard, triggering the security lights and waking Stan and Ruth. Boobaloo bayed frantically. Stan stood on the bed, looked out the window. He couldn't tell what the smoldering hulk was—a smashed car, maybe? He knew it was bad news. "Damn!" he said. Then the thing cracked open and shiny gray bugs the size of toasters crawled out on spiky legs. Boobaloo charged them, then backed away when they raised their forelegs. The hound turned in a circle, bayed, and charged again.

"What is it?" Ruth stood beside Stan to look out. "What in the world?"

"Call the police!" Stan went to the garage for the twelve-pound maul he'd bought with his employee discount. By the time he reached the yard, gray bugs were everywhere. Boobaloo, growling, had a few cornered by Ruth's peonies, but others were in the bushes or climbing the walls of the house. One clung to the window frame where Ruth's cat, on the other side of the glass, stood hissing.

The bugs saw Stan coming. They froze. One of them approached Stan cautiously on five legs, waving the sixth leg before it. Then it hissed and shook its body. The air was suddenly thick with the smell of rotten eggs stewed in turpentine. Stan gagged, lifted the maul, and crushed the thing.

He went after the others. Some scrabbled away through gaps in the fence. Most stood their ground, shook their bodies. Each one emitted its own stink before Stan's maul landed with a crunch. One smelled like dog vomit. Another like burning rubber. The next was like rotten meat. The one after that . . .

Stan paused in his backswing. The smell was like oranges. Two of the bugs skittered close to the one he'd been about to smash, and the smell was even stronger, sweeter.

As the bugs shook themselves, scenting the air with oranges, Stan noticed that their middle legs were shrinking back into their bodies and their shells were sprouting fur.

They growled at him. Stan lifted the maul and killed the middle one. It didn't crunch like the rest had. The resistance of its body was fleshier. While Stan absorbed that difference, the other two orange-scented creatures dashed for the fence and escaped. In fact, they were all clearing out through the fence or over the roof. Boobaloo had one in his jaws and was shaking it. Stan made him drop it. The dazed creature looked at him with brown eyes. Its furry face was like a cross between a cat's and a monkey's.

He heard the back door open. "Stan?" Ruth stood on her tiptoes, straining to see the thing at Stan's feet.

The creature opened its mouth and groaned. Stan said, "Don't look, honey," and put it out of its misery.

By the time the police arrived, every dog in the neighborhood was barking.

Six months later, as Stan finished dressing for work and pinned on his Handy Hardware badge, Ruth called out, "Come see what's on TV!"

Lucy Arnold, president of the Poddling Fancier's Association and author of *Don't You Just Love Your Poddling?* was on *Good Morning, America*. She held a black-and-gold-striped poddling in her lap and stroked it under the chin. The animal's eyes were half-closed. "They're very easy to care for," she told the interviewer. "They'll eat just about anything. Mine do very well on cat food."

The interviewer said, "Aren't you worried about harboring an alien life-form?"

"Yeah," said Stan. "What about that?"

Ruth shushed him.

Lucy Arnold laughed. "You've never held a poddling in your lap. You wouldn't ask that question if you had. Want to see what I mean?" She handed the animal to the interviewer. The poddling sniffed the man's shirt buttons, then rubbed the back of its head against his chest.

"It's purring!"

"Sometimes they purr. Sometimes they drone, which is sort of like purring, but steadier."

"What about reproduction?" The interviewer scratched

the poddling behind the ears. "They have litters, what, once a week?"

"That's a good thing, as far as the Fanciers are concerned. There was all that talk of making poddlings illegal, of rounding them up and locking them in cages for research. But poddlings were everywhere before any of those stuffed shirts could get the laws passed."

"But a litter a week! That's a lot of pups!"

"They're ready to be on their own in two days, and there's certainly no trouble finding them homes."

"Your association has how many members now?"

"About eighteen million worldwide. Of course, not every owner joins the PFA."

Stan said, "Jeez! They're taking over the world!"

Ruth shushed him again.

"Oh, yes," Lucy Arnold was saying in response to some question, "in every country. All sorts of people can afford to keep them. If you can't afford cat food . . . well, just imagine what people must be feeding them in places like India. But even very poor people have no trouble keeping poddlings."

"One thing our viewers can't appreciate," the interviewer said, "is the way that poddlings smell. This one smells like vanilla and fresh-baked bread."

"It varies," said Lucy Arnold. "The first ones smelled like oranges. . . ."

Stan said, "Like hell!"

". . . but there's a wide variety, and the same poddling may smell different on different days. I call this one Cinnamon. That's usually what she smells like, but I think she's showing off for you."

"She's darling. I have to ask you, though, about all those people who say we shouldn't be so complacent about bringing an alien life-form into our homes."

Lucy Arnold said, "There are always going to be a few people whose first reaction to anything is fear. But really. Look at that little face. Can you believe that the first man who encountered poddlings started killing them?"

Stan shook his fist at the television. "Their little faces didn't look anything like that!"

"I want one," Ruth said. "You know Luisa up the street? Her poddling just had pups."

"No. Ruth, don't you remember what they were like when they first came out of the pod? I don't want one in the house!"

At first, the other men at the hardware store were Stan's allies. He'd often repeated the story of the poddlings' arrival, and the guys all agreed that poddlings were deep down disgusting, even if they didn't show it now. Gunderson, Johns, Smitty, Wallace, Beck . . . they all said they were going to stick to dogs even if the whole world started keeping poddlings. But one by one, the poddlings wore them down. Before long, only Stan and Smitty lived in households that were alien-free. One day, the two of them arrived to see a black poddling riding on Beck's shoulders while he worked to restock the plumbing aisle.

"I don't believe it," said Smitty.

"Beck," said Stan, "you brought your pet to work?"

"Gunderson said it was okay." The poddling ran its fingers through Beck's hair, grooming him.

"Ugh," Smitty said, "how can you stand to let that thing touch you?"

"What?" Beck said. "It feels good!"

"So do a lot of things we don't do at work," Stan said. "I'm sure Gunderson didn't mean you could come out on the floor with it. You're out where customers can see you!" And he nodded toward the front doors where, at that very moment, a customer came in with a golden poddling cradled in his arms.

Beck said, "How do you know what Gunderson meant?"

"We'll just have to fricking ask him," Smitty said. "Won't we?"

So Stan and Smitty went back to Gunderson's office

where they found him leaning back in his chair with his shirt open so his spotted poddling could groom his chest hairs. He didn't ask them what they wanted. He just looked up and smiled. The poddling hopped onto Gunderson's shoulders and started kneading the muscles of his neck. Gunderson grunted with pleasure.

Smitty said, "Come on," and made sure that Stan followed him to the far end of the stockroom. "You thought much about how serious this is? I seen a cop with one of those things this morning. The President has one. Think about what we just saw in Gunderson's office. Think of that same thing happening in the White House, in the Pentagon."

"Jeez."

"Exactly. It gets worse. Gunderson and Beck, they just got theirs. But people who've had 'em for a while, they act suspicious around you if you *don't* have one. Like pretty soon they're going to starting making everyone who doesn't have one, get one."

"The only person who bugs me about getting one is my wife. But I won't have it in my house."

"My friend, she may have one already. My wife did. She was hiding it from me. The little frick was having pups when I found it in the basement. I put a stop to that, I can tell you."

"You put a—"

"Listen. Me and some other guys, we've been talking. You ready to take some action?"

"What kind of action?"

"Come on," Smitty said. "If you gotta ask, you ain't ready."

Stan thought about it. "No," he said. "It's too late. I had a chance in my backyard. But now . . ."

"Concerted action," Smitty said. "It's never too late for concerted action."

Stan hadn't taken part in the uprising, but that wasn't good enough for the neighborhood vigilance committee.

He had killed poddlings before. Everyone knew that. The only reason they didn't burn him out was that Ruth was in the house, and everybody knew Ruth had a poddling.

Stan kept himself out of sight in the closet while Ruth stood at the front door talking to the committee's chairwoman. "He's really a sweet man," Stan heard his wife say. He also heard a low humming sound, the contented drone of the poddling on Ruth's shoulders. Stan was still getting used to the idea that she'd been hiding it from him for weeks. For *weeks*.

"He just doesn't understand," Ruth concluded.

"He has to be made to understand," said the chairwoman, "or else he has to be dealt with. You can't expect your neighbors to live in fear of what he might do."

"I suppose you're right," Ruth said pleasantly.

Stan's heart hammered he heard the front door opening, heard the tread of many feet in his entryway. The closet door swung wide. He saw grim faces, shotguns, pistols. On every pair of shoulders he saw a poddling. One of the creatures wore a bandage on its head—a casualty of the uprising.

Ruth stood in front of the others. She held a little ball of black fur in her hands. Violet eyes opened and looked at Stan.

"Honey," Ruth said, "everyone agrees that it's time you had a poddling of your own."

A man with a pistol chambered a round and said, "Don't you hurt the little guy!"

Stan reached for the poddling with trembling hands.

Sometimes Stan would take a walk with Little Guy, who had actually been full-sized for quite a while, and he'd see things that made him sad. The burned-out husks of houses, for instance. Smitty's house. It was sad to think that Smitty had been so full of miserable thoughts and had done such miserable things that it had been necessary to put him out of his misery.

There was the hardware store, too. That made Stan sad

because of all the miserable time he'd spent there doing miserable work to get miserable money to buy miserable things. He'd been like Smitty, as miserable as that.

He was also sad to see the broken windows, the scattered merchandise, not because he thought looting was wrong—it wasn't wrong to take whatever you needed for your poddling. But it distressed him to think that there might be things that Little Guy would need, like a new water dish, and Stan wouldn't be able to find one because all the stores had already been looted by other owners who needed water dishes for their poddlings.

Sometimes he was sad when he saw packs of dogs or, rarely, a stray cat, because he didn't have a gun and dogs and cats were pretty hard to get now without one. Other sorts of meat were even harder to get, but anything that wasn't meat had long since been eaten up.

The feel of his skin tight over his ribs, his occasional light-headedness, these made him sad, too. It meant that he was weak, that he might not be as good at getting things for Little Guy as he wanted to be.

Sometimes he was even sad to be home because home reminded him of Ruth. He had been fond of her—nothing like what he felt for Little Guy, of course. One day she had gone off to find something for her poddling to eat, and she hadn't come back.

None of these things made Stan sad for long. Whenever Stan started to feel sad, Little Guy knew it. Little Guy would start to drone and knead Stan's shoulders and fill the air with perfume, and everything would be okay. Stan would stop being sad.

Stan knew that there was more happening than the droning, kneading and perfuming. He knew that there had to be something else, some molecules in the air or secretions from Little Guy's paws that entered his bloodstream to make everything all right. He was so very happy so very soon after Little Guy noticed he was sad. It had to be a drug.

That was fine. Whatever Little Guy did, however he did it, it was fine with Stan.

When the ships came scorching through the atmosphere and crashed down, one of them smashed into the elementary school. Stan took Little Guy to see if the ship brought anything for the poddlings to eat. For a long time, the craft sat smoldering among the school's ruins. Other people from the neighborhood gathered, too. Some brought guns in case some dogs happened by.

At last the giant pod cracked open. One spiky leg appeared in the opening. Then another.

Stan felt himself getting a little sad, or maybe a little worried. But Little Guy was droning and kneading his shoulders like crazy. Poddlings on the shoulders of the people all around him were doing the same. The air was rich with delicious smells.

Another leg appeared, and then a gleaming body like a chrome-plated microbus emerged from the crack. The alien skittered down to the ground.

Nobody seemed to think these aliens looked like something a poddling would eat. No one wasted a bullet by taking a shot at one. Stan and his neighbors just watched as alien after alien skittered out of the ship and started sorting through the ruins of the school, tugging at any pieces of metal they found, pulling up wires and girders and steel doors, hauling them to the center of the playground. One of the aliens started tearing up the schoolyard's chain link fence. When they had assembled a great heap of junk, something spidery came out of the pod, ambled over to the pile and burrowed into the middle. Then there was light so bright that Stan had to look away. When he looked back, he could see that a sort of building was starting to take shape. Or a hive. A metal hive.

The aliens started down the streets now, pulling the roofs from houses, sucking up nails, tearing out wires and pipes. Everybody had turned to watch them. Stan guessed that everybody, for a moment at least, felt sad about that. Where would they sleep with their poddlings? Where would Little Guy sleep? But Little Guy wouldn't mind sleeping under the stars. He purred and droned to say so. He massaged Stan's neck.

Every person that Stan could see was getting a good massage, was feeling the calming vibrations of poddlings as they droned. Cinnamon, ginger, baking cookies, spring blossoms, rain-washed air, it all smelled so wonderful as the aliens marched down the streets smashing houses. Every one of Stan's neighbors had a poddling to care for. And all the poddlings were taking really good care of their masters. That was wonderful. Stan felt deep down how wonderful it was.

5. The One Thing You Don't Like

Back home, people said you were a fool for contracting to return to Zodor's world as his pet. But aside from the one thing you don't like about it, it's been a good deal. You can lie in your waterbed all morning reading novels or listening to music. Zodor subscribes to all the data squirts for you, so you have your choice of texts and recordings.

And if you don't feel like lying around in bed, you can use the lifters to stand up and go to your garden. Zodor appreciates your garden, and he always brings his house-guests to see it. Host and guests shuffle carefully around the perimeter like gigantic beach balls with extruded feet. They squint in the artificial light and gasp to breathe the heated air. But in spite of their discomfort, they squeak and shudder in expressions that you know are admiration.

You don't have mirrors. Zodor has mirrors, but you never have to pass one. You hardly ever leave your rooms and garden. It's too cold. Even with your modifications, the rest of the house is just too cold. Outside, of course,

it's colder still, so cold that it can be dangerous even to
Zodor.

But you're not the sort to get cabin fever. Reading,
music, tending your garden . . . this is the sort of life you
always wanted. There is the one thing you don't like, but
it's just one thing.

The food is divine. Zodor has an extensive library of
Earth meals, and there's even a kitchen where you can do
your own cooking if you want to. You don't want to. It's
hard enough to garden, poking seeds into the ground
with long-handled tools. The kitchen would be worse.

The garden has a pond. Sometimes you can't avoid
seeing yourself reflected there, a beach ball with feet and
hands.

Naturally Zodor would want his pet to be pleasing to
the eye, to have a shape like Zodor's own, a heat-holding
shape, a nice round shape.

It's the one thing you don't like.

6. Retirement

As the ship limped toward the edge of the galaxy, Ktak
repeated: "We will make quick repairs, rejoin the fleet,
and strike the enemy hard." Three lies, and both of the
crew members knew it.

We will make quick repairs . . . The reef was dying.
Polyp after polyp collapsed into mere matter, mere energy. Without a reef, the ship that bore Ktak's name
would have no engine, no weapons, and no replication
cells to finish mending the hull where the enemy's di-
gester swarms had breached it. Already, the patches
leaked, but Ktak kept the cells busy healing the crew's
radiation burns anyway. The burns were bad. The reef
governess' fur had fallen out. The guide had been blind
for a time. Ktak himself had nearly died. With the life left
in this reef, Ktak could probably save his ship or his
crew, but not both. And it would take a century to spark
another reef.

. . . rejoin the fleet . . . But there was no fleet. Any ships that had made it out of the swarms had staggered away, like the *Ktak.*

. . . and strike the enemy hard. In a thousand years of fighting the enemy, they had never even slowed it down. It kept creeping outward from the galaxy's center, infecting local group after local group, turning planets into factories for making more of itself, firing its spores farther into space.

The ship with its zero-point reef, the cells with their molecular manipulations, these technologies pressed the limits of what science could even conceive, yet they weren't enough. Not even a fleet of such ships had been enough.

The reef governess said, "The enemy will not be stopped."

"No," Ktak admitted. He said to his guide, "Choose a planet with breathable atmosphere."

They orbited the planet while the cells made and dropped Searchers. Remote scans showed primitive industry. The Searchers reported two biochemical lineages, one so fragmentary that it could only be exotic: interplanetary colonizers. The primitive industry was theirs.

"Put us down on the night side, near a settlement," Ktak said. "Be discreet. I want to keep an eye on our hosts, but I'd rather they didn't know about us."

The *Ktak* landed in a forest. The reef governess took the engines off line, so the cells could concentrate on healing the crew. Ktak dispatched more Searchers to watch the colonizers, and he studied the pictures they sent back.

The colonists were bipedal, nearly hairless except for their heads. From their own world they had brought food plants, industrial plants, food animals, and some microorganisms. A few of the colonists' quadrupeds, however, clearly weren't for food. They were companions.

Pets. Ktak had heard of this practice in some backward species.

Some of the pets, like Ktak and his crew, were about a meter long and covered with fur.

Ktak said to his reef governess, "Could the cells give us stomachs that could digest food from both the native and colonial lineages of this world?"

"Of course," she said.

Ktak bared his teeth thoughtfully. The cells could also dismantle the ship. "Let us sleep so that the cells can finish repairing us. While we sleep, let us consider the time it would take to spark a new reef. Let us consider what difference, if any, we could make if we returned to the fight."

The guide said, "What would we do instead?"

Ktak said, "We could retire."

"How long you had that furry?" asked the offworlder.

"All my life," said the colonist, scratching her pet behind the ears. "It belonged to my great-great grandfather."

"They really live that long?"

"Guess they have to. They don't seem to reproduce."

The offworlder looked at the animal's face. "Those eyes are so intelligent. I bet it understands what we're saying."

The colonist laughed.

The furry rolled onto its back and looked up. Stared up. Stars shone through gaps in the jungle canopy, and the offworlder had the uneasy impression—he just couldn't shake it—that the furry knew what stars were and that it was watching them, waiting for something to happen, waiting for something to arrive.

7. What We're Looking For

What are we looking for, out in the sea of stars?

Most people want a dog, but not always *exactly* a dog. I've got Earth dogs in this shop, sure, but also Tansoor pacers, cheegaits, and spindle crownbacks. They're all dogs. They're all cursorial hunters, running their prey to exhaustion. In the wild, they hunt cooperatively with tail signals, vocalizations, bioluminescence. . . .

They're like us. We once ran our prey down like that. That's why we take to dogs and why they take to us. We know how to give them orders that they know how to obey, that they *want* to obey.

Not every biosphere fills this niche. There aren't dogs on every colonial world. But look at the really successful colonies, the worlds where we mesh, where we fit, where the first generation felt right at home. Tansoor. Noterr. Spindle. All those worlds have native cursorial hunters. They all have dogs.

What are we looking for, colonizing worlds, spreading humanity across the stars?

We're looking for the lost pack.

WINNER TAKES TROUBLE

Jane M. Lindskold

Despite competing claims by interested parties, neither cats nor guinea pigs provided the author with the original for the alien pet introduced in this story. If there is a single source, credit must go to that master of imaginative writing and art, Dr. Seuss. Jane Lindskold resides with both cats and guinea pigs (and husband, archaeologist Jim Moore), in Albuquerque, New Mexico. Her most recent novels are *Changer* and *Donnerjack* (in collaboration with Roger Zelazny).

I won it in a card game.

Though the players came and went as luck and finances dictated, there were two of us who were in from the start—me and this big Marine.

His first name was Bill. I don't recall if I ever knew his last name—I don't think I did. What I recall is that he played a good game while the cards were with him, but when he started getting lousy hands, he didn't have the sense to pull out.

After a while, even the deep pockets of an active duty Marine drawing combat bonuses were empty. I let him bet his watch, his earrings, his three gemstone-studded rings. I drew the line at him betting his medals, and so did the other players.

That was sentiment on my part, but I don't know how it was for the rest of the players. All the other stuff could be turned into cash at any one of the several hock shops that lined the space station's entertainment rim. Selling medals was illegal, so they'd bring only whatever price the pawnbroker felt like paying for their metal weight.

And so we came to a hand where everyone but Bill and me had folded. The pile waiting on the table was pretty fine, enough to put Bill back into the game in style, if not enough to make back his losses. The problem was, I'd just put down my bet and he couldn't even match me, much less raise.

The tension around our table was palpable, so great that even the casino security officer (who'd long ago decided—correctly—that I wasn't cheating) strolled over for another look. Bill fingered the case holding his medals, but I shook my head firmly.

"No, bud," I said. "My brother was a Marine and he died in an action against some pirates. My mom and dad have his medals in a shrine back at our house and that's where your medals belong, not melted down."

Bill winced like I'd kicked him, but he didn't protest. He just ran his hand over his shaven skull, fingering the input ports. It was a nervous tic with him, one he'd suppressed when we'd started playing but one that had become more and more pronounced as the night wore on.

"Listen, Allie," he pleaded. "They're all I've got. The casino won't let active military play IOUs."

"That's right," the security officer put in.

"Sorry," I said. "I'm not taking your medals."

Bill glanced around the table, but no one there was going to give him a loan. He'd cleaned out too many of them earlier in the evening. Besides, it was a showdown now, just me and him, and putting up the cash would be taking sides. No one wanted to do that in case I might remember some other day, some other game.

Bill's head sank toward his chest. Just when I thought he was going to fold, he jerked his head up again, looking for all the world like a puppet on strings.

"I've got something else," he said hoarsely. "It's in my locker at the front."

"What?" I asked, curious despite myself.

"It's unique," he said, "and I'd have to show you."

I glanced over at the security officer. "Can you put a shield on this game?"

"Done, Allie," he agreed, as interested as any of the rest of us in learning what Bill had left to gamble.

When the shield flickered on, Bill and I crossed to the lockers where customers store anything too bulky to carry around. A few other players trailed along, but they faded back when Bill glowered at them.

He was a big guy, and his broad shoulders effectively blocked peepers. With a practiced hand, he twisted through the touchpad's maze combination, and popped open the door.

The locker was big, meant to take vacc suits or body armor when necessary, so the carrier inside fit quite tidily. Without taking it out, Bill unlatched the lid and let me look inside.

A pointed little head that rather reminded me of a fox terrier my brother and I had owned when we were kids looked up at me, blinking enormous eyes. These were a shade of amethyst no fox terrier had ever possessed. There were also five of them, two just about where you'd expect eyes to be, the other three on the end of long stalks that extended from the creature's fluffy head.

All five eyes had long eyelashes—dark purple, which was fitting since the creature's silky coat was a pale blue that faded into lavender tipped with pink.

The creature looked at Bill, perked enormous ears, and inquired, "Vrrook?"

Bill didn't reply, his gambling fevered gaze on me. "That's what I've got to offer, Allie. She's unique. I've only seen four others and they were all male. This is the only female. My buddies and I bought them about a year ago from a tramp trader out by a system that isn't on the records yet. We smuggled them aboard the *Retaliator* and kept them as mascots.

"I'm getting transferred to a new unit, though, and I've been wondering what to do with her. I had pretty much settled on selling her to Croesus Boutique so she could become some rich lady's pet, but I'll put her up as my share of the bet."

I wanted to protest, wanted to remind him that trade in alien life-forms was highly restricted, wanted to say lots of reasonable things. What came out of my mouth was:

"What's her name?"

Bill colored. "I call her Margaret, after my great-grandmother, since she's a formal little thing. The trader called her 'Gittchy.' I'd guess you could call her whatever you want."

"How about I buy her straight?" I asked.

The gambling fever burned brighter. "Nope," he said firmly, closing the lid on the carrier and snapping it down. "She's my stake or nothing."

I shrugged, pretending a nonchalance I didn't feel. "Then we're back to the cards. I've got to warn you, my hand's pretty good."

"So's mine," he said happily. "So's mine."

There was a further pause while Bill filled out a voucher that we both signed, indicating his offer and my acceptance. After this was sealed and turned over to the security officer, we went back and turned over our cards.

Bill's hand was good: four Aces. Mine was better: a Straight Flush.

After I collected my winnings, I looked at the security officer. "Has the casino locked him," I gestured to where Bill sat unmoving at the table, his head in his hands, "out?"

"Right after your game."

"And he won't be able to play anymore?"

"Not this trip. He ships out tomorrow."

"Good."

I walked over to Bill and put a credit voucher under his hand. It contained enough so that he'd be able to afford small pleasures until he drew his next check. I've heard from my brother what the Marine mess was like.

Then I gathered up the carrier containing my prize and got out of there fast. I never saw Bill again, but I was to think of him on one of the more unpleasant days of my life.

I ended up calling her Gittchy, since I'd never had a great-grandmother named Margaret. Also, she didn't seem terribly formal to me—maybe she'd just been reacting to living on a troop transport with a bunch of noisy guys. Once we were together, just two girls and a single-ship, we were instant pals.

As soon as I had brought her aboard, Gittchy wanted out of her carrier. When, against my better judgment, I let her out, she darted here and there, showing the most lively interest in everything.

Gittchy wasn't formal, but she was terribly vain. Bill must have been serious about selling her, because he had all her gear with her. In addition to a life-support unit (which he'd needed in order to keep her on a military transport), some food and bedding, there was a flat case that held an assortment of combs and brushes, ribbons and bows. There were even a few collars—necklaces might be a better word—since they were clearly for adornment, not restraint.

I laughed at the doodads, that is until Gittchy herself made it quite plain that her grooming was not complete without a bow in her hair. She liked at least one in her topknot and, whenever possible, "vrrooked" at me until I tied one around her tail as well. I felt a bit silly about doing that at first, but I justified it since the grooming sessions gave me a good chance to learn how my new pet was put together.

Her pointy fox terrier face housed a mouth, nose, and two of those big eyes. The eyestalks didn't come out of the top of her head, the way it had looked to me when I saw her the first time. They were rooted in her spinal column and, when not needed, vanished back in there, eyes and all. Usually, Gittchy kept at least one eyestalk extended to watch behind her.

She also had feathery antennae that started where eyebrows would be on a human. These could be kept coiled or extended to either side of her face. She didn't have any whiskers, so the antennae probably did some similar job.

Gittchy was a quadruped. Her little paws possessed semiretractable claws and the long tail she carried curled over her back was fluffy but not prehensile. All in all, she was a cute little creature, but not terribly well adapted for survival. I figured that her race had been bred as pets by some alien race, just like humans bred Pekinese from fierce wild dogs or Persian cats from stealthy desert felines.

Actually, if I'd had the naming of my new pet, I'd probably have ended up calling her "Vrrook," since that was all she ever said. She had lots of intonations for it: the query I'd heard first, the demand, the happy-sound, the disappointed sound, the complaint, the "Hey, where are you?" and dozens more. She tended to talk in other ways. The tilt of her head, the angle of her ears, the extent to which she uncoiled her antennae or eyestalks all added meaning to that one "vrrook."

I had a lot of time to get to know the subtleties of Gittchy's conversation since she was my only companion aboard the *Mercury*. The *Mercury*'s my ship, of course. I'd named her for a Roman god who carried messages, stole things, and guided people into the underworld.

I thought the name was pretty appropriate, myself, but whenever anyone asked me about it, I either told them what most people knew, that Mercury was the name of a planet or, if I was feeling flippant, that Mercury was a twentieth century American god of florists. If that wasn't enough, I told them I'd named my ship for the metal, since its other name was "quicksilver" and I liked the intimation of speed. That provided a good transition into business.

My business was the same as the god's. I carried messages. Ever since the human race bought the first Faster Than Light ships from the Tesseracts a century ago, we've been fanning out of the Sol system, colonizing new worlds, bumping into other spacefaring races, and in general doing all the things humans have always done when in the middle of an Age of Exploration.

The one thing that slows us down is that though we have FTL drives for our ships, we don't have FTL communications.

Those first ships, the ones that were purchased a century ago, were remodeled Tesseract ships. Just like everyone else, I've heard the folk tales about how there was a place on the ships' consoles for communication equipment, but that the original stuff had been pulled out and replaced with gear that was nothing better than the microwave communicators we use today.

Whether that's true or not doesn't matter to me. What matters is that the only way to get news quickly from system to system is to have it carried by ship. The various governments and the military have their couriers, but for the average person the best and most secure way to send information is to entrust it to a private carrier.

That's where the *Mercury* and I come in. For the last decade, we've been running messages on the fringes of civilization, and making a very good living at it. Eventually, some big company sets up routes, but by the time they do I'm tired of that set of colonies and space stations, and am ready to leave them behind to see what's just been opened up.

There are other people who thrive on the new frontiers

as well: entrepreneurs, smugglers, miners. Not pirates, though.

Contrary to what both the entertainment industry and the military want the folks at home to think, pirates don't like the frontier. In order to turn a profit, they need established trade lines, military convoys, and colonies to raid. A passenger on some big liner is at far more risk than some two-bit mining vessel out to strip asteroids before the corporations get in their claim.

On request, and for a big fee, I'll make connections for people who want to buy blackmarket goods or purchase ore at below market rates. That's the "underworld" to which the *Mercury* and I are guides. And the thieving? Well, you should see what I charge!

Gittchy filled in the one part of my life that had been less than satisfactory. Company. In a pinch, the *Mercury* could carry a passenger, but to allow the maximum amount of space for engines and power plant, I had sacrificed on things like living quarters.

My father, when touring an earlier version of the ship, had compared it to a studio apartment. I had everything I needed, but it was all in one room. Fortunately, I'm not very tall, coming as I do from Earth Asian stock, and I don't suffer from claustrophobia.

There were advantages to life on the *Mercury*. I could do a course correction without getting out of bed or cook a meal while brushing my teeth, but it did mean that except on very rare occasions I traveled alone.

Gittchy was about the size of a small cat and liked to snuggle into various odd corners. I mounted her life-support unit at the bottom of the locker where I kept my vacc suit and practiced with her until whenever I went for my suit, she went into her case. She caught on fast, but I figured that was a residual from her Marine training rather than any indication of intelligence on her part.

Then, about a month after I got her, I learned Gittchy's secret.

I'd been doing some standard maintenance in the engine compartment in the back. When I'd left, Gittchy had been asleep on my chair. When I came back, the chair was empty and standing on the galley counter was a Venusian fire dragon.

At least it looked like a fire dragon, but when I noticed that it had been eating Gittchy's favorite snack food—saltine crackers—I started wondering.

"Gittchy?"

The image flickered slightly, just a shifting of the burnt orange highlights on the dragon's dark green scales into lavender. The three eyes, one on either side and a third on the top center of the head, looked less topaz and more amethyst.

"Gittchy!"

"Vrrook," admitted the creature resignedly. Then the fire dragon vanished and Gittchy, her yellow tail bow untied and her expression distinctly sheepish, stood on the counter. She had crumbs on her muzzle.

It took me a while to convince her to perform again— a thing I achieved at the expense of my remaining stock of saltines. After she realized that I wasn't angry with her, she happily ran through her repertoire. In addition to the Venusian fire dragon she could do several ferocious creatures I'd never seen before. One looked something like a bulldog with porcupine spines. Another looked like a mountain with teeth. A third resembled an antelope with fangs and needle-sharp antlers.

In addition to these monstrosities, Gittchy could look like a human female with breasts of a size and buoyancy usually only seen in male fantasy; a Marine officer, perfect down to every crease in his uniform and the jackports on his shaved scalp; and a severe looking man with dark hair and eyes.

When I tried to talk with the human forms, I confirmed what I had suspected from the start. Gittchy wasn't changing shapes, she was projecting illusions.

Each illusion came provided with its own movements

and sound effects. The bimbo, for example, wriggled and cooed, "Sweetheart! Darling!" followed by several convincingly orgasmic noises. The Marine snapped "Attention!" and "Prepare for inspection!" Each of the predatory animals emitted appropriate snarls and howls.

The last human illusion was the most interesting in a way. He didn't have a routine, just stood and looked tough. Then, every so often, he'd turn his head, look straight at me, and say "Karlsen Nappert" in tones that can only be described as deep and thrilling. I resolved to learn if he was a real person just as soon as I got back into more civilized systems.

Meanwhile, I worked out a theory to explain why Gittchy's species might have developed this odd ability. Her long silky fur, her tiny size, her pretty color all might have been bred into her species to make it a more attractive pet, but the projection ability seemed too basic, like claws on a cat. It had to be part of the original equipment.

I guessed that even in her basic model, Gittchy's species—call them the fluffheads—wasn't the most survival prone of animals: no long claws or fangs or poison. They were quick on their feet, but not so quick that they could outrun one of those killer antelope. Instead, they had eyes that could see behind them, an acute sense of smell, sensitive antennae, and great big ears. In short, creatures built to anticipate trouble—not to fight it or escape it.

When something does sneak by those defenses, a fluffhead projects an illusion of something a whole lot more ferocious than it is, like one of those monsters I'd seen. The other illusions, the bimbo, the fire dragon, the Marine, and Karlsen Nappert could all have been learned later. I was willing to bet she'd learned them from Bill and his buddies on the *Retaliator.*

Gittchy munched a saltine contentedly, apparently unaware of my scrutiny—or perhaps flattered by it. Today she was wearing a new violet ribbon with a little flower in the middle that she was being very careful not to disarrange. Around her neck was a *faux* pearl choker that went nicely against her freshly brushed coat.

We were just starting our return into civilization, about two months or so after I had won Gittchy, when the black ships caught up with us.

I'd been making tightbeam links with clients' private databases to deliver mail when a message came through for me.

"CAPTAIN AH-LEE. PREPARE FOR BOARDING. STANDARD INSPECTION. FIFTEEN MINUTES."

I cursed a little but didn't think anything of it. The Sunline colony had hit the ten thousand resident mark, putting it just inside the lower limit of interest for the bigger communication companies. Usually their first move is to chase out freelance competition. Convincing the local government to indulge in some gentle harassment is a common tactic. I figured that this was more of the same.

Gittchy saw me reach for my vacc suit and scampered into her carrying case. I scratched her head (she had a pink bow on today) and promised her a brushing when we were done here.

"Now, you be good and quiet when the inspection crew comes on board," I said as I locked the latches, "and we'll be done with this all the sooner."

"Vrrook," she agreed and curled into a silky blue ball.

I suited up, anchored everything, and then depressurized. That's my standard procedure for making inspectors as unwelcome as possible. The *Mercury*'s cabin is cramped at the best of times. It's really uncomfortable when two or more people in vacc suits are bumbling around.

I can always justify my actions by saying—honestly—that my life-support plant can't handle more than two. Since most inspection teams come in pairs to prevent bribery and other collusion, and since they can't roust me out of my ship without a better reason than a routine inspection, we have a polite stalemate. They do their inspection, and I get to make a protest against the intrusion without saying a word.

I had time to return to routing messages before the inspectors arrived, requested permission to board, and anchored their lines on the *Mercury*'s hull.

When I opened the cabin door, I was glad that my helmet's automatic polarization was at work because the tinting meant that there was no way they could have seen the involuntary "O" of astonishment that I immediately hid behind my best poker face.

I had expected to find one of the usual clunky in-system boats coasting alongside. At Sunline they're painted two-toned, pink and gray with a rising sun coming over the horizon. It's a good motif, but it can't make the ship look any more sleek.

What was out there across from the *Mercury* was no in-system boat. Sleek and needle-pointed, it hung there, a black shape against the stars. It bore no name, no registration code, nothing but big engines, discretely concealed weapons ports, and a reputation that was more terrifying than either in the circles in which I ran.

Originally commissioned for pirate hunting and "internal security," the black ships have become a law unto themselves. Faster than even my little courier, more heavily armed than anything that size should be, they streak between the systems, chasing the only things faster than themselves—rumors.

Watching as two black jumpsuited figures sprang across the void, disdaining the anchor ropes that prudence demands be set up whenever a person goes EVA, I had a sinking sensation that I knew just what rumor they were chasing this time.

"Captain Ah-Lee, we request permission to come aboard," said the one in front.

It was a woman, I thought, but her jumpsuit was made to conceal such things. The members of the Silent Watch, as they like to be known, cultivate anonymity.

"Come aboard," I said, stepping back. "It's a bit close."

"We will take care not to damage anything," the Watcher replied politely. "Our inspection should only take a few minutes."

"Thank you," I replied. Years of poker playing were coming to my rescue now. I actually sounded like myself despite the fact that my heart was racing and my mouth felt dry. A sip of water from the nipple in my helmet did little to alleviate the dryness, but hearing myself sound calm paradoxically convinced me that I was.

The second trooper stood in the doorway while the first made a swift but complete search of the front compartment. My stupid pulse started racing again when the trooper opened the locker which held Gittchy's carrier.

Since I was helpfully trailing after the inspector, I saw that except for a spare pair of EVA booties at the bottom and some hosing and filters on the shelf above, the locker was completely empty.

I was still swallowing down the various excuses I'd been about to make to explain Gittchy's presence ("Oh, that's nothing important." or "In there? Just my pet terrier.") when the first trooper asked me to open the door to the engine room. Ready and alert, her backup stepped into the front compartment, so as to have a clear line of fire.

I hadn't been in-system long enough to take on any contraband, even if I'd been planning to, which I wasn't, so the engine compartment was as clean and bright as a recent overhaul could make it. The Watcher took a bit longer here, then, coming out she went over the front compartment again.

By now I'd figured out what Gittchy had done and, that puzzle solved, I could spare the energy to wonder who had tipped the black ships off about her—since it had to be Gittchy they were looking for.

I hadn't shown her to anyone at any of my stops, not wanting her to be stolen by some lonely frontier colonist as a present for the kids. That left Bill, his buddies, and anyone on the *Retaliator* who knew about the fluffheads, too many possibilities for me to narrow down.

The Watchers left after they had completed their third inspection. They had clearly expected to find Gittchy, but I suspected that they were not certain enough of their information to be rude or to impound the *Mercury*.

Although I longed to rush to the locker and learn if my guess about what Gittchy had done was correct, I began the repressurization sequence first, got the life-support plant up and running, and then scanned the ship for ears and eyes. I found two, one in the engine compartment, one right over my desk. They were easy enough to deactivate, and I did so immediately.

Since they're illegal to use without a search warrant and none had been presented to me, the Silent Watchers could only shrug and bitch to each other when their snoopers went blank. I didn't plan to be around long enough to give them a chance to get that warrant.

Then I zipped out the rest of the mail and moved out of the system. Less than fifteen minutes after the Silent Watchers had left my ship, I was off to an unregistered destination.

Only then did I open my locker. As I had expected, those extra EVA boots had vanished. In their place was Gittchy's carrier. She was too pleased with herself to even pretend indignation that I'd kept her locked up after the company had departed.

"So that's how you survived all those inspections on the Marine troopship!" I exclaimed, fussing over her, happier than I could say. Life, I realized, would be pretty lonely without her. "I'd always wondered, but figured that the officers were looking the other way."

"Vrrook!" Gittchy said happily. Perking up her ears and flourishing her antennae she leaped up and brought her jewelry case down off the shelf.

"I think you deserve it," I agreed, fastening her favorite necklace around her neck—a new one with amethyst beads that I had bought for her at an outlying colony. To

celebrate, I slipped another one of her necklaces around
my wrist where it made a good bracelet and tied a ribbon
in my hair.

Even as I got out a hoarded box of saltines, I was busy
worrying about what to do next.

Item One: Someone wants Gittchy. Probably government since the black ships work (mostly) for various
government agencies.

Item Two: I don't want to give Gittchy up.

Item Three: Why do they want Gittchy?

That one was easy enough to answer. No living creature we'd encountered thus far had demonstrated this
ability to project illusion. A creature like Gittchy (suit-
ably controlled) could be quite useful for espionage or
military operations. A person with Gittchy's abilities
would be even more useful. Even with all the electronic
identification measures in routine use, most people still
go by what they see and ask questions later.

Item Four: There's no way they'll learn what they
want without submitting Gittchy to "study."

I shivered at the thought of my vain little pet stuck in
some laboratory cage, poked and pried at. No one would
comb her fur or put ribbons on her topknot. When they
fed her treats, it would only be to get her to perform.
She'd just be a "subject."

What if they cloned her? My mental image mutated to
show a host of shave-headed little Gittchies imprisoned
in laboratory cages, electrodes stuck to their scalps, lots
and lots of fingers poking and prying, scalpels glittering,
computers humming . . . .

"No!" I said aloud.

Gittchy looked at me. "Vrrook?"

"I can't let them have you," I said aloud, "and I don't
know how I'll stop them."

"Vrrook," she agreed, flattening her ears. I'd guessed
a while ago that the ears and antennae were at least partially redundant systems. When the big ears needed to be
hidden, she deployed the more fragile but equally accu-

rate antennae. When in a really confusing situation, she used both.

"We can hide for a while," I continued, "but not forever. The *Mercury* won't need a power plant recharge for a couple years. We took care of that at Sunline, but we'll need food a lot sooner. The ship doesn't have the storage to carry much."

"Vrrook," Gittchy said, not really saying much, just keeping me talking. She did that a lot when we were out between systems. I flattered myself that she liked the sound of my voice.

"I wonder what happened to the four other whatever-you-ares that Bill the Marine mentioned?" I continued. "Do the black ships have them already? Are the males as gifted as you are in the illusion department?" I paused.

"You know," I added seriously, "there's a whole lot I don't know about you, given that we've been shipmates for two months."

"Vrrook," she said smugly. (At least it sounded smug to me. I was, of course, projecting, as humans have always projected onto their pets).

"First step, then," I said, "is to do some research—not just about you, about what happened to the *Retaliator* as well, and I should finally look into that mysterious Karlsen Nappert."

One thing I hadn't skimped on when I'd ordered the *Mercury* was communications equipment, so it was no trouble at all for me to go to the Fyolyn system and tap into the public library network.

First thing after my arrival in-system, I'd arranged a covert supply drop through some of my underworld connections. Once I hauled the concentrates on board, I was set for a while.

I'm not going to describe the Fyolynese and their various habits here since, like all the other alien races humanity has encountered (but one), they have been the subjects of exhaustive study by xenologists.

What I want to note is that I chose Fyolyn because the libraries there are extensive and, by human standards of security, extremely public. Additionally, the Fyolynese trade with every race that humanity does and have been doing so for much longer.

The only difficulty with using their library is that the Fyolynese methods of cataloging defy human logic. However, since information is my stock in trade, I'd long ago learned how to work within their parameters. Within a few hours of my arrival, as the *Mercury* lay passive on the edge of the system, hooked into the library array by the tightest beam possible, I had learned everything I needed to know about the fate of the *Retaliator*.

She had been lost with all hands in a battle with pirates. That didn't tell me what had happened to Gittchy's companions, but it gave me a pretty fair idea. Bill the Marine was harder to trace, but I finally managed by checking the rosters of every military ship that had been at the space station the day we met against every variation of a name that could be diminutized as "Bill."

Gittchy's Bill had been a casualty a week after our meeting. He had died with honor, which is why I found a listing for him as easily as I did. The article on his deeds filled two full columns, but what brought tears to my eyes was the picture of his mother and father coming to claim their son's medals, including the new one for heroism beyond the call of duty.

I told Gittchy about what had happened to Bill, but she seemed more interested in licking the salty tears from my face than in mourning her former owner. Heartlessness or just practicality? Or maybe she didn't connect my words and the flat picture with the guy who had liked her enough to buy her necklaces and combs.

"Well, girl," I said. "We've got to operate on the assumption that you're the only one of your kind in circulation and that's why the Silent Watch wants you. Even if they managed to get all the others, they'd still want you, especially if someone told them you were the only female in the lot.

"As I see it, the only way to make them leave you alone is to find where you came from. Then not only won't you be a unique commodity, your entire species will be covered by the agreements governing trade in alien life-forms."

"Vrrook."

"Of course," I added, "those same agreements might make things more difficult for us, but we can't hide out forever."

Going into the Fyolyn Library and asking questions directly about Gittchy could quite possibly set alarms blazing and get the black ships back on my tail, so I decided to do my research by indirect means and save asking about Gittchy's race itself for the last. I'd get out of system as soon as I had an answer.

I'd already discovered that Gittchy's illusions could be photographed, so my next step was to transfer photos of the three "monsters" in her collection into my computer and then see if the Fyolyn library system recognized them.

The bulldog with spines chunked a negative, but I hit paydirt with the other two. The entry for them contained names in an alien script, unpronounceable equivalent pronunciations, and the legend: "POSSIBLY MYTHICAL BEAST OF TESSERACT ORIGIN. SEEN ON COATS OF ARMS EARLY IN INITIAL CONTACT PHASE. NO ACTUAL REPRESENTATIVES OF THE CREATURES HAVE BEEN SEEN. BEAST CEASED TO BE SHOWN AFTER (PRESUMED) GOVERNMENTAL SHIFT IN . . ."

The date was in the Fyolynese format. When I translated it, I came up with a time about fifty years (Sol standard) before the human colony on Pluto had been contacted by the Tesseract.

Xenologists, frustrated by the Tesseracts' refusal to enter into any cross-cultural exchange, had speculated that our alien benefactors had been in the midst of a change of policy at the time we were contacted and sold the FTL drive. This theory explained why the Tesseract would, on the one hand, have sold us the means to get out of our isolated system while on the other hand stubbornly maintaining their own isolation—an isolation that they had not maintained to a similar degree with earlier trade partners (though they had consistently refused access to their home world).

Selling us FTL technology could have served a couple of purposes. It could have upset an existing balance of power and trade among the various alien races. It could have brought a particular Tesseract clan influence. Although we had no proof, we had the impression (reinforced by comments from other alien races) that Tesseract clans could claim an exclusive relationship with a trade partner for some period of time only known to the Tesseract themselves.

These theories also explained why no one (except possibly the Tesseract themselves) had FTL communications. These gave the Tesseract the advantage over everyone else, an advantage that it might well be treason for an individual or clan to share.

The "governmental shift" mentioned in the Fyolyn Library was something I had come across elsewhere, hints of a time when Tesseract policy had not been centralized, but had been handled by individual clans or nations. Paradoxically, the Tesseract isolationism had become stronger after they sold those first ships with FTL to the scientists on Pluto. They had continued to do business with us, but had worked through agents—human and otherwise.

So where did that leave Gittchy and me?

"With a headache," I muttered aloud. I powered down and got something to eat. When I went to sleep, Gittchy curled up on my pillow. Her fur smelled of cinnamon and tea.

*   *   *

Eight or so hours of restless sleep later, I was ready to see what I could find out about Karlsen Nappert. All I had was a name and an image—and I couldn't even be certain that I'd spelled the name right since "Karlsen" could be spelled with a "C" rather than a "K" and the "sen" at the ending could be "son" or "ssen" or "sson" or . . .

I decided that line of thought would defeat me before I started. Giving every variation of spelling I could think of and appending the picture, I paid for a wide-ranging intuitive search. To help limit the search further, I added that there might be a possible connection with the Tesseract.

Even with the peculiar logic circuits built into the Fyolyn library system, it took their computer several hours to get back to me with an answer. My man's surname, it appeared, was spelled "Knappert," but I'd had the Karlsen right.

The condensed summary attached was brief, but tantalizing: "Linguist, specialization, Tesseract dialects. Trade liaison, specialization, FTL parts. Retired. Current residence, Eb've. List of publications follows." That last ran for several pages and was full of titles like: "Subtleties in the Use of the Verb 'To Run' " or "Poetry of Fear" or " 'Dig' as a Verb and as a Noun."

"Looks like," I said to Gittchy, "we're going to Eb've, but first . . ."

I sent the Fyolyn Library a request for information about the fluffheads, narrowing the search by tagging "presumed Tesseract origin" onto the picture.

The message "NOTHING ON FILE" came just as my commo rig alerted me that someone was trying to tap our beam. I cut the connection and hit the preprogrammed FTL sequence. Hopefully, we were out of system before the Silent Watch realized we'd ever been there.

The *Mercury* arrived on the fringes of the Eb've system, unheralded and undetected, but I didn't expect that state of affairs to last.

Eb've started as a Fyolynese settlement, but it's pretty

mixed now, so I wasn't worried that one more human ship would attract attention. What I was worried about was that whoever had tried to tap me at Fyolyn might do some fancy searches into recent requests from the data banks. With the right investigating program, the black ships could show up any time.

How long would it take them to ask the right questions?

When you know where you're headed, the end is obvious. (That's why it's cheating to start a maze from the wrong side). So even though logically I knew that the black ships might take weeks, if not months, to find us again, I was on edge.

Besides, I'd done some thinking while we were in transit and I'd come to some conclusions that left me wondering if I was in over my head. If I was right, then the Silent Watch might be waiting right here.

Knowing that I was taking a big gamble, I asked Port Authority for clearance to land. While I waited to see if my request would be granted, I downloaded the residential directory, located Karlsen Knappert, and reserved a rental vehicle.

When, to my surprise, clearance was granted (I'd expected to be arrested or held for questioning as soon as the Port Authority had my ID number), I brought the *Mercury* down at a little-used landing field on the fringes of a tertiary population center. The rental vehicle I'd requested was waiting at the landing pad.

"Come on, Gittchy," I said, opening her carrier. "We're going out."

She leaped into the carrier with enthusiasm. I one-way opaqued the side panels so she could see out, but no one else could see in. Then we were off.

Karlsen Knappert's house looked for all the world like an English cottage set amid fields of blooming anemones. I'd pulled up local real estate listings, however, and had learned that this unostentatious dwelling was considerably larger underground, possessing its own water supply, power plant, and thick walls that (though not listed as such) looked remarkably like shielding.

Another point for my growing theory.

I parked the rental car in the gravel driveway and, taking Gittchy's carrier, went and rang the front doorbell. A series of chimes was followed by the sound of footsteps on a wooden floor.

I felt Gittchy shift and knew from past experience that she had just sat up straight. Doubtless all five eyes were deployed, and her ears and antennae were both spread wide.

The door opened and Karlsen Knappert, just like he looked in Gittchy's projection, motioned me inside.

"Captain Ah-Lee, also called 'Allie,' of the good ship *Mercury*," he said, giving a slight bow but not offering his hand. "Do come in. I suspected you might call."

I did as he requested, feeling considerably safer once the door was shut behind me. That feeling of safety was an illusion, of course, but I couldn't help it. At least I'd reached my goal before the Silent Watch got to me.

"Is that Gittchy?" Knappert asked, leading me into a room furnished in the English cottage theme.

"Vrrook!" she answered. I heard her paw scratch against the door to the carrier.

Knappert smiled, looking far less severe. "Might she come out, Captain Ah-Lee?"

Still not speaking, I undid the latches. Gittchy bounded out, coiling her antennae, and leaving only one of her three eyestalks deployed. After circling my ankles once for security, she started exploring.

"So she's been here before," I said, hearing my voice sound a bit rusty. "I thought she might have."

"Yes. She and her littermates lived here with me for a brief time."

"After you brought them from Tesseract, right?"

"I . . ." Knappert fell silent.

"Some of her projections are of Tesseract animals," I pressed. "Where else could she have seen them?"

"I stole her," he replied, speaking very quickly now. "From . . . never mind where. I stole them. Things were getting too hot for me, so I unloaded them on the Marines and got out."

"Vrrook," Gittchy commented reproachfully.

"That might be true," I agreed, "but I've been thinking about the FTL drive, how we got it, some of the conjectures that were raised later, when people started wondering about where the Tesseract came from, about the possible dynamics of their internal politics."

"Oh?"

"Humans have fingernails," I said, "because our ancestors had claws."

"Captain Ah-Lee, are you insane?" he demanded.

"Are you a Tesseract?" I countered.

He stared at me. "You *are* insane!"

"You are, aren't you?" I laughed, stepped forward, and very deliberately poked my finger at his shoulder. It went right through, just like I had thought it would, but the reality still left a very funny feeling in my gut.

Even weirder was watching his projection flicker, reestablish for a moment, then snap off. Before me stood a golden-furred Tesseract. I sank down into a chair. It's one thing to expect something, it's another to see it happen.

He was about average height for one of his species, which meant that he was taller than me but skinnier. Tesseract are built on lines similar to a human's— bipedal, two limbs for walking on, two for manipulation. That's why we could use their space ships, where we would have been at a loss to use those built for the squat, insectoid Fyolynese.

I learned later that the Tesseract I had seen up to that time were trained explorers, modified with bio-armor, polarizing skin implants, internal computer systems, and much more. The Tesseract standing in front of me resembled those sleek creatures like an overweight Labrador retriever resembles an attack-trained Doberman.

The dog analogy is unfortunate, since, as everyone knows, of all Earthly mammals, Tesseract resemble nothing so much as giant rabbits: long ears, big eyes, wiggling noses, and all.

Knappert's nose was wiggling full force now, and Gittchy "vrrooked" softly in sympathy.

"You're a rebel," I said, keeping my voice level when faced with his obvious terror, "just like the ones who sold us the FTL drive, except that instead of selling us something technological, you were going to sell us pets."

"Everyone at home," Knappert wailed, "was so afraid of you humans! You're so aggressive. Clan Killer-Antelope," (he used the animal's real name, but I can't spell it in this alphabet), "was removed from the registers and the Home Protectors came into political power over the sale of the FTL drives. I wanted to show them that humans are capable of gentle emotions, as well as of violence.

"I smuggled Gittchy and her littermates out when they were just pouchies." He straightened a little, remembering the act with pride. "And sold them to the Marines. They treated the fluffheads with great loving kindness— and they were humans who had been trained to kill. Disaster struck just as I was about to reveal my experiment to the public."

"The Silent Watch learned about them," I guessed.

"Yes. The Marine contingent of the *Retaliator* was rotated. Several of the new soldiers did not approve of the mascots and reported them—including suppositions on their projection ability. However, by the time the Silent Watch learned of the report and decided to act, the *Retaliator* had been destroyed."

"You had nothing to do with that?" I demanded.

"I swear!" he squeaked, his ears flying up in alarm. "I mourned deeply for the little innocents. I had never considered that *they* would be at risk since Marines fight on planets or other ships, not ship to ship.

"The Silent Watch," he continued, "learned that one fluffhead had escaped death and they came after you."

"You certainly know a lot," I said suspiciously.

"I have been following the progress of my experiment," he countered mildly. "Additionally, in my little way I am something of a spy. I have worked as a translator for many years, disguised as a human, living among you. That was how I learned to believe in the better qualities of your race, for even as I saw some of the worst at work, I learned that these were the great minority."

"Do the Silent Watch know you were the one who sold Gittchy to Bill the Marine?" I asked. "Not that this isn't fascinating, but I came here to try to convince you that I want Gittchy left alone, not turned over to some security lab."

"I don't think they have made the connection." He made a smug little gesture, similar to one of Gittchy's. "I don't believe they even know that I am not a human. How did you figure it out?"

"Gittchy projected your image as part of her repertoire," I explained. "When I researched you, I learned you were a specialist in Tesseract languages. I wondered then. The Tesseract are remarkably chary about who they associate with, and you seemed to know an awful lot about the subtleties of the language and culture."

"Oh!" His ears flopped up in alarm. "My vanity will be my undoing!"

"You and Gittchy, both." She ran over to me at the sound of her name. I scooped her up and cuddled her close, "You two have a lot in common. Now, are you going to help us?"

Knappert frowned. "I fail to see how I can."

"Tesseract creatures," I explained, "are protected under alien trade laws. Identify her as a Tesseract native and she's protected from seizure—and especially from experimentation."

"Ah, that might work. But wouldn't those same laws force you to return her to Tesseract?"

I'd done a lot of research during the trip here, and I thought I had the answer. "Not if you give me permission to keep her as a pet—specifically as a pet, not for breeding, resale, experimentation, or cloning."

"Cloning!" he yelped. "I'd forgotten that."

"You were a bit impulsive," I agreed, "but we can fix it."

"But if I admit she is from Tesseract, they'll want to know where I got her."

"Tell them!"

"But then they'll want to know how I know where the planet Tesseract is located!"

I poked him in the chest again. "Show them what you are. You're retired. The worst they can do is follow you around. They're probably doing that anyway."

"Oh!"

"Did you really think you could start a revolution without taking some risks?" I scratched Gittchy, who sat on my lap and stared at him with all five eyes. "Or, I should say, by letting someone else take all the risks?"

"Vrrook!"

"I . . . I'll tell them," Knappert answered firmly.

The Silent Watch took two days to catch up with us. I learned later that they had stopped direct surveillance on Knappert sometime before but had put a flag in place for them to be notified if I called on him. The two-day delay was the time it took for a courier ship to get to the nearest black ship.

I was glad for those two days. I learned that not only did Karlsen (we settled on that since I couldn't pronounce his Tesseract name, my front teeth being far too short) resemble a rabbit, he rather acted like one, too. The slightest shock would send him running to his basement which was—as I'd guessed—a complete survival shelter.

Fluffhead evolution had been much as I'd surmised. While humans and wolves made friends by hunting things together, Tesseract and fluffheads made friends while hiding from the hunters. The more I learned about the panic responses hardwired into my alien friends, the more I respected the courage, as brave and true as that of any Marine, that had helped Karlsen to defy his more isolationist kinfolk.

Appealing to that courage, rather than browbeating him, proved to be the way to get Karlsen to draw up the agreement giving me custody of Gittchy. That same courage upheld him through a rather unpleasant interview with the local Tesseract diplomatic corps and our ultimate encounter with the Silent Watch.

In the end, they slunk away, while Karlsen marveled at his own valor.

And me?

Gittchy and I are back in the business of running messages from system to system, guiding folks to the underworld, and charging high for our services.

It's the same job as before, but now I do it with a friend at my side and a ribbon in my hair.

THENAGAIN

Gary A. Braunbeck

Gary A. Braunbeck writes poetically dark suspense and horror fiction, rich in detail and scope. Recent stories have appeared in *Robert Bloch's Psychos, Once Upon a Crime,* and *The Conspiracy Files.* His occasional forays into the mystery genre are no less accomplished, having appeared in anthologies such as *Danger in D.C.* and *Cat Crimes Takes a Vacation.* His recent short story collection, *Things Left Behind,* received excellent critical notice. He lives in Columbus, Ohio.

> "O for a Muse of fire, that would ascend
> The Brightest heaven of invention . . ."
> —Shakespeare, *Henry V,* Prologue

THEY *were named the L'lewyth-i by the Welsh sheep rancher who found their ship embedded in the side of a grazing hill one cold September morning. It was the talk of the village for days, then the world.*

No one had witnessed the ship's crashing—if indeed it had *crashed. A few minutes before dusk that grazing hill had been undamaged; a few minutes after dawn, when the rancher was herding his sheep to their favorite spot, there it was, still smoking, buried in the hill, the size of a city block.*

There had been no comets during the night, no fires in the sky, no howl of celestial destruction as it plowed into the Earth, no explosion, no vibration, earthquake, nothing.

It was simply there.

And when the shell cracked open, they came spilling out, scuttling toward the rancher and his sheep, ready to begin their friendship with humankind.

When Athos awoke, he found that sometime during the night he'd turned back into Simon Kaiser and the woman who was his Lady De Winter had broken into particles of dust that drifted before his eyes like so many unobtained goals.

He dragged himself out of bed, stoop-shouldered, and made his way to the motel room's small kitchenette where, for the umpteenth time, as if he were still back home, he prepared himself a breakfast of toast, tea, and half a grapefruit, all of which he'd purchased at an all-night convenience store before arriving at the motel. He ate in silence, trying to recapture the scent of Lady De Winter's skin, the soft fullness of her lips, the sparkle in her eyes that promised passion. No good; gone but not forgotten.

Simon Kaiser finished his breakfast, started the day's first cigarette, and thought about his life, all thirty-six years, four months, two weeks, six days, seven hours, and—he looked at the clock—eighteen minutes of it. It was not an extraordinary life—he was no poet, no visionary, no heroic leader of men—but it was usually a good life, if a bit solitary; but what else could an acne-scarred, slightly overweight, prematurely balding bachelor who was still technically a virgin expect?

He crushed out his cigarette and went into the bathroom, where he showered and shaved. As he stood in front of the mirror drying what was left of his hair, he studied his average face and wondered why it was that everyone had to be exceptional these days. It wasn't good enough just to do your best and get by; no, that was a bit unadorned for most people's vision of success—not that he could lay claim to even that much anymore.

God bless corporate downsizing and the greedy bastards who coined such quaint terms as "outsharing" because it was no longer PC to call it "firing."

And so here he stood, in a motel room one-hundred-and-fifty miles from his cramped apartment in Cedar Hill, with only enough money for another night's rent, two meals, and enough gas to drive back to Ohio—and even that was going to leave him a little short for the rent come the first.

Dammit.

On mornings like this, it was everything he could do not to cut his throat.

If you were broke and unemployed at twenty-one, people smiled and said, That's okay, you're young; if at seventy you were in the same boat, they smiled and said, That's okay, you're old; but if you were thirty-six and unemployed, if a glorified-gruntwork job you'd worked at for sixteen years had suddenly been deemed superfluous by the corporate powers-that-be, if you found yourself, through no fault of your own, a month away from filing bankruptcy despite your outstanding work record and glowing references and having taken care not to indulge in any luxuries since being "outshared" fourteen months ago, well, then, these same people looked at you only briefly and whispered to one another, "Failure."

"Always start the day on a cheery note, eh?" he said to his reflection. It was a pleasant if unmemorable face (and if anyone *did* remember his face, they remembered only the terrible acne scars), and he decided—as he always did during this morning ritual—that he was happy with it and the man who accompanied it. If only there were someone in his life with whom he could share his fear at this moment, to whom he could voice his doubts, if only he could find someone who would—

—ah, the hell with it. That's why he had Lady De Winter at nights (or Esmeralda, or Roxanne, or Whomever), occasionally in the afternoons, sometimes during lunch, but she was always with him, more a part of his memory than those few people who were actually a part of his life.

As he was adjusting his tie, a sudden, loud *whump!* from the room next door shook the wall over his bed with such force that the cheap painting hanging there fell off its hook and dropped right onto his pillow.

Good thing I didn't sleep late, he thought.

He took the painting off the bed and was attempting to hang it back up when there was another, louder, more violent *whump!* next door, followed by the sound of a man screaming, *"Leave me alone, bitch!"*

Simon froze, then leaned toward the wall, and could hear, very plainly, the sound of a woman crying.

Clenching his teeth, he started toward the door, ready to go over and see if the woman was all right. He'd grown up in a house where his father thought nothing of taking out his frustrations on Simon's mother in the form of a fist to the face or stomach or a couple of hard slaps, and Simon was not one to turn away from a battered woman.

He exited his room and stormed over to his neighbors' door, took a deep breath, and knocked.

Very insistently.

The door opened only so far as the chain lock on the inside would allow it, and one half of a beautiful woman's face, tear-streaked and red, peered out.

". . . y-yes?"

"Are you all right? I heard—"

"I'm fine, thank you."

"Are you sure? It sounded—"

"Please mind your own business!" she hissed at him, her voice equal parts hiss and heartbreak, then slammed the door.

Simon raised his fist to knock once more, pulled it away, raised it again, then shook his head and dropped his hand to his side.

Coward, he thought to himself, then sighed.

Christ—didn't anything ever work out for people in this world?

And so Simon Kaiser, an average, lonely, unimaginative but decent man, left for the attorney's office to carry out his duties as Surviving Grandson, still trying to recapture the scent of his dream lover's skin.

Just another day. No fanfare, please.

The L'lewyth-i were more than willing to submit themselves to scientists' testing—not that it helped Humankind to understand their nature or origins any better.

They were a combination of crystal and supercooled liquids that could not be precisely identified. Each L'lewyth-i was a single-celled creature with a faceted wall. The solidified fluid which gave them form was a type of colloid with an index of refraction like that of polystyrene, and each contained a complex nucleus the likes of which no scientist had ever seen before, and so could not hope to understand.

The L'lewyth-i gladly agreed to submit to a series of intense heat, corrosion, and bombardment tests, tests that should have destroyed their crystalline characteristics but did not. When it became apparent to even the most uninformed layman that modern science was never going to be able to determine the L'lewyth-i's biological/chemical makeup, it was decided to delve into their method of communication.

These tests yielded no better results until one night, in a fit of sleep-deprived frustration, one of the scientists on the project glared at the creature on his table and, not completely subconsciously, sent a wave of angered thought in its direction—

—and was answered by a sound, of sorts. Nothing that could be detected by any audio equipment, but a sound, nonetheless; a pressure in the scientist's mind. No word, but the pressure was an equally angered negation, a "no"-flavored impulse.

Being familiar with the phenomenon of piezoelectricity, wherein a crystal of quartz of Rochelle salts would yield a small potential when squeezed, or would slightly change its dimensions when voltage was applied across it, the scientist attempted another connection, and discovered that the L'lewyth-i used piezoelectricity in a way that had not, until their coming to Earth, been considered viable: They adapted their electronic impulses to be in synch with the brainwave patterns of whomever was focusing on them.

And so they came to be called, in the popular culture, the "electric starfish."

"Leave me alone, bitch!" screamed Jean Guillou (whose real name was Andrew Hill, but only he, his family, his girlfriend, and agent knew that), throwing the second chair across the room and enjoying the sound it made when it crashed against the wall.

Robin cowered near the bathroom door, Jean's syringe kit in her hands. Bitch should've known better than to just come into the john like that. He didn't know whether to laugh at the memory of her face when she saw what he was doing or just punch her lights out. She'd startled him so badly that he'd dropped the heated spoon and its expensive contents right into the sink. A thousand bucks right down the drain—figuratively *and* literally.

He stomped over to her, slapped her across the face, and wrenched the syringe kit from her shaking hands.

She nervously brushed some hair from her puffy, red, moist eyes, and looked up at him like a scared puppy.

". . . *why,* baby? Why'd you have to go and start on that stuff again?"

"None of your damned business!"

Robin pointed at the syringe kit. "Is that . . . is that why we're staying in this hole instead of a good hotel? Have you gone through that much of our money?"

He drew back to hit her but was stopped by the sound of someone hammering on the door. He grabbed her hair and yanked her in front of him, then gave her a shove. "Tell 'em to go away, whoever it is!"

He retreated to the bathroom, this time locking the door behind him.

He listened to her open the door and speak in whispers to whoever it was . . . sounded like that guy from the room next door: Was she all right? Was she sure?

She snapped something at him, then slammed the door.

Jean nodded his head, popping the top of the vial and delicately tapping out the powder into the spoon. He tightened the rubber tourniquet around his arm and set about getting the dose ready.

God knows he was ready for a dose, what with all the pressure he'd been under lately. It wasn't easy being a rising star on the Art Circuit, but after too many years of struggling to have his works acknowledged, building a cult following in galleries in the tristate area, and finally finding an agent with solid connections to the New York and L.A. gallery scene, he was on his way . . . and he deserved to treat himself. The Indianapolis show was the last one before moving on to New York, and he was *an artist,* he had things to grapple with that no one else could understand, and after tomorrow night it was on to the Big Time. So what if he hadn't produced anything new in over four months? He had enough old stuff that hadn't been shown to buy him a few more weeks, long enough for inspiration to strike, everything was gonna be cool, but in the meantime he needed release, he needed a treat.

And the junk *was* a treat, that was for sure. It helped when the work wasn't going well, when he couldn't get the images in his head onto the canvas so they'd be perfect reflections of one another; the junk, it was *bliss,* baby, it held you like you'd never been held before, singing lullabies in your brain—*Shhh, don't worry, I'm here with you now, you're a part of me*—and it loved you like no woman ever could; it never argued, never judged you, never gave you any lip; it knew what you needed, and that it loved you; it knew where you needed to be licked, and when to stop before the sheer *sensuality* of it broke your mind and spirit.

He sank the plunger.

Instant bliss. Better than any painting ever done by anyone anywhere anytime.

Oh, yeah. . . .

When they wanted to, the L'lewyth-i traveled just like electrons do: They were able to jump from point to point without crossing the space between.

"Blinking," as it came to be called.

Scientists discovered this after Government agents attempted to take the L'lewyth-i away. If the creatures didn't want someone to touch them, they simply "blinked out," of one spot and "blinked in" to another—sometimes halfway across the room and then, later, halfway across the world.

Which is how they came to be so widely scattered, and why so many people started taking them in as pets— though that implies that the "owners" had a choice in the matter, which they did not. If a L'lewyth-i wanted to be your pet, then it allowed you to keep it. If it sensed something about you that it didn't care for, you couldn't catch it to save your life. There were hunters who tried poison, tranquilizer darts, electric prods, you name it, they tried it in order to catch one against its will, but no go.

The L'lewyth-i chose their keepers.

* * *

"Have a seat, Mr. Kaiser," said Walter McGinn, the attorney who was the executor of Melinda Kaiser's estate. "Would you care for something to drink? Coffee or a soft drink, perhaps?"

"No, thank you," replied Simon, already feeling uncomfortable in the attorney's austere and expensively furnished office.

"I want you to know how deeply sorry I am for your loss," said McGinn, taking his seat behind the large oak desk that served as the centerpiece of his office. "Your grandmother was a wonderful woman. You know that she worked here for several years as—"

"—as your cleaning lady, yes, I know." The words came out with more bitterness than Simon had intended to demonstrate, and he immediately apologized for his tone of voice.

"No need to apologize," said McGinn. "I can fully understand how a man in your current circumstances would feel about . . ." He gestured outward at the office. ". . . about all this, and about your grandmother's position. I never looked down on Melinda, Mr. Kaiser; she was far too sharp a person to put up with any sort of condescending treatment." McGinn laughed, sadly. "More than one night, she sat in here and listened to my problems, be they personal or professional, and she always gave the best advice. I considered her a good friend and always will. Which is why I helped her draw up her will and agreed to be executor—and before you ask or even think it, I did all of this *pro bono*. I would not have charged Melinda for my services for anything in the world."

"That's awfully nice of you," whispered Simon. "I know she thought a lot of you."

"Did she? That's good to know. Really, it is."

For a moment the two men sat in silence, each with his memories of the woman whose absence was almost a sentient force in the room.

Finally, McGinn cleared his throat and leaned forward,

shuffling some papers, in full legal mode. "I'm afraid that your grandmother's estate isn't as considerable as you might have been led to think. Most of her assets—stocks, the house, some savings bonds—were liquidated upon her death so the moneys could be divided up equally between—"

"I would've come to the funeral."

McGinn looked up. "I beg your pardon?"

"I would've come if I'd known. I was . . . I was up in Seattle for a job interview when she died. Nobody called to tell me or I would've been at her funeral."

McGinn shook his head slightly. "If I've said or done anything for you to infer that I have judged you in some way—"

"No, no, you haven't. I just . . . I just wanted to tell *someone,* you know?"

"Of course. I understand."

"It's just that nobody let me know."

"Your father or one of your sisters didn't try to get in touch with you?"

"My sisters don't much bother with anyone outside of themselves, and my father and I haven't spoken since Mom died." He shrugged. "I don't know, maybe I should've called Grandma more than I did this last year or so, but with losing the job and everything—"

"If it's any help, Mr. Kaiser, she spoke of you often. She loved you very much." He leaned forward. "Between us, you were her favorite grandchild."

"That's only because no one else called or visited. Sorry—I guess I'm feeling a little sorry for myself today. The job search isn't going well and on top of everything else, I didn't even get to kiss her good-bye. Does that sound corny?"

"Not at all." McGinn lifted a sheet of paper from his desk. "Melinda was aware of your circumstances, and in the cash portion of your inheritance—three thousand dollars—she instructed me to give you one-third of it in cash. 'Poor guy probably can't afford to make the trip, but you bet your butt he'll come.' That's what she said." He produced a brown envelope from a desk drawer and handed it to Simon. "A thousand dollars in fifty-dollar bills, and a cashier's check for the remainder."

Simon looked inside the envelope. "What's this key?"

"That's to a local storage facility where the rest of your inheritance is waiting. It's not much—some knick-knacks, her cross-stitch work, hobby supplies and several photo albums, old '78 records and an antique gramophone to play them on—but these items were the most precious things she owned, and she specifically wanted you to have them. 'He's the only one who'll know how to appreciate them.' Her words. Here are the directions to the place." He handed Simon a folded slip of paper. "It's in a very good section of town—an up-scale storage facility, if you can believe it—and the rent's been paid until the end of the month."

"I'll, uh . . . I'll clean it out tomorrow before I have to head back to Cedar Hill."

Simon closed his eyes and allowed himself a few tears for the loss of his grandmother—and not simply the big things, her voice on the phone wishing him happy birthday every year, the card with a twenty-five-dollar gift certificate from the Book-of-the-Month Club every Christmas, her laugh, the way she'd gotten all misty-eyed the Thanksgiving he gave her a silly owl-shaped cookie jar, the way her bear hugs stuck to your ribs for half an hour after her embrace—he remembered these things, yes, and always would, but the things he mourned, the things he would miss the most, were the underlying currents of her that were always there in his life, separate but converging, the minute details that filled in the cracks between the larger memories: a news-paper left draped across the arm of a chair, a coat hanging on the hall tree not-quite-rightly, the crumbs of freshly baked cookies she didn't wipe off the counter, the way she crossed her sevens, the scent of her old perfume clinging to his shirt. . . .

The underlying currents. Gone now. Forever.

"There is one last item," said McGinn. "The matter of your grandmother's pet, ThenAgain."

Simon laughed. "ThenAgain. Christ, what a name. She never told me how she came up with it."

"Nor me," said McGinn, reaching down beside his desk and lifting the glass jar into view.

Simon had known that his grandmother kept one of the alien creatures as a pet, but until this moment he'd never seen one in person; oh, sure, he'd seen pictures in magazines, videotape on the news, all that, but it was completely different from actually being in the presence of one of them.

It was starfish-shaped, but there the similarities ended. Where regular starfish had a crusty, bottom-of-the-sea-and-look-what's-clinging-to-it quality, the L'lewyth-i in the jar appeared to be composed of isinglass filled with tiny bursts of lightning giving way to perpetual fractured prisms of color. He knew from the news that all of this activity had something to do with the way they communicated with their "owners," and he knew also that they were, so far, perfectly harmless, but the sight of the thing still frightened him. There was an aura of *otherworldliness* to it that made him feel at once even more insignificant than he already did, and that was the last damn thing he needed.

"Look, Mr. McGinn, I don't think that I'm the best person to take care of this—"

The rest of the sentence died in his mouth when he placed his fingertips against the jar in order to push it away from him.

For a brief second there was an impulse, overpowering but definite, of his grandmother. And this Grandma-impulse had come from within the L'lewyth-i.

"Jesus," he said.

"I know," said McGinn. "I felt her, too, when I went to pick it up." The attorney leaned closer to the jar but didn't touch it. "They say that these creatures can know everything there is to know about a person with one touch. I suppose that's why so many people want them. Can you imagine having something like this, something that knows your every thought, every impulse, your golden qualities as well as your darkest corners, and accepts you, anyway?"

"I can't imagine it, no," said Simon, rising from his seat and gathering up everything except for the jar. "Look, Mr. McGinn, I can barely take care of myself as it is, let alone any kind of pet, let alone one that came from . . . from . . ."

". . . outer space?"

"Still sounds weird, doesn't it?"

"Yes, indeed it does." McGinn offered his hand. "I fully understand your wishes, and I hope things turn around for you soon."

Simon thanked the attorney for his kindness and was opening the door when the Grandma-impulse came to him again, much stronger than before, and stopped him in his tracks.

I can't take care of you, you scare the hell out of me and . . .

. . . and there was something else there, deep beneath the Grandma-impulse . . .

. . . *I wouldn't know what to do with you, how to care for you, I just can't . . . I mean, I really don't think I could . . .*

. . . swimming to the surface from under the Grandma-impulse, yet still carrying her essence with it . . .

. . . *I don't think I can . . .*

. . . closer, closer, shhh, I've a secret promise to carry out . . .

. . . *then again,* Simon thought and turned back toward the creature.

*   *   *

Andy:

I've had it. I refuse to go through this a third time, especially now that we were so close to Making It like we'd always dreamed. I worked for you, took the extra jobs so you could stay home and paint, and after all these years this is how you repay me, by shooting that shit into your system. Well, you can have it. I'm finished. I'm taking half the money we still have left and will take half the money in the savings and checking accounts—if there still is any, you bastard.

I'll have my stuff moved out by the time you get back from the show. I hope it goes well for you, I really do. You were a great talent once, and maybe you will be again someday if you stop squandering it. I don't think you've ever really appreciated the gift you have. A lot of people would give anything to have half the ability that you've wasted.

Don't think I hate you because I don't. I pity you too much to hate your sorry ass. When I think of you, I will remember what you might have been.

Robin

Jean wadded up the note and threw it in the trash.

Yeah, well, fuck her and the horse she came in on. He'd manage. This Indy show was going to make him famous, and that's all he'd need for a while. The show itself would go to L.A. or New York, and that would buy him a couple of months, maybe more, and if he didn't come up with anything new, he still had the old stuff and—

—and for just a second the thought crossed his mind that maybe she was right, maybe he'd squandered his talent and the well was dry, one needleful too many and enough brain cells fried—

—no. He could control it this time. A little inspiration, that's what the junk gave him, and as an artist he had the right, the fucking *right,* to choose how to get inspired.

To hell with her.

He looked at the note in the wastebasket.

"To hell with you—*fuck you!*"

And decided to celebrate his freedom with a beer.

Finding the fridge empty of brewskies, he threw on a shirt, washed his face, and grabbed up what cash he needed. There was a market down the road and he needed some munchies, anyway.

He slammed the door on his way out and wasn't looking at where he was going and so almost bumped into that pizza-faced bald dude from the room next door.

"Oh, hey, sorry 'bout that, man," he said.

"Sure," said Pizza-Face, sidestepping to let Jean pass.

"Hey, what'cha got in that jar? Izzat—oh, wow—izzat one of them starfish things?"

"Yes, it is." And without another word—but giving Jean a real dirty glance, as if to say *I know what you did to her, you prick,* Pizza-Face went into his room and locked the door behind him.

And all the way to and from the store Jean kept remembering everything he'd read and heard about the creatures, how they could expand your consciousness if they chose to, how they could tell you things, teach you things, *show* you things, images from deep space, maybe from their home, their planet, images, images, images, enough images to keep him in supply for the rest of his life, enough images that he'd never again have to worry about going dry, images enough to keep him famous— oh, yeah; images.

So he made a decision.

He would take the creature from Pizza-Face. After all, what the hell was some loser like that going to do with it? He probably had no idea what it was capable of, what could be done with it if you knew how—hell, a loser like that didn't *deserve* to have a gift like that, no way, no how, no sir.

But Jean knew that *he* did deserve it.

And in a little while, he'd do something about it. . . .

*   *   *

For the longest time Simon couldn't bring himself to open the jar and touch the L-lewyth-i, but eventually he did, as he knew he would.

He removed the lid and reached in, and the thing *blinked* into nothingness before he could touch it, and Simon almost cried because he knew what that blinking meant, that it didn't want to have anything to do with you, and why the hell not? He was nothing special and never had been, just look—

—look—

—look there. Right on his shoulder, warm and snuggly like a napping kitty.

He touched its surface, reveling in its softness and the chill of space.

There was an impulse, a Sleep-Now impulse, and Simon found himself, despite not being all that tired, lying back on the bed and closing his eyes while the creature sang within him a song of distant places and galaxies. . . .

Jean waited until after midnight before opening the door which joined his room to the one next door. He had a credit card all ready to force the lock on Pizza-Face's adjoining door—dude couldn't be that much of a loser that he'd leave it unlocked—but unlocked it was, and Jean smiled to himself, pushing the door open in slow increments, hoping it wouldn't squeak, and it didn't, and that was good because now he was in the room and moving slowly, very slowly, light on his feet, toward the bed where Pizza-Face looked down for the count, and there was the creature next to him, just as out-there as you please, and Jean reached for it but the thing must have known he was coming, must have *wanted* him to come, must have known he was the one who deserved it, because before he could touch it the thing blinked right into his hands, and then he was back into his own room, closing and locking the door and falling down on the bed, his heart hammering against his ribs because he'd *done it!*

He examined the creature in his hands.

Psyche-fucking-delic, those colors.

He could barely contain himself at the thought of what it was going to show him.

So why not enhance the experience even more? he thought, and did a couple quick lines of coke to get himself stoked and rockin'.

"Show me the magic," he said.

And the thing blinked out of his hands and onto the side of his head, clutching at his skull like a vise.

The Vedic religious traditions believe in the "vibration metaphor": throw a pebble in a pond, and the vibrations ripple outward in concentric circles; strike a bell, and it vibrates in waves of sound; meditate on a thought, and it will echo through the realm of the collective unconscious. Though the L'lewyth-i knew nothing of these concepts—at least, not in Earth terms—nor anything about theoretically applying the vibration metaphor to recent discoveries about the susceptibility of brain-wave patterns to nonphysical stimuli, it nonetheless put these theories into action as it merged with the man on the bed, employing a blended and sequenced series of binaural sound pulses to induce a frequency-following response in his brain, creating a ripple effect that altered his EEG wave patterns and generated expanded states of consciousness. Resting-state alpha activity was suppressed and replaced by synchronous slow-wave activity in the median of the central cortex; it then increased the amplitude and frequency of the sound impulses, and the resting-state alpha and slow-wave activity were induced to operate simultaneously, accompanied by temporal gamma brainwave activity, enabling the man on the bed to perceive nonphysical energies outside the confines of the physical-law belief system; not only that, but he perceived these nonphysical phenomena as constituting his whole field of awareness, lifting him into a state that was as nearly perfectly blissful as any human being had ever achieved.

And that's when the L'lewyth-i did what its race was sent out into the universe to do.

It fulfilled its purpose.

Simon awoke violently, his chest hammering, his body covered in sweat, his limbs shaking, his breath coming in bursts, gasping as if the oxygen in the room had suddenly been sucked out.

He looked down at the L'lewyth-i on the bed next to him and was compelled by an impulse, a Do-It-Now-impulse, and without questioning why he rose from the bed and put on his shoes and grabbed all the keys and ran out to his car and drove to the storage facility and found his grandmother's "locker."

He unlocked and opened the door, turned on the light, and climbed inside, carefully rummaging through all of her hobby supplies until he found what he was looking for, the old oil paints and some unused, prestretched canvases, and it stunned him how easily he was able to get started, first with a charcoal pencil to sketch the outline, then with a light sealant on the base, then the colors themselves, blinking onto the brush and then the canvas, and he painted—God, how he painted!—as if he'd been doing it all his life, even though he'd never so much as tried a stick-figure before—hell, he was lucky to get a paint-by-numbers kit to come out right, crying clowns and bland landscapes and dogs playing poker—but *this*, this was unlike anything he'd ever known before, he was opened up to the glories of the world and the universe, hurtled into the void and all that lay beyond, shedding the fragile prison of his flesh, flung wide open, dizzy and disoriented, seized by a whirling vortex and spun around, around, around, spiraling higher, thrust into the heart of all Creation's whirling invisibilities, a creature whose puny carbon atoms and other transient substances were suddenly freed, unbound, scattered amidst the universe—yet each particle still held strong to the immeasurable, unseen thread which linked it inexorably to his soul and his consciousness and his flesh and the canvas before him; twirling fibers of light wound themselves around impossibly fragile, molecule-thin membranes of memory and moments that swam toward him like proud children coming back to shore after their very first time in the water alone, and when they reached him, when these memories and moments emerged from the sea and reached out, Simon ran toward them, arms open wide, meeting them on windswept beaches of thought, embracing them, accepting them, absorbing them, becoming Many, becoming Few, becoming One, knowing, learning, feeling; his blood mingled with their blood, his thoughts with their thoughts, dreams with dreams, hopes with hopes, frustrations with frustrations, and in this mingling, in this unity, in this actualization, he became more than he was, more then he'd ever hoped to be, becoming—

—*the inhabitants of a planet millions of light-years away, swimming in endless seas of liquid lambda, merging with the atmosphere instead of merely surviving in it, and these creatures, these glorious creatures, floating beings of hydrogen, bobbing to and fro in the conscious refrain of chemical processes that kept them buoyant and alive, a race that had inhabited the breadth of time and space, each one an artist of such unknowable genius that their most primitive thoughts, their most repulsive perversions, were the most beautiful and moving poetry Simon had ever read/hear/known/experienced, and among them was one named Tutrah who took the clay of his planet and from it fashioned the Indruh Ukreeahlah, the creatures called the L'lewyth-i here on Earth, and they were Tutrah's most magnificent creations, but when the Others saw them, how simple they were and therefore*

*dangerous, a throwback of sorts, they condemned Tutrah
to a planet of outcasts and demanded that his creations
be destroyed, but he refused and so was hunted down and
himself destroyed, for there can be no hint of backward-
thinking here, but before they took his life which he
gladly gave up for the sake of his race's art, he sent his
creations out into the universe with instructions to find
Worthy Ones and give to them some of the genius that his
race had fostered for enternities upon eternities, and in
this act, in these transferences, each one of the Worthy
would contribute some small part to recreating Tutrah
on a new planet in a new universe—now go, my children,
my creations, be fruitful and multiply—*

—and Simon fell backward, drenched in wonder and
sweat, his arms and hands and eyes and back aching,
agonized, and saw that he had gone through seven canvases, each one in succession telling some small part of
Tutrah's story, and that of the L'lewyth-i, in turn, promising more to come, the story of images and impulses not
even close to reaching fruition, and Simon wept at the
realization of what ThenAgain had given to him, for he
was not the same as he was, nor would he ever be again.

For he had been deemed Worthy.

A new beginning was his for the asking.

A new life was his for the taking, and, in time, when
every L'lewyth-i had fulfilled its purpose and recreated
their creator through the Worthy Ones, then Simon's new
life would be the world's as well. . . .

They found Jean hanging from the shower in his motel
room with enough junk in his system to kill three people.
There were very few clues as to why this young artist, on
the brink of stardom, had chosen to end his life in such a
seamy way.

No one knew what to make of the dozens and dozens
of sketchbook pages found scattered around the room,
nor the childlike scribbles on those pages; the hand

which created these pitiful pictures wasn't even capable of drawing a stick figure.

I was never worthy, read the note pinned to his shirt. *I was never worthy.*

And Simon Kaiser awoke every morning to find that he *was* Athos, and always had been, and always would be.

BONGOID

David Bischoff

David Bischoff is active in many areas of the science fiction field, including writing his own novels such as *The UFO Conspiracy* trilogy, collaborating with authors such as Harry Harrison, writing three *Bill The Galactic Hero* novels, and writing excellent media tie-in novelizations, such as *Aliens* and *Star Trek* novels. He has previously worked as an associate editor of *Amazing* magazine and as a staff member of NBC. He lives in Eugene, Oregon.

"I want one," said Jimmy.

And, of course, Jimmy got one. What else *could* have happened?

His parents, after all, were fans, too, and they wanted one, in their own kiddie Planet Hopper matrixed and substratumed minds as well. They watched the old show, the older shows, the ancient, and the prehistoric versions. When they looked up to the stars, they really could see that familiar spaceship parked in Earth orbit, radiating with meaning and truth and universal goals and general feel-good philosophy.

So, when the Captain flashed into the living room

entertainment stage and blithely announced, his gay twinkle in his eye, that yes, the news reports were true, there were Bongoids out there in the great blue-and-purple beyond, the twinges that traveled through heart-strings were not only in ten-year-olds.

It was, after all, a Planet Hopper Earth.

That was, if it wasn't a Mega BattleMoon Universe.

"Hi there, lo-sci-fi fans! It's me, Captain Felix Alphonse, leader of the Starship *Let's-Take-A-Peak*." That twinkle, that rakish smile. The echo-twizzle in rooms across the world shiver and effervesce—ah, the dopamine spikes in kiddies and oldsters alike. Who can forget the semi-sacred place in the pantheon of vid-Gods this figure holds! "I've teleported down with great Beyond Solar News!"

The Captain has a touch of crow's feet around those blue eyes, and the hair looks a bit—well, acrylic. There's a slight paunch above the raunch here, and that smile is somewhat subsincerity speed. Still, the old Capper doesn't look bad for being on the dicey side of two centuries old.

"Yes, Earthees! In yet another astonishing example of coincidental evolutionary development, our valiant space farers, working for you in the Great Beyond, have discovered a planet full of Bongoids!"

The brain chemistry detectors at the Central Nodes around the Earth have been prepared for this one, but still the surge is impressive. Across the world, the registered Hoppees, in front of their entertainment stages, utter whoops and gasps.

Immediately, the beloved image of the Captain floats stage left, to make room for a delicious cloud of mystery that billows up, resolving finally into a form.

Oh, boy! Oh, joy! It's a Bongoid!

First of all, the fur! Yes, what would a lovable scamp of an alien critter be without lots and lots of golden, lustrous, snuggly-wuggly fur! It appears at first to be one great ovoid of fur, but then slowly, it rises up on six ha-ha-look-at-that! hinged limbs atop duck-webbed feet. From its posterior sprout two antennae looking like nothing so much as early Dumont TV rabbit ears. But ah! the grabber—here they are—peeking from the mound that is presumably the head: a pair of limpid oval eyes, filled with doleful emotion, glistening with a strange combination of pathos and hope, that make the sad child eyes that stare from black velvet look malevolent.

Even as the oohs and ahhs whoosh through the Hopper camps of the world, a small limb breaks through that mass of fur, rolls out, reveals. From a paw, a plant protracts step by step. From pistil, blossoms emerge. Something like a sunflower grows and glows—an offering, a gift, a kind of melt-your-heart expression of universal Hallmark happiness.

"Hey! Aren't they cute? Aren't they absolutely adorable?" said the Captain. "And guess what? This species—and I've got the real name from the xenobiologist but only my scientific officer Sergeant Major Zapp can pronounce it, so let's just stick with Bongoids—this species doesn't cause any of the—uhm, problems—they caused in Episodes 10, 34, 59, 88, 145, 233—or the offshoot animation series DEEP SPACE BONGOIDS. They're one-hundred-and-twenty-percent faithful and supportive and adorable!"

In living rooms across the Earth, the Bongoid Eyes—those limpid, expressive orbs—grow like moons of love looming in living rooms. Hypnotizing with yearning, only slightly vibrating with subsonic subliminals, they loom and grow until every Hoppered-up family is convinced on a subatomic level that the deep well of love in those eyes is the Ur-universe upon which all joy of being is founded.

In the background: the Bongoid theme—a pastoral flute and whistle bouncing over hill and dale in playful pursuit of the Heart's Desire.

Then—voice thick with joy and tears and at its hammiest best—the Captain continues:

"And the best part is—they want to come and live with us! Yes, that's right— You see, their planet is in big trouble. The sun is going superduper-nova. Yes, one step worse than supernova, people, and that's worse for a species than having a black hole in the toilet!"

A flushing sound. The horrific wailing of little screams rotating down into a funnel of oblivion into the sewage pipes of dark matter.

"So we've got to help them! And in return, every family that signs to take one in will not only be getting all the love and affirmation and joy implicitly promised by the OverCreator himself—the creator of the Hopper universe, Dorg Keiser—"

The signature theme of Planet Hoppers—a symphony of faintly off-key theremins in a kind of John Philip Sousa march tempo—slips under the narration. From a glorious dawn the familiar grin of the Fabulous Meister flickers, waving at the minions and then recedes.

"Thanks, Dorg. You're the best!" says the Captain. Then he turns his eyes, with a dead-earnest cast locking into the brainstems of the viewers. "Please! Help us take in these dear creatures. They're only semisentient, so they need our help. The Great Human Burden in the universe is vast. How can you not give but a little of your vast wealth toward the care and upkeep of these beasties . . . ? And, in turn, your very own Bongoid will be the best pet a Hopper Heart could ever want to have!"

The Hopper symphony segues into the Bongoid theme—rocked up a bit—and those great lovable eyes superimpose and mesmerize.

"So plug into your Hopper cred connection and bring this new uplink to the Great Mystery beyond deeper into your Science Fiction lives!"

Another voice reverbs into audio view, as usual with Planet Hopper shows: " 'Science Fiction' is a Trademark of the Planet Hopper Corporation."

And, as in many and myriad a living room, a cry arises from the children.

Here, represented by little Jimmy Hydra.

"I want one!"

The Bongoid was delivered to the Hydra family on May the third, two thousand one hundred and ninety-two. The senior Hydras—father Richard and mother Judy—had the regulation one-and-a-half children for their income bracket. These were Jimmy, age ten and Freddy, aged negative two.

The Hydras lived in New New Jersey, an island off the Jersey shore created by landfill. Richard was a computer program. Judy was a vestal nonvirgin of the High Church of Science Fictionology created by Dorg Keiser in the Great One's monastery years.

Little Jimmy wanted to be a computer program just like his old man, but he was a bit troublesome because he was allergic to Diet Coke and pizza, the traditional contents of computer program's feedbag when he plugged into the MegaLink. Geneticists were expensive, and the Hyrdras were saving up to make their youngest at least three quarters of a child, so Little Jimmy had to find other dream occupations. Right now, for instance, he dreamed of being a starship captain. This was encouraged, because, even though there might only be reconstituted soy and bean sauce for dinner, by Dorg, each and every family in the world (that didn't side with the evil BattleMoon faction, anyway) had the International Americus Global Enterprise right to watch Planet Hoppers and dream about the future. As Hydra pater and Hydra mater themselves were stone Hopper freaks, every interest in Hopperdom was encouraged.

So, when the delivery was made that day, the family gathered in their living room (stacked with Hopper cubes and Hopper books, Hopper memorabilia, Hopper posters and, of course a Hopper Science Fictionology shrine, complete with a plastic Dorg Keizer idol, a jolly belly ballooning from its Hawaiian Nebula shirt) to examine the newly arrived crate, covered with air holes and spaceships.

"I'll get my tools," said Richard Hydra.

A familiar squeak sounded from the box.

Little Jimmy bounded up from Littler Freddy (half-children made great furniture) and knocked on the crate.

Again that evocative squeak emerged from the crate—something halfway between a bird's caw and a monkey's complaint.

"Just like in Episode 94 of the Planet Hopper Classic Series!" said Jimmy, clapping with delight.

"Yes, yes, dear," said Mrs. Hydra. "Isn't this wonderful? Watch out now that you don't step in Little Freddy's drool."

Drool, however, was the last thing on Jimmy's mind. His spine tingled with Planet Hopper joy. His brain was frothing from medula oblongata to cerebrum with Planet Hopper serotonin. All the electrical blips that surged across his synaptic gaps were shaped like starships.

Imagine! Even though he and his family seemed doomed to wallow in the mire of Earthly cess all their lives, performing repetitive and meaningless and redundant biological and work functions in a pointless and overcrowded planet, they could not only dream of a brighter future—they could actually share the adventure and delight of that future in their very own little hole. La, la, la, it made Jimmy even more giddy than when he ate Planet Hopper Long ShelfLife HyperChoc Cupcakes!

Father Hydra emerged with Engineer McBagged's Patented Spanner Plus device. This was actually only a crowbar, but it had wicked Planet Hopper Go Faster stripes. He pulled out a few staples quickly, pried off the top of the crate. They all stepped back as the sides of the crate flopped open like petals of some wooden blossom.

Crouching before them was a bundle of fur. A sign was around its neck. "Feed me, please," said the sign.

"Oh, isn't it adorable!" said Mrs. Hydra, hands clasped together with maternal delight.

"Hi!" said Jimmy.

From one side of the fur (and what a wealth of roly poly fur!) a pair of eyes emerged. Big saucerlike orbs they were, with a richness and fullness of color and detail and pure adoration and love that no entertainment stage anywhere could have predicted.

The thing squeaked.

With a bound, it pushed up from its six strange legs and was all over Jimmy, a meter-long tongue licking his face with far more affection than a mere besotted St. Bernard could ever hope to manage. Then, each in turn, it bestowed its attention on Mr. Hydra and Mrs. Hydra, each getting a thorough washing by the enthusiastic alien tongue.

Then, the Bongoid turned to the littlest Hydra, Freddy, and ate him.

"Freddy!" shrieked Mrs. Hydra.

"Out there!" said Jimmy, impressed at how big the creature's mouth was.

Richard Hydra chuckled ruefully. "Heh, heh, these Bongoids. Always full of tricks. But then, the universe *is* full of adventure!"

"Freddy!" shrieked Judy again.

The Bongoid burped.

"Don't worry, dear," said Mr. Hydra. "Remember Episode 52 of the Bongoid animated series? This happens sometimes when Bongoids get too excited."

So saying, Richard stepped over and thrust Engineer MacBagged Patented Spanner Plus in the part of the fur where that mouth had opened to engulf the half child.

The Bongoid made a sound somewhat like a playful growl, and honestly didn't seem to care much for getting an adult human arm thrust down its throat, but nonetheless yielded. Freddy was pulled out. The half-child gurgled and giggled, the only damage a dent in his skull.

As there was only a rudimentary brain within, no harm was done.

Little Jimmy stepped up and wagged a finger at the Bongoid, affecting the pouting tone of the Shirley Temple Folk of Series Twenty: PLANET HOLLYWOOD HOPPERS. "Naughty Bongoid! Don't ever eat Freddy again."

The big eyes emerged from the fur, looking adorable and woeful. They blinked. The Bongoid looked decidedly sheepish. The fur turned white and fleecy.

A tiny teardrop fell from one of those eyes.

"Ah, shucks, fella. That's okay," said Jimmy. "Give us a hug."

Jimmy Hydra's arms were suddenly full of squeaky, adorable alien love.

"I thought that Captain Alphonse said that these things wouldn't cause the problems they cause in Planet Hoppers," said Judy Hydra, picking up Freddy and pushing his skull back into shape.

"I'm afraid, dear, that those were the premium grade that don't cause all the problems. This grade comes with not-at-all-serious problems, and it's the only kind we can afford and, besides, look at those two. They were just made for each other! And really a Bongoid is much more satisfying than the alien fish we've been settling for— and it doesn't need liquid hydrogen to swim in!"

The skull of Freddy had popped back into place and he seemed none the worse for wear, so Judy Hydra's querulous remarks (much in the manner of the annoying Leary O'Squeamish, poop-deck commander in Series Seventeen, the Sitcom Mission: Planet Hopheads) ceased. After all, whether or not this Bongoid was of the tippy-top grade, it was a genuine Bongoid, miraculously transplanted from the actual universe into their living quarters. This was a living, breathing, nictitating, phosphorescing, undulating, and above all furry missionary of cuddlyness from the bedrock of the Hydra existence, Planet Hoppers, and by all the Heavens, whether or not they ever stepped up to the economic status to get little Freddy a full brain, they had a biological connection to the wonderland of stars out there? Right?

And so their lives continued, Father Hydra helping to run the machinery of the Earth in his little plug-in way, Mother Hydra servicing the corporeal needs of the Science Fictionology Priests and chanting the praises of the Great Creator, Freddy Hydra finding creative uses for Planet Hopper diapers and Jimmy attending Planet Hopper PS Academy Two Hundred and Twenty-Nine Thousand Eight Hundred and Twenty-Three, hoping to fly starships one day but probably fated for Monad Unit Sanitation. Still, thanks to the imagination of the Planet Hopper folks, they had dreams and purpose. . . .

And now, of course, they had a Bongoid.

They named him Jackson.

Jackson served every function of a cat or a dog or a parrot or any other kind of normal Earthbound pet. If someone rang the buzzer of the domicile, it barked. It would bring dead rats from the nearby forest as gifts to the family. It would clamber into a large cage and chirp 'Polly want a cracker' at appropriate moments. Bongoids, after all, according to the Planet Hopper tradition, were marvelously emphatic creatures. A Bongoid could tell by psi feelings exactly what *kind* of pet the Hydras needed. Even when it was time to chew up a leg of the coffee table or take a dump on the kitchen floor, to declare its petness, it knew exactly the right time to perform these pet functions.

Even so, the family could never doubt that it was a Planet Hopper critter just like they were. When the Entertainment theater was on for the latest adventures of the various noble crews or space station inhabitants, Jackson was right there, eyes no longer doleful but alert, watching right along with the family. When other Bongoids appeared, it would do various entertaining Bongoid dances.

And whenever other Planet Hopper merchandise was offered, it wailed woefully until Papa Hydra hit the appropriate button to order it.

Little Jimmy did, however, wish that Jackson the Bongoid did one thing that it did not do that pets were supposed to do. Jackson would not sleep in his bed with him at night. In fact, one of the conditions that Bongoids came with was that each night, they would be placed in their own room for eight solid hours, and not be disturbed.

At first, Jimmy did not mind. Such was the joy of having a Bongoid that he slept well at night and dreamed his starry dreams alone, quite happily. But then, after two months of this, Jimmy realized that, at night, he craved company. He would wake up and wish for something furry to hold onto. Such, perhaps, was instinct as Jimmy was descended from a long line of Planet Hopper watchers, and the longing for Bongoids perhaps genetically inlaid as far back as the first irradiation of Hopper Watchers in the mid-twentieth century.

One night, Jimmy awoke, a light sheen of sweat upon his brow. He had just had a terrible dream, in which a terrorist group of BattleMoon watchers had strafed a bunch of innocent Bongoids with sizzler rays and then served them with rice and Teriyaki sauce to the PowerMad Gods who had created that awful media series.

Jimmy got up. He got out of his unit, traipsed past where Freddy was vegetating and out into the hallway. At the end of the corridor, draped in shadows, was the closed door of the room in which Jackson the Bongoid slept.

A strange sound drifted around the edges of the door.

Driven on by helpless curiosity, and the need to see his beloved alien pet, young Jimmy ventured forth. He placed his hand on the doorknob.

Twisted it.

Opened it.

Peering in, he saw the nighttime form of Jackson the Bongoid.

"Oh, my Dorg!" he gasped.

Rip Markel, the beloved actor who portrayed the dashing Captain Felix Alphonse on many of the television series, the movies, and animated trading cards of Planet Hoppers examined himself in the mirror, not caring much for the way his hair was parted.

"Nine centimeters above the left ear, dammit!" he shouted.

The thick weave atop his head wriggled a bit. Strands undulated, and a half-hearted attempt was made by the hair to create the exact part desired. However, finally, the effort caused the ends of the hair to fall limply and hang forlornly down over the brow of the star. A kind of unearthly sigh escaped the thing.

"Dammit! I paid good money for this thing!" said Markel.

A stage assistant peeked into the room. "You're on in five minutes, Captain."

"Goddammit. I can't take it. I just can't take it! I'm a starship captain, not a performing monkey!" Markel reached down for his makeup trowel. He stuck it under his pate and, with his other hand, pried the hair-creature from off his head. Underneath, cyborg batteries winked dully in the mirror. As quickly as he dared, Markel yanked the connections to his base cutaneous underlay. Then he threw his hair down to the floor. It began to whimper like a hurt dog; the strands of hair wriggled about like an agitated anemone.

Snarling and sneering, Markel began to jump up and down on the thing. It wailed and cried and gasped. A blot of green blood spurted onto the floor.

"What the hell is going—Jesus!" said Theodore Evans, Corporation Representative on the set. Evans was one of the Suits who looked after Markel. He was paid well for his trouble, and trouble it often was. However, generally Markel honored his alien toupees and at least had the sense to get help with them. The man had had violent temper tantrums before, sure—but if he went too far with this business, there could be more rebellion than in just an ancient egotist's addled brain.

"Goddamned thing," said Markel. "I'm the Captain. You'll obey my orders!"

Evans tackled him. He pushed the man back onto the trailer couch and pinned him against it. The old man kicked and screamed, and it wasn't like the ancient thespian didn't have muscles. Still, Evans was young, and he had been picked for just this kind of possible violent moment. He was able to keep Markel pinned just long enough for the guy to calm down. A spritz of the old dermic certainly helped matters. Markel untensed and lolled back a bit, twitching.

Evans looked at the pile of hair smeared upon the floor. He twisted a finger and spoke into it. "Bio clean up. Workover detail, Markel trailer, immediately. Delay commercial shoot—" He looked at the starship clock on the wall. "Three hours. Explanation: psycho/ego eruption. Classified info. Repeat. Classified."

He looked back down at the bald actor. Already there was a distinctly gray hue to his skin, and his right arm was twitching.

The operative adjusted his dermic and gave a blast into the arm. Then, just to be double sure, he pulled up the man's side, opened up a cabinet and put the bio-cells into stasis. There might have to be some kind of mem-wipe later.

The dressing room wardrobe door whacked open.

One of the Planet Hopper uniforms deopaqued and grew eyes on stalks. "We demand to know what is going—"

Evans acted promptly. He pulled a spray can from his pocket on the way over to the door and gave all the clothing a good blast of Numbler. Then, just for good measure, he went over the unconscious uniform on the Markel and blasted it with a good spritz of Numbler as well.

Above a desk, a comm-face took form.

Abner Raintree, Corporate Ops.

"Psych-Ego eruption, huh?" said the face.

"Guess he took a dislike to his hairpiece. Ripped it off and stomped on it," said Evans.

Raintree grunted. "Just another couple of years. That's all we need the son of a bitch for. Patchwork holding together otherwise?"

"I numbled them. I know we own their asses, but with exos, you never know."

Raintree shook his head. "Well, this is going to cost. We wanted that commercial for tonight's showing. The President wants the accounts in the hyperblack, and the new products are ready. They always go faster when the Captain hustles the star-schmoes. You got the team coming in?"

"I figure he'll be worked up in three hours and ready. What about a live feed?" said Evans.

Raintree pursed his lips. "Chancy. With one of the new actors maybe, but with the Captain . . . We don't want him mooning the audience mid-transmit."

"Some would pay to see that!"

"I'd pay not to see that, myself." The Suit looked thoughtful. "Look, we've got another option. I think there's too much money at stake to blow this today. Just stay there and oversee the team when they get there."

"What are you going to do?"

"You'll see in about fifteen minutes."

Evans shrugged. "Okay. I'll babysit. That's my job."

"You tell the vid boys the shoot only gets nudged back an hour. Markel will be ready for taping, I guarantee."

The face faded.

Evans pulled out a cigarette, stuffed it into his mouth, and lit it.

"Okay, Captain. You heard that," he said to the unconscious actor. "The show must go on."

He blew smoke into Markel's face. He'd always wanted to do that, every since he was a kid. Meeting the real Markel just made him want to do it more.

"Oh, my Dorg!" said Jimmy.

The crepuscular activity continued.

Music! It was music—some kind of music that Jimmy couldn't recognize. There was nary a sign of a theremin or any kind of electronic and synthesized quality to it. This sounded very strange indeed.

And the smells that emerged . . .

So odd!

Stranger still was the Bongoid.

"Oh! Hello there, James!" said the creature. It lounged upon a reclining chair, wrapped in a silk dressing gown. In its hand was a wooden pipe from which curled aromatic tobacco smoke. Or what Jimmy presumed to be tobacco smoke, since tobacco was supposed to have been declared illegal last century on Earth, and Jimmy had never actually smelled the stuff before. (The Hopper Corporation of course sold Adromedan cigarettes—the marvelous kind of smokable vegetation that, should you get cancer from smoking it, you can just *think* the tumors away.) It smelled rather nice, but he really was too alarmed by the sight before him now to sniff too much.

"Jackson! What happened to all your wonderful fur!" said Jimmy.

Indeed, the only quality of the creature that had been the furry bundle of joy named Jackson the Bongoid was those limpid, doleful eyes. Gone was all that furry loneliness. Gone were the six legs. Instead, on the recliner was a humanoid shape with slicked-back matinee idol black hair.

"Transmutation, dear boy!" said Jackson. "I could have returned it all again to the rear ventral spinnerette, but I really am not in the mood. In fact, I was hoping that your curiosity would get the better of you. Please! Close that door before those dimwit parents of yours hear my music."

The eyes still shone with sincerity and now the melonish humanoid face actually had a mouth, which smiled in a comforting reassuring way.

Jimmy closed the door.

"There! Now then, I can turn up the music. Here, listen to this for a moment. Do you know what it is, Jimmy?"

Jimmy stepped forward. The alien that had been their pet but now seemed something slightly different wiggled a pair of stumpy fingers and gradually the volume of the music increased. A solo instrument described a beautiful figure of melody, rich and multidimensional, into the air.

"What's that?" said Jimmy.

"It's a clarinet, Jimmy. This is Mozart's 'Clarinet Concerto,' actually, lad. Have you heard of Mozart?"

Jimmy's brow scrunched together with thought. "Wasn't he a villain on the third Planet Hopper series? I didn't know he did music, too."

The alien chuckled. "Oh, no, no. Forget Hopper matters for the nonce, please! Mozart is part of your rich heritage as a human. Why Jimmy, your race comes from a richly cultural past, and Mozart is but one of your great composers. But of course the Hopper Corporation has suppressed his music just as they have suppressed so much for their own particular purposes."

"I don't understand. And why are you speaking English?"

"Because you wouldn't understand my native language."

"No . . . no, you're supposed to be semisentient!"

"Rumors and damned lies!" said Jackson, still smiling.

Jimmy shook his head. "And if you're an alien creature, how can you like human music?" The boy smiled smugly and tapped his forehead. "You see, I've been trained to think reductively by the excellent teaching provided by the brilliant dialog of Planet Hoppers!"

"Simple. A special transpositional device." The alien lifted a small wafer from a tray by the recliner and popped it into his mouth. "Hmm. Sturgeon caviar on water crackers. Delicious."

"What?"

"Kind of like an artistic and sensory universal translator," replied the alien. "This pile of salty fish eggs on baked yeastless flour, for instance, comes across to me like naglak nodes on gryphonfly wings. Absolutely divine."

"I don't understand—"

"Wait!" The alien cupped a hand to spiked earlobes. "The Adagio. Listen."

Jimmy listened. For a moment all he heard was the pulse in his ears and the pound of his heart. After a moment, though, a pleasant reedy sound backed by an orchestra fluttered and emoted. Seconds later, he was immersed in the experience. The melody was so beautiful and pure he felt shivers on his spine. When it was over, he felt a tear drip down onto his cheek.

The alien stuck a pipe in his mouth. "You know, that came across to me like Fixnik's "Estrogenic Escapade," but I have to say, it's so good I almost got a human take on it."

"Wow!" said Jimmy. He had to sit down.

"You see kid, it's like this. You Earthfolk have been slipped antipodal fluke up your elimination cavities. I shouldn't be telling you this, my contract is very specific—but hell with it. I like you, I trust you. You got a good heart, kid. I don't think you're going to rat on me."

"You . . . you're really not a Bongoid . . . are you?" said Jimmy.

"See what I mean? You catch on quick."

"But why . . . ?"

"That other universal translator, pal. Dough. Scratch. Moolah. Money."

"You mean . . . the Planet Hoppers are paying you?"

"That's right. And with more than money, actually.

You see, Jimmy . . . I'm from the planet Hargia. We Hargians evolved in a pretty competitive environment and we had to learn to biologically change ourselves. So we can grow hair or different orifices and limbs. Stuff like that. Things are kinda tough on Hargia. So when your Hopper Corporation landed and contacted us and found out what we could do . . . Well, they hired us to imitate the beloved Bongoids. We're kind of indentured servants here. But we get eight hours a day to kick back and enjoy contraband stuff—like this terrific Mozart here."

"I still don't understand."

"Look. Jimmy. Can you say these words? 'Fascism.' 'Political and cultural control.' 'Power-mad maniacs.' That's the people who put the feedbag on your old man and plugged him into a machine. That's the people who stick your head into Planet Hopperville and turn on the brain-puree button. Take it from me, kid. You humans have been had."

"But—but we have a glorious future."

"Oh. Right. The old orange clava root dangling from the ka branch! Keeps you in your place. Look, I've been reading up. Let me tell you what happened to you poor bozos:"

What happened was a peculiar kink in history.

As happens in capitalism and the ocean, big fish eat small fish. By the second decade of the twenty-first century, one gigantic corporation not only owned most media, but certain American states and small Third World countries as well. In its fierce gobbling, though, it had swallowed not only the world-renowned Star Hopper franchise, but the religion of ScienceFictionology. ScienceFictionologists, having been taught guerrilla infighting tactics and the tenets of cultural fascism, naturally slowly took over the corporation. Before long, it was the Planet Hopper Corporation, and it owned most of the world. In the hallowed tradition of capitalism, it fed its captive consumers with product slowly and thusly mutated into what it was now in the twenty-second century.

When the Hopper Corp. actually developed a Star-drive which boosted it to other planets, things were a far cry in the actual universe from what was predicted in the Hopper Philosophy. The Hopper Corporation realized that if it actually allowed its captive Earth population to know what really went on in the Great Beyond, all interest in the Planet Hopper franchise would die. They'd not only lose control, they'd lose money.

And so they simply did what big Corporations traditionally did. They lied.

The biggest lie was that it was really the twenty-fifth century, not the twenty-second. The Corporation had managed to hoodwink the public to such an extent that hundreds of years had been taken off the calendar, lost in a fog of status quo. The owners and rulers of the Corporation, however, utilized the money earned to not only line their own coffers, but build fabulous space castles and beautiful colonies, all of splendorous luxury and fabulous taste.

"You see," said the alien. "By feeding you the gruel, the Corporation gets the sweetmeats and roast beef, to say nothing of the champagne. They've managed to build quite an empire out there in the galaxy—and they know just what cracks the whip. Power and money!"

"But that music . . . why do they withhold it from us?"

"Ah! Not just music! Drama and literature! Fine cuisine and great art! Great philosophy and architecture. All the things that make our pitiful lives worth something—the richness of our hearts and souls. Yes—you see, they hold all that back . . . and higher education as well . . . and feed you with constant twentieth century junk and pulp culture to keep you oinking in the slop and mire."

"But . . . but that's not the Hopper Planet Equal Opportunity Way!" objected Jimmy.

"Oh, right. Nothing like cheerfully corrupt egalitarianism to keep the boot squarely on the peasants."

Jimmy's brow scrunched down. "You . . . you aren't a secret agent for the BattleMooners, are you?"

"Oh, please. I'm your friend, Jimmy. I'm your dear Bongoid. . . . I'm doing my job, I'm getting my rewards. . . . And maybe I'm being subversive, I don't know. But really, Jimmy. Planet Hoppers is just an opiate for the masses. Your people deserve better."

Jackson took a glass of wine from a side table.

"What . . . BattleMoon?"

Jackson choked on the wine. "Battle. . . . Dear boy—BattleMoon is owned by the same people that own Planet Hoppers. It's just a ruse of competition to lure the rebellious . . . and keep them away from the true goodies of culture. The truly fine things that mitigate the existential pain of life."

"The same . . ." Jimmy shook his head in disbelief. "But that's like—the Stellar Union being in league with the Turd Quadrant!"

"Worse. Because the suckers aren't fiction. The suckers are real people. Victims, like you."

Jimmy's world view twisted like an Escher pretzel. Anger fused with despair. Still, as the music lightened the room and he began to think of other things, he remembered that, come to think of it, he was getting pretty damned tired of tight bangled star suits and stilted dialog.

"Hey. Can I have some of that wine?"

"You bet, Jimmy." The pseudo-Bongoid poured him a glass.

It was red. Jimmy sipped it, and made a face. He gave it back. "Maybe when I'm older. And forget that pipe. More of this music, though. And you mentioned books?"

"Intuitive wisdom, lad. We shall have a fine time together late at night. And who knows. One day you may emerge the New Messiah, a complete collection of Shakespeare under one arm and a Van Gogh under the other. And I shall be the John the Baptist to your Jesus Christ."

"Who's Jesus Christ?"

"Oh. Kind of like Dacko in 'The Sacrificial Empath

Mutant' in Series Twenty-Nine, Episode Three Hundred and Two."

"What a minute," said Jimmy. "If it's really the twenty-fifth century, that means that Captain Alphonse is really, really old."

"That's right Jimmy. Now—let's listen to some music by a man named Beethoven."

Operative Evans opened the door, and men in black turtlenecks hustled in the vat on wheels.

"What the hell is that?" said Evans.

"Emergency alien," said a Turtleneck.

A man in a lab coat and thick black glasses stepped in, holding an electronic clipboard. He shook Operative Evans hand peremptorily. "Dr. Carlson, Secret Scientists Squad. That is Markel on the couch?"

"Yes."

"Would you please remove his clothing?"

"I don't get paid enough."

The Secret Scientist raised an eyebrow. "You do now, Operative Evans."

Evans went over and began to unbutton and unVelcro. The saggy, veiny flesh oozed and sagged and thumped. Finally, when Rip Markel was bald and naked, Dr. Carlson went over. He felt the pulse, then attached a band with electrodes around the bald pate. He examined his clipboard and pursed his lips.

"Brain activity still strong. Amazing. There's enough ego-stuff in there to fill up ten starship captains. Ah, well . . . He'll last for a while longer. He just needs a little help." The scientist looked over to the vat. "Begin, gentlemen."

Evans watched as one of the men in black turtlenecks spun the vat around, revealing a wheel on one side. He spun the wheel, and dials began to wobble. With a MacBagged Spanner Plus, the other pried off the top of the vat. A splash of mucousy stuff spurted and whapped onto the floor.

Frowning, the Secret Scientist tapped instructions into his computer clipboard with a small pen.

The vat began to shake. A roundish, translucent body began to lift up from the liquid with the unnerving sound of tentacles scraping a chalkboard. Colloidal flaps flopped over the side, and finally the thing from the vat crept down the metal sides onto the floor. Tiny nerve strands and organs pulsed and glowed within the amoeboid body. Cilia aided by undulation drove it along the rug toward the unconscious body of Markel on the couch. Evans noticed that the room no longer smelled of Tough Starship Caption cologne, but rather burned Hopper Cherry Pop Tarts.

"What the hell is that thing?" asked Evans.

"New creature discovered on Orion Six," said the scientist, smiling grimly. "The Franchise shall continue!"

"Hail the Franchise," murmured Evans, more from rote than any conviction.

The thing speeded up. Evans watched with horror and déjà vu as the roiling creature dragged itself over the prone actor. Slowly but surely it rolled over, metastasizing in a gooey, multispectral way. Evans blinked. The plasma of the thing seemed to weld and meld with Rip Markel's flesh, at first assuming the bright crimson of arterial blood and then slowly pixelating into a shifting diorama of patterns.

"Jeez! Just like the Oinkoid beastie on Planet Hoppers Redieux: The Third Sequel."

"Yes."

"You mean, there actually *has been* a *true* case of coincidental evolution in the real universe?"

The Secret Scientist looked at Evans as though he were crazy. "Of course not. This alien is quite special, and not only does it have a contract—it's got full residuals."

"Residuals. Not even Dorg Keiser got residuals."

"Shut up. Now watch."

Evans turned and watched. By now, the alien covered

Markel entirely. The shifting protoplasm seemed to be hardening. Slowly, it formed a chrysalis.

"Spanner-Plus, gentlemen!" said Dr. Carlson the Secret Scientist. "Handy things, eh, Operative Evans?"

The Turtlenecks cracked open the rind on the chrysalis and pulled it back. From the crisp covering emerged Markel dressed in a snappy Starship uniform, bright with brass buttons and laser-sharp creases, to say nothing of epaulets and money.

Evans did a double take. Not only did the resplendent uniform look new, so did Markel. He was, without a doubt, the *young* Captain Alphonse who had set out on that three-and-a-half-year mission so many centuries before—not the stitched-together Frankenstein's monster of longevity he'd become. Plus, his hair was real!

"Amazing!" said Evans.

"Yes. Talk about a genetic shift. The alien has integrated itself with Markel—and transformed the man into a version of his younger self."

"A marvelous concept. But I think I'll stick to artificial fibers, thanks," said Evans.

Markel opened his eyes. He rose, looked down at his spotless uniform. Then he went to the mirror with a spring in his step. He looked at himself and there was a pronounced gleam to his sharp, piercing blue eyes.

"Ah! Now that's more like it!"

Evans smiled. "You ready for the spot now, Rip?"

"Let's go surf some stars!" The trademarked phrase snapped off the actor's tongue with sass and ease. Cockily he walked toward the door.

"Money in the galactic bank," whispered Evans to Dr. Carlson.

At the door, though, Rip Markel stopped. He turned around and Captain Alphonse had a twisted, pinched look on his face. The actor shuddered and shook for a moment.

". . . docking . . . nuclear spasm . . . surround . . . surrender . . ." he choked.

Dr. Carlson frowned. "Hmmm." He stepped over and whacked the newly young actor on the head. The pinched look relaxed.

"At ease, Captain!"

Markel shook his head. "Wow! What a lightshow. Okay. Ready for the spot. Show me the 3D Prompter."

As he left, Dr. Carlson turned with a smug smile. "There. Slight adjustment."

Evans was still frowning.

Something felt wrong about this. Real wrong.

The Hydra family were gathered about the nuclear family multimedia, watching a Planet Hopper repeat, munching their reconstituted pseudo-soy gruel pizza ramen dinner, when the world changed.

Little Jimmy lay stretched upon the comfy and furry expanse of Jackson the Bongoid, wearing his earphones. In fact, he was not truly listening to "Planet Hopper Theremin Hits," but actually to Beethoven piano sonatas. Somehow, this "classical music" grew on you and not only was it good, but he found a secret thrill in rebelling against his parents' tastes, which lately had been pretty much revolving around "Planet Hopper Easy Listening Disco."

Freddy Hydra, quite suddenly, stood up in his pile of drool and pointed at the nuclear theater, which was now glowing with a soft nimbus. "Heil, Captain!" he said. His little arm executed a stiff and perfect salute.

"Freddy talked!" said Mother Hydra. "Freddy talked!"

Father Hydra looked up from his Planet Hopper novel. "Huh?"

There, instead of the Planet Hopper episode was Captain Alphonse, looking shiny and clean in a brand new uniform.

"Captain Alphonse!" said Jimmy. "My Dorg—he looks—like in Episode 1 of Classic Planet Hoppers!"

A baritone voice boomed from the speakers. "Oh,

Hopper Crew of the Planet Earth. Hail, Well, Met . . . and
attention! I have nothing to sell you today, oh, Hoppers!
I have only this announcement."

The Captain's eyes began to glow. The illumination
grew and grew, beaming out in concentric circles of light
that bashed against the theater, shaking it. Light-pods
from the studio in which he stood crashed to the floor.
Staging hands began to scream.

"I am now taking over the Planet Earth, Hoppers! Behold your Master—Captain Alphonse of the Star Patrol!"

Jackson the Bongoid stood up on his hind legs. "My,
my. Sooner than I thought."

The Hydra family—except for Jimmy—jerked to attention. They lifted their arms in salute to the new Dicta-
tor. Jimmy could not help but notice the ragged beams of
energy that leaped from the multimedia theater and
jammed into their heads.

"What's going on, Jackson?"

Jackson was metamorphosing into his true form. "Its
the Mungbick. Hereditary psi-spawn enemies we call the
Black Vacuoles From Beyond Space."

"What's it doing with Captain Alphonse?"

Jackson—no longer a Bongoid—clacked a mandible.
"Psychic symbiotic infiltration, Jimmy. I'm really a secret agent of my people, sent to guard against just such
attacks. It's happened much sooner than I thought!
Quickly! Before your family grabs us!"

Sure enough, Mr. and Mrs. Hydra and little Freddy—
their eyes radiating a strange energy—tilted before them,
arms outstretched and clutching.

"Gee! Just like in Series Ninety-Three, Episode 10—
Universal Freeloaders!" said Jimmy, skedaddling. "Where
are we going, Jackson?" he asked as they loped away
down the hall.

"Planet Hopper Studios," said the psuedo-Bongoid. "I
am the Khronos, Force-Buoy of the Empire of Light.
There's a Cosmic Confrontation about to occur!"

* * *

In the ruins of Planet Hopper Studios stood the Captain Alphonse intergalactic creature. His bare biceps and gleaming naked pectoral muscles shone through the ripped threads of his starship uniform. His strange eyes flashed a steely spectrum of lights. Energies zapped off into the ether, connecting him into the nexus of Earth control. About him lay the charred bodies of Hopper operatives, scientists, and staging folk.

A boy and his pseudo-Bongoid strode into the ruined studio.

Tendons tensed as Captain Alphonse turned and surveyed them.

"Khronos! Ancient Enemy! We meet!" said the Dark Thing.

"Yes," said Khronos. "Stand back, Jimmy. This is the reason I am here upon the Planet Earth. I have been chasing this villain for star-centuries."

"Prepare yourself for annihilation, meteor barnacle!"

"Bite me."

Great beams of force spritzed from the creatures' foreheads. White beams crashed into black beams, thrust and parried. Great gobs of melodramatic music filled the air.

"Sounds like Beethoven's *Fifth!*" said Jimmy.

As the two interstellar titans dueled, Jimmy crept behind the Captain Alphonse thing and hit him in the shin with a MacBagged Spanner Plus.

"Ouch," said the Dark Thing, and he caught a jagged quark beam up the left nostril right up to the neocortex. He dropped to the ground, and the Earth was saved.

"Good job, Jimmy," said Jackson.

A thunderous sound filled the sky as two strangely shaped spaceships descended from the sky. The things were studded with lenses and microphones. They hovered above the ground.

"Cut! That's a wrap! Good show, guys!" barked an amplified voice. That's the climax to PSI Rangers Series

Ninety-Nine—THE PLANET HOPPER MENACE. We've got some great intergalactic entertainment, and we've saved a species from cultural atrophy to boot."

The Dark Thing got up, rubbing his thing. He shot Jimmy a Dark Look. "Hey, kid. You didn't have to hit so hard," he said as he hobbled off to get boosted onto the ship.

"Well, Jimmy," said Jackson. "I guess this is it. We're going to take the pseudo-Bongoids and the other alien creatures your corrupt Planet Hopper Corporation economically enslaved and return them to their rightful homes!"

The alien turned and walked toward the starship. "Jackson!" cried Jimmy. "Jackson! Take me with you! Take me home with you! I want to be *your* pet!"

Jackson turned. He shook his head sadly. "You've got work to do here on your home planet, Jimmy." Swells of emotional strings choked the air. "There are billions of confused people who are lost and must be saved."

Jackson the ex-Bongoid pointed a finger and a dove materialized. Carrying a crystal laurel leaf in its talons, it flapped toward Jimmy, where it turned into a magnificent paisley halo, strobing about his head.

"I have now programmed the whole of Earth's culture—minus Planet Hoppers—into your subcortex, Jimmy. Go—teach—heal. Learn social skills. Farewell."

Jackson, on beams of pure antigrav force, lifted up and was enveloped by a spaceship. The ships bounded off toward their ethereal homes, leaving Jimmy alone.

"Jackson! Jackson . . . don't go! Don't go! Jackson!"

But the stars were silent.

Something tugged at Jimmy's pants. Jimmy had to adjust his halo to look down.

"Help me, Mister. Please!" piped a little voice.

A strange straggle of hair and scalp stood, bandaged, upon a pair of crutches.

"Who . . . Who . . . are you?"

"I am Coiffonicus—former slave to Captain Alphonse . . . also known as Rip Markel. I am—was . . . his hairpiece."

Jimmy reached down and touched the crippled wig. A blaze of hirsute light erupted—And then, as it faded, Jimmy beheld a beautiful, but very short and stylishly combed, creature.

"Oh, thank you! Thank you!"

The healed wig fluttered off to spread the gospel.

Jimmy looked up to the cold stars and then down to the ruins of the Planet Hopper studios. He realized that a crowd of bewildered and lost-looking people had gathered, gazing at his halo with awe and reverence.

Then, Jimmy, filled with conviction, knew what he had to do.

He took off his halo and used it for a podium.

"Fellow humans," he said into the microphone the halo had so thoughtfully provided. The halo began to pipe out some Bach. "We've done nothing here— And we're here for a reason."

Then Jimmy Hydra, Messiah, told them what they had to do.

AS THE ROBOT RUBS

Dean Wesley Smith

Dean Wesley Smith has sold over twenty novels and around one hundred short stories to various magazines and anthologies. He's been a finalist for the Hugo and Nebula Awards, and has won a World Fantasy Award and a Locus Award. He was the editor and publisher of Pulphouse Publishing, and has just finished editing the *Star Trek* anthology *Strange New Worlds*.

MY name is Mike Blackmoon. And I got this story. It might be called a romance, but it's not a romance. Some folks might call it a mystery. Nope. Wrong again. If the story were printed, some silly bookstore owner might stick it in the horror section. Slap that person with rolled-up page proofs. There's just no way this story can be anything but science fiction.

That's right. Science fiction with sex. And a really strange twelve-legged alien dog named Spot.

Of course, in science fiction, all the sex is like a Norman Rockwell painting. But it's still sex, so what the hell. However, a dog is still a man's best friend in science fiction, except when he's been turned into a dog from a human. Then all bets are off.

My daddy, Howling Blackmoon, was the greatest storyteller to ever sit beside a campfire. He always said that if you want to hold a listener's attention, you gotta start your story right in the middle of the good part. The problem with this story is figuring out the best *good* part. This story could start with Buckey the Space Pirate, the dashing hero. He's a good part. Or it might start with his twelve-legged dog, Spot, since Spot sort of saves the day. But to really grab you, readers, the story should start in the absolute best part. So here goes.

"Don't stop," she panted.

How's that for a start? I'll bet right now your mind is skipping right along with pictures of a young, big-chested girl. In the old pulp magazines that was a must in science fiction. And this girl (woman to be politically correct) would be breathing heavily as this young space pirate named Buckey nibbles on her ear while at the same time unbuckling his blaster. Buckey, you should know, is a real ladies man in his white tights, white plumed hat, and black boots. He also wears a saber strapped on one hip and a blaster on the other. A true galactic hero.

Now, if you're thinking Buckey is going to take off his blaster, you're wrong.

Wrong. Wrong. Wrong.

Buckey is nowhere to be seen. What's really going on is that this woman named Sarah—who is an escaped slave from the horrid alien prison camp—is telling her fellow escapee, Loreina, one of the main characters of this story, to keep running toward the ancient hidden ship with Buckey's dog, Spot. Sarah has decided that she must stay behind and hold off the prison guards in the narrow desert canyon with her phaser pistol that's almost out of charges.

Loreina argues with Sarah for only a moment, then

gives her one of those looks. You know the look, don't you? The same deep understanding look that every mother has when she sees wads of used Kleenex in her teenage son's garbage can. You know . . . *The Look!*

Loreina hugs Sarah. Only a sparkle of tears form in their eyes. (It's the desert so they can't waste much water.) Then Loreina turns and runs up the canyon carrying the dark-haired, many-legged Spot. Why Spot can't run beside her is simple. Spot only minds Buckey, and at the moment Buckey isn't in this narrow canyon trying to get away from nasty alien prison guards.

So, Loreina runs away with Spot while Sarah faces the quickly approaching alien guards who will for sure either (a) kill her, or (b) torture her, or (c) do whatever else mean and nasty alien guards do to young women in science fiction stories.

At this point, it is good storytelling technique to jump forward in time. Or, sometimes back in time to explain the good time all the characters had getting to the present time. Of course, anytime you jump in time, you must let the story listener know you're signaling time out.

In the movies, they do it with fade-outs. In fiction, they use white spaces. In this case I'm just going to pause.

(Pause)

Pause for effect, then hook the listener again, my old man used to say. (He could tell a whopper with the best of them. I'm here as living proof of that fact, since it must have really been a great story to get my mother to agree to jump in bed with the guy.) So, being a good listener, I'm going to follow my old man's advice and jump back into this story right at the most interesting part.

"Don't stop," she panted.

*   *   *

I bet I know what you're thinking. Loreina is sitting in the copilot's chair (Right?) of this small spaceship (Right?) while the handsome Buckey (the space pirate who rescued her from the prison planet) nibbles softly on her big toe and then starts working his way north. Right?

Don't you wish.

Remember, this is a science fiction story. Norman Rockwell sex, remember?

What's really going on is that our heroine, Loreina, is lying naked, facedown, with only a towel over her butt on a massage table at Galactic Headquarters while a robot carefully works all the soreness out of her muscles.

Leaning against a post (yes, they have posts in Galactic Headquarters) is Loreina's boss and possible future love interest, Jerome. At least their love might be possible if they don't find out that they are really brother and sister later in the story. (Of course, they aren't brother and sister because that's just too silly to put in a story. And my daddy said never put anything silly in your stories. Besides, having sex with your sister isn't science fiction. It's something . . . well . . . you just don't put in science fiction stories.)

(Of course, you also might stop and ask yourself why Loreina would be interested in anyone by the name of Jerome in the first place. But I wouldn't. It would just complicate the story too much. Trust me that Jerome looks like no Jerome I ever met. Besides, Loreina likes the fact that he doesn't wear underwear under his tight-fitting Galactic uniform.)

As the robot rubs (Note how really swift the title of this tale worked in?), Loreina tells Jerome all about how she and Sarah were captured when they were zapped by a Lomax Ray which shut down all their food processing and bar equipment, as well as their main Wild-Blue-Yonder Drive just as they were about to learn how the dreaded aliens were managing to steel fruit off Eden, the most heavily guarded planet this side of the core.

Jerome just shakes his head, so Loreina goes on to tell

him about how horrible it was in the alien prison, and about how Buckey's dog, Spot, just sort of suddenly showed up, and how Sarah stayed back so that one of them could get through with the message, save Spot, and get a good massage.

Again, Jerome just shakes his head. He knows Loreina likes the strong silent type in her science fiction. He also read on her job application for heroine that she liked men who didn't wear underwear.

Loreina gives Jerome that serious stare, raising up on one elbow so that she can see him better—and he most certainly can see her better. (The robot doesn't notice. Stupid robot. It just keeps rubbing.) She then tells him, in a very deep tone, that she must return to save Sarah if Sarah is still alive. She (Loreina) just can't leave her (Sarah) there in that awful place (the alien prison), she (Loreina) says.

Again, Jerome just nods, never taking his eyes off of Loreina's chest. (Which means in science fiction that while Loreina talked, he had moved his face right up against her chest and, as in all good science fiction sex scenes, it is now time to fade out, white space, or pause, and thereby miss all the good description that follows when Jerome removes his eyes from her chest and puts other body parts there while the robot rubs.)

(Pause . . . damn it anyway.)

"Don't stop," she panted.

Take your mind out of the gutter. I am not starting the story back on the massage table where Jerome and Buckey the Space Pirate have drawn a dotted line down the center of Loreina and are having a duel to see who can get their half the most excited.

I wouldn't do that in a science fiction story. Besides, Buckey likes his women whole.

But during all that white space around the last pause

Jerome has done the regular manlike, middle class, try-to-take-over-the-story thing and told Loreina that she can't go to rescue Sarah. He has assigned her to a desk job in Galactic Headquarters where he can keep her under his thumb (as well as other body parts).

Loreina didn't take kindly to that kind of power play from above, so, not really being a "company" girl or terribly fond of the missionary position, she captures a guard at the spaceport and is following the guard up a long, circular staircase in the launching tower of the new Bigger, Longer, and Taller spaceship. The BLT has nifty screens that make the ship almost invisible to aliens and blocks out the aliens' Zapper Beam. That will allow Loreina to get close enough to the prison camp to rescue Sarah and still have lunch.

This part of the story opens as the guard stops suddenly in front of Sarah halfway up the huge tower. (There's a lot of stairs, and they are both out of breath. *"Don't stop," she panted.* Remember?) Sarah keeps him going and then, at the top, once she has gotten into the ship, she stuns the guard. As he falls, she notices that he, too, doesn't wear underwear under his tight-fitting uniform. (The guard, who is a friend of Jerome's secretary, also got a peak at Loreina's application.)

Of course, at this point, Loreina is heavily occupied with stealing the ship and getting Sarah out, so, with only one mouth-watering glance at the guard, she jumps into the Captain's chair, straps herself in, and blasts off, only to discover a few moments later that Buckey the Space Pirate's dog, Spot, was sitting in the control room, panting. (More than likely from the climb up the tower, too.)

Blasting off should not be noted here with a bunch of noise. She just floats up through the rain clouds quiet as you please. The drive on the BLT is very silent and doesn't need a match to light it. Real advanced science fiction stuff. And Spot doesn't even get knocked off his twelve legs.

Of course, out in space, she gets chased by the entire

Patrol Fleet which happened to be home on leave. She doesn't want to Atomize them (or even fire a warning shot across their bows) because she knows The Patrol is on her side, and that some men in those ships may have read her application. Instead she does a few really nifty moves around the sun, loses about ten pounds when the inside of the ship heats up, then pops off through the Time Warp Instant Trajectory. When in a TWIT, no one can follow, or would really want to, so she's safe.

Next she goes about getting herself ready for instant sleep to pass the sixty-four days it will take to reach the alien prison world, where she will somehow rescue Sarah. She strips down to only her skimpy bikini underwear and a sweat-soaked T-shirt and crawls in. But just before she's about to close the lid and drift off into sleep, Spot reminds her that he's there, too. She manages to find enough food scraps in the galley to fill about ten bowls. She hopes it will be enough to last Spot.

She pats Spot on the head, tells him to guard the ship, and crawls back into her sleep chamber that looks like a hollowed out cucumber. The last thing you see is her breathing slowing as she passes out and her nipples get hard. And again, you guessed it, it is time to . . .

(Pause)

Now where should the next part of the story open? My daddy said never let a listener down. (Or a bartender, for that matter, but that's another story.) He said that if you've got someone's attention, don't disappoint them, especially toward the end of your story. So, following old man Blackmoon's advice once more, I return to the story at a "good" part.

"Don't stop," she panted.

Wow, don't you just love an exciting story? I mean, imagine Loreina there with Sarah and Buckey the Space Pirate on the filthy dirt floor of Sarah's cell in the alien prison. The three of them are tied up, naked except for

Buckey's white hat. Buckey has one foot between Sarah's open legs and his other foot between Loreina's open legs. He's working on untying the girl's ropes with his toes. Of course, his heels are making the escape a somewhat pleasurable experience for both women.

Now that you've imagined all that: dirt floor, moldy smell, low moaning, and all, I'm glad you got it out of your system because that's not what is going on. Remember . . . science fiction story? I know, I know, I hate repeating myself, too. But sometimes I must, I must.

In the real story, Sarah wakes up after sixty-four days, crawls out, and does the classic yawn. We've all seen it in a hundred movies, so no point in going into the yawn scene too much, except to say that her little panties seem even smaller and the T-shirt still looks wet. (Don't ask how. That's beside the point.) Without dressing, she runs to the cockpit of the ship and checks her instruments. Spot is sleeping on the pilot's chair and is very, very happy to see her. She spends the next hour petting Spot in all sorts of spots.

She discovers she is almost to the alien prison planet. Now what is she going to do? She looks quickly around nearby space for the intervention-of-the-machine (sounds better in Latin) that will end the story quickly, but she doesn't see one.

Failing that, and still petting Spot, the plot must thicken like overripe soup. Loreina clicks on her screens and sneaks up on the alien prison world. It just so happens that the entire alien fleet is circling the prison planet. (Probably on vacation. It's that time of the year.)

Loreina decides it would be suicidal not only to her and Spot, but to her lust for men who don't wear shorts, if she went in alone. Probably get Sarah killed, too. She thought and thought and wracked her brain trying to figure out what to do. That wasn't a pretty sight, even with her still in her bikini shorts and wet T-shirt. A smoking, ruined brain is never fun to look at. Even Spot left the room.

Finally, after reading two issues of *Playhunks of the Spaceways* magazine and a good night's sleep, she realizes the answer has been right there in front of her in the story line all the time. Spot. He's Buckey the Space Pirate's dog, and more than likely Buckey would be happy to have him back, enough that he and his Space Pirate fleet of ships might help her rescue Sarah.

She patted Spot's head and said, "Good boy." Of course, Spot was an alien dog, with a large number of legs, and she didn't really know if he was a boy, a girl, or something really different. (In science fiction stories, trust me, it can be really, *really* different. But that, too, is another story.) Spot didn't seem to care since as she patted his head, two hind legs thumped on the floor, and a long, long tongue hung out of his mouth.

While petting Spot, she thought about the old days. (Petting an alien space dog is always a good time in a science fiction story for a memory scene.) She and Buckey go way back. Her first true love. She really loved his saber. Only after a year or so she went corporate and he stayed in the private business sector, and it had all ended with a net loss. Why hadn't she thought of having him help Sarah before? She used to think of him often, usually in the bathtub.

She sat there in the Captain's chair, petting Spot, and thinking about sitting in the bathtub and thinking about Buckey. Pretty soon she is thinking a lot about Buckey and petting Spot even harder. Slowly her T-shirt is getting damper and damper and she is panting and petting and it is right at this point, with her eyes closed, and Spot's tongue almost on the floor, that Loreina utters the opening words of this section. (Bet you thought I'd forgotten, didn't you? You remember, don't you? *"Don't stop," she panted.*)

Spot's three hind legs are thumping the deck so hard it snaps Loreina alert (before her hands turn this into a romance). She realizes she's not in the bathtub after all and that Sarah is still sitting down there in that stinking, dirt-floored, alien prison waiting to be rescued. Buckey is the only hope.

Loreina brushes her damp hair back out of her eyes, tells Spot to lie down, does a few quick calculations, and inserts the ship back into TWIT. Three quick days and she'd be with Buckey the Space Pirate's fleet.

She did a few instrument checks, gave Spot one more good patting, then headed for the bathroom. She wouldn't deep sleep this time. She needed a long, long bath far more.

And, as the door to the bathroom hisses softly closed, this story again does the correct thing and . . .

(Pauses.)

"Don't stop," she panted.

Nice hook to the climax of the story, huh? My daddy would be proud of me, if he hadn't died in a bar fight over losing a bet over who could spit farther, him or an old lady named Marge.

So, the tension of the story builds. Where is Loreina now? Is Sarah still alive? Does Loreina get Buckey to help spring Sarah from the prison camp? Does Buckey wear underwear? What does petting Spot really mean? Tough questions that must be answered in this section because this is the last damn chance. That's right. No more pauses. It's all downhill from here.

If this were a standard science fiction story, this section would have opened with Loreina in the bathtub thinking of Buckey when (suddenly) alarm bells go off all over the ship. Of course, Loreina would have had time to struggle into just enough clothes to be almost decent before facing the problem of one of Buckey's ships attacking her ship. She would have finally gotten through to Buckey who would have saved her in the last moment so that they could both go rescue Sarah. Now that's pure pulp storytelling.

But that's not the way it happened. This is a liberated

world, remember? Loreina has got to do it herself, with Spot's help, or it just won't mean anything.

On the third day of Loreina's bath, she gets to Buckey's home base and discovers from Buckey's second in command, Fred, (who has a large nose, very white teeth, and a small part in this story) that while on a raiding mission on an alien world, Buckey's ship blew a warp and Buckey had been captured and was being held on the prison ward. (Wow! That explains the entire alien fleet being around the prison world much better than them just being there on shore leave.)

Fred doesn't know what to do. But Loreina, after three days in the bathtub thinking about Buckey, has a desperate idea. She decides to give Buckey's fleet the secrets to the screening device in her BLT so that they can all sneak inside the alien fleet. Buckey's ships can keep the aliens busy while she rescues Buckey and Sarah. Neat plan, huh?

Fred likes the idea (and why wouldn't he?) and so, for the next two weeks, while Loreina takes a lot of baths and she and Fred do a lot of careful rescue planning, the screening devices are built and installed in all sixty-plus ships in Buckey's fleet.

Finally, the fleet is ready, Loreina is well wrinkled, and the plot must go on.

At this point I could go into another pause, letting the three days' travel back to the alien prison world pass quickly. But I promised I wouldn't. And besides, I still haven't got to the point where the story starts after the last pause. So, let's just suffice it to say that the three days do pass like a bowl of chili and Buckey's fleet, with Fred in command, sneaks inside the ring of alien ships and attacks them on their naked, exposed undersides, right where they least expect it.

I could go into long detail about the battle. Blood and violence are okay in science fiction, and in fact are currently fashionable as long as the violence occurs in the

future and has a high-tech feel. But I don't like violence.
I like sex. So to hell with the battle scene.

Trust me when I tell you that except for the loss of two
of Buckey's ships, Fred and the crews were completely
successful in blasting those mean and nasty aliens out of
space. Loreina flew the BLT right down to the prison and
landed in the main yard, killing all the aliens in sight with
her ship's nifty weapons that fired bright red beams.

But now her problem was how to find Sarah and
Buckey in that huge prison. Then she realized that again
her answer was right in front of her. Spot. He was a dog,
he could lead her to his master.

"Find Buckey," she says and opens the door.

Spot just sits there.

She tries again, but again Spot doesn't move. Finally
she kneels down in front of the multi-legged dog and
stares him right in the eyes. And for the first time, she
realizes those eyes are green, and that Spot has a brain
behind those eyes.

"Look" she says, "you find Buckey, and I'll pet you
for an hour straight, without stopping."

Spot was out the door almost faster than she could follow. Spot led her through tunnels and down and down
until finally she didn't think they could go any more. And
she was right. They hit bottom, where Spot found Sarah
sitting in one cell staring at Buckey in the next cell. Both
Sarah and Buckey were fine, except Sarah was a little
glassy eyed from staring at Buckey all those weeks.
(Buckey never wore underwear either.)

Now remember that all that nifty action really happened in the last pause. The last part of the story really
hasn't started yet. But it's about to, *finally,* with Loreina
leading Sarah, Buckey, and Spot back through the narrow tunnels of the prison at a full run. (They don't know
that Buckey's fleet is winning the battle out in space.)
Loreina guards one side corridor as she tells them breath-
lessly not to stop. (Remember: great opening line of this
section. *"Don't stop," she panted.*

They somehow make it safely back to the BLT, with Spot scaring off two aliens with a bark Loreina didn't know he had.

So as this story closes with the ending that of course will leave enough open for a trilogy, Loreina sits in the Captain's chair with Buckey kneeling at her right, Sarah standing beside her on the left, and Spot on his back at her feet, all twelve legs up in the air. (Loreina has just finished her promised petting session.)

Picture this: Sarah's hand is on Loreina's shoulder. Buckey's left hand is on his saber. Buckey's white hat is tipped slightly to one side. His right hand is on Loreina's knee. Loreina's shirt is still wet. All three are smiling like damn fools into the view screen in front of them, as if posing for a wedding picture.

This kind of scene is always in every good science fiction movie. Shown on the screen, the BLT leaves the nasty alien prison world behind and inserts itself (with a rainbow of colors) into TWIT, going who knows where.

"Don't stop," she panted.

Loreina gives her last command and, as the story fades to a close, leans back, closes her eyes, and sighs.

Buckey's hand moves softly on Loreina's leg.

Sarah glances down and licks her lips.

Spot pants.

The end.

DOG IS MY COPILOT

Karen Haber

Karen Haber's short fiction appears in *Warriors of Blood and Dream*, *Animal Brigade 3000*, *Elf Fantastic*, and *Wheel of Fortune*. Her novels include the science fiction trilogy *Woman Without a Shadow*, *Sister Blood*, and *The War Minstrels*. She lives with her husband, author Robert Silverberg, in California.

"OOOOOO." Charlie covered his eyes with his mutated paws. "That was a close one, Frank."

The asteroid, so huge in the viewfield a moment ago, dwindled in the wake of our cruiser to the size of a pebble, got smaller, and winked out behind us in the dusty black void.

"Listen, pal," I said. "Last time I looked I was still the pilot of this buggy. Now just let me maneuver through this asteroid field without your feedback, okay?"

"Oh, God, oh, God, no! Don't turn there. Watch out! You got too close to that one."

"Do me a favor. Shut up and enjoy the scenery."

"Ooooooo, that was too close."

"Do you know what you sound like when you do that? A hound dog."

"Only on my mother's side. On my father's I'm part dinosaur."

"So you said." I skirted a floating rock the size of North Dakota and watched it spin away out of range. "Pretty small part, I'd say."

"Are you going to play tag with asteroids all morning—despite my warning—or is there some actual point to this flight plan?"

"Keep your spots on. We're nearly there. Looks like a big mother lode of recombinant Feragon. Should keep us in biscuits and champagne for a couple of months."

"Sure. Just like the diamond lode last month that turned out to be mostly ice and carbon. And the hydrofer ore before that, the lode that rusted on the way to the orbital processors."

I didn't like his sarcastic tone. "Hey, I wasn't the one who forgot to dry the bins after flushing them."

"It was a computer glitch, I told you."

"Any time you get tired of this, you can be replaced by a mutated Siamese."

"Hah."

He knows and I know that I don't mean it. I've never been a cat man. And Charlie, despite his tendency toward hysterics, is generally good company.

I'm an ore-buster by trade, like my daddy. And like him, I'm dark-haired, dark-eyed, with a weakness for a pretty smile and a good joke. Ore-busting isn't a bad life. Problem is, it gets lonely out here on the edge of the galaxy. Too much time spent alone and a pilot gets to thinking strange things and doing stranger ones. Setting his autopilot on a one-way plunge into the nearest planet's surface. That kind of thing.

But the company discovered that if men and women were shipped out together, they spent most of their time screwing and arguing. Productivity went to hell. Company policy was rewritten: male and female miners were to just visit occasionally. So that left us all flying solo again.

The company decided that a companion was the answer. A pet. Cats were too unpredictable. Lizards were better, but they slept too much. But dogs, well, dogs always like to go for a ride, don't they?

Dogs genetically altered to sustain the stress of space travel, with extended lives, and the ability to walk themselves into the artificial-g toilet, are the perfect antidote to the deep space blues. Nearly the perfect pet. Just one problem. That engineered gene that allows them to talk? It sometimes gives them ESP powers, too. And dogs, they worry. Out loud.

Charlie is mostly terrier—for smarts—with a cooling touch of Labrador thrown in for stability. There's some lizard in there, too, grafted on to give him a longer life span, cute rubbery fingers with pads on the end, and the ability to change his color. Right now he's in his sophisticated, "Call me Charles" mood. Black on black, with just a hint of white around the muzzle. Distinguished.

When he's "Just Chuck," he sports tawny close-cropped fur, dark muzzle, and large triangular ears. But I think I like his "Charlie" mode best, all smiley mouth, bi-colored pelt—predominantly white with gingery ears and nose. Very jaunty. He seems happiest when he's Charlie.

When he's upset, he can undergo some pretty amazing physical changes: grow purple crests and weird red horns over his eyes: those old dinosaur genes kicking in under stress, I guess.

For example, this morning I looked up from bolting my caffshake and saw him sprout weird pink dots all along his spine. I decided to take the direct approach. "What's bothering you?"

His mouth worked for a moment before he answered. "I've got a bad feeling about today."

I've learned to pay attention to Charlie's hunches. "Bad-dangerous or bad-pain-in-the-butt?"

"First choice."

"Give me a range on a scale of one-to-five.

"Five."

"Big dangerous." I sat back in my pilot's chair.

"Yep. Big bad dangerous, as in asteroid. As in collision."

"Okay, I'll watch it."

"Sure you will."

The ship shuddered in an ungood manner.

Ping! Ping, pa-ching!

Something was rattling around the cockpit.

A buzz began in the life-support panel and became a full-fledged alarm. The impact beacon flashed on the front edge of the cockpit, red, red, red.

"Impact?" I yelled. "With what?"

"Microasteroids," Charlie said. He sounded disgusted. "Got in under the shields. I warned you to get our defense system upgraded!"

The klaxons were screaming. Mist filled the cabin. A couple of the damned little bastards had gone right through and exited, double-holing the hull.

"Oooh, I warned you!" Charlie's whine threatened to slip a decibel into a full-throated howl. "Pressure is at eighty-seven percent and slipping. Oooooh. We're gonna die, I knew it."

"Shut up and keep feeding me pressure readings." Was that a whistling sound I heard or my imagination?

I hit the emergency sealant. It misfired. I'd have to hit reset and wait sixty seconds. Meanwhile, atmosphere was rapidly leaving the ship.

"Eighty-five. Eighty-one."

We could last to sixty.

"Seventy-five."

The seconds ticked away.

"Seventy."

Come on!

"Sixty-eight. Sixty-four."

I hit the restart on the sealant, nearly cracking its armature.

"Sixty." Charlie paused, and with dramatic zest, said, "Holding steady at sixty-four."

The numbers on life support climbed swiftly.

"Pressure holding steady."

"Well, that's over. I hope that was your emergency."

Charlie nodded. "Yeah. I thought it would be worse."

"You always do. I hate those mini-rocks. The scanner never sees those little bastards in time."

We scarcely had time to relax before another warning chimed. But this was the telemetry meter sounding. We were nearing our target asteroid.

Charlie said. "ETA in five minutes. I'll get the probes ready for launch."

"This time, set them down nice and easy."

Charlie pressed the probe release. "Probes away. Impact in thirty seconds."

"Twenty. Ten. Five . . . probes are down."

I began scanning the readouts from the surface of the asteroid. The numbers were better than I'd dreamed they would be. "Bingo! What did I tell you? It's a mother lode, ninety-five percent pure. That new prospecting hardware was worth every credit. For once your ESP was wrong, wrong, wrong."

Once we had lasered and lifted the ore into our main cargo hold, I weighed our find and registered it with Records Central. I couldn't wait to see those new numbers at the top of our Gross Income to Date file. The new figures would be ready almost instantly.

I dialed up the file—and stared in disbelief.

Despite today's haul, we were in the red to the company credit union into quadruple digits.

"Charlie!"

He was sitting in his seat, covering his eyes with his paws, again. It was an atavistic gesture, I knew. Pure instinct.

My instinct was to wring his spendthrift neck. "Have you been watching the Catalog 'Wave again?"

The only reply was a miserable and guilty grunt.

"What did you buy this time? A cedar-scented floater bed with its own gravity generator? No, that was on your last binge. Well, then it must have been those dehydrated liver biscuits I saw you mooning over, and a matched set of water dishes good to three g. Or maybe some more *Bitches in Heat* videos?

He was lying on his back, feet feebly waving surrender, waiting for the Alpha Male to rip out his throat—or let him live.

I let him live. But to make certain that he wouldn't be excessively grateful for the gesture, I reminded him of how many times his overspending has gotten us in trouble in the past. The whole lecture. "How do you expect us to ever afford a bigger cruiser?"

He was still on his back, whining.

I was beginning to feel like a bully. "Get up."

"You should get rid of me, Frank. Get a Saint Bernard. They hate to shop."

"Don't be stupid. Not one of them has a decent sense of humor."

"At least they're dependable."

"I don't want one."

"Then somebody else."

"Yeah, great. Maybe some damned fool who barks his head off at every passing freighter? Or even worse— remember what happened to Joey Martin?"

"Of Joey and Hugo?"

"The very same."

Charlie's eyes rolled back in distaste. He knew the story as well as I did: Joey was a good-natured ore jockey who had the bad luck to hitch up with Hugo, a Sharpei/Jack Russell mix. Six months into their assignment, Hugo mutinied, stranded Joey on one of Pluto's moons, and stole the ship. Hugo didn't want to kill him, I think. Just wanted him out of the way. He even left him some generating equipment and survival gear. Joey Martin, the pilot who let the dog drive. Joey got rescued in a week, but he never lived it down. I think he finally gave up the business, probably putting in time at a desk somewhere for Honsubishi.

No, I didn't want to switch partners. But we were still in trouble. "You know what this means," I said. "Double shifts and short rations."

It was our third red-eye run of the month and we were both a little giddy with fatigue. It was a stinker of a payload: salvage parts from an orbital partially destroyed by a runaway freighter. Hours of hard, dirty work in null-g suits, and we had to rad-proof the hold just to be on the safe side. Let me tell you, anti-rad paint is slimy nasty stuff.

I'm not sure which one of us wasn't paying attention as we onloaded the junk. It doesn't really matter now. But the ship got away from us. Literally. We were left there dangling behind it, two pull-toys towed by our suits' umbilici through the cold dark night. Who knows how far we might have gone? Our oxygen feed was strong, our suit life-support systems were chugging away. If we didn't die from starvation or have lifelines disconnected by a passing meteor, we could last a long—long—time.

Our suit-to-suit transmitters still worked, which was a mixed blessing.

"Y'know," Charlie said. "This is embarrassing."

"Tell me about it." I was remembering how much I hated zero-g and its effects upon my equilibrium.

Charlie was oblivious. "I can't decide which option is worse: if we get rescued or if we die."

I knew which I voted for. And soon, please, God. "If we die, we won't have to hear everybody laughing at us."

"Quieter."

"Peaceful," I agreed. "No one blows their lunch in their space suits in the afterworld."

A star moved closer, grew larger until there were definite outlines and shapes to distinguish it from some natural galactic phenomenon. Its glow diminished, silvered.

"Bad news," I said. "We're saved. Then I saw the call letters on the ship's hull. USFSPX9742. "Uh-oh." I could feel the gooseflesh rising under my space suit.

"What do you mean, uh-oh?"

"Charlie, Do you happen to remember the call letters of Joey Martin's old cruiser?"

"The one that Hugo—" he paused as the implication seeped in. "You don't mean?"

"I could accept being wrong here."

Of course I wasn't.

A rescue pod scooped us up, severed our lines and deposited us inside the cruiser. It was a near-match to ours, but worse for wear. The place hadn't been cleaned in a while, and it was coated with dog-hair. Let me assure you that dog-hair in low-g is nothing to sneeze at. The whole place smelled, well, doggy.

Hugo looked a bit mangy around the ears, and definitely down in the muzzle. Command can do that to you. His Sharpei side was in the ascendant, giving him a hulking bearlike appearance. Tawny unreadable eyes peered at me from out of his dark face. But when he spoke, it was in a high Jack Russell tenor, sharp-edged and impatient.

"I've got your ship under radio control."

"Great," I said. "Thanks for the rescue. We'll just be moving along—"

He ignored me. All of his attention was on Charlie. "Want a drink?" he said.

"Who, me? No. No thanks."

"Sure you do. C'mon. Relax. I've got something I want to talk to you about." Hugo herded Charlie out into the main ship. As I made to follow, the hatch of the rescue pod slammed down, rendering me prisoner. I watched through the port window as they moved into the pilot's quarters. The door closed.

Days passed, or so it seemed. I think I fell asleep. I

came awake to see a huge bearlike head looming through the window. It disappeared. "Hey!" I cried. "Hugo, how about letting me out?"

The pod engines fired up.

"Charlie? Where are you?"

The cruiser's hatch opened and I was out the door, chugging through darkness, heading for God-knows-where.

One thing about dogs—when they form habits, they stick to them. I was being stranded, just like Joey Martin. I hoped that Hugo had at least been as generous with supplies.

Thunk!

The escape pod hit, bounced, settled. I peered out the viewscreen at a marbled landscape, blue-green. I was on some planet, somewhere. Great, just great.

How could Charlie have abandoned me? We were pals. I fumed over this for a while before deciding that Charlie had been compelled by Hugo. Had to have been. To distract myself from these unhappy ruminations, I began to catalog my supplies. I had enough grub to last several months, so long as I didn't mind a steady diet of grape-flavored synth protein in tubes. At least it would keep me going.

The pod's sensors registered that the air mixture was safe to breathe here, and that the gravitational strength was slightly less than that to which I had been accustomed. I removed my helmet and took an experimental sniff. Aside from an odd tang, the air seemed breathable. Off came the gloves and the bulky outer survival suit. As a precaution I removed the suit's utility belt and fastened it around my waist. Looking up, I glanced out through the viewscreen.

Strange vertical shapes were pogoing on the horizon. I watched them jump up and down, wondering if this was some unusual version of the local flora, a life-form, or a hallucination.

The pogoers were getting closer. I could hear the sound of their impact each time they landed.

Poing! Poing!

Too loud for flora, I decided. Probably not a hallucination either.

My scanners registered several distinct life-forms approaching. I was definitely going to have a close encounter.

Now they were near enough for me to smell them: Sweet, like some sort of fizzy drink or powerful perfume. They were much larger than I'd initially thought, as big around as logs and covered in feathers—or scales that looked like feathers: yellow at the heart, raying outward to iridescent green.

"Hello," I said. "I come in peace."

The scales fluttered and rose like miniature window blinds. Beneath them I saw round orange eyes staring fixedly at me. The feather-scales were eyelids, and the pogoing tubular aliens were covered with eyes. Immediately I dubbed them Eyehoppers. They inspected me for a considerable amount of time, every eye glued to every move I made.

I decided to assist them in their examination. I pivoted, holding out my arms. "See?" I called over my shoulder. "This is the backside of a Terran." I spun back to face them. "And this is the front side. I'm friendly. Really. Do you understand anything I'm saying?"

We traded stares. Then the Eyehoppers began jumping up and down, faster and faster, moving closer. I backed away. They followed. We continued this game for some time. Gradually I perceived that they were herding me ahead of them. To what end I didn't know. I began to get nervous.

They forced me into a glade of what looked like silvery thorn trees. At the heart of it was a shelter—a big rounded hut. Theirs? They wanted me to enter it, that much seemed clear. What was inside, their queen? What if they were merely the appendages of some horrible

giant carnivorous thing that had sent its legs out hunting
for breakfast?

A tiny rational voice in the back of my brain said:
"Eyes with legs that hunt independent of the main
body?"

Of course eyes with legs, I countered. How else could
they see their prey?

The rational voice was quiet after that.

I gazed at the open shelter uneasily. What if it was just
a camouflage? What if I were being nudged into the open
mouth of some hideous ravenous alien?

I stopped dead in my tracks.

Two Eyehoppers crashed into me. One fell down.

I felt kind of bad about that.

The fall didn't seem to hurt it. It bounced back to its
feet and recommenced hopping at me as though nothing
had happened. They were single-minded, these Eyehoppers. That was okay. Group minds can be tricky to
deal with.

Now I was being nudged again. But before I could
make a move, there came a muffled sound from the hut,
and several life-forms emerged. Tawny and golden, they
were ticked here and there, with subtle shades of brown
and lavender. Each of them had two large liquid lavender
eyes set midway in a triangular head above a lipless
mouth. They had two limbs upon which they stood and
walked. There were at least five of them, and all were a
head taller than me. One had white feet. They looked
about as dangerous as kittens.

The one with the white feet ventured a soft, deep inter-
rogative chirrup. A second later, the others chirped as if
in agreement. I got the impression of a family cluster.
And, as they stood close together, I got a further impression of strange but distinct intelligence.

The Eyehoppers had retreated. What were they in rela-
tion to these beings, I wondered—sheepdogs?

I felt a strange tickle in my limbic brain, almost a
physical sensation. A questing touch, there and gone. It

made me shiver all over. Somehow I knew that an alien intelligence had attempted to penetrate my thoughts and contact me, mind to mind. The impression it left behind was benign, curious, welcoming. I felt no fear. These aliens must communicate via telepathy. Although I couldn't understand any words, I could understand emotions. And so, apparently, could they. I radiated as much friendliness as I could.

White Foot chirruped again, and several of the others moved closer.

"I'm really very friendly," I said. "Honest. My name's Frank. Frank Hogan. Friend."

At the first sound of my voice, they jumped as though stung by an electric shock. And yet they had no ears nor any other organ indicating aural perception. In lockstep they retreated to stare at me—from a safe distance—in obvious fascination.

I held up my hands, palms open. "Peaceful, see? Nothing to fear."

Each set of lavender eyes was fixed, unblinking, upon my hands.

Slowly, the littlest alien edged forward and inclined its head toward my right palm. The tip touched it. I wiggled my fingers. It squeaked and jumped backward, snuggling against a larger critter that might have been its mother or father, or both.

White Foot approached and poked my hand with its head. I allowed my hand to rest on its head, then moved it slowly down its neck. Its flesh was warm and silky. White Feet closed its eyes and chirped softly.

Immediately, the others were crowding around, wanting their necks petted, too.

It was the beginning of a beautiful friendship.

They never seemed to eat, at least, not when I was looking. As for my food needs, I used the analyzer on my suit's utility belt to scan the local flora and found that nearly everything growing within reach would prove toxic for a Terran. Miserably I swallowed my purple paste and hoped that the emergency transmitter I had triggered would bring help before my supply ran out.

Their days were spent in quiet contemplation. Now and then I saw one of the adults engaged in peculiar repetitive movements that I suspect had a ritual nature. They wove odd textiles from the dry grasses, studied them, then deliberately tore them apart. Perhaps it was a game. Now and then they would throw their weavings over my head and chirrup loudly, then pull them off and drag them away.

They appeared to communicate by some means of telepathy, huddling together for a pow-wow. Occasionally I would feel a gentle mind-touch, nothing intrusive, that left me tingling with well-being.

At night I was allowed to snuggle among them in the warmth of the hut. Their exhalations had the faint scent of honey. They didn't suffer from morning breath either. And their gentle mind-touches were soothing, enabling me to maintain a good outlook.

I began to give them names, to make distinctions between them. White Foot remained White Foot for me. And there was Big Head and Beeble and Pip. The littlest one I christened Jimmy out of sentimental memories of my kid brother.

I lost track of the days. My perpetual battery failed on my wristwatch, and the calendar with it. I lived by the twin suns in the sky, getting up and going to sleep with their rising and waning.

My hosts' shelter was pretty flimsy and I helped them rig a double-layer of woven grass, making the walls practically impervious to wind. I even set up a lodge pole at the center of the hut, to support the walls. It felt good, helping them out.

At night, warm in the hut with them, I could almost forget where I had come from. I could almost forget Charlie. But not quite. I worried about him. What if Hugo had turned on him and thrown him out of an air lock? What if he was in trouble?

A small voice in my head reminded me that I was the one who was in trouble. But it was the most comfortable trouble that I'd ever fallen into.

Meanwhile, Beeble showed me how to find the best, most fragrant grasses for bedding. Pip came around for neck scratches. Big Head led me to a grove of fragrant trees, quirching in counterpoint as I whistled old show tunes from the twentieth century.

The only thing they drank was a thick green liquid gathered from a deep lagoon at the end of the trail. It wasn't water as I knew it and I politely abstained whenever it was offered to me. But I didn't mind helping them fetch the stuff. I quickly became the water-fetcher, and Jimmy often came with me, skittering ahead along the trail, chirping brightly. Sometimes I let him balance the bucket on his head.

The days passed quickly. I figured out a way for them to braid the dried grasses using a foot-activated loom that I lashed together from stout bushes. Aside from my grape-flavored meals, it wasn't a bad life. The suns rose, the suns set.

One morning I awoke to find them agitated, in high confusion. I did a quick head count and saw that Jimmy wasn't there. Where had he gone in the night? The thought of unknown predators chilled me, especially the image of his soft little head caught in the grasp of some murderous giant spider-thing.

I grabbed up my stungun and utility belt and began searching.

He wasn't playing in the shade of the cinnamon trees.

There was no sign of him in the meadow near my escape pod.

I was beginning to give up hope when I approached the green spring, and saw him up to his neck in green goo, clinging feebly to a rock, too far away for me to reach him.

I pulled the rope gun from my belt. Aimed. Clicked.

Nothing happened.

I checked the power levels and saw that something had drained the gun of all power.

Now I needed help if I was going to rescue Jimmy.

I covered the ground back to the hut in record time. "Come quick," I yelled. "Jimmy fell into the lagoon."

They ignored me. I yelled and screamed. Finally, I grabbed White Foot by the neck and dragged him after me. Then the others came. When they saw the situation, they circled in agitation, chirping, then began to pull up the long grass along the shore. They wove it between their toes, making a rope of sorts. I seized it and tied it around my waist, securing the other end to a wide-trunked tree.

"Hang on, Jimmy. I'm coming!" If he couldn't understand the words, perhaps he would intuit the sentiment. Taking a deep breath, I waded out chest-deep into the green liquid. It was repellently warm, with a thick greasy feel. Disgusting. I shivered and forced myself to move.

The footing was treacherous, slippery and slow. I brushed against unseen objects and forced myself not to think about what they could be. Any second I expected to be dragged under the surface. There was a weird prickly feel to the liquid, almost fiery, but after a moment it passed. Then I realized that my feet were getting numb, and I couldn't really feel my hands.

By the time I grabbed hold of Jimmy's pelt, my hands were mostly numb. I held him in a dead-man's carry, my elbow crooked around his neck, and thrashed my way back toward shore, partially towed by the tether.

Nauseated and dizzy, I collapsed on the ground, Jimmy on top of me. I don't remember much after that. What I do remember is awakening in the hut when White Foot gently prodded me.

The next thing I felt was a blaze of warmth, of incredible well-being and almost orgasmic pleasure. It faded gradually, and I closed my eyes, thinking that a nap would be nice.

Then it hit me.

White Foot had just given me my reward.

I sat up, appalled.

A reward. I was their dog. Their pet. Hadn't they trained me to fetch, to heel, even to rescue their young? I was glad that Charlie wasn't there to see it. But at the same time, I missed him more than anything.

I turned away from White Foot and the rest, and curled into a ball of misery. I *had* a dog—somewhere out there between the stars.

I slept poorly that night and awoke early, feeling an urgent need to see the escape pod and my emergency beacon.

When I got close to it, I saw that something was wrong. The pod was nearly dark, with only a faint green-ish glow flickering from the emergency lights. What had happened to the generator?

I got inside and began a systems check. All power levels were unbelievably low, as though something had come in and just drained the entire ship. My beacon could only manage a feeble blip.

What could have caused this?

I thought of the odd episodes with my "owners." My wrist watch had stopped despite its perpetual battery. My rope gun had died. Now this.

I couldn't believe that they had deliberately sabotaged my only hope of escape. No, it had to be something inadvertent.

I decided to check my suspicions using a half-drained battery pack. It was no good to me in its current state, but it still held enough juice to register on its readout. I brought it back to camp with me and set it on the floor of the hut.

One by one, my friends slowly gathered around it, chirruping happily. As I watched, the remaining power level dropped until the readout was at zero. Then—and only then—did the group of them drift away, burping, to sleep it off.

That clinched it. No wonder I never saw my gentle

owners eating anything. They absorbed energy directly. And their appetites had trapped me here with them.

I couldn't sleep that night, and crept outside to watch the sky. It gave me bittersweet pleasure to contemplate the face of the heavens and remember that once I had winged my way between the stars. A comet shot across the horizon and drew a tear from me in its wake. But I didn't have long to weep.

With a crash and a roar, a hideous monster came pounding toward the hut. It had one huge eye in the middle of its forehead, and its appendages, if that's what they were, rayed out around its head like sharp oily spears. It was disgusting to look at, and it smelled bad, to boot. When it opened a mouth lined with jagged teeth, I decided it was time for a quick retreat.

I backed into the hut and tried to awaken White Foot.

No response.

I shook him.

He was completely unconscious, as were the others.

My stun gun was useless, its energy drained. I pulled my knife out—it was better than nothing—and contemplated how much strength it would take to penetrate the monster's hide.

The thing was trying to get into the hut. The walls shook with the fervor of its attack. Luckily, it was too large to fit through the door, but I had no confidence that the flimsy structure could withstand a continued attack. I smacked my knife against the lodge pole at the center of the hut. "Danger," I yelled. "Wake up! Danger, danger!"

I shrieked and swore, but it had little effect. Only when I put two fingers in my mouth and whistled did White Foot stir. Muzzily it got to its feet, took in what was happening, and, quirching loudly, spread the alarm. Soon the entire crew of them stood in the center of the hut, heads together. As I watched, a greenish glow began to build from their center and moved outward, washing over me and spreading to the very walls of the hut.

The beast became quiet. It backed away.

The glow pushed out into the forest, shoving the beast before it. I watched from the doorway as, squalling, the thing fled toward a rift in the canyon walls, squeezed through it, and was gone.

I watched it go, then noticed something else strange. My escape pod had come back to life. It was lit up and signaling the heavens with its emergency beacon.

The sky slowly shifted in color from the icy black of dead night, softening toward dawn. Another shooting star came across the horizon, followed an arcing path and hovered overhead.

Hovered?

I was running, screaming and waving my hands over my head.

The pod set down. Charlie was standing in the doorway, a broad smile on his face, nearly barking with joy.

I pounded toward the hatch. "Quick," I said. "Get us out of here before your power drains."

"Roger." He was already in the pilot's seat and powering up for takeoff.

I strapped myself in. Through the viewscreen I could just see the hut, and one small face peering out of the door: Jimmy.

I hoped that he would find a new pet soon.

It was well past the cocktail hour. The ship was on autopilot, heading for an ore-rich planetoid a week away.

We were relaxing, sharing celebratory drinks—his, water, mine, whiskey.

"So you tracked me via the transponder in my mess kit?"

"Yeah," Charlie said. "It was really weak, but it kept broadcasting. I had some idea of where the pod went, thanks to the ion signature, but your beacon died before I could triangulate a secure fix. Luckily it came back to life just now."

I tried to keep myself from asking, but the whiskey

and I just had to know. "Did you go with Hugo because you wanted to, or because you had to?"

Charlie rolled his eyes. "He was even worse company than you are," he said. "Anyway, I didn't exactly have a choice. He jettisoned your pod while I was in the w.c. When I came out, he had a gun on me. It took me a hell of a long time to win his trust. That paranoid pooch would shackle me to the comm before he went to sleep and lock down communications when he went to the john."

"How'd you get away?"

"Finally I convinced him that I was more effective with all my paws free. When he was asleep, I set the ship on autopilot for the nearest Port Authority, took an emergency pod to cut the radio towline, boarded our ship, and got out of there."

"And Hugo?

"He's in custody as we speak." Charlie turned black on black, his formal mode, obviously pleased with himself. "And the reward money has not only paid our debts, there's a little something left over in the kitty. So, it took a dog to catch a dog."

"Amen. He was one crazy sucker."

"Yeah, but mostly, he was lonely. Dog wasn't meant to fly alone."

I was surprised by how sympathetic and sad he sounded. "You'd never turn on me, would you, Charles?"

"I'm not crazy."

I was relieved, but all the same, I couldn't help asking. You see, dogs aren't the only ones who worry.

A BOY AND HIS ALIEN

John Helfers

John Helfers is a writer and editor currently living in Green Bay, Wisconsin. His fiction has appeared in anthologies such as *Sword of Ice and Other Tales of Valdemar*, *The UFO Files*, and *Warrior Princesses*, among others. He is also the editor of the anthology *Black Cats and Broken Mirrors*. Future projects include coauthoring several novels. In his spare time, what there is of it, he enjoys disc golf, inline skating, and role-playing games.

JACK struggled up the hill, the shouts of his pursuers following him. He had just reached the tree line, and knew if he could make it far enough into the forest, he could find a place to hide. After that, he would figure out what to do—

His foot slipped as he tried to scramble over the hilltop. *Worry about saving your ass right now, Jack, then think about later when it comes.* If the three boys that were chasing him caught up, he wouldn't be thinking about anything but pain for a good long while.

"Dammit! Get that little bastard!" came a cry from below. Jack righted himself and scrambled over the hill,

skidding to the bottom of the other side. Just a few steps
more—

The forest lay before him, the rustling trees covering
dense thickets of underbrush and grass. Jack didn't waste
time admiring the scenic view. As he raced into the
woods, a shower of rocks pelted the tree trunks around
him. One large stone slammed into his shoulder, causing
him to stagger and gasp in pain. Jack heard laughter behind him.

"Nailed him! Good shot, Chris!"

"Now let's teach that little asshole a lesson about respect." The relentless footsteps started again.

Jack ran faster, looking for a place to hide, or at least to
catch his breath. He stumbled farther into the forest, hoping to find a thicket or copse he could take cover in. The
voices of the boys following him echoed off the trees,
making it seem as though they were coming from all
directions at once.

If I don't find something quick, I'm history, he thought.
He could see an open space ahead of him, and made
for it.

Jack ran to the clearing, skidding to a stop at its edge.
Before him lay the usually placid river, now swollen and
turbulent from the spring rains. The water had carved its
way through the forest for centuries, creating a deep
ravine which was tricky climbing on a good day. Now,
with the current violently throwing up spray onto the
rocks, it looked impossible.

Panting, Jack looked back at the forest, wincing at the
pain in his shoulder as he turned. The boys were maybe a
minute away. Running along the riverbank would only
cut off escape in that direction. And if they caught him,
he was a goner. But maybe he could find a place to hide
in the tumble of rocks. . . . He looked for a spot to begin
climbing down. If he couldn't hide, maybe he could
cross the river, maybe even lose his pursuers for good.

Right there, he thought, and started working his way
down the riverbank.

The rough rocks scraped patches of skin from his hands, and his shirt and jeans were soon soaked. He had just reached the first flat rock in the riverbed when a cascade of pebbles bounced down the earthen walls behind him.

"Trades, you pansy-ass. Come back here!"

Jack ignored the taunts and kept going. Only when the first stone whizzed past him and into the river did he look up. All three of the boys were searching the riverbank for suitable missiles. Jack knew what a wealth of ammunition they'd find. He kept edging out farther on the slippery boulder, looking for another rock he could jump to. He didn't want to risk wading the river unless it was absolutely necessary.

Then the choice was made for him. When the next volley of stones flew at him, a rounded rock clipped Jack on the side of the head. Stunned, he lost his balance and toppled into the roaring water.

The icy spring current shocked him back into full consciousness. Jack clawed his way to the surface, choking and spluttering. He tried to get his bearings, but was tossed about the river like a fallen tree trunk. For a brief, desperate moment his world consisted of flashes of sky alternating with facefulls of chilling water. Jack struggled to keep air in his lungs, to keep from being swept underwater, and to avoid smashing himself against any of the large boulders in the riverbed.

He suddenly had more important things to worry about than the boys following him.

About fifty yards away, the river disappeared, dropping out of sight in a foaming waterfall. Caught in the middle of the current, Jack was having trouble just keeping his head above water. He knew he couldn't swim to the riverbank in time to save himself. With a yell, he shot over the falls and into the rolling water below.

Just before he dropped over the edge, he heard the three boys' laughter echo off the ravine walls as they walked away, leaving him to his fate.

*   *   *

About a half-mile down river, Jack reached up from the water and grabbed an overhanging tree limb. Holding on against the current, he dragged himself over to the river's edge. Half-drowned, so tired from fighting the current and keeping his head above water that he could barely muster the strength to save himself, he grabbed a handful of grass and pulled. Slowly, painfully, he hauled his body partly out of the water. *Safe at last,* he thought, as he collapsed on the bank. He convulsed once, then vomited up a stream of brackish river water.

Against all odds, it seemed he was going to live through this.

Coughing, he took stock of his injuries. His whole body ached dully, with sharp flashes of pain coming from his head, shoulder, and leg. *I should have stayed and let them beat me up. I'd probably be in better shape,* Jack thought.

Getting a better grip on the tree limb, Jack hauled himself completely clear of the river's grasp. His left knee hurt, so he pulled himself up with his hands. When he had made it to the riverbank, he rolled over on the grass and let the sun soak into his cold, battered body.

I nearly died because Chris is such a jerk-off, he thought. *Just because he's too stupid to do his own homework he expects everyone else to "help" him. Bullshit. Well, I didn't do it for him last night. I'm not sure I'd go through this again to avoid it, though.*

Jack lay on the bank a few more minutes, then rolled over and slowly stood up, fighting a wave of dizziness that whirled through his head. His shoulder hurt even worse now than it had before he'd fallen in the river, and he could feel his left knee starting to swell. He knew his leg wasn't broken, though. Putting weight on it brought a groan of pain to his lips, but he remained standing. The leg would support him. Maybe things weren't as bad as he thought they were.

That's when the next wave of despair hit him.

I'm standing up, all right. But I'm standing on the wrong side of the river.

For another minute, he just stayed where he was, weaving a little from pain and exhaustion, looking around. He had explored almost all of the riverbank's other side, but hadn't ventured very far over here. It all looked pretty much the same, but with the sun starting to set, the lengthening shadows were a little creepier.

Jack yawned, feeling weariness settle over him as the reaction to his narrow escape set in. But as tempting as it was, he couldn't afford the time to rest. He had to follow the riverbank downstream until he found a shallow enough place to cross. Then he could head back to the home, thinking up suitable excuses for his lateness, his injuries, and the damage to his clothes along the way. With any luck at all, Chris and his gang would be in bed and asleep by the time he got there, but Jack knew just how thin his luck had been running lately.

He had been walking for a few minutes when he smelled something burning. Was he now going to be burned alive in a forest fire? Maybe not—it was an odd scent, not like the campfires the boys' home sometimes had. This was different, more like a gas or chemical fire.

Jack followed the scent, heading deeper into the forest. *Maybe some hunter's camp has gone up in flames,* he thought. If so, somebody would have called the fire department. Maybe he could catch a ride out of here and back home, if that was the case. The smell grew stronger, and as he headed toward the source, he noticed that there was no noise in the woods he passed. No birds sang, no squirrels chattered, no rabbits ran through the grass.

Most likely the fire scared off the local animals, that's all, he told himself. By now the smell was almost overwhelming, and Jack could see something ahead of him sparkling in the fading light. His curiosity made him forget his aching body, and he half-trotted, half-limped toward whatever it was.

After a few minutes, Jack came upon a scene unlike anything he had ever seen before.

Before him was a large circle of scorched and burned earth. Some of the scrub brush and grass at the edge of the shallow crater was still smoldering, though the woods and ground were probably too wet for a wildfire to start. In the middle of the blasted patch was a pit where something had crashed into the ground—a large rock of some kind, broken in half and studded with shiny smaller rocks that glittered in the waning sunlight. Jack realized what had made the flash he had seen.

Cool, a meteorite, he thought.

Looking around, Jack saw no one else nearby. The air was intensely warm, as if the meteorite had hit quite recently. *I wonder why I didn't hear the impact,* he thought. Jack was about to examine the meteorite when something else caught his attention.

On the far side of the crater, a small pool of what looked like silver gleamed in the blackened grass and dirt. As Jack tried to get a closer look, he saw that it didn't look like a charred birch branch. Nor did it look like the bones of an animal burned up in the collision. He warily circled the crater to take a closer look.

The stuff in question resembled a puddle of silvery liquid, veined with threads of black. *It kinda looks like that sample of mercury Mr. Hawes showed us in science class. I bet it came from that meteorite,* Jack thought, looking back at the crater. He saw a hollow polished space in the center of one of the pieces. Hawking loudly, Jack spit on one of the meteorite halves. When it didn't sizzle, he used a large stick to drag one half of the meteorite out of the pit.

Whatever this is, it's perfect for my science project. Who knows, maybe it's some sort of remains left when aliens crashed on Earth. Being careful not to touch the meteorite with his hands, Jack took off his T-shirt and maneuvered the rock into it with his stick. Placing the meteorite half on the ground next to the puddle, he took his stick and poked the silvery mass, ready to leap away if it showed the slightest sign of being dangerous. Jack had seen too many sci-fi movies not to be careful. Nothing happened. Satisfied that it wasn't going to do anything weird, Jack gently scraped the silvery blob into the polished cavity in the meteorite with his stick. He was about to bundle up his shirt into a sling to carry the meteorite in when a most unexpected thing happened.

The silver stuff moved.

Faster than he could react, the amorphous puddle flowed out of the meteorite and slithered toward Jack. Before he could drop his shirt, the silver covered his hand and was sliding up his arm. Frantically he tried to rake it off, but it seemed to flow right around his fingers. Jack scraped with the stick, trying to pry it off, but with no better results.

Jack screamed helplessly as the stuff reached his neck. It coiled around his throat, squeezing until Jack, still trying to claw it off, felt the blood pound in his head and saw everything blur in front of hm. The last thing he remembered was a silver tendril blindly feeling its way up toward his face. . . .

Jack awoke to the sharp smell of antiseptic and the coolness of clean sheets. He opened his eyes and saw the familiar walls of the boy's home infirmary around him. He was in one of the beds that lined the wall.

The second thing he noticed was that his shoulder and leg didn't hurt very much. Moving them experimentally, he found the pain and swelling were mostly gone. His head itched, and when he reached up, Jack found a bandage taped above one eye. He sat further upright on the bed, trying to piece together what had happened. Through a window on the opposite wall, he saw that night had fallen.

How in the hell did I get back here? he wondered. There was a strange metallic taste in his mouth, as if he had been swallowing blood. Then he remembered what he had found out in the woods. Sitting upright, Jack's hands shot to his neck, searching for the silver liquid. He felt nothing there but his own skin. Sighing in relief, Jack leaned back against his pillow and relaxed. *Just some sort of hallucination, I guess. But that still doesn't explain how I got back here. Unless I dreamed the whole thing.*

In the hallway, he heard a door open and close, then the sound of footsteps on the stairs. Jack quickly lay back on the bed. A minute later, a middle-aged woman in a white uniform walked through the door. "Ah, Mr. Trades, it's good to see you're awake. At least you don't look as bad this time as you usually do," she said with just a hint of an aristocratic British accent. Jack smiled and started to raise himself to a sitting position, but was stopped by the nurse. "Just a minute, young man. I want to make sure nothing's seriously damaged. Let me take a look at that leg first."

She peeled back the blanket and sheet, revealing Jack's thin legs sticking out of the infirmary gown he was dressed in. Jack shivered and goose bumps popped out on his skin as the cold air of the room hit his bare skin. "Sorry," the nurse said.

"That's all right, Miss Rimes. Just unexpected—" Jack started to reply, then stopped as he saw the frown on the nurse's face. "Um . . . is something wrong?"

"Well, yes, I mean, no . . . I'm not sure. When you were brought in here, your knee was swollen to the size of a softball. Now . . ." she trailed off.

Jack lifted his head and looked at his leg. The left knee looked just like the right, except for a faded yellowing bruise that looked about a week old.

"Can you move it for me?" Nurse Rimes asked. Jack flexed his knee experimentally, slowly at first, then faster.

"Any pain?" she asked.

Jack shook his head. "Not even a twinge."

She nodded. "How about that shoulder?"

In response, Jack rotated his shoulder and raised his arm above his his head. The nurse sat him up and checked it as well, finding the same slight bruising, but no other damage. His head checked out exactly the same, once the bandage was removed. Nurse Rimes was at a loss to explain it.

"Those injuries should have taken at least a week to heal, but they've cleared up in a matter of hours. What happened to you out there, anyway?"

"I was walking along the riverbank, and the next thing I knew, I fell in the water. I went over the waterfall and downstream a ways, and managed to swim to shore. That's all," Jack said.

"That's all, hmm? It sounds like more than enough to me. I've told the governing board more than once that the river should be fenced off. I don't how many times we've warned you boys to stay away from there. Sooner or later we're going to lose one of you permanently. You were lucky this time, Jack," the nurse said.

"Yes, ma'am," he replied.

"Well, there's really no reason to keep you here any longer, unless you feel the need to rest up a bit longer. If you hurry up and dress, I believe you might be able to catch the evening meal."

"Beef stew, sounds great," Jack said as he sniffed the air.

Nurse Rimes gave him an odd look. "Why, yes, how did you know?"

"What, can't you smell it?" Jack asked.

She shook her head and smiled. "I guess my nose isn't as sensitive as a hungry boy's is."

A loud rumbling from Jack's stomach punctuated the nurse's last sentence. Jack smiled and looked down. "Anyone within hearing distance can tell I'm starving. Is there something here I could change into?" he said.

"Of course." Nurse Rimes walked over to a supply closet and returned with a pair of jeans and a long-sleeved shirt, some socks and sneakers. "You can change behind the partition there." She turned to go to her office.

"Thank you, ma'am. By the way, who found me? How did I get here?"

Nurse Rimes stopped at the doorway. "One of the custodians said he saw you walking across the backyard looking like you had been in a nor'easter. He brought you directly to me. Surely you remember that?"

"Oh, umm, yeah, now that you mention it, it's kind of coming back to me. I guess that knock on the head scrambled my brains a little more than I had thought. Thanks for everything."

"You're welcome, Jack. Now please, try to stay out of trouble for at least a few days this time," the nurse said over her shoulder as she walked into her office.

Not much chance of that with Chris and his goons around, Jack thought as he pulled his clothes on. *I still don't understand how I got back here. The last thing I remember was that silver gunk all over me . . . but somehow I must have got it off and found my way back here.*

Another gurgle from his stomach reminded Jack that, at least for now, he had more important matters to attend to. He tied his shoes and trotted down to the dining hall.

The dinner hall was, as usual during mealtime, organized chaos. Rows of boys sat at long wooden tables with their trays of food, eating and talking. Staff personnel walked up and down the aisles, making sure the boys didn't get out of hand. Cooks and kitchen staff bustled behind the serving tables, making sure the food trays were well stocked. A line of boys circled around the room and shuffled past the metal serving tables. The noise was incredible.

When Jack walked in, a ripple of conversation buzzed around the room. Just about everyone looked at him. Some boys gave him a few quick glances; several stared at him outright. Jack ignored all of it and went to the line, grabbed a tray, and piled food on. Just as he had gotten it heaped to his liking, a voice from behind him made him turn.

"Jack?"

Jack looked up to see his science teacher, Mr. Hawes, standing nearby.

"Feeling all right?"

Jack nodded. "Just hungry."

"Missed you in class today," the man said.

"Yeah, I was in the infirmary. Had to lie down for a while. But I'm much better now. I'll get today's assignment from one of the guys," Jack said, picking up his tray.

Mr. Hawes looked at him for a long moment before replying, "All right. Be sure you do. Enjoy your dinner."

Jack grinned. "Thanks." *Phew,* he thought, *that could have been trouble.* He walked over to an empty table and sat down, looking around as he did so. Except for the occasional glance thrown his way, the hall had returned to its normal activity. Jack noticed Mr. Hawes keeping a closer eye on him than usual, his tall figure crowned with a shock of salt-and-pepper hair easily distinguishable in the crowd of boys. Jack began forking his food down, barely aware of how it tasted. Instead, he was listening to the murmur of conversation around the room.

"—I'd hate to be in his shoes—"

"Chris is going to mess him up even worse now—"

"He be fucked—"

Jack looked up when he heard the last words. He recognized the voice as that of an African-American kid from the projects in Boston. Jack scanned the room until he found the boy, sitting at least thirty feet away, and talking in a low voice. That was weird . . . Jack had heard him as if he were sitting right next to him.

Before he had time to think about what was happening to him, he had more trouble than he could handle on his hands. Three guys pulled out chairs at his table and sat down, one on either side and one across from him. He was trapped—but even Chris wouldn't be dumb enough to pull something here, would he? Jack curled an arm around his tray and kept eating, not looking up. Maybe if he refused to play their game—

"Trades, I can't fucking believe you're as stupid as you look. I would have thought that the little swim you took would have knocked some sense into your blockhead. But I guess you still need a lesson in how things work around here." The voice paused. "Look at me when I'm talkin' to you."

Jack raised his head, staring straight into Chris's muddy brown eyes, feeling the larger boy's stale breath waft over his face. Jack knew his type, had seen variations of his kind in the other homes he had been in. A bully, a larger, stronger kid who ruled everybody else by intimidation, taking what he wanted and beating the shit out of anyone who dared stand up to him. He kept this up until someone bigger or stronger did the same to him, then the cycle continued.

The trick to handling these guys, Jack had learned, was twofold. One, never let them get you alone. Two, never show fear. He lifted a forkful of food to his mouth and ate it, chewing slowly. He considered another bite, rejected it, set the fork down.

"What's the matter, food not up to your high standards?" one of Chris' flunkies, a towhead named Kelsey, taunted.

Jack shook his head. "No, I just looked up and lost my appetite."

Chris mistook the insult for fear. "Good, that's more like it."

Jack looked at the goons on either side of him. "Aren't you guys at the wrong table?" The three kids exchanged glances, then looked back at Jack, who said, "The table reserved for assholes is over there." He pointed across the dining hall.

Chris grabbed Jack's shirt and yanked him across the table. "Listen, dickhead—" was as far as he got before a shadow fell over the group.

"Is anything wrong, Mr. Desjardins?" Mr. Hawes asked, all conversation at nearby tables dying down as the other boys watched the conflict.

Chris released Jack, smoothing his shirt out. "No, sir, I just wanted to make a point in our conversation."

"That true, Jack?" the teacher asked. Jack nodded and picked up his fork.

"Well, why don't you three let Jack finish his meal in peace?" Mr. Hawes commanded. The three boys slowly got up, Chris last. As the bully rose from the table, he put his face close to Jack's. "We're not done yet, new fish."

"I'll be waiting," Jack replied, casually taking another bite of his food.

As the three boys left the hall, Jack could hear snatches of their whispered conversation as if he was walking right next to them. "Tonight—mess his shit up good—nobody makes a fool out of me."

Why can I hear them from here? he wondered.

"Jack?" The voice next to him sounded like a clap of thunder. Jack winced and looked up, seeing Mr. Hawes still standing over him.

"Yes, sir?"

"Are you sure you're all right?" the science teacher asked. "You kind of looked like you were spacing out there for a moment."

"Yeah, yeah, I'm fine," Jack said, concentrating on looking at his food. Some things had to be settled without grown-up interference. At least if they were going to stay settled.

Instead of leaving, Mr. Hawes sat down across from Jack. "Those guys weren't bothering you, were they? I know their type."

"Yeah, so do I," Jack said. "Always looking for an angle."

Hawes nodded. "It's hard being new in a place like this. If you have any more trouble with them, come see me, all right?"

Jack regarded him for a moment, then nodded. "All right."

Mr. Hawes got up to walk through the now mostly empty dinner hall. Jack watched him go, then shook his head. *If only it were that simple.* Jack had done enough time in state homes to know what would happen to him if he did talk to Hawes. *The only thing these kids hate worse than a bully is a rat. Thanks, teach, but I'll take care of this on my own.* He finished his meal and took his tray up to the window, then left the dining room.

As he headed to the stairway, a burst of laughter caught his attention. Looking back, he saw Chris and the other two boys lounging near the dining room doors. Chris smiled at him and made a gun out of his thumb and forefinger, pointing the imaginary weapon directly at Jack.

"Bang," he said. Jack smiled back at him and went upstairs.

Once he'd reached the large stark room that housed Jack's bed along with nineteen others, Jack looked around to see who else was there. The room was deserted except for one other boy, a skinny kid with glasses who was reading a thick textbook. Classical music played from a small radio on the window shelf above his head. Trades heaved a small sigh, then slowly walked over to his bed.

The kid on the bed—Charles Williamson—looked like a stereotypical bookworm, but nobody at the home had messed with him after his first and last fight. The kid who had started it had lost a finger. Williamson had bitten it off. Since the other boy was a habitual offender, and there were twelve witnesses who swore that Williamson acted in self-defense, he was still at the boys' home instead of doing time at some youth detention facility. He had spent two weeks in solitary, however. Since then Williamson had been the model of self-restraint, but most of the other kids had given him a wide berth. Nobody wanted to test his limits again. Jack kept his hands behind his back as he approached.

"What do you want, Mr. Trades?" Williamson asked, not even looking up from his book.

"I need the batteries from your radio," Jack said.

That got his attention. Williamson looked up, blinking in surprise. "I didn't know Handel bothered you so much. I can certainly turn it down."

"No, it's nothing like that. I just need the batteries for a little project I'm doing."

"You wouldn't be planning a little aversion therapy for some of the more misguided youth around here, would you? Batteries for battery, perhaps?"

"No, but it's better you don't know what they're for," Jack said.

"Hmm. And what do I get out of it?" Williamson asked.

Jack smiled. The other well-known fact about Williamson was that he had an immense sweet tooth. "My desserts for two weeks."

"One month," the smaller boy countered.

Jack didn't even argue. "Done."

Williamson reached behind him and pulled the small radio off the shelf. "Pity, Beethoven's Second is the featured symphony tonight. Oh, well." He tossed the six double A batteries to Trades. "Mind you, they'd better work when I get them back, or I might not need any dessert," he said, snapping his teeth as he spoke. That was the trouble with Williamson, one never knew if he was kidding or not. Jack smiled weakly as he headed back to his bed and lay down.

Soon the rest of the boys in Jack's wing started filing in. Except for the occasional glance his way, none of them spoke about what was going to happen later that night. Conversations were low, and this time Jack couldn't hear what was being said. It seemed the heightened hearing he had enjoyed earlier was gone. *Too bad, I sure*

*could have used it to hear Chris and his goons coming.
Guess I'll have to do this the hard way.*

The overall mood in the room was subdued that evening, as if the promise of future violence was casting a
pall over the other boys, but Jack knew he was on his
own when it came to trouble with Chris. The first rule of
any home was always "don't get involved unless you
have no other choice." The other nineteen kids had already decided that what was going to happen tonight was
going to happen no matter what, so it was just better to
stay out of the way.

After what seemed like forever to Jack, one of the staff
came in to do the evening head count. Five minutes later,
the lights went out.

Immediately Jack stripped his pillowcase off and put
the batteries in it, making sure they were all packed in
one corner of the pillowcase. He then tied a knot above
them, trapping them firmly in place. He hefted the
makeshift weapon experimentally. He wished he could
have gotten his hands on something larger or heavier, but
this would have to do. If he swung it hard enough, his
makeshift cosh would leave a sizable lump on someone's
skull.

Jack lay on his back, the hand holding the pillowcase
dangling off the side of the bed. He wrapped one end of
the pillowcase firmly around his palm, so he could swing
it harder. Now all he had to do was stay awake and wait.

Strangely, even after the day he had been through,
sleep was the farthest thing from Jack's mind. He felt as
alert as if he had just gotten a full night's sleep, every
nerve tingling, his muscles relaxed yet ready to move at a
second's notice. About an hour later, that second arrived.

Jack heard the measured footsteps of one of the staff
doing their patrol. The footsteps retreated down the
stairs, then silence reigned. Jack stared at the ceiling, listening for the slightest noise.

The door handle turned slowly and the door opened. A
shaft of light speared into the room, followed by three

shadows of varying heights. The light vanished as the door swung shut. Jack closed his eyes, his chest rising and falling rhythmically as he feigned sleep.

He had to admit, they were good. They didn't whisper to each other as they approached his bed. They moved almost silently through the room. If he hadn't been expecting them, they'd most likely have caught him by surprise. Jack's grip tightened on the pillowcase. He could actually sense them coming closer, not just by hearing their footsteps on the tile floor, but more with a strange spatial awareness, like a bat's sonar sense or a snake sensing motion with its tongue.

Jack didn't waste time pondering his newfound abilities. He just reacted. When he felt someone lean over him, he brought the pillowcase up and across, cracking the guy solidly in the face. Jack heard a muffled grunt and a creak of bedsprings as the boy rebounded off his mattress and crumpled to the floor.

Jack opened his eyes to discover he was looking at a nightmare. The two boys, one on either side of his bed, weren't even recognizable anymore. Instead, they were humanoid forms glowing brightly in brilliant reds, yellows, and oranges that flared against the darkness. Too aware of what would happen if he did, Jack didn't scream, but scrambled to his feet, standing at the head of his bed. He held the battery-filled pillowcase in front of him, whirling it slowly, ready to nail the first kid who made a move toward him. He saw that the pillowcase now looked black against his hand, which was colored in the same bright shades as his two attackers.

So it's not them, but something that's happened to my sight instead. Jack could hear the two boys whispering, but this time he couldn't make out what they were saying. Their intent, however, was obvious. Each one took a step closer to Jack. They were ready to rush him. After a tiny pause, they ran toward him as fast as they could.

Jack watched them approach, waited for them, not moving an inch. He felt a confident calm settle over him.

His entire body was tingling, as if every muscle was overloaded with adrenaline. Jack crouched down on the bed, still whirling the pillowcase. He knew exactly what he was going to do.

When the two glowing forms came at him, Jack sprang forward off the bed, leaping high in the air. He had planned to land in the aisle and head for the door. But he'd misjudged the power of his jump, and he sailed across the room, nearly landing on the bed of the boy who slept across from him. Jack dropped the pillowcase and flailed his arms and legs, trying to aim for the floor next to the kid's bed. His wild gyrations caused him to land wrong, and he felt a flare of pain in his left ankle as he hit.

Off balance from the fall, Jack never saw the foot coming. The kick hit him square on the side of his face, knocking his head into the bed frame and causing a bright flash of light to explode behind his eyes. He opened his eyes again—but this time saw nothing but darkness.

Another blow rocked him, this time in the rib cage. Jack grunted and he slammed against the bed frame. Blinking back tears, Jack began to see dark blurry shapes in front of him. Someone grabbed him by the hair and yanked his head up. Another kid wrenched his arm behind his back and shoved his hand up between his shoulder blades. The boy behind him shifted his grip, bring his other arm up to encircle Jack's throat.

"After this, you'll be begging to do anything I say," a voice Jack recognized as Chris' hissed in front of him. He followed up the threat with a pile driver to Jack's stomach. Oddly, it didn't hurt as much as Jack thought it should have. In fact, his whole body felt kind of numb. He could still move and feel the pain where he was being hit, but it was dulled, as if his body were covered in impact-absorbing padding.

"Reach behind you and grab the boy's throat," a firm voice commanded in Jack's head. Jack didn't even think.

His free hand shot backward and found soft tissue. As soon as he felt it, Jack began to squeeze. He felt the pressure on his own throat increase, but his mind felt clear and sharp, not bothered by the lack of oxygen at all.

"Use your knee," the calm voice suggested. Jack lashed out with his foot instead, catching Chris, who was just winding up for another flurry of punches, squarely between the legs. The stocky boy screamed and collapsed to the floor, curling in on himself.

Jack heard gagging sounds emanating from behind him, and the pressure on his throat and arm slackened. He kept up his stranglehold, ignoring the struggles of the boy behind him as he tried to pry Jack's hand off of his throat. The boy was growing heavier in Jack's grip, and Jack finally released him, just as the room was flooded with light.

"All right, break it up, break it up!" Two night wardens ran to Jack and Chris, separating them. A third one ran to the boy who had been behind Jack, who was now lying on the floor, making strange choking noises. His throat bore mottled bruises in the shape of four fingers and a thumb.

"I think you'd better get Nurse Rimes. This looks serious," the warden who was bent over the thrashing boy said.

"He started it, the son-of-a-bitch attacked us for no reason!" Chris shouted, still rocking on the floor and holding his groin.

The night warden, a beefy guy Jack knew only as Sykes, poked Chris in the chest once with his baton. "Shut up." He motioned for the one behind Chris to go get the nurse.

Jack didn't say a word, he just looked at the other teenager, who was crumpled at the foot of his bed, blood oozing from his mouth and nose. Jack grinned, then gasped as his arms were pinioned behind his back.

"Okay, tough guys, it's solitary for both of you until we straighten this out," Sykes said. He grabbed Jack and

Chris, holding each by one arm, and propelled them toward the door. He had to half-drag Chris, who was groaning and limping. Sykes' hand felt like a steel band squeezing Jack's bicep. "Now, we're going to take a nice quiet walk down to detention. If I hear a word, even one peep, out of either of you, your stay in solitary will be extended. Nod if you understand." The two boys nodded. "All right, let's go."

Sykes marched the pair down the stairs to the basement of the hall, where the detention cells were. He escorted Chris into one, locked it, and took Jack across the hall into a similar room, containing a cot, a sink, and a toilet. The door slammed, and Jack was left alone in the darkness.

Jack blinked his eyes several times, but nothing happened. *Well, whatever's happening to me, I apparently can't control it,* he thought. He stretched out his arms and felt his way across the room to the cot. A dull ache was spreading from his chest and ribs outward to his arms and legs. With a grunt of pain he lowered himself gingerly down onto the thin mattress.

The events of the day whirled through his mind like a dust devil. The forest, Chris, the river, the silver blob, the meteorite, the fight, Mr. Hawes, the strange things happening to his body—everything spun through his mind in a confusing jumble until, without registering the change, Jack slipped from consciousness into a deep sleep.

The click of the fluorescent lights overhead woke Jack. Blinking, he tried moving his arm. No pain. He tried his other arm with the same result. Taking a deep breath, he lifted his head, tensing in anticipation of stabbing pains he knew would shoot through it. The bare white walls of the detention cell still surrounded him.

Something was bothering him, and it took Jack a minute to figure out what it was. *Breathing,* he realized *I'm breathing just fine.* Jack couldn't remember how many shots he had taken to the chest and stomach, but even the first one had cracked some ribs. Yet he was breathing with barely any difficulty at all. He lifted up his T-shirt. Once again, he saw the same kind of yellowing and faded bruises he'd seen yesterday on his knee and shoulder. Except for a slight twinge of pain every so often, he felt like he had been resting in bed for a week.

"What the hell is happening to me?" Jack whispered, still staring at his pale chest discolored by the ring of healing bruises.

"At the moment, your body is repairing itself at approximately five times its normal rate," a voice said.

"Yeah, right, how would . . . you . . . know?" Jack started to snap as he looked up toward the door, where he thought he had heard the voice come from. The judas hole was still closed, as well as the door itself. Jack was quite alone in the room.

"Who said that?" he whispered.

"I did," came the quiet reply.

"Where are you?" Jack asked

"I'm with you."

"Uh-huh. Jack, you are losing it," Jack whispered to himself. He rolled to his feet, and walked over to the sink. A few splashes of water in his face later, he was starting to feel like himself again. "It's gotta be hallucinations caused by the rock slamming me in the head. Maybe a concussion I got going over the waterfall. What I saw last night, maybe the nerves in my eyes are fucked up. I'd better tell the nurse about that before it gets worse."

"I'm afraid that this 'nurse' will find nothing wrong with you. There is certainly nothing wrong with your head now." Jack swore he could hear the voice take on an injured tone. *"Your eyes are currently operating at 99.1% efficiency. As I grow accustomed to your body, that percentage will increase."*

"Will you just shut the fu . . ." Jack began, then

stopped as the voice's words sank in. "What do you mean, 'grow accustomed to my body'?"

"A visual demonstration will prove most helpful in assessing our current state. Please look at your left arm."

Slowly, Jack's gaze swung down to his arm. As he watched, his skin started exuding droplets of a familiar silver liquid, as if he were sweating quicksilver. Jack reached over with his right hand and tried to scrape the stuff off, but it just slipped through his fingers. He shook his left arm, trying to fling the stuff away from him, but when he looked again, it was still there. As he watched, it slowly melted back through his skin.

"It is too late. We are joined now. I am as much a part of you as you are of me."

Jack didn't say anything, he just kept staring at his arm where the silver goo had been.

"Jack? Jack? Are you still there?"

"Just like in *The Hidden*," he said. A scene from the movie came back to him. "How did you . . . get inside me?"

"I entered through what you would call your mouth. Why?"

"Oh, no particular reason," Jack said, hawking up phlegm and spitting in the sink several times. He drank two glasses of water, then splashed some more on his face.

"I am sorry if it caused you discomfort, but at the time it was the easiest way to gain access." For what it was worth, the voice sounded apologetic.

Jack stared at himself in the mirror. Same brown hair, freckled features, small nose, clear blue eyes. *Nothing at all to suggest that I have anything wrong with me,* he thought.

"I really wish you would stop using that term. At this time, apart from the damage you appear to invite from others of your kind, your body is in excellent shape. And now it will be even better than before."

Jack nodded slowly. "So that rock in the woods wasn't just a meteorite, was it?"

"Correct. It was the craft I came to this planet in," the voice said.

"So you . . . really . . . are not just alien remains, but you're the alien?" Jack asked.

"Correct again. You are a quick learner."

"Wait a minute. You're telling me I've got an alien organism in me that talks."

"Not talking, I am communicating directly with your mind. That's why you are able to understand me—"

"Just shut up a minute, will you?" Jack digested this information. It was as if someone had just told him what the dinner menu for that evening would be. He felt totally calm, completely in control. It was the exact opposite of what he thought he should feel like. "Why aren't I like, you know, freaking out over this?"

"Because you have read about these kinds of interactions between alien organisms and humans for years," the voice said.

"What? What the hell are you talking about?" Jack asked. "How do you know what I have or haven't read?"

"I have been processing the information contained in your brain for the past day while you have rested and eaten. There are several articles by humans known as Asimov, Heinlein, and Silverberg which discourse extensively on human-alien encounters—"

"Wait a minute, you idiot, that stuff you're looking at isn't real. Those are made-up stories. If they were true, we'd be visited by aliens on a weekly basis."

"How do you know you are not?" the voice replied. *"The fact remains that you are able to deal with this situation with more of an open mind than others of your kind. However, I'm sure the fact that I'm suppressing your adrenal glands from producing adrenaline probably plays a large role in your lack of reaction as well."*

"Oh." Jack was able to follow the alien's logic fairly well. Science was one of the few classes he stayed awake for. "So you're a—what did Hawes call them—it's not a parasite, but—"

"A symbiote?"

"Exactly." Jack replied.

"That is also correct, I coexist with my host, unlike parasites which only take what they need. After all, it is in my best interest that you remain as healthy as possible."

"What do you mean?"

"Once one of my kind has found a host, the union is permanent. If you die, I die."

"What happens if you die somehow?" Jack asked.

"That rarely happens without the host dying first," was the calm reply. Jack shivered at the thought. He paced back and forth in the small room, pausing for a second to examine his knee. The swelling and bruises were practically gone.

"So that would explain my leg, shoulder, head, and everything else?"

"Yes. I am capable of controlling your bodily systems much better than your own brain. I simply repaired the damage there much faster than normal."

"And my eyes?" Jack asked.

"Regrettably, that was my fault. I was only trying to help you see better. Unfortunately, I had not yet mastered the finer points of your visual system, so I compensated for the wrong wavelength spectrum. You were seeing heat when I was trying to make your eyes use the available light more efficiently."

"Ah, well, a word of advice, next time you want to do something like that, make sure you let me know first," Jack said.

"Of course, but at the time, I didn't want to surprise you by making my presence known. It seemed that you were rather . . . involved at that moment."

"Yeah, that's one way to put it," Jack said, scratching his head. He looked at his hand. "You said you were controlling my adrenal glands so they didn't produce any adrenaline. Does that mean you can activate them as well?"

"That's correct."

"So . . . I could lift a car, or punch open that door, and not get hurt?"

"Not exactly. The burst of energy could very well let you do those things, but you would very likely strain your muscles or break your hand. Broken bones, like the ones you would assuredly have after hitting the door, take time to repair. I could stabilize them and surround the break with a protective membrane, which would cut the time to heal to about half of what it normally is."

"So how much could you heal?"

"That depends. Severe injury to the brain cannot be repaired. Major organs can be difficult, depending on the degree of injury. Muscle, ligaments and bones are the easiest to repair. You have many advantages over most humans now, but you're not invulnerable," the voice said.

"Advantages, eh? Like what else?"

"Well, as I am regulating your bodily functions, which includes your immune system, you'll never become ill again. I've even absorbed the small tumor that was growing in your brain."

"What? There was a what in my head?" Jack asked, looking at himself in the mirror.

"A small tumor. It's gone now. I also will care for your internal organs much better than your own body can. This will prolong your life span exponentially."

"Really, how long?"

"By at least a factor of four, perhaps longer."

"No shit? Wow, that's . . . that's at least three hundred years." Jack marveled at the implication, then his brow furrowed as a thought struck him. "Does that mean I don't age as fast?"

"Correct. Cell death and replacement will become much more efficient—"

"Oh, God!" Jack did the math in his head. "I'm gonna

be a teenager until I'm sixty? I'll be going through puberty for forty years!"

"*But I thought that humans desired their youth for as long as possible.*"

"Maybe, once we're old enough to appreciate it. Right now, it's going to be a major pain."

"*You forget the control I have over your functions. This "puberty" should not be more than a minor annoyance.*"

The alien's choice of words brought back another scene from the movie. "Are you a good alien or a bad alien?"

"*Well, good and evil don't really apply to us, but . . . I guess I'm more-or-less good. After all, I am letting you control your body.*"

"What?"

"*Of course, how do you think you got back here? With my control over your nervous system, I can command your entire body almost perfectly right now. You walked back to this place, went to the infirmary, and the nurse took care of you. After what had happened, you looked like you needed the rest.*"

"Did I—you—did we say anything to her?" Jack asked.

"*I didn't want to take the chance of not getting your personality correct, so you said nothing.*"

"Why didn't you take over during the fight?"

"*It is easier to control an unconscious body at first. It will take time for you to become accustomed to your body moving without you controlling it. Your heightened stress levels might have caused you to try to resist my control, which could have caused you more serious injury. Also, I didn't want to frighten you at a critical moment. Simple suggestions appeared to be the most logical course of action.*"

"Okay." Jack was still trying to absorb everything the alien was telling him. "Wow. My very own alien."

"*Listen, someone is coming,*" Jack fell silent and, sure

enough, the sound of approaching footsteps could be faintly heard.

"Are you boosting my hearing?"

"That is correct."

"And you can do that with sight, smell, everything?"

"Yes, all of your senses can be greatly improved."

"Cool."

"That means good, yes? Your body's core temperature is within the acceptable range."

"Yeah, that means good. Hey, what am I gonna call you? You already know my name," Jack said.

"My designation is unpronounceable to you."

"Well, you're a symbiote, so why don't I just call you Sym for short? How's that sound?"

"Whatever you think is appropriate. I would probably be quiet now, as I do not believe you humans look kindly on people who talk to themselves."

"You got that right," Jack said before he could stop himself. *Can you read my mind?* he thought.

"Of course. Just think what you want to say, and I will answer," Sym replied.

The cell door opened, and Sykes stood outside, tapping his baton into his hand. "Let's go," he said, motioning Jack to walk ahead of him.

He escorted Jack up the stairs, out of the detention center and through the main building until they had reached the head administrator's office. Sykes rapped on the door with his baton.

"Send him in," a muffled voice said. Sykes opened the door and prodded Jack forward. Jack half-turned and glared at him, only to be met with an impassive gaze and the steady thwacking of the baton into his hand.

"Compensating, eh?" Jack said as he walked through the door. He looked back and was rewarded by the flicker of a frown on Sykes' face.

"Antagonizing our captor will not improve our present situation," Sym said.

Ah, he's an asshole, Jack thought.

In the office were the administrator, Mr. Keller, and a man Jack had never seen before. He did, however, recognize a cop when he saw one. This guy was practically screaming it, from his rumpled off-the-rack suit to his stern by-the-book facial expression. Both men stood up when Jack entered.

"Just a minute, son," the rumpled man said. In his left hand was a strange-looking device resembling a *Star Trek* phaser. The man passed it over Jack's head and body, watching a small readout screen all the while. After a few seconds, he turned it and turned to the administrator. "He's clean."

Clean? Sym, what's he talking about? Jack asked. There was no reply. *Hey, Sym, you awake in there?* Still no answer. Jack felt a twinge of worry. As far as he could remember, Sym had never mentioned needing rest. *Of course, that doesn't mean he wouldn't if given the opportunity. Still, he picked a fine time for a snooze.*

"Did you hear me, Mr. Trades?" a voice cut through his thoughts. Jack blinked and turned his attention back to the two men.

"I'm sorry, sir, I just . . . drifted off. You were saying?"

"Agent Whelan here was asking you about a meteorite in the forest nearby." Mr. Keller said.

"What meteorite?" Jack automatically countered.

The rumpled man spoke. "Now, Jack, you're not in any trouble here. My analyzer detected traces of rock on your hair and hands that match what we're looking for. We have three witnesses that place you fairly close to the meteorite impact site. All I want to do is find out what you saw, that's all."

Chris, that prick, he sold me out, Jack thought, shifting his gaze from the man to Mr. Keller. The balding administrator looked back at him. "Telling the agent what you know may just help you in your, ah . . . current situation, Mr. Trades."

Jack turned back to the man. "Let me see some identification first."

The man grunted and reached into his jacket pocket, pulling out a black leather wallet. He flipped it open and held it out for Jack to examine. Jack did so, not knowing what he was looking for exactly. The Federal Bureau of Investigation ID card certainly looked authentic enough. After a few seconds, Jack nodded and leaned back in his chair. "All right, what do you want to know?"

"Just start from the beginning and tell me what happened," Agent Whelan said, taking out a small notebook and pen.

And Jack did so, omitting anything having to do with Sym. "Then I walked back to the home and went to the infirmary, and that's pretty much it."

"So you didn't see anything, besides the meteorite itself, unusual at the impact site?"

"No," Jack said, "Just the broken rock." *Sym, any time you want to wake your lazy alien butt up would be fine with me,* Jack thought. There was still no answer. In fact, Jack could not sense any glimmering of consciousness from his friend. *What the hell is going on?*

"Hmm." Agent Whelan flipped his notebook shut. "Mr. Keller, with your permission, I'd like to take Jack here down to headquarters and get his story officially recorded.

"Hey, since when did the F.B.I. take such an interest in meteorites anyway?" Jack asked.

"Jack!" Mr. Keller exclaimed. Whelan smiled and held up his hand.

"It's all right, Mr. Keller, I think Jack has a right to know. There have been several reports of contamination from meteorite impact sites. We're just following up any leads on people who have been in contact with a meteorite," Whelan said.

"Contamination?" Jack asked, fearing the worst.

"A strange illness humans and animals seem to pick up from the site. Preliminary tests have revealed it to be some sort of heavy metal poisoning. Don't worry, as I said before, you're clean. We just want to document what you saw and run a couple of tests."

"I certainly have no problem with it, Agent Whelan. How long do you think this will take?" Mr. Keller asked.

"I'd say not more than two or three hours at most. We should have him back in time for dinner," Agent Whelan said.

"Well, then, he's all yours," Mr. Keller said, standing up and shaking Whelan's hand. "When you get back, Mr. Trades, we'll discuss that other matter."

"Yes, Mr. Keller," Jack said. His attempts at rousing Sym had all met with failure. *I wonder if he's sick or something,* he thought. *Maybe I don't agree with him.*

Agent Whelan placed a hand on Jack's shoulder. "Let's go, son." They left the administrator's office and headed down to the main entrance. Whelan was quiet as they crossed the parking lot to his car, a nondescript blue four-door sedan.

"Get in," Whelan said, unlocking the passenger door. Jack did so. The inside of the car smelled like a corn chip. His feet were buried in fast-food bags and cardboard containers. Jack fastened his seat belt and looked at the back seat, which was swimming with more of the same. He noticed as he pulled the door shut that there was no release handle on the inside. No window handle either.

Whelan crossed to the drive's side and got in. He started the car and drove them out of the lot toward the highway. An eerie calm had settled over them. The silence was broken only by the rustling of the paper bags on the floor of the car.

Goddammit, Sym, wake up! I'm not kidding! Jack thought so hard he figured he might blow a blood vessel.

"It can't hear you," Agent Whelan said.

"What?" Jack asked.

"I said your symbiote can't hear you. It's stunned," Whelan said as calmly as if he had just asked Jack who his favorite football team was.

"What the hell are you talking about? I don't have . . ." Jack trailed off as Whelan looked at him and blinked. When his eyes opened again, they both looked like they were composed of a familiar silver liquid. He blinked again and it was gone, leaving only his watery blue eyes looking at Jack.

"God, I love doing that. Newbies make shitty liars. That's all right, though, you'll have plenty of time to work on it," the agent said.

Jack just sat there, his mouth open. Finally he had to say something. "There are more of us?"

"Sure. The ones that have been around for a while can sense others of their kind. That's how I knew about you. So, I just used my neural inhibitor," he said, patting the weapon at his hip, "to turn yours off for a while. Wouldn't want you to get any nasty ideas about putting my head through the windshield."

"Why didn't it knock me out as well?" Jack asked.

"Human cognitive processes are on a different wavelength than the symbiotes. That's why they have to be inside us, so they can communicate directly with our minds."

"Is it—he hurt?" Jack asked.

"No, are you kidding? They're far too valuable to be hurt or killed. The inhibitor just scrambles their thinking processes for a while. Communication or any kind of interaction with the host is impossible," Whelan said.

"Where are you taking me?" Jack asked, swallowing hard to keep the lump of fear from growing any larger in his throat.

"I'm taking you to a group of scientists who are going to test every fiber of your body to find out what makes you tick. You see, normally the symbiotes have to be attuned to their host bodies. You, however, are the exception. We want to find out why. Don't worry, most of it is perfectly safe for you. For him, that's another story," Whelan replied.

SYM!!! Jack thought-screamed. This was getting worse by the minute. And still no response from Sym. *Calm, remain calm,* Jack thought, remembering his encounters with the school bullies. *Never show fear.* The thought soothed him somewhat, and he was able to relax a little bit.

"So, you're really with the F.B.I.?" Jack asked.

"Of course. It's the perfect cover for information gathering. And the authority afforded by my position is an excellent advantage at times, like when I was sent to recover you."

Jack sighed in what he hoped sounded like relief. "Boy, I sure am glad you found me. I didn't know what I was going to do when I found out what had happened to me. I thought I was going nuts for a while. I hope you guys can help."

"Help?" Whelan chuckled. "Son, you've just been helped more than you can possible know. These guys make us nearly immortal, give us amazing healing and mental powers, and so much more. They'll be the perfect governors for this planet."

"Governors? You mean—"

"Of course. Once there are enough for everybody, we will literally achieve peace on Earth. No more conflict, no more strife. It will be a glorious merging. Total harmony."

"Oh, yeah, of course. That's why the thing inside me was talking so weird. Always talking about 'joining the collective' and all that. That's what he meant, huh?"

Agent Whelan looked at Jack for a moment, his eyes cold. "Jack, you may not have figured this out yet, but the symbiotes are excellent lie detectors. And we know you're trying to feed us a line. Don't ever try it again. It won't work."

He returned his attention back to the highway. "Your symbiote must have been injured in the crash, which is why it doesn't exert the necessary control over you that it should. We should be able to fix that."

"Oh, great," Jack replied. If Whelan heard the sarcasm in his voice, he didn't react. The pair drove in silence for a few minutes. A growl from Jack's stomach reminded him that he hadn't eaten anything since last night.

"I don't suppose you have anything fit to eat in here?" Jack asked, kicking at the grease-stained fast-food bags beneath his feet.

"Sure, there should be something down there. I didn't finish my breakfast. It'll be cold, though," the agent said.

"That's okay," Jack replied, bending down and rummaging through the various containers.

Agent Whelan chuckled. "You know, before I was chosen, I had just had triple bypass surgery. No more burgers, no more fries. Everything was no-salt, no-fat, no-cholesterol, no-taste. Now I can eat anything I want and not have to worry about clogging my arteries. It's fantastic."

"Mmmm," Jack agreed around a mouthful of egg muffin. He tipped the bag to get at the hash browns on the bottom when a small white packet fell out into his palm.

As soon as Jack saw what was in his hand, a plan formed. Jack rummaged among the other bags, searching for other similar packets. He continued munching as he did so. One of the things he had learned in the state homes was to eat whatever you could, whenever you could. After all, you never knew when your next meal might be. By the time he was done, he had collected several of the packets. Still bent over near the floor, he tore them open and poured the contents into his other hand. Shoving the empty packets under the seat. Jack straightened up and checked the road in front of them. At this time of the morning, traffic was nonexistent.

"Get enough?" Whelan asked.

"Yes, I found exactly what I was looking for," Jack said.

The odd statement made Whelan look at Jack for a moment, which is what Jack had been hoping for. His right hand came up toward Whelan's face, the mixture of salt and pepper flying directly into his eyes.

Whelan cursed and clawed at his eyes with one hand while stomping on the brake. At that exact moment, Jack reached for the steering wheel and yanked on it with all his strength. The sedan was just starting to slow down when the sudden change in direction made it flip and roll over and over. Jack could see the sky and highway change places as they tumbled. He heard someone yelling, and thought it might be himself. Then the car rolled off the road into the ditch, and Jack knew nothing more. . . .

"Jack, Jack, wake up. We have to get out of here," a voice inside Jack's brain seemed to scream at him, making his already throbbing head pound even worse.

"Oops, sorry. Here, let me help." After a minute the headache subsided, and Jack cautiously opened his eyes.

The morning shone through the remnants of the windshield, now shattered and broken. Jack could see muddy water above his head, and he realized that he was upside down, suspended by his seat belt. Jack felt wetness on his face, and smelled a coppery stench mixed in with the smells of gasoline and hot rubber.

"Seat belt . . ." he said, looking over at Whelan.

The F.B.I. agent had not been so lucky. As he hadn't been buckled up, he had been thrown about like a rag doll as the car had barrel-rolled. On one of the revolutions it looked like he had gotten caught between the steering wheel and the windshield. The corner of the roof on the driver's side was punched inward, with Whelan's head caught on the jagged metal. The steady drip of blood mixed with silver liquid was the only sound in the wrecked car.

"Well, that's just about the most awful thing I've ever seen," Jack said shakily. He still felt calm, and realized that Sym must be helping him. *Better living through chemistry, eh?*

"Jack, we have to get out of here before anyone comes. I don't hear any cars or anything approaching, so now would be a good time to start moving," Sym's usually quiet voice held an edge of fear in it. Jack waited a few more seconds for the cobwebs to finish clearing and nodded.

"Is he . . . ?" Jack asked, motioning to Whelan.

"No, he's quite dead. As I mentioned earlier, brain injuries cannot be repaired."

"Whew. All right, let's make like a shepherd and get the flock out of here," Jack said.

"I was not aware that Whelan had any sheep in the vehicle," Sym replied.

"It's a joke . . . never mind," Jack said, unfastening his seat belt and dropping to the floor of the car, which was now the passenger side window. "Oh, great," Jack said as he looked up at the only way out.

"The sooner you start, the sooner it will be done. I'm going to turn off your olfactory senses for this," Sym said.

"Yeah, that's a good idea," Jack said as he searched for suitable handholds. A moment later, and Jack felt like he was breathing through a cotton sack, the air in his nose and throat dull and heavy. Taking a final deep, tasteless breath, Jack pulled himself up toward the driver's door. He tried not to think about what he was grabbing for or pushing off of. He just fixed his eyes on that bright patch of blue sky and hauled himself toward it for all he was worth. Another step, a last desperate pull, and his head poked out of the car. Jack scrambled out as quickly as possible, then stopped. Reaching down, he grabbed the neural inhibitor off of Whelan's body, then jumped down into the muddy ditch.

"Self-defense?" Sym asked.

"Well, I'd rather have it and not need it that need it and not have it," Jack replied. He could hear the distant wail of approaching sirens.

"Someone must have seen the accident and called the cops. We'd better bail," Jack said.

"Yes, run due east," Sym said.

"Which direction?" Jack said, spinning around.

"Toward the . . . oh, just let me do it." For a second Jack had the odd sensation of watching his body move itself without himself at the helm. After he was facing the right direction, Jack felt control return.

"Sym?"

"Yes, Jack?"

"Don't ever do that again unless you absolutely have to."

"All right."

With that Jack took off like a deer through the forest, leaving the accident scene far behind.

Two hours of hard travel later, Jack stopped to rest in an abandoned farmhouse some miles from the boys' home. He knew he couldn't stay there long, but he had to rest for a while. He also had to ask Sym a few questions.

"Sym?"

"Yes, Jack?"

"Why didn't you tell me there were others?"

"I didn't know there were any here yet. I was supposed to be a scout, controlled by the military arm of my people, the—" Sym made a noise that translated into chirps and hisses in Jack's mind. *"I was supposed to land near a military base and study this planet's defenses using a military officer they had kidnapped. My insertion craft malfunctioned and I ended up in your forest."*

"And that one that almost got us?"

"That was one of the military symbiotes. Now, there will be others." Sym said.

Jack leaned back against the wall of the deserted house. "So you're saying that Earth is going to be invaded."

"Eventually, yes."

"Great." Jack got up and stretched. "Um, Sym?"

"Yes, Jack?"

"This is going to seem like a dumb question, but—"

"No, I really don't have any designs on taking over your planet. Back on my world we have a rigid caste structure, with our . . . what you would call careers . . . planned for us from birth. I find the freedom here rather intoxicating. I don't really wish to go back."

"That's good, 'cause I don't think they'd be too happy with you right now," Jack said, smiling.

"Jack, you know they're going to come after us."

"Yeah, I've been giving that some thought," Jack said.

"And?"

"Well, first we're gonna put some more miles between us and that home. Then we'll figure out what to do."

"What do you mean?"

"Well, someone's got to warn Washington, or the President or whoever's in charge down there. And I guess that somebody is us," Jack said.

"And just how do you intend to do that?"

"Well, I figure you'll make a pretty convincing demonstration."

"Then what?" Sym asked.

"Then we'll figure out a way to scan for you guys and stop your buddies before they get us."

"Somehow I don't think it will be that easy."

"Probably not. But we'll worry about that when the time comes. Trust me. It always works out in the books I read," Jack said. "That base you were supposed to go to, that might be a good place to start. If we can capture one before they get into a host, that might help."

"Maybe," Sym replied. *"But my race has been doing this for thousands of years. And as you said earlier, those books you read were fiction."*

"True, but now that this is the real thing, I'm gonna make sure *we* do it right. So we'd better get moving," Jack said, standing up. He looked out of the door of the farmhouse at the winding dirt road that led south. Jack smiled, thinking of the new life that stretched before him, much like that road.

"Sym?"

"Yes, Jack?"

"I think this is the beginning of a beautiful friendship."

THE PET ROCKS MYSTERY

Jack Williamson

Jack Williamson was born in 1908 and has been writing science fiction for the past seventy years, with the novels *Darker Than You Think, The Humanoids, Star Bridge*, and *Lifeburst,* as well as many others as a result. He has also written nonfiction on such topics as the teaching of science fiction and a study of H. G. Wells. A winner of the Nebula Grand Master Award and the Hugo Award, he lives in New Mexico. His most recent work is the novel *Black Sun.*

STRANGERS may wonder why anybody wants to live in Portales, but we try to be proud of our town. It stands on the high, dry plains of Eastern New Mexico, fifteen miles from the Texas line. A sign on the highway claims a population of 12,000 solid citizens as well as three or four old grouches. We have a small university, a soft drink canner, and a new Wal-Mart. The Cannon air base is only eighteen miles away. To get here, if you are anybody but the odd little man who gave his name as A. Magellanic, you fly into Lubbock, rent a car, and drive through a hundred miles of flat, empty nothing.

Nobody knew how Magellanic got here, or who he really was. A thin dark little man of uncertain age, he might have been from Mexico if he had spoken Spanish. He didn't. He might have been retired military from the air base, but nobody there had ever heard of him. He may have come in on the midnight bus, though nobody at the station recalls any passenger arriving. Maybe he hitch-hiked into town. Maybe he simply walked. The first person to see him, so far as anybody knows, was Jillian Maybird, a waitress at the Inn. He was her first guest that morning, and she says she will never forget him.

He came in just after six that morning, limping in a pair of tall yellow cowboy boots too large for him. He wore ragged blue jeans, cut off at the knees, and a grimy black T-shirt. The morning was chilly, and he had on a pink terry robe, the pocket sagging to something so heavy that she wondered for a moment if it might be a gun.

He seemed not to understand anything she said till he stuck something like a hearing aid in his ear. He had what she calls a weird accent at first. It faded away as they talked. He asked to use the bathroom and wanted breakfast. The accent made her wonder if he was a foreign professor out at the university. When she asked where he came from, all he said was "South." He took a table in the back of the room, sat staring at the menu, and finally asked what coffee was.

She brought him a cup and found him bent over a chunk of rock he had laid on the table. A peculiar rock, she says. A jagged chip of some dark-red stone, nearly as big as his fist, it glittered with fine diamond points when he moved it under the light. He sat rubbing dried mud off of it till she set the cup under his nose.

He tasted the coffee and frowned at her till she told him to try it with cream and sugar. He seemed not to understand till she stirred them in, but then he gulped it down and wanted another cup. Pointing at the menu, he asked her about *Huevos Rancheros* and made her try to explain what an egg was. The salsa was too hot for him, but he asked for another tortilla and wiped his plate clean.

He had no money when she brought the check, but he showed her a diamond he wanted to sell. It looked oddly cut and too big to be real, but she told him to try the pawn shop. He sat at the table, polishing the rock with his napkin, waiting for the shop to open. Back with real money, he paid his bill and made her understand that he wanted a place to live.

She phoned Victoria Strunk, who was in hard shape, with her husband dead and her son in prison and not well herself. To meet the payments on her house, she was trying to rent out her guest room. Magellanic pawned another diamond and took the room. From then on Victoria gave him his breakfast, whatever she had. He walked back to the Inn for lunch and sometimes for dinner. He learned to like liver and onions, Jillian says, and the taco plate.

Mostly he kept to his room, though sometimes in the evening he walked around town, looking into shop windows, or wandered through Wal-Mart. He never bought anything except newspapers, never spoke much to anybody till he met Oscar Korley. Oscar lives on a ranch forty miles out toward the Pecos River, but comes to town on Fridays for the Rotary lunch meeting. He wears a bolo, mounted with a chip of red stone that could have come off Magellanic's rock. Magellanic saw it when they passed in the lobby.

"It turned him crazy," Oscar says. "He pointed at it and jabbered at me till I finally understand that he wanted to know where I got it. No mystery about that. The rainbow shimmer of it caught my eye when I ran across it close to a sink hole out toward the river Pecos. The jeweler offered to buy it when I showed it to him, but I had him mount it on the bolo. This little Magell— whatever his name was—got more excited the longer I let him squint at it. He kept asking about the sink hole, till I drew him a road map and said I wouldn't care if he came out to see it for himself."

Victoria said he was gone three days, walking in a pair of her husband's work shoes she gave him, a better fit than the cowboy boots she never knew where he got. He came back sunburned and hungry, with a grocery bag of rocks. His pet rocks, she called them. He laid them out on a bridge table in his room and spent hours fitting them together. She said they stuck when he got them just right, to make something like her old grindstone that came from Texas in the covered wagon.

It had a big gap in the rim. He took a box lunch she fixed for him and went back to look for the missing piece. Gone most of a week, he came back try it in the gap, so happy he yelled out loud when it made a smooth fit. A heavy red disk, a foot across and half an inch thick, it was still lying on the card table in his room when Jason Strunk made his prison break and came home to see his mother.

The troubles of the Strunk family had filled the news for a week, half a dozen years ago. A pitiful little tragedy, with no villain except the weather. Here on the high plains, our climate is a fickle friend. Some years are good, some soul-killing. Old Amos Strunk had come out of East Texas with his family in a covered wagon, back near the turn of the century. They settled on a homestead in the Richland community. Generation after generation, the family hung on there, through hard years and harder years, till Truman crippled himself in a tractor accident. He could have put his land into the government soil-saving program, but he and Victoria found money for a down payment on the old McCabe house here in town. He deeded the farm to his son.

A tall, rawboned kid with thick black hair, Jason had been a high-school basketball star. He went on to State for a degree in agriculture and came home to the farm. "All we ever had," his dad told him. "Never give it up."

He promised, with his right hand on the old family

Bible, but the weather went against him. After one dry year, in debt for a new tractor, he had to borrow money to plant again. The next year was just as dry, and the dealer repossessed the tractor. The third might have been better, but a hail storm wiped out a fine stand of milo and a hundred acres of promising cotton.

The fourth year, he begged the bank for one more chance. The rains had come again. He had three hundred acres of winter wheat nearly ready for the combine. He was engaged to Shawnel Doyle, a lively redhead who taught third grade at the new Valencia school here in town. His hopes ran high till his bank had to tell him that it was no charity.

He lost everything, Shawnel and the land and his pride. Lost his head on auction day, when the bank had foreclosed and put the farm up for sale. Most of the morning he spent on his knees, praying for a miracle that never happened. He ran out of the house when he heard the auctioneer and tried to stop the sale. Crying and cursing, he was waving the old Colt .45 his great-great-grandfather had carried to Cuba with the Rough Riders in '98.

He swore at the trial that he hadn't known the gun was loaded, swore he never meant to pull the trigger, but his bullet killed a state cop who was there at the bank's request to keep order in the crowd of Jason's friends. The sale went on when the ambulance was gone, and cops look after themselves. Sentenced for life, Jason was a model prisoner until he got the letter from his mother about her cancer.

She never wanted him to make the break. We saw her letter, printed in the *News-Tribune* during the investigation. Writing to say tell him good-bye, she had filled five long pages with her shaky script, tenderly recalling moments from his childhood and closing with her prayer for his pardon. No pardon was likely. With nothing else left to live for, Jason wanted to see her before she died.

Maybe Shawnel paid for his escape. Nobody knows,

but a prison guard was later suspected of accepting bribes, and a stolen car seems to have been waiting for him on a side street after he got out of his cell and over the wall. The cops overtook him a few miles out of Portals. Driving desperately, he got to his mother's place with the rear tires shot out and a bullet through his thigh.

He staggered into the house and locked the door. The cops got there half a minute behind him, sirens still howling. He had left the car in neutral on the sloping drive. When it started rolling back toward the street, a jittery cop ordered it to halt and shot the glass out of the windows before it stopped at the curb.

Half a dozen police cars were there by then. Piling out with guns ready, the cops ran to circle the house and yelled through a bullhorn for him to come out with both hands on his head. He was in a no-win fix. Surrounded. Bleeding like a stuck hog in the car and on the walk. He needed medical attention. His mother's minister wanted to talk to him. They promised to hold their fire for half an hour, to give him one last chance to come to reason and save his immortal soul.

His answer was a bullet through a window. A front tire on the nearest police car blew out with a bang louder than the gun. The cops hunkered down behind their cars and the man with the bullhorn yelled for him to keep his cool and wait for the pastor. He didn't want the pastor. The siege went on till Shawnel got there from school and begged the cops to let her go inside.

She had heard about the standoff on the radio. Jason and his mother were friends she loved and trusted. She knew Mr. Magellanic, who was also in the house. She didn't want anybody killed, and the cops let her call through the bullhorn. Somebody opened the door. She went inside. Another bullet spattered concrete chips off the walk just ahead of a cop edging after her. The door slammed behind her. An hour later it opened again. She came out, walking unsteadily, a tear streak through a smear of blood across her cheek.

"They're gone," she said. The cops asked where. She didn't know. They made her lead the way back inside. Jason had left the old .45 on a bloodstained sofa, two shots left in the chambers. Part of a bed sheet lay on a coffee table; his mother had torn strips from it to bandage his thigh. The card table was folded up, she says, leaning against the wall in Magellanic's room. The red rock was gone. The house was empty, with nothing left to tell how Jason and his mother and Mr. Magellanic had got away.

What the cops did find was a little pile of oddly cut diamonds lying on an unsealed envelope on the dresser in his mother's bedroom. In Victoria's spidery script, the envelope was addressed to Shawnel. The cops let her read the document inside, took it away to make a copy, and later returned it to her.

It was written in Jason Strunk's bold hand, in evident haste, with errors crossed out. Headed *Bill of Sale,* it was signed by ARISTO MAGELLANIC (all in bright green metallic capitals), Victoria Strunk, and Jason himself. Claiming that the signers were the legal owners of the diamonds, it conveyed all rights of ownership to Shawnel Doyle.

The cops had questions about the diamonds and the document and the disappearance. Newspaper and TV reporters had more. Shawnel had no answers for anybody till after the story brought two men with lawyers who challenged the document as undated, not witnessed, never recorded, and without legal effect.

Both men wanted the diamonds. Mawson Kleeman was a Kansas City life insurance salesman, who claimed to be Victoria's cousin and her legal heir. An Albuquerque banker named Scarlo claimed that the diamonds had been part of the Strunk estate, illegally concealed from the bankruptcy court and therefore property of the bank.

Shawnel went to a local attorney. In view of Jason's record and all the unexplained circumstances, he doubted that she had much of case, but he did agree to represent her on a contingency basis for half of anything he might collect. More details came out in her testimony at the pretrial hearing, when she and the prison guard were suspected of conspiring to aid Jason's escape. In the witness box, she wore no makeup. She looked nervous and distressed, her voice barely audible.

The district attorney was a waspish little man with a hawk nose, coyote eyes, and a buzz-saw voice. He'd brought his Harvard law degree to New Mexico to recover a political fortune he had squandered in New Hampshire. Basking in the lights of a TV crew the judge had allowed in the courtroom, he kept probing hard for any clue to Jason's whereabouts. He asked Shawnel if she knew him. Her answers are in the court record.

"We were together—" Her voice came out so faint he made her start again. "Together in grade school. We were planning to marry before—" She stopped and swallowed hard. "Before what happened. The end of everything for him. He wrote me a good-bye letter from prison and had his mother give me the gold band he had bought for me."

"So you knew Mrs. Strunk?"

"Since I was in her eighth grade class. A great teacher. We all loved her. She had taken the job to help her husband hold on to the farm through the bad years. They loved the land."

"Did you know Mr. Magellanic?"

"I saw him." She hesitated, frowning over what to say. "Lately, since Victoria's cancer spread and the doctors couldn't do much except try to ease the pain, I'd been coming by after school to bring her a basket of fruit or a bowl of soup or anything I thought she could eat. If she couldn't eat it, she would have me knock on his door and give it to him."

"A. Magellanic?" The district attorney looked at his notes. "What do you know about him?"

"Nothing, really." She shook her head. "Nothing except what Victoria told me about him and his rocks."

"What was that?"

Her voice was louder now, but again she paused to think.

"Nothing you'll believe. Victoria said nobody would believe anything he told her. Not even about the diamonds."

"Why not?"

"He claimed to be a galactic guide."

"Galactic? What's that?"

"I don't quite know." Shawnel shook her head and turned to look at the judge as if begging for help. When his stony face promised none, she drew a long breath and tried to sit straighter. "I don't think Victoria knew."

"But she did tell you something?"

"She was sick and lonely." The judge had leaned a little, listening, and she went on more easily. "She thought he—Mr. Magellanic—must be as lonely as she was, sitting in his room all day with no friends and nothing to do. When she felt well enough in the afternoon, she used to make tea and set out a plate of cookies or cheese and crackers and ask him to come in. They got to be friends. He talked to her, the way he never did to anybody else. Talked about the rocks."

"What about the rocks?"

"Victoria said they came from far outside in the Milky Way. That's a galaxy, he said. A big one, with two smaller ones close to it that he said we call the Clouds of Magellan. He said the galaxies are swarms of stars. Millions of stars. He said a lot of them are inhabited by civilized beings. Mostly not much like us, but just as smart as we are. Some maybe—maybe smarter."

She faltered and stopped, shrinking from the district attorney's impatient scowl. The judge nodded slightly when she looked at him. She caught her breath and went on again.

"About Mr. Magellanic, he said his own people came down from a group of human specimens picked up by explorers who landed in ancient Greece two thousand years ago."

"He really said that?"

"Magellanic's story." The judge had his hand cupped to his ear, and she seemed more sure of herself. "Not mine."

"What was his business here?"

"He told Victoria he was a professional guide. He talked about a galactic culture on thousands of civilized planets scattered all across the three galaxies. They live in peace, with regular transportation between them in ships that move faster than light. But he said a lot more planets are still wild. Too hot for any kind of life. Too cold. Their atmospheres chemically poison. Infested with hostile life-forms. Dangerous in all sorts of ways.

"But explorers want to visit them. To prospect for precious elements or anything of value. To survey them for what he called terraforming—making them fit for settlement. Sometimes just for adventure or sport. They hire the guides to get them there and keep them safe and get them back. The guides have the know-how and equipment. They understand the problems, and they can cope."

"Here in Portales?" The district attorney had thick black eyebrows that lifted in scornful unbelief. "How was he coping here?"

"As for that—" Shawnel stopped to fidget with Jason's gold band on her ring finger. "Of course Victoria wanted to know, but he wouldn't tell her anything till after he came to trust her, and then just enough to frighten her. He never really said so, but she came to think he was hiding here with the red stone till he could make some kind of deal. She thought it had been stolen."

"Stolen?" The district attorney was on his feet, shouting as if accusing her of the crime. "From whom?"

"A museum." Shawnel flushed and sat straighter. "Victoria said the rock was priceless. Damaged, but she said he was proud of the way it was healing itself when he got all the pieces fitted back together."

"A rock?" The district attorney glared in disbelief. "Healing itself?"

"That's what Victoria said he said."

"It must have been a remarkable rock."

"Victoria said it was. Mr. Magellanic told her that it stored information like a computer chip. He said it was the journal of the greatest author on his home planet, containing a holographic record of his life and the original versions of all his plays and poems. A unique artifact, it had disappeared from the museum a hundred of our years ago. Mr. Magellanic was first here guiding a search party that traced the thieves to Earth. They'd crashed here, trying to land in a rocket-assisted shuttle. The impact dug the pit the rancher took for a sink hole. The rock was shattered. The thieves must have died. The search party left with nothing, but Mr. Magellanic never gave up. He came back alone, with a little chip off the rock he had picked up. The fragments are all linked together by something like radio, and the chip helped him locate the other pieces."

"Stolen goods?" the district attorney barked like an angry dog. "He was hiding with it?"

"I don't know what he told Victoria, but she thought he was trying to work out a deal to let him return the object for a reward."

"Another thief!"

"Maybe not." Shawnel shrugged. "He got the diamonds. They're what his people use for money. I guess he made his deal."

"You were here when they left." The district attorney cleared his throat and scowled at his notes. "Where did they go?"

Shawnel flushed. "I told you I don't know."

"Don't you have any kind of clue?"

She frowned, trying to get her words together. "He hadn't known how sick Victoria was. The news from

Jason distressed him. He told her he wanted to take her back to his home planet to doctors who could save her life and heal Jason's wound."

"Hogwash!" A scornful hoot. "She believed him?"

"Does it matter?" She shrugged again. "Victoria knew she was dying. Jason was still bleeding. But still at first she didn't want to go. She thought Magellanic would be risking his own life. Jason's answer was to nod toward the siren sound of an ambulance coming up the street. He had to get away."

"You saw how they did it?"

"I saw a machine in his room. Something with seats like the seats on a bicycle. A canopy over it that looked like yellow plastic, and a net around it that looked like woven silver wire. He put Jason and Victoria on the rear seats and climbed on the front seat and pulled the net around them. I heard a crackling like corn popping; maybe some kind of static. They flickered and disappeared."

"They did?" His bushy eyebrows lifted. "What else did you observe?"

"Nothing, sir. Nothing at all."

That was the end of Shawnel's testimony. The judge recessed the hearing with nothing else to explain the escape and no evidence to support any charge that Shawnel had conspired with anybody. The disposition of the diamonds was settled later in civil court, when the attorneys for Kleeman and Scarlo worked out a compromise to have the stones sold and the proceeds split between them, on condition the judge would declare Shawnel's bill of sale invalid.

She must have been disappointed, but not for long. On the first day of the school vacation, her landlady reported her missing. Carrying the morning mail to her room, she knocked and heard nothing from Shawnel. The door opened when she tried it. She was slow to talk about what she thinks she saw, but now she swears she caught a glimpse of a strange machine standing in the middle of the room. It had three seats, like bicycle seats. A small dark man sat on the front seat. She thinks she saw Shawnel and Jason Strunk on the two behind, but they were gone before she was really sure

None of them has been seen again. Shawnel left no note. Her car was repossessed. A sister came from Deming to clean out her room and claim her effects. People laugh at pet rocks, and most of us are uncertain what to believe. We're commonly absorbed with the everyday events of small-town life, but when we look out across the Milky Way on a moonless New Mexico night, we sometimes search the sky for one bright star where we hope Victoria and Jason and Shawnel are well and happy, learning the ways of a stranger world than we can imagine.

IN THE STORM, IN THE STARS

Paul Dellinger

Paul Dellinger is a longtime reporter for the Roanoke (Va.) *Times*, which is the only place where he's worked with computers (the newspaper was upgrading from manual to electric typewriters when he started there). He still manages to crank out an occasional high-tech science fiction story, despite being cyber-impaired. Other stories by him appear in *Wheel of Fortune*, *The Williamson Effect*, *Lord of the Fantastic*, and *Future Net*.

THE early-morning colors painted by the sun rising over nearby mountain peaks were spectacular—almost worth waking up to see. Almost. Once more, I asked myself why a city boy was spending two torturous weeks among people whose idea of fun was riding wagons and horses along trails that pioneers might have used more than a century ago.

But, then, I knew the answer. I was the only one in the world who knew the answer—in this world, at least.

"Tim Sexton, you ought to be ashamed of yourself," an all-too-familiar voice from the past cut in on my bleary-eyed appreciation of the view.

I turned around to another lovely view, conscious of my unshaven state even though it hardly mattered anymore. These days, Holly Lloyd couldn't have cared less.

"Good morning to you, too, Holly. Beautiful day, isn't it? And thank you for starting it off so on such a positive note."

She ignored my attempt at levity which, I had to admit, didn't amount to much. "Don't you think you could take the halters with those stupid horns off your animals at night?" she said. "They could poke them into the ground while they graze, Tim. They could hurt themselves."

I smiled. "Don't worry, my two muley-corns are used to horns in the middle of their foreheads. They've always had them, you know."

"Muley-corns!" She gave an impatient little stamp of her tiny booted foot. The familiarity of that movement brought back a year's worth of memories, from when Holly and I had been a pair. I fought them down. I couldn't afford them right now.

"Lighten up, Holly. Heck, they draw a crowd every place we stop, whether people believe they're real or not. That's more donations from onlookers to the riding therapy program for handicapped kids, which is supposed to be what this little odyssey is about in the first place. Right?"

Holly shook her head in another familiar gesture. "You're impossible." I watched her walk away, back to where she had Shaker, her black Tennessee Walker, tied to a tree. Most of the riders hobbled their horses overnight, but Shaker had an occasional weakness in his right front leg, from having caught it in fence wire as a colt. It usually didn't hamper him, even traveling every day like this, but she always took precautions. I couldn't argue with that, even if veterinarian Joyce Carlson was along in case any animal needed medical help. Shaker was one of my favorites, too.

I wanted to follow her, to give Shaker a friendly nose rub for old time's sake and to show him that I still held no grudge for his spinning me out of the saddle once when a groundhog startled him. But Holly was a smart lady. The less I gave her to ponder about me right now, the better.

The nearly two dozen people in our caravan were all seeing to their livestock, so I did the same. The two brown mules sporting those horns that upset Holly looked up from munching on grass as I approached. One of them gave me a solemn wink.

"Cool it," I said under my breath.

The pistollike crack of Daniel Nesbitt's bullwhip broke the early morning stillness. "Okay, people, listen up," he bellowed, dressed today in a cowboy hat, vest and jeans reminiscent of Ward Bond in the old "Wagon Train" TV series. "The eggs and bacon will be ready in a few minutes. If we get lucky today, maybe I can nail us some deer meat to roast tonight. We've only got two more days before we finish up in the Mount Rogers National Recreation Area. It's all downhill from here."

Actually, it was all pretty much uphill. Mount Rogers was the highest peak in Virginia, and we would be far up its slope when we connected with the other riding club members, bluegrass musicians, maybe a few local politicians and others who would be waiting to help celebrate the end of our fundraiser.

By then, my task would be about over. All I had to do was release my animals a little farther up the mountain so they could continue to their own rendezvous point. I'd worry the next morning about explaining their absence when we all started down again.

I waited until I saw Holly with her tin plate in the breakfast line before I slipped around to where she had Shaker tethered. "Hi, fella," I said softly. "Remember me?" His ears perked up as he looked me over. "Just wanted to say hello again, old boy," I told him. "I've missed you. Both of you," I added with another glance in Holly's direction.

He ducked his head, and I ran a hand over his shiny

black coat. Holly was obviously giving him the best of care. He didn't even make that jerky nodding motion he used to when someone approached him, or anything made him nervous. Holly must have finally soothed him out of the habit that had given him his name.

As usual, I skipped breakfast to make sure I had my animals harnessed properly to the covered wagon I'd borrowed from a Civil War reenactor. I didn't have the expertise at hitching them that all the others did. My friend, Curt, had to give me a crash course in where to put the various poles and straps and everything before I could even get accepted on this jaunt.

Some of these horse-and-wagon hobbyists made this trek every year. For them, it was a vacation. For me, it was—well, I guess, atonement of a sort. At least, that was the impression I'd gotten from the alien.

Later that day, when the trail we were following widened enough for a horse to come alongside a wagon, I found Holly and Shaker walking along next to mine. "You seem to be holding up pretty well, Colonel Tim," she said, using her little gibe from when we lived together comparing my riding skills with authentic westerner Tim McCoy. "What are the names of these mules you're using?"

I almost responded with the truth, that I couldn't pronounce their names. "Moonbeam and Crowder," I blurted, dredging up a Walter Brennan movie I'd seen on TV about two mules, so old that Natalie Wood had been a child actor in it. "I'm doing okay, I guess. But I may not sit down for a week after tomorrow."

"I can imagine. What prompted you to do this, anyway?" While I was still trying to come up with an answer for that one, she added: "Did you know I'd be here?"

Actually, I hadn't known. It was just that this particular ride at this particular time offered the opportunity for me to do what I'd agreed to do. But I couldn't tell her that. Besides, I found myself thinking that maybe she hoped my answer would be yes.

"I've missed you, Holly," I said, giving the most honest answer I could under the circumstances. "Heck, I've even missed Shaker."

"I know. I saw you with him when I was eating." So much for all my stealthy skills. "Tell me something, Tim," she said and pointed to my mules. "Is this some new scam for a supermarket tabloid?"

I tried to laugh it off. "You don't believe my muleycorns are the real thing?"

"Don't be ridiculous. Even the people who gawk at them at our stops know better. But I could just see you using this bit of publicity to generate another of those articles of yours."

That had been our problem. Holly was too honest for the way I made my living—writing tabloid pieces and books about Bigfoot, flying saucers, the Bermuda Triangle, the Loch Ness Monster, and whatever else I could amplify into some bit of entertainment. I'd first met Holly when I came to Wytheville, Virginia, a few years ago to work up something on the UFO flap going on there. So she'd known what I did from the start.

She called it pandering to a gullible public. I called it giving the public what it wanted. That started a gentle back-and-forth chiding which eventually grew into a divide neither of us could cross.

Well, I could honestly say that I'd never do an article about this, and actually started to do so. But I caught myself in time. If I told her it wasn't that, what could I tell her it was? I couldn't suggest that someone who wrote fake news items about UFOs would be the safest human for aliens to contact. After all, who would believe him?

So I took a deep breath, and lied. "Well, sure. Why not? A few photographs of people lined up to pet them during our stops is all the art I'll need. Can't you see the headline? 'Strange New Animals Hiding in Virginia Mountains' . . ."

"I might have known!" she said. "You'll never change. I hope . . ." She seemed to be searching for the most virulent curse she could possibly put upon me. "I hope you catch cold when it rains tonight!" With that, she touched Shaker with her heels, and he racked away from my wagon.

"Rain?" I whispered. "It can't rain. The weather report was no rain for the whole two weeks. We're supposed to be in the middle of a drought. What's this about rain?"

One of the mules cast a worried look back at me. "It's all right," I said. "I've got more dye if we need it. But I didn't figure on rain. Hey! Charlie!" I called to another rider, Charlie Eagle, dressed in buckskins and a head-band celebrating the Cherokee heritage he claimed once a year when he abandoned his computer shop to make this trek. "What's this about rain tonight?"

Charlie slowed his brown-and-white pinto until my wagon caught up. "That's right, paleface," he said, stay-ing firmly in his two-week character. "The drought ends this evening. Rain starts right after sundown and keeps coming until one or two o'clock in the morning."

"How can you possibly know that?" I demanded, hop-ing he was wrong. "Putting your ear to the ground? Watching the behavior of migrating birds? Following cloud formations?"

Charlie grinned, reached into his saddlebags, and pulled out one of his little electronic toys, this one with a dial, two knobs, and a folded antenna. "Channel Seven weather report," he said.

Aristotle had apparently believed in unicorns. At least he put forth a theory about how the material that formed their hooves left only enough of its substance to grow a single horn. The earliest report I'd found in my recent reading dated back to about 2500 B.C. in China, where the animal was called Ch'i-lin and made a sound, it was said, like the chiming of bells. A Greek named Ctesia told of such creatures living about 400 B.C. in India, which people readily accepted despite the fact that he had never been there. Another Greek called Magasthenes heard about them from Buddhist monks, or so he claimed. Even the Bible mentioned unicorns in Psalms, and a number of artists insisted on including one in their conceptions of the Garden of Eden.

Writers of the Middle Ages depicted unicorns all over the place. Of course, they also talked about hippogriffs, dragons, griffins and manticores—not to mention other outlandish-looking animals like elephants and giraffes, which actually turned out to be real. But there was one difference between all of them and the unicorn: its horn developed a reputation as an instrument of healing and purification. Even today, a famous tapestry in New York's Metropolitan Museum of Art depicted various animals waiting to drink from a stream after the unicorn has cleansed it by touching its horn to the water.

By the sixteenth century, apothecaries were selling bits of unicorn horn as cures for any ailment you could name, and apparently there had been plenty of takers, even, or maybe especially, among the intelligensia. Now we think of them as gullible, tricked into buying the horn of a rhinoceros, a narwhal, or something else. Anyway, the unicorn moved gradually from the real to the mythical.

And it was up to me to keep it that way.

Lightning flashed, illuminating the clearing I was watching from inside my wagon, somewhat shielded from the pounding rain. In the flickering radiance, I could see them running, leaping, cavorting like a couple of kittens, their sparkling white coats washed clean by hours of cool precipitation. After nearly two weeks of pretending to be beasts of burden, they obviously couldn't restrain themselves any longer, and I couldn't blame them.

I'd known the brown dye I'd applied to them two weeks ago, and touched up occasionally at night, wouldn't stand up against the kind of storm we were getting. I'd moved my wagon about half a mile from the rest of the camp. In the confusion of settling in and securing the livestock and getting out of the rain, I didn't think I'd be missed before morning. We'd be back in place by then. The rain was supposed to end by early morning, according to Tom Eagle and his home-made weather receiver, which would give me time to dry them off, apply the coloring, reattach the long ears and put on the head straps with holes I'd arranged to make the horns look like they were attached to the halters instead of the animals.

You could cover some things and disguise others, but not the most distinguishing feature of a unicorn. The only solution I'd been able to come up with for that was misdirection. Of course people would assume the horns were fake. What else could they be? There was no such thing as a unicorn, much less a mule so endowed. Muleycorns—that obviously had to be a joke, right?

I hadn't believed in unicorns either, or UFO aliens, for that matter, until very recently.

Arthur C. Clarke and Stanley Kubrick had it wrong. It wasn't mysterious black monoliths that extraterrestrial overseers had placed on various worlds for evolving intelligences to discover. It was innocent, frolicking little creatures from the stars, and they weren't there to be found—they were there to help us in other ways.

I had no idea if they took the same form on other planets where they might be stationed. Probably not—a fleet four-footed creature would look even more out of place where life had gone in some other direction than vertebrates. I didn't even understand exactly what they did for the inhabitants of the worlds they occupied; what little information I'd been given was apparently limited to need-to-know. Maybe they nudged a line of development here, nipped another in the bud there, saved some key figure in our future history from plague germs or some other kind of death so a particular destiny could be fulfilled, all the time concealing themselves from those they were helping. I also got the impression that they themselves were instruments of genetic manipulation, so maybe they even guided the process of our evolution—ours, and the other creatures that lived on our world.

And now, as closely as I'd puzzled it out, it was time for the last of them to go. We were developing our own knowledge of genetics and cloning and all those other arcane achievements. I didn't know how many of what we called unicorns had been placed on Earth in the dim mists of our past, but it was made clear to me that only these two remained, and apparently they had now done all they could of whatever they did. Now things were being left up to us, to purify our own streams and take charge of our own evolution.

I wondered if our guardians might have slipped up and allowed some impurities into our gene pool. Many of our varied species—from ants to cats to ourselves—had certainly developed into predators over time. I could see some of us—like Nesbitt, our wagon master, the poor man's Lash LaRue—hunting these beautiful creatures for their horns, or just to mount their heads on the wall of his den as trophies.

I couldn't let that happen. I wouldn't.

They fascinated me. I couldn't take my eyes off them. I had never seen them like this, off by themselves where no human eyes could pry, none but mine, and able to behave however they did naturally. When I had gone to their hiding place, a cave in a remote section of the county that I hadn't known existed, they were quiet and docile, and almost too friendly—one of them in particular insisted on rubbing against me, almost catlike, as I applied their dark coloring and I ended up with about as much of it on myself.

In all the stories I'd made up about alien contact, I'd never gotten it right. I'd never written a scenario where the alien appeared on someone's television screen, interrupting a Roy Rogers movie, and began communicating with the viewer.

It wasn't communication in words. It wasn't even

communication in thoughts, not quite. The closest I can come to describing it is communication by impressions.

The TV image had been unsteady. In fact, I'd assumed something had gone wrong with the set when a vaguely humanoid chalky-white face replaced Roy and Trigger galloping across the prairie, and was reaching for the remote when that first impression hit me.

For a few mad seconds, I expected to hear the voice of actor Vic Perrin: "We control the horizontal. We control the vertical . . ." Then I knew without a doubt that I was facing someone who had never walked the surface of my world.

I couldn't get a clear look at the face, if that's what you could call it. A flickering spike, almost like a horn, seemed to extend and then retract from its forehead, and again I thought it a glitch of the TV. But somehow I knew that I was the only one seeing this particular broadcast, wherever it was from. I got the impression that I had been chosen, specifically, to do some payback for the fraudulent use I'd made of alien contacts and freakish beasties all these years.

Afterward, I almost convinced myself that I had fallen asleep in front of the TV and dreamed it all. But I couldn't resist going the next day to that part of the county where I'd "dreamed" there was this cave. . . .

The rain had finally slowed, I noticed from the sound of it hitting my wagon cover. The lightning flashed once more—and I blinked. The clearing was empty. Panic rose within me. Had I misunderstood? I was sure these were intelligent creatures. Was it possible they were wild, instead, and had taken this opportunity to run off? Had I lost them, so close to the end of their journey?

I slid out of the wagon, ignoring the dwindling rain as I sloshed to where I'd seen them last. The storm seemed about over, but a subdued glimmer of lightning showed me movement, I thought, in the trees near the clearing's edge. I moved in that direction, frustrated in that I could not even call out the names of those I was seeking.

As I closed in, I spotted movement again—but not from either of the creatures I sought. I caught my breath as I realized that the form I was seeing was human.

The figure wore a dark raincoat, so I could tell nothing about it—only that it receded into the trees as I ran toward it. I had no chance of catching it in the dark. And what would I do if I did find it? Beg that my secret be kept? Try to convince it that the sight had all been imagination, or illusion?

The unicorns must have sensed the presence before I did. They had lifetimes spanning more years than I could imagine, centuries, perhaps, or millennia. They had survived, for however long, through concealment. No wonder they disappeared so fast from the clearing.

But suppose the watcher, whoever it was, had seen them?

What then?

Charlie Eagle had tears in his eyes when my newly disguised "muley-corns" and I met him just outside the encampment the next morning.

They had returned to me about an hour after my unknown visitor had vanished. I assumed they would know, better than I, when it was safe to reappear. I just hoped they had scampered out of sight before whoever it was had spotted them.

"Charlie? What's the matter?"

"Miss Holly," he said hoarsely.

I felt a chill that had nothing to do with the wet clothing I'd been wearing most of the night. "Holly? Has anything happened to her?"

"Not her," Charlie said. "Her horse. His front leg—it's broken."

"Oh, no!"

Shaker had slipped his tether in the storm last night, Charlie explained. He didn't wander far, of course. Horses are instinctively herding animals; they know they're prey and their safety is in numbers. But when he came in this morning, he was hopping on three legs. Nobody knew how it happened. It was one of those freak accidents. Shaker might have stepped in a depression, or caught his hoof on some uneven ground, and with that weakness in his leg . . .

I found my way to the opposite edge of camp where the crowd was gathered around him and Holly, and Joyce Carlson, the veterinarian. Holly had her arms around Shaker's neck—and Dr. Carlson had her bottle of whatever it was that she used, as the euphemism had it, to put down large animals. There were tears in her eyes, too.

The fetlock of Shaker's right front leg hung loose, as though attached only by a strip of skin—a truly sickening sight, even for those with strong stomachs, as was evident by the way everyone looked everywhere but at that leg. Shaker stood calmly on the other three legs. Oddly, he seemed to be in no distress, as far as pain was concerned.

I noticed one of my disguised animals moving in behind Shaker, lowering its head to point the horn at one of Shaker's flanks. I started to warn him that Shaker had a tendency to kick, but then I doubted that he could kick in his present condition.

"I don't think we can get him to move any farther," the veterinarian was saying. "I'll have to do it here. We won't be able to get a 'dozer into this area, so we'll have bury him here—dig the grave ourselves, some of us. I hope we have enough shovels . . ."

Holly looked up at that point, and her glistening eyes found mine. Unaccountably, hope seemed to flare up in them. I couldn't think of any reason why.

And then I could.

Then I knew who had followed me last night, and that she had, indeed, seen the unicorns. And she was obviously thinking about their legendary healing powers.

I found myself wondering if she might be right.

I looked for the one that had gotten close to Shaker, that may have poked his horn into Shaker's flank. It was standing away from Shaker now. It looked directly at me, and I could have sworn that it shook its head, just slightly.

I turned back toward Holly, and shook my head as well.

"The break must've severed the nerves, too," Carlson was saying. "But it won't be long before he begins feeling it, Holly. We've got to go ahead now."

Still Holly stared at me, then inclined her head toward my animals in an unspoken plea. "She's right, Holly," I said. "There's nothing that can be done."

She flashed me a look of pure anger, so strong it almost rocked me physically. Could she possibly believe that I was deliberately withholding aid, out of spite from our breakup? She had to know me better than that.

Charlie Eagle walked up beside Holly, holding a bucket of oats. He began feeding some to Shaker. Others, including Holly, joined in. I started to protest that they might cause the horse to founder. I remember Holly warning me that horses would eat oats too quickly for their surprisingly delicate digestive systems, unless they had some hay first. Then I realized how silly it was for me to worry about something like that, when Shaker would soon be gone from us, anyway. Heck, let him eat all the oats he wanted. Charlie was exactly right, and maybe it helped both him and us get through this.

I'd never seen the process of killing an injured horse before. Dr. Carlson attached the bottle of deadly medication to Shaker's side, and plugged an intravenous tube with a needle at the other end. I noticed that she examined what looked like a scrape in a small area of Shaker's flank, and I caught my breath, wondering if she would connect it with my animal. But horses get scrapes and nicks all the time and, to my relief, she didn't dwell on it. She inserted the needle under Shaker's skin, where it would feed the contents of the bottle into his veins.

"Holly," she said, "you'll have to stand away from him. We can't be sure which way he'll fall."

Holly whispered something in Shaker's ear, and gave his nose a final rub before stepping away. Carlson held the lead line from his halter, as the process continued irrevocably. We waited in silence, broken only by an occasional sob that someone couldn't hold back. I started to reach out to stroke him as well, but pulled back at the expression on Holly's face when she glared at me.

Shaker must have started to feel the drug. He staggered just a little. I heard Holly's breath catch in her throat. Then Shaker began that nervous nodding movement of his, the one I'd thought he'd overcome. He must have begun to realize something wasn't right. The nodding continued for a minute, then slowed. The light seemed to fade out of his large, expressive eyes. He wavered briefly, then fell heavily to the ground and moved no more.

Holly's cry of anguish was almost lost among those of many others, horse lovers all, people who had bonded with these animals even beyond my own understanding and liking for them. But I could understand the pain of Shaker being gone, the faithful horse I'd come to know so well during my year with Holly. And I couldn't cry. I felt the tears trying to come, but then I'd remember Holly's last angry look at me and they would dry up.

I turned abruptly and walked away.

It had taken us several hours, despite the number working, to shovel out a grave big enough for Shaker. It wasn't easy to ride off and leave the mound under which he lay, for any of us, but we couldn't simply ignore all those who would be waiting for us farther up the mountain. There had been some talk of simply sending a rider on ahead, with the message that the wagon trek had ended prematurely. Holly had been the first one to veto that. Now she was riding on the lead wagon with Dan Nesbitt. I wondered what she might be telling him.

I got the impression my "mules" were concerned, too. If a unicorn could wear a worried frown, these two were doing it. I don't mean they were laying their ears back flat against their heads, as horses do when they are preparing for trouble. I don't really know what I mean. Maybe I was becoming more sensitive to their attitudes, as our association continued. I still didn't know how intelligent they were, but they were certainly more than preprogrammed entities designed to carry out an inflexible set of actions. Those little winks and nods I got from them occasionally had shown me that, as well as that these beasties had a sense of humor.

It was evening by the time our wagon train reached the camping area where we were to meet other members of the riding organization and those who were joining us to celebrate the end of our trek. As I'd done the previous night, I continued a little farther up the mountain past the main body of people, far enough to be out of sight even though there was no rainstorm tonight to cover our activities.

I released the creatures from the wagon harness for the last time. There was no way I could communicate directly with them, but once more I had the feeling that they understood me when I told them good-bye. I had no idea where up there in the starry sky their real home lay, but I wished them luck in reaching it. One of them leaned forward and rubbed its soft nose against my cheek, then the other nuzzled me in similar fashion.

Then they turned, and began walking up the small mountain trail, slowly at first and then gathering speed as they ascended into the growing darkness.

I continued looking up long after they had disappeared from sight, and slowly turned to make my way back down to where I could now see the light from a campfire, and hear the sound of many voices and fiddles, guitars and dulcimers being played. I'd have to borrow someone's spare horse or hitch a wagon ride back down the mountain in the morning, and arrange with someone to come back up here later with a pair of animals to haul my friend's wagon back down where he could get it . . . .

"There you are!" It took me a minute to recognize Nesbitt in the darkness. "Holly thought you might have gotten lost or hurt yourself," he said, in a tone making it all too clear he wouldn't have been surprised, himself, if I was clueless enough to have done either of those things.

I murmured something about returning from a call of nature. How much had Holly told him? Had she told him anything? Or everything? But he seemed to accept my comment at face value, and started to fall in beside me as I continued down the path.

Then he stiffened. "Hey . . ." He was pointing higher up the mountain, and I turned to look. A bright, fluorescent-seeming light outlined a broad band of trees up there, as it seemed to settle down into them from out of the sky. "What in the hell is that?" Nesbitt whispered.

"I don't know," I replied. "Swamp gas?"

He didn't bother to respond, but started up the incline at a dead run. I barely managed to keep up with him. The light seemed to have stopped moving, and its brightness muted just a bit. I thought I could hear, or maybe just feel, a kind of thrumming sound that hinted to me of engines with power beyond anything I could conceive. There had been an unspoken understanding between myself and the entity who sent me on my mission that I would not follow the animals after our parting, but I had to know what Nesbitt saw. I was hoping he wouldn't see anything.

I almost got my wish. By the time we reached the stand of trees silhouetted against the light, it had started to rise again. As Nesbitt and I stared, the huge light rose slowly and silently above the trees that blocked a clear view of it, and faded slowly into the night sky.

A residual spot danced in my eyes as I blinked them in the darkness. It was at least a minute before either of us spoke. "Did you see that?" Nesbitt said, still staring upward.

"Yeah," I said.

"A damned UFO," he said. "We've seen a UFO!"

"I guess we have."

"Come on," he said, grasping one of my arms as he turned. "We've got to tell the others."

"Okay," I said.

I stumbled over forest things at least three times as he dragged me after him, running back to where the revelry was taking place. "Hey," he shouted, waving his hands for silence. "Hey, did any of you see it? Up there on the mountain?"

"See what?" one of the musicians asked.

"A flying saucer or something! It came down near that peak up there, and then it took off back up again."

There was an uneasy silence. Then somebody laughed.

"I'm serious!" Nesbitt shouted. "It wasn't just me. Sexton saw it, too," he said, turning toward me. "Tell them. You saw it, didn't you?"

"Sure did," I said agreeably.

There was more laughter this time. "You gonna write it up for the tabloids, Tim?" Charlie asked with a grin.

"Sure am," I said, smiling back.

"Right," he said, turning away along with most of the other onlookers.

"Hey, this is no joke," Nesbitt called after them. "We saw it! We've got to tell someone, get some military investigators up here . . . ."

Someone else took my arm in a warm grip, much more gently than Nesbitt had. "Don't worry, Dan," Holly said, barely suppressed laughter in her voice. "Tim will spell your name right."

Nesbitt said a few more things, none of them particularly memorable, but no one was listening. My own attention was riveted on Holly. The light of the big campfire reflected a warmth like that I used to see in her eyes every day. I didn't need flying saucers. That warmth was miracle enough for me.

Before long, the music started up again.

* * *

It took me two days to arrange to borrow some horses from a local riding stable, as well as a trailer to haul them into the national forest. I rode one of them, and Holly rode the other, up to where I'd left the wagon. Both were also broken to harness. We'd have no trouble driving the wagon back down.

We'd done a lot of talking in the past forty-eight hours. Somehow, it didn't feel like a betrayal of my trust to tell Holly what I'd been doing, and feelings had been my main bellwether for what I'd done at each stage of the proceedings.

"I'd seen them. I knew they were real," she'd told me. "When I saw you standing there, I remembered the superstitions that had come down to us about such animals. I pinned such hope on the idea that it seemed to me you were just being stubborn in saying no. The whole idea of beasts like that was so fantastic, I just wasn't thinking straight about them."

"They weren't beasts. I'm not sure just what they were. I think maybe one of them actually did try to help Shaker. It seemed to be probing at his flank with its horn. But I guess nothing could be done, even with whatever powers they had."

She nodded. "I came to that conclusion, eventually. At first, all I could think about was Shaker. . . ." Her voice choked off momentarily. "Finally I decided that you must be protecting those two animals, Tim. It showed me a side of you I never quite recognized before. Of course, I didn't know what you were bringing them to, until Dan came running into the middle of the camp with that ridiculous story." She actually managed to laugh at the recollection.

"I don't know why those other beings couldn't just land wherever those two were hiding," I told her. "Maybe there's a problem with our lower atmosphere, although Mount Rogers isn't high enough to make any difference I can see. Or maybe it had to be some high, isolated point because of something to do with how their craft work. I don't know. I just know I had to get them up here, without anyone knowing, if they were to survive."

She squeezed my hand. Before long, we had the horses unsaddled and harnessed to the wagon. We were about to climb aboard and start down when I heard it—the high-pitched little whinny.

I looked at Holly. "It must be one of the wild ponies that roam up here in the high country," she said. She shook her head. "I suppose I have to get used to everything sounding like the little fellow I raised from a colt. . . ."

She broke off, and we both stared open-mouthed at the small, black, long-legged form that scampered into the clearing and looked up at us with obvious horse curiosity.

"Oh, how cute!" Holly said. "But that's not a pony," she said, walking slowly over to him. To my surprise, he stood his ground. "Where's your mother, sweetheart?"

"Holly," I said, "I don't think we're going to find a mother."

She stared at me, as the implication began to sink in. "Tim. Do you think they . . . ?"

"DNA from a scrape along the flank?" I said, half-musingly. "Cloned, and force-grown somehow past the eleven-month gestation point? I don't know, but it sure looks like him. . . ."

Holly had managed to touch him. The little black colt stood his ground. "How about it, little fellow? Would you like to come with us, and let us take care of you?"

The colt made a nervous motion with its head, which looked remarkably like nodding.

EVERY HOME SHOULD HAVE ONE

Tim Waggoner

Tim Waggoner wrote his first story at the age of five when he drew a version of King Kong vs. Godzilla on a stenographer's pad. Since then he's published over forty stories of fantasy and horror. His most recent work appears in the anthologies *Prom Night, Twice Upon a Time, A Dangerous Magic,* and *Between the Darkness and the Fire.* He lives in Columbus, Ohio, where he teaches college writing classes.

"WHAT are you playing with, Curt? Some new kind of video game?"

From the couch, Owen Conway watched his eight-year-old son work the controls of what looked like a small silver oval. Curt sat cross-legged in front of the TV, but he paid no attention to it, despite the fact that the Steelers—his favorite team of all time (or at least this season, at any rate)—were ahead by two touchdowns. He was completely absorbed by the electronic whatever-it-was in his hands.

Owen leaned forward to get a better look. He told himself he wasn't being nosy; he was merely taking an interest in his son's activities, as a good father should.

Owen tried to see over Curt's shoulder, but the object was so small, it was hard to make out specific details. It had a tiny display screen across which some sort of crudely animated character cavorted with jerky motions. Owen wasn't sure what the thing was supposed to be. It kind of looked like a cross between an insect and an octopus. Strangely shaped letters were molded in the plastic above the screen, with similar letters running down each side. They resembled Japanese, but the letters didn't seem quite angular enough. They were too fluid, so much so that they almost appeared to bend and twist in the light from the television.

Whatever the thing was, Curt didn't seem to be playing it, exactly. At least, not in a way Owen recognized as play. There were no blazing guns, no racing cars. Just the little creature on the screen waving its tentacles and letting out an occasional soft EEP! Curt pushed the buttons on either side of the silver ovoid in what looked to Curt like a completely random fashion, but there must have been some pattern to it, for the creature stopped EEPing and opened its mouth wide. Owen thought he saw tiny rows of jagged teeth, but the picture was so small, he wasn't certain. Little dots came in from off screen and bounced around a couple times before going into the animal's mouth. It closed its jaws, licked its lips with a forked tongue and rubbed tentacles over its suddenly bulging belly. Owen wasn't sure, but he thought the animal looked slightly larger than before. Taller, wider.

Curt swayed for a moment as if he were dizzy, then he smiled. "You're welcome," he said softly. Owen noticed him gently stroke the side of the silver case with his forefinger. For some reason, the gesture disturbed him.

"What you got there, boy?"

Curt turned, startled. Then he smiled. "Sorry, Dad. I guess I forgot you were there."

Owen smiled back. "Words every father longs to hear." He nodded toward the ovoid, which Curt had covered with his hand. "What's that?"

"Nothing. Just something I traded Jamie Schuhl for."

Owen frowned. It wasn't like Curt to hide something from him. "What did you give him?"

"Not much. My Willie Mays baseball card."

At first Owen thought Curt was joking. But the boy looked dead serious. His eyes were a trifle bloodshot, the skin beneath them puffy. Owen wondered if his son was getting enough sleep.

"I thought Willie was your favorite."

Curt's only reply was to shrug, as if to say, *That was yesterday; this is today.*

"Well, I hope whatever you got in return was worth it."

"It was." Curt stood, careful to keep the egg hidden. "I just remembered, I have some homework I need to do for tomorrow."

Who are you and what have you done with my son? Owen thought. Aloud, he said, "What about the game?" Curt lived for sports. Football, baseball, basketball, soccer, hockey, it didn't matter. If you could play it or watch it, Curt loved it.

"It's not that interesting. Everyone knows the Steelers are gonna win by a mile. And I really need to get this homework done, Dad. It's important."

While Curt wasn't a poor student, he didn't exactly bring home straight As. "Far be it from me to discourage you from doing schoolwork. Need any help?"

"No thanks." Curt ran for the stairs, bounded up two at a time. "Let me know how the game turns out!" he called over his shoulder.

"Sure thing." Owen sat back and focused his gaze on the TV screen, but the images didn't register. He was too busy wondering why Curt had been so secretive about his new toy. Of course, kids did keep secrets from their parents. God knows Owen had kept his fair share from his mom and dad. Still, that didn't mean he had to like it.

Pittsburgh scored another touchdown, then made the extra point. But Owen didn't notice.

* * *

"Do you know what Curt's new toy is? The silver thing?"

Leona stood in her robe before their open closet, trying to decide what to wear for work tomorrow. Owen had no idea why she went through the same ritual every night. It took her half an hour to decide and come the morning she'd end up wearing something else anyway.

"Hmmm? Oh, that." She didn't turn, kept shifting clothes around on their hangers. "He told me it was a DigiPal, whatever that is."

"Never heard of it." Owen sat on the edge of the bed in his underwear, trying not to notice how his gut blobbed over the waistband.

Hangers slid, clacked together. "You know how it is, they come out with a new toy every day. There's no way to keep up."

"I suppose."

Leona paused, hand on hanger. She turned to look at him, brow furrowed. "Something wrong?"

"Not really. I guess I just don't like being out of touch. Makes me feel old."

She let go of the hanger, turned around. "I know something that'll make you feel young again." She smiled and began to undo her robe.

Owen forgot about Curt's new toy.

Later, Leona was curled up in bed, snoring softly. Owen tried to get to sleep, but he couldn't. He had to go to the bathroom. He fought it for as long as he could, too tired and lazy to get up, but in the end, he had no choice. He sighed. He should have known better than to have that last soda before bedtime.

He got out of bed slowly, so as not to wake Leona, put on his own robe, and left their bedroom. He padded quietly down the hall toward the bathroom, not wanting to disturb Curt. The boy was a light sleeper, and once he was up, he—

Owen reached Curt's door and paused. A faint bluish-white light issued forth from the crack beneath the door. He listened, heard faint whispering. Curt, surely, but it almost sounded as if someone else was in there with him. The boy didn't have a TV in his room—Owen wouldn't permit it; it would've been too difficult to monitor what Curt watched that way. He heard giggling now, in a voice much higher pitched than Curt's. The sort of voice that might make an EEP! sound.

Owen rapped the door with a knuckle. "What's going on in there?"

As if a switch had been thrown, the giggling cut off and the light winked out. He heard the sound of covers shuffling. "Nothing, Dad. Just having trouble sleeping, that's all."

Owen thought of how Curt's eyes had looked blood-shot and puffy that afternoon.

He debated whether or not he should go in. On the one hand, Curt was definitely up to something, probably playing with that new Digi-whatever-it-was. On the other, Owen didn't like coming across as a hard case. His own father had busted his chops something fierce the entire time he'd been growing up, and Owen had sworn to himself that he'd never treat his child that way.

Besides, he really had to pee.

"Go to sleep, Curt."

"All right, Dad. I will."

Owen waited another moment, listening. But he heard nothing. Satisfied, he continued on his way toward the bathroom and relief. But he decided that first thing tomorrow, he was going to find out just what a Digi-Pal was.

"C'mon, don't tell me you haven't heard about Digi-Pals! They're the latest thing, bigger than Tamagotchi ever were. My granddaughter has three of them."

Owen sat on an uncomfortable chair in Fay Narayan's carrel. Fay, a bird-thin woman in her late fifties who dressed more like a stereotypical librarian than a loan researcher, was the office Know-it-all. And Tell-it-all.

Owen thought he'd heard of Tamagotchi before, maybe read about them in a newspaper or magazine, but he wasn't certain. The only information he retained on a long-term basis were sports stats and interest rates. In that order.

"Okay, I admit it: I'm farther behind the times than Fred Flintstone. What exactly are DigiPals? Some new kind of game?"

Fay leaned an elbow on her desktop and propped her chin in her hand. "Wow, you really *are* out of the cultural loop, aren't you? Do you remember Pet Rocks?"

"Sure, they were a fad back in the seventies. My older brother had one. Stupid idea, but I guess it made somebody a ton of money."

"DigiPals are kind of like Pet Rocks, except they're alive. Well, not really. They're virtual pets, programmed to simulate life. They need to eat, sleep, be played with, soothed when they're afraid, comforted when they're sad. Kids can take care of their DigiPal's needs by pressing certain combinations of buttons. If they do a good job caring for their animal, it grows strong and healthy. If they neglect it, it dies."

"What do you mean, it dies?"

"Deactivates might be a better word. The program shuts down for good. Although some varieties of virtual pets have reset buttons so you can start over."

"What do you do when one . . . deactivates? Just throw it out?"

"Some kids become so attached to their virtual pets that they hold funerals for them, even post tributes on the Internet."

Owen shook his head. "That has to be one of the dumbest things I've ever heard."

"Not if you're a kid. Did you have any pets when you were growing up?"

"Sure, we had a Dalmatian and a couple of cats. We

had an aquarium for a while, too, but the fish kept dying, so my dad got rid of it."

"Did you ever lose one of your pets?" Fay asked. "Not counting the fish."

"Yeah, our Dalmatian—Tippy was her name—got hit by a car. We had to take her to the vet's and have her put to sleep." Even now, all these years later, his throat tightened at the memory.

"To a lot of these kids, losing a virtual pet is just as traumatic as losing a real one. Children always have a favorite doll or stuffed animal they pretend is real. It's that much easier for them to believe a virtual pet is real, since it moves and makes sounds, begs for food, does tricks. Pretty much everything a real pet does. Even poop." She grinned. "Though they are a lot easier to clean up after."

"So this is just a hi-tech fad, then."

"Maybe. But taking care of a virtual pet teaches a kid responsibility. If they don't respond to their pet's needs— feed it when it's hungry, play with it when it's bored—it withers away and dies, just like a real animal. My granddaughter has really been affected by her DigiPals. She does her chores with less grumbling, and she's more attentive to her schoolwork."

Owen thought about how Curt had passed up watching the football game so he could go do his homework.

"Do you have any real pets at home?" Fay asked.

"No. I'd like to have some, but Leona has terrible allergies. If she so much as comes within a block of an animal, her eyes water and her nose runs like a faucet. We took her to the zoo once, and she nearly went into a coma."

"Well, there you go. This is Curt's chance to learn what it's like to take care of a pet without making your wife miserable."

Owen had to admit that sounded pretty good. "But then why did he hide it from me?"

"You said he stroked the DigiPal, right? Maybe he was afraid you might not understand his feelings. To a grown-up, a DigiPal is little more than a computer chip encased in plastic. But to a kid, it's as real as . . . well, a Dalmatian named Tippy."

That evening, as Owen turned onto his street, he saw Curt with a group of neighborhood children. That in itself wasn't unusual. Curt was always up for a game of street hockey or a little one-on-one. But these kids weren't playing sports; they sat in a circle, hunched over tiny plastic objects they held tightly in their hands. DigiPals.

Owen slowed and pulled up to the curb. He rolled down his window. "Hey, Curt, what are you up to?"

His son didn't look up, didn't acknowledge Owen's words or presence in any way. None of the other kids reacted either. They appeared completely unaware of him, of each other, for that matter. Their attention was focused solely on their individual DigiPals.

Owen started to get angry. He didn't appreciate being ignored by his son. He put the car in park, reached for the door handle, intending to get out and Have a Few Words with Curt. But he hesitated. He remembered what it had felt like when he was a boy and his dad read him the riot act in front of his friends: total humiliation and burning resentment. Not only had Owen made damn sure not to pay attention to anything his dad said, he did the exact opposite the first chance he got.

So maybe this discussion should be tabled for now. "It'll be dinnertime soon, Curt. Don't be late."

Curt didn't respond; he just kept working the controls of his DigiPal.

Feeling completely ineffectual, Owen pulled away from the curb and continued on toward his house.

"Sorry, Dad. I guess I was . . . concentrating too hard." Curt took another drumstick—his fifth—and tore into it like he hadn't eaten in a week. His eyes were even more bloodshot and puffy than they'd been yesterday.

Owen glanced across the dining room table at Leona. She gave a tiny shrug that meant, *Don't ask me.*

"How much sleep did you get last night?"

"I don't know," Curt mumbled around a mouthful of chicken. "Enough, I guess."

The boy sure didn't look like he'd had enough rest. Not only were his eyes tired-looking, but his face was pale and his cheeks slightly sunken, as if he'd lost weight. "No more staying up at night to play with that DigiPal of yours. I know it's probably a lot of fun, but you need your—" A soft EEP, EEP, EEP! cut through the air, interrupting Owen.

Curt pulled his DigiPal from his pants pocket, pressed a few buttons, gazed at the display screen. He nodded once, then put the toy back in his pocket.

"Sorry, Dad. My DigiPal has a pause function. I'll use it tonight; that way, he'll sleep when I do. Okay?"

Owen opened his mouth to speak, but he wasn't sure what to say. It wasn't supposed to be this easy. There should've been more protests and feet-dragging, maybe with a little whining thrown in for good measure.

"All right, then," he said finally. "Finish your dinner."

Curt nodded, then returned to his assault on the chicken leg. But Owen noticed the boy reach down with his free hand and reassuringly pat the DigiPal.

That night, Owen made it a point to stay up so he could walk past Curt's room and check on him. No light came from beneath the door, no whispers, no giggles. Feeling like a father who had successfully done his duty, Owen returned to his bedroom. But as he settled into bed next to his wife, he wondered why he'd never seen the Digi-Pal produce any light during the day.

Three weeks passed. Curt continued eating as if he were sixteen instead of eight. He always looked tired, and he was definitely losing weight. But no matter how hard Owen tried, he hadn't been able to catch Curt staying up late to play with the DigiPal. Owen would've really worried if Curt's grades began to slide. But lately, all the homework and tests he brought home were A pluses, and at the top of his papers his teachers wrote comments like *Excellent, Fantastic,* and *Way to Go!*

Curt had changed in other ways. On those rare occasions when he sat down in front of the TV, he turned on CNN. And he never went outside anymore, unless it was to meet with his fellow DigiPal owners. No more football or basketball. He didn't even want to talk about sports anymore.

"He's just going through a phase," Leona said when Owen brought up his concerns to her one evening before bed. "Didn't you ever obsess about anything as a kid? Besides sports, I mean."

"I don't know. I had a beer can collection. One hundred and fifty-two different cans, from all over the world. I used to walk around town, looking in ditches for cans, digging through people's trash. It drove my dad crazy."

"There you go. This is the same sort of thing." She smiled. "Only more hygienic."

"Maybe. But doesn't he look thinner to you?"

"You've seen how he's been eating recently. He's probably getting ready for a growth spurt. Besides, it looks good on him. He was starting to get a little chunky." She walked over and patted his belly. "You could stand to lose a few yourself, Mister."

She started telling him about a new health club that had opened up down by the mall, but he didn't pay attention. He had decided to pay Curt—and his DigiPal—a little visit tonight.

Owen lay in bed, staring up at the darkness clinging to the ceiling. Beside him, Leona let out soft nasal rumblings as she slept. Ordinarily, he would have gone downstairs and watched TV to help keep himself awake, but he didn't want to make any noise that might alert his son that Dad was up and about. Owen hoped for one of two things: to catch Curt playing with his DigiPal and confront him about it once and for all, or to find Curt asleep so he could sneak the toy out of the boy's bedroom and examine it. Either way, Owen intended to find out just what the DigiPal was and why it had such a hold on his son.

He did everything he could to stay awake. He thought about work, mentally replayed the last three football games he'd seen, even counted Leona's snores. He made it to three hundred forty-seven before his eyes closed and he drifted off to sleep.

He woke with a start, looked at the clock radio on his nightstand. 3:21. He almost rolled over and went back to sleep, but then his mind cleared and he remembered. The DigiPal. He slipped out of bed quietly, donned his robe, and tiptoed to the bedroom door. As he turned the knob, Leona's snores increased in volume. She sputtered once, twice, and he feared she would wake. But she rolled over, sighed, then returned to emitting her normal soft reverberations.

He opened the door just wide enough to pass through, stepped into the hallway, and closed the door behind him, making sure to release the knob gently so it wouldn't click too loudly. Then he began making his way down the hall toward Curt's room.

He felt foolish, like a man attempting to burglarize his own home. Leona was probably right. Curt was just going through a phase, and there was nothing sinister about his relationship with the DigiPal. If Owen got caught, he'd damage his relationship with his son, and his wife would think him ridiculous. Better to forget this sneaking about, go back to bed, and talk to Curt in the morning about the DigiPal.

He hesitated, started to turn around. But then he thought of the way Curt had responded when Owen had confronted him at dinner several weeks ago, how the

DigiPal had beeped and Curt had looked down at it, nodding, as if it had told him exactly the right things to say to shut Owen up.

He continued tiptoeing down the hall.

It seemed to take a long time, but finally he reached Curt's room. He listened at the door, heard nothing. Looked down, saw no light. He gripped the knob, started to turn it, glad there wasn't a lock on Curt's door. He pushed gently, but the door refused to budge. He pushed again, harder this time, but the door didn't move. It felt jammed. He released the knob and knelt down, ran his fingers along the crack beneath the door. His fingertips brushed the smooth tip of a wooden wedge. Evidently, Curt had spent a little time out in the garage making his own lock.

Owen stood, more determined than even to get inside the room. He stepped quietly to the bathroom, opened the medicine chest and took out a hard plastic comb. Then he returned to Curt's door, bent down again, and inserted the comb through the crack beneath the door, pushing and prying at the wedge. Since Owen didn't want to make any noise, he had to go slowly, and it took a while to force the wedge out. But eventually he succeeded. He stood, stuck the comb in his robe pocket, and tried the door again. This time it opened easily.

He entered.

The room was pitch-black, and for the first time since Curt had been a toddler, Owen regretted that his son no longer needed a night-light to sleep. He walked cautiously across the room, putting his feet down gingerly, toes probing for the sharp edges of any toys. He crossed to Curt's bed, alert for any sign that the boy was stirring. But Curt's breathing was slow and regular. Owen made it to the nightstand, heart pounding in his ears. He forced himself to breathe shallowly through his nose so he wouldn't wake his son. He felt around on the nightstand, fingers searching for the oval plastic case of the DigiPal. But he felt nothing.

He probably sleeps with the thing, Owen thought. *Keeps it in his pajama pocket, or maybe clutched in his hand.* Once more, he considered aborting his mission. He wasn't a pickpocket; he doubted he would be able to get the virtual pet away from Curt without waking him. But Owen had come this far. He had to know.

Slowly, Owen drew the covers back from his son, then leaned over the boy's sleeping form. Curt slept on his side, almost in a fetal position. Owen reached out toward the useless chest pocket on Curt's pajama top. He found it empty.

In his hand, then.

Owen chose the hand closest to his, the left. It lay in front of Curt's flat, almost concave belly. Owen touched the boy's hand, felt for the opening between thumb and forefinger. Nothing.

Curt took a sudden deep breath, shifted on the bed. Owen jerked his hand back, experienced a guilty urge to turn and run. But he held his ground, and Curt grew still again, his breathing slow and even. A bead of sweat ran down Owen's chest, pooled where the swell of his gut began.

Curt's other hand lay beneath the pillow. Owen lifted the pillow's edge, reached in, felt around, came in contact with soft boy-flesh and, at last, cold hard plastic. He smiled grimly in the dark. Bingo. He took his time working the DigiPal loose. Curt wrinkled his nose and frowned, but he didn't wake. Finally, the DigiPal slipped from Curt's grasp. Owen grinned, feeling as if he'd just pulled off an impossible diamond heist.

Now to get away with the goods.

But just as Owen turned to go, the DigiPal let forth a loud EEP-EEP-EEP!

Curt bolted upright in bed, instantly awake. "Dad!"

Owen struggled to find an excuse, some justification for why he was pilfering his son's bedroom in the middle of the night, but he couldn't think of anything. He decided to lead off with *I'm sorry,* and hope the rest would follow. But Curt spoke first.

"Dad, Dad, Dad." Owen could see Curt shaking his head in the dark. "I really wish you hadn't done this. It's most inconvenient."

It was Curt's voice, but the words and manner were completely different. Older, cynical. Their casual detachment made Owen's skin crawl.

"My pet's not quite ready yet. It takes some time for his species to become fully acclimated to our world. They need to grow into it bit by bit, to connect with a life-force native to this plane which can teach and nourish them." He sighed. "Still, I suppose we have no choice now but to proceed."

"What in the hell are you talking about?" Owen nearly shouted, his words edged with hysteria. "It's just a god-damned toy!"

Owen felt the DigiPal jerk in his hands, heard a soft cracking sound.

Curt grinned as blue-white light danced in his eyes.

"It's not a toy, Dad. It's an egg."

ELMER

Peter Crowther

Peter Crowther is the editor or coeditor of nine anthologies and the coauthor (with James Lovegrove) of the novel *Escardy Gap*. Since the early 1990s, he has sold some seventy short stories and poems to a wide variety of magazines and chapbooks on both sides of the Atlantic. He has also recently added two chapbooks, *Forest Plains* and *Fugue on a G-String*, to his credits. His review columns and critical essays on the fields of fantasy, horror, and science fiction appear regularly in *Interzone* and the *Hellnotes* internet magazine. He was appointed to the Board of Trustees of the Horror Writers' Association. He lives in Harrogate, England, with his wife and two sons.

LESS than an hour after he concealed his father's body, Oswald Masylik stared into the early-morning sky and thought of the past.

Thinking of the past was something Oswald had been doing more and more since he had hit fifty-nine, and now, with the big six-oh straddling the horizon of his future like a stormcloud, what had already gone seemed a sight more appealing than what lay ahead.

There are some places where the past seems to sit on the air like a ribbon tangled up around an overhead wire, blowing and fluttering in the wind like it's about to spin off somewhere . . . but always staying right where it is.

Oswald had heard other folks talk of these special places: sometimes they were triggered off by the wafted scent of a familiar old perfume, sometimes by the shape or coloring of a once-familiar building, and sometimes by a long-ago familiar sound . . . like a floorboard settling down for the night that sounds just like a throat being cleared by someone you don't see anymore.

Oswald Masylik's "place" was a mixture of *all* of these.

For Oswald, the past would always be two things: the first being a sensory amalgam comprising the acrid smell of diesel fumes, the sight of the old aluminum sidings of a thirty-four-ton freight rig, and the unmistakable sound of shifting gears and air brakes; and the second being the memory of the old schoolhouse from his childhood days.

And maybe there was a third place: the old ravine where he made The Great Discovery.

Out of all the weeks that stacked like building blocks to form the many-roomed mansion of Oswald's early life, one stood out as being special. And that was the week of The Great Discovery.

Looking now out over the once-barren rockface of the ravine, the events of that week came tumbling back to him.

It was April 1946.

In those days, Oswald was simply "Ozzie." His father was a long-haul driver for the Pacific Intermountain Express Company—or PIE for short—handling the Illinois leg of the ten-man tag-team needed to get freight from Oakland to Chicago.

Ben and Eleanor Masylik and their son lived in a little

town called Pecatonica, about twenty miles west along US20 from Rockford.

To say Pecatonica was "little" in those days was kind of underplaying the truth. The fact was that it was tiny. The best example of this was the school.

District School No. 94 was one of the best one-room schools in the country (or so everybody kept on telling the students), with one teacher—Miss Meyer—teaching all of its fifteen-strong, six-grade "Class" of '46 at the same time.

A typical day in that bygone era might have seen Miss Meyer assign a study problem to the seventh grade and then get the first graders busy crayoning. Second graders were then put to work at the blackboard doing arithmetic, and the fifth grade were sent into a corner to compose a letter. She might then assign some reading in geography to the sixth grade while she went through homework with the third. There was no fourth grade in 1946, which maybe made things a little easier that year.

The simple fact of the matter, however, was Miss Meyer never seemed flustered by anything she had to do. She would stand there in front of the blackboard as calm as you please, a book open in her hands while she read to one of her grades, one foot standing toe-down behind the other like she was one of those big birds that sleep standing on one leg.

In 1946, Will Jenner and Ozzie were the entire third grade. They were seven years old, reaching impatiently and anxiously toward double figures like kids on a carousel reaching for the brass ring that meant a free ride.

The days leading up to Ozzie's Great Discovery were exceptionally dull ones—that's "dull" in meteorological terms.

The weather was stormy, even for early April, and most recesses saw the students of District School No. 94 confined to the classroom staring out of the long windows as rain lashed down on grass they should be out playing on. The privy was out there, too, so they were all having to work at holding bowels and bladders.

The immediate postwar years were another world as far as kids of the late 1990s were concerned. Most of the kids at District School No. 94 walked to their studies each day—sometimes two or three miles each way—although one or two got lifts from their fathers in beat-up pickups and rusting Pontiacs, Fords, and all manner of other autos with mufflers that sounded like low-flying aircraft.

Pecatonica was not a wealthy town. Not by any means.

Ozzie's mother never learned to drive and his father was away most every weekday, so Ozzie's feet were his transport. Will Jenner suffered from the same problem.

Will had a younger sister, Irene—who was in 1946's first grade—and an older brother, Homer, who worked for a delivery company in Belvidere. Homer was twenty-two years old and the family didn't see much of him since he'd moved away from home.

Irene was a cute kid, with wavy blonde hair and a smile that Shirley Temple would have died for, but she drove Will batty, always running up to him when he was talking to Ozzie about comic books or radio shows, asking him things. But, while Ozzie could see how frustrating she was—with her lisp and that wild shriek she had when she was happy—he also kind of envied Will having someone he could talk to if he really needed to.

Ben and Eleanor Masylik had just the one child.

Ozzie's mom used to delight in telling him, while she was ironing her husband's uniform or Ozzie's school shirts, that it meant they could give all of their love to him. But, over in the corner of the room on these occasions, reading the newspaper or listening to the radio, Ben Masylik would add that a good motto was "never make the same mistake twice." Eleanor would glare across at him, and he would just raise his eyebrows and shuffle the newspaper or shake a cigarette out of the creased pack in his shirt pocket, a *what did I say?* kind of look that he would always postscript with a wink and a smile to his son when Eleanor, hiding a knowing smile, wasn't looking any more.

This little ritual always made Ozzie laugh, even though he had seen it a hundred or more times.

But the truth was, Ozzie was lonely.

Some of the other kids had pets. Dogs and cats, mostly, though one or two who lived on farms and other smallholdings kind of adopted things like chickens and sheep.

Billy Morrison had a pet pig that went by the name of Lamont (after the guy in *The Shadow* radio show) and Martha Toffel told everyone she had befriended a woodchuck that she called Millie, but nobody ever saw it. But that didn't bother Martha because she had a twin sister and the two of them seemed to be together all the time. Ozzie didn't have anybody: no brothers or sisters, and no pets.

Ellie Masylik had an allergy to fur, which made her wheeze like a stalled train, so the idea of keeping cats and dogs was out. And they didn't have a farm or any land to speak of—even though the house was surrounded by woodland—so keeping some other kind of animal was out of the question. Ozzie's mom, who felt mightily guilty about her affliction, said Ozzie could have a bird if he wanted, but somehow, keeping a bird in a cage didn't seem as attractive as having something to take out for a walk.

Then, right at the end of that dismal, overcast week, Northern Illinois got the mother and father (plus a few aunts, uncles, and cousins!) of all storms. None of the kids had ever seen anything like it and even the usually placid Miss Meyer seemed a little rattled by all the banging and crashing of the wind against the old schoolhouse and the sight of the privy door pinwheeling across the field before taking off like something out of *The Wizard of Oz*.

And so it was that school let out early that day and all

the kids got taken home by Billy's father in Mr. Morrison's old backboard truck, all of them sitting huddled up in a mess of interlinked arms and legs against the back window of the cab, being lashed by the wind and rain and laughing fit to burst.

There were fourteen of them that day—Martha Toffel had stayed home with a temperature—and Will, Irene, and Ozzie were the last ones dropped off at the end of the road that split into two and led down one way to the Jenners' house and down to the Masyliks' the other. Right in front of them, an uprooted tree lay across the road.

Mr. Morrison leaned across Billy and rolled down the window. "Can't take you any farther. You kids gonna be okay here?"

Ozzie and Will nodded enthusiastically, the wind blowing rain-soaked hair down over their eyes and then whipping it back again. "Sure thing, Mr. Morrison," Will shouted, holding up his sister's tightly clasped hand as evidence.

"Okay," Mr. Morrison said, a note of reluctance in his voice. "You run right on home now and stay indoors," he shouted over the whine of the old truck's engine and the steadily increasing wail of the wind. "It'll blow itself out before too long, but it's my guess we haven't seen the worst of it yet."

Will and Ozzie followed Mr. Morrison's gaze across the flat grassland leading down to the highway. Every now and then they could see pieces of tree whipped up into the sky and just whisked out of sight, and what was left of the trees themselves was bowed right over toward the ground as though they, too, were trying to get out of the storm. It was only a little after one o'clock, but black enough to be near nine at night.

The three kids nodded and Will pulled little Irene close to him, clasping her hand still tighter.

"I'm fwikened," Irene said, her face so screwed up she looked like she was going to start bawling. Will waved to Mr. Morrison's truck as it trundled back up the road and then hunched down by his sister. "There's just a few minutes' walk and we'll be home," he said, pulling the collar of her jacket up around her neck and managing to give her a reassuring hug in the process. He turned to Ozzie and nodded with all the gravity that a seven year-old can muster—and that's a mighty lot of gravity—and patted his friend's shoulder.

"You take care, Ozzie," he said.

"You, too, Will." Ozzie glanced over at little Irene and couldn't help but smile. "You, too," he said. "Look after your brother now, hear?"

Hanging onto Will's left hand, her face suddenly lightened. She had a responsibility, she now realized. Someone other than herself to worry about. "I will," she said somberly, suddenly grabbing hold of her brother's arm with her free hand. But her words were lost in the wind.

A couple of minutes later, over the tree and running through every puddle he could see, Ozzie turned around to wave, but Will and Irene were gone. For a few seconds, he just stood there looking at the distant horizon. Clouds were roiling in clumps, tumbling over each other like playful puppies. About midway, on the flats, uprooted bushes were rushing across the grassland like tumbleweed, bouncing occasionally high into the air when they hit a patch of uneven ground. Now and again one of them would flash high into the air, pirouetting madly before falling back to earth.

Ozzie turned back to the track that led home and started to run again, tucking his chin deep into his chest to preserve the ability to breathe. He could hear the high-pitched whine of the wind now, like the siren attached to the old schoolhouse to warn of a possible nuclear strike.

He was suddenly scared. Maybe that's what this was. Maybe it wasn't a storm at all. In a strange way, the sound of his own whimper comforted him.

The first leg of the dusty track that eventually led to the wood-frame house he shared with his parents wound flat for a couple hundred yards beyond the fallen tree before curving to the right, overlooking a steep ravine, a place of barren rock and scrawny bush skeletons, and up to a tree-lined crest. Looking up briefly, his legs pistoning forward, feet occasionally catching lumps of rock and clumps of grass, Ozzie could see that some of those trees had gone.

Ozzie knew, staring into the wind through watering eyes, that the track dipped sharply and without protection in an ambling curve around the mouth of the valley and several square miles of flat and exposed scrubland. That single thought gave him additional cause for concern when the wind bent a tree alongside him all the way to the ground before uprooting it entirely and sending it cartwheeling across the track, where it suddenly disappeared out of sight down into the ravine.

The surge of wind stopped him almost dead in his tracks and he bent even farther forward, noting as he did so that his body was virtually horizontal to the ground. He could have stretched out a hand and touched the grass beneath him.

With renewed effort, Ozzie reached the crest and fell down beside a stump of tree. Pushing his body in against the bark, he turned his face into his chest and gasped for air, glancing back the way he had come.

That's when he saw it.

Coming out of the clouds in the distance, lightning flashing all around it, seeming even to be originating from it, came what looked like a cross between one of the planets illustrated in Miss Meyer's science books and a giant mudball, like the ones Ozzie used to make with Will Jenner when they were both little kids out in the Jenners' backyard.

Without even realizing he was doing it, Ozzie raised his right arm like he was going to salute the thing, lifted it so that the forearm was almost over his eyes, lifted it so that it might protect him when that thing hit him square on, pounding him into a million zillion bits of bone and gristle. All serious thought vanished: he did not think of escape or of hiding or of the pain the thing was going to cause him. All he thought of was . . . where did this thing come from? It wasn't a bomb, and it wasn't an aircraft: it came from *out there*.

Out there!

Just the words filled Ozzie with awe. The thing was some kind of comet or meteor, hell-bent on hitting the Earth after spending—what? After spending how long out in space? Maybe this thing was older than the Earth itself. Maybe it had been flying around out there when Jesus had trudged up the hill with His cross . . . maybe it had been zipping around when the dinosaurs had idly looked up, wondering at the high-pitched whine as they munched the tree tops.

He watched as the planet/comet/meteor spiraled and glimmered, shimmered and twirled, huge forks of light glancing across its gnarled surface

He didn't have time to consider moving, to think about shielding himself or flattening out against the ground. All he could do was stare at it, leaning over at the very last second as it came hurtling by, feeling its heat, smelling its surface—a mix of old vegetables, the inside of aluminum cans, and clothes fresh from a windy day on the washing line out back.

At the very last second, as the thing hurtled down toward him, Ozzie covered his face and shouted, although he could hear only the sound of the high-pitched whine, making sure he kept a small gap to see through.

The thing filled his vision then, a seething mass of ridges and knolls, of troughs and valleys, promontories and clumps of what looked like thick, stringy hair, whorls of gray and blue and black, eyeless sockets formed of silt and dirt and mud, made hard by time and the airless cold of outer space.

No sooner was it in front of him than it was past, missing him by what seemed like only a few yards, its whine like a police siren passing him by and moving off. Out of the corner of his eye, Ozzie saw the gigantic mudball strike the ground to his right, just above the ravine. For a few seconds nothing seemed to happen and then, still twirling around and spinning, grass and dust and dirt billowing into the sky like a curtain, the thing just rose up again, still spinning, already growing smaller.

It was only then that the ground beneath him shook and Ozzie jumped up to his knees, fearing that it was going to open up and swallow him.

He jumped up and down, jumped sideways, first one way and then the other, swapping feet, holding the one foot in the air, arms stretched out, watching the ground, waiting for the first splits to appear. But nothing happened. He landed from one of the jumps and stayed put, both feet on the ground, spread wide, half crouched like a mountain cat waiting to spring away.

He looked to his right, up after the mudball, and squinted into the settling dust. He could just make out the shape of the meteor through the haze, growing steadily smaller, still spinning and twirling, up into the sky and back into the depths of space.

Ozzie staggered a little, feeling like a freshman sailor on the deck of his first ship. He plopped to the ground against the tree stump and waited, though he had no idea what exactly he was waiting for.

The wind had dropped. Now there was only a pleasant breeze.

Ozzie looked up and saw a slight break in the clouds, a tear in all that gray and darkness through which gold rays shone. Okay, it was only a slim break, but it *was* a break.

Dust was settling all around him, settling on his outstretched arms like bathroom powder. He looked down at himself, checking to make sure there were no tears in his jeans or sweater. Everything seemed intact. Then he looked down at the ground to his right, where the meteor thing had hit before bouncing out to Alpha Centauri and all points north, and he gasped.

There was a thick gouge out of the earth that looked like the heaviest airplane in the history of aviation had just taken off carrying the entire contents of Fort Knox in its belly. There was a deep runnel starting just a few yards from where Ozzie was sitting and carrying on to just a few feet shy of where the land dropped away into the ravine.

Plants—most of them weeds—had been either crushed or uprooted; a bush seemed to have been torn in two, one half sitting same as ever and the other half gone out of sight; and the whole area of ground seemed indented, as though a boulder had been rolled to the ravine and just let go over the edge. But most of all, the ground was torn, soil and dirt channeled into deep gouges and tears, the grass and brush razed away like skin peeled off, exposing the glistening surface of earthy blood and muscle that lay beneath. Ozzie stared.

Something was happening to that ground.

He blinked and rolled to one side, thinking maybe it was the light from that gap in the clouds or maybe his close brush with death and destruction had left him a little light-headed. But no, what he'd thought was happening was still happening, no matter which angle he looked from or how many times he rubbed his eyes.

Keeping his body as close to the ground as he could manage, Ozzie crawled forward on his stomach, pulling the rest of himself along behind like he was some kind of human snake. When he got to just a few inches away from where the comet must have made its glancing blow, he stopped and watched.

On the ground in front of him, covering the grooves and runnels and smashed earth, lying up alongside and across the bruised ground, were what looked like the amoeba things Miss Meyer had talked about one time in her introduction to biology, all flattened out and frilly around the edges. They looked like a cross between a frying egg, a wad of gum, and the bald head of Elmer Fudd, the little guy who was always the butt of Bugs Bunny's antics in the cartoons they showed on Saturday mornings at the movie theater over in Rockford. The things were a kind of dull, light brown, like an adhesive bandage strip, and they seemed to undulate when they moved along, their sides rippling.

Creeping nearer, Ozzie stared.

The things seemed to be merging themselves onto the ridged soil. They would shuffle along, their sides rolling up and down, and then they would stop and . . . and they would just kind of disappear. There was no other way to describe it.

There seemed to be hundreds of the things, each one just a few inches in diameter. As he looked around the ruined path left by the comet, Ozzie saw that the things seemed to be congregating at the edges of the swathe, then they would stop and disappear. Seconds later, more would reach the edge of *that* spot and then they would disappear. And the piece of ground that they had covered, momentarily smooth, would change.

Ozzie gasped in astonishment. "Wow!" he said to the gently soughing wind and the upturned earth. The pieces of earth recently covered by the things had started sprouting green stalks, each shoot slowly nuzzling its way free and standing proud.

He got to his feet and moved still closer, bending over where the things were working—he supposed "working" was a reasonable description of what they were doing. The grass coat destroyed by the comet was being replaced.

He looked up away from where he was standing and allowed his eyes to travel along the comet's graze to the edge of the ravine. The width of the path between the untouched grass was narrowing. Soon there would be no sign of the comet having been there at all, save for a gently rolling indent of the grassland.

Already, the section directly beneath him had met in the middle. And as the graze was healed over, the process seemed to speed up, with the amoeba things having less of a distance to travel in order to carry out what could only be termed a healing or restoration process. Now,

Ozzie saw, the ground was recovering some of its earlier greenness, albeit with a distinctly hollowed-out appearance. It looked for all the world as Ozzie imagined a piece of ground might look after something huge had been removed from beneath it.

With the whole process having taken only what seemed to have been a minute or two, there were few of the things left. Those that remained settled on small areas of exposed soil, some of these areas no bigger than a dime or a nickel, and simply faded from view. Then Ozzie saw one of the things shuffling across some recently "reseeded" grass heading for a thin welt of exposed soil.

His heart pounding in his chest, Ozzie tentatively reached out his hand and, grimacing, tenderly took hold of the thing between thumb and forefinger. He was prepared for pain, maybe a stinging sensation or some kind of shock, but there was nothing. What did happen was that his finger and thumb suddenly felt quite numb.

He placed the thing on the palm of his other hand and watched it closely. For a few seconds, Ozzie thought that it was dead, that the sudden pressure of his fingers had somehow traumatized it, but then, with a flick-and-swirl of its tiny skirts, it shuffled slowly across his palm toward his fingers.

"Whatcha doin' fella?" he said softly, moving his free hand beneath the fingers of the other so that the thing would plop to safety when it reached the tips of his outstretched fingers. There was no answer, of course.

Once on its new surface, the thing simply trundled its way toward Ozzie's wrist, apparently exploring.

Ozzie looked up at the sky and saw that the sun was definitely now out. The ground in front of him was completely healed. There was no sign of any of the amoeba-things.

He looked down at the thing on his hand and smiled as it continued to swish its sides as it moved slowly over his wrist. Then he placed the other hand beneath his arm and allowed the thing to crawl back onto his palm.

"You sure are a wittle wascal," Ozzie chuckled, trying to mimic Fuddsy's voice. "I'm gonna call you Elmer," he whispered, cupping both hands, ensuring that the thing had no way to escape. Then he set off for home.

Ozzie had expected his mother to be full of excitement about the comet—after all, she must have seen it—but she said nothing, although she was pleased to see him home safely.

"That was quite a storm," she said, looking out of the window. "But it looks like it's clearing up just fine now."

Ozzie nodded. He had trapped the amoeba-thing in his right hand and that hand was now thrust deep into his pocket.

"You go get washed up now," his mother said. As Ozzie turned and ran out of the kitchen, she called after him: "Supper will be ready in a few minutes."

In the sanctity of his room, Ozzie carefully placed Elmer into a glass bowl he had been using to store marbles. Across the top of the bowl, he placed a thin sheet of cardboard. As an afterthought, he used his penknife to cut three small holes in the cardboard in case he suffocated his new friend. Then he placed a carton of toy soldiers on top of the cardboard for added security, making sure that the carton didn't obliterate the life-preserving holes. When he was satisfied that the thing was both safe and secure, he went downstairs.

That night, it being a Friday, Ozzie's father was home. But there had been a problem at the depot. One of the drivers scheduled to take a rig out on Saturday had called in sick, so Ben had to do the drive from Moline across to Chicago. It had all been arranged, he explained to a disappointed Eleanor while Ozzie lay on the floor reading comic books. Tom Nelson was due to take a rig from Iowa City across to the West Coast and so he was going to take Ben down to Moline, drop him off and continue on to Iowa City where he would pick up at the PIE depot there. Ben reckoned he would be back late on Saturday night and that they would at least have the Sunday together as a family. Unaware of the fine points of this conversation—or of the silent glances and nods between his parents—it was a surprise when Ben Masylik suddenly announced that he could use a little company.

"You feel up to that, Ozzie?" Ben inquired, his face looking serious.

"Huh?!" Ozzie was amazed. He loved to sit in the big rigs and he had never been out in one when it was actually moving. "You bet!" he said, getting to his knees.

"Your father has to be up and away early, now," Eleanor announced as she stacked clean dishes by the sink. "Means there'll be no time for dawdling around."

"Yes, ma'am!" Ozzie said. "I mean, no ma'am," he corrected himself. He thought about reminding his father about company policy stating that drivers' kids couldn't travel with them on the rigs but decided against it. Nevertheless, he was reassured that his father wouldn't be getting into trouble when Ben Masylik explained that he had had a word with the crew foreman and, seeing as how Ben was helping them out of a tight spot, it was going to be okay for Ozzie to make the trip.

Even better, Ozzie thought. It's official.

Up to bed earlier than usual that evening to make sure he was rested for the three A.M. get-up the next morning, Ozzie was surprised to see that the holes in the piece of cardboard over the bowl containing the amoeba-thing had disappeared. The cardboard was as good as new. For a second, fearing that his friend from the comet had suffocated, panic set in. Ozzie lifted cardboard off the bowl and reached inside. He breathed a long sigh of relief when Elmer responded to his prodding finger.

"So, you don't need no air, then," Ozzie whispered to the thing as it trundled around his palm. "That makes things a little easier, anyways," he said. He had been wondering how he was going to carry Elmer around with him when he and his father went on their adventure the next morning. The fact that the thing didn't seem to need oxygen the way humans did meant that he would be able to carry it in one of the jars his mom used to store her homemade jam.

Feeling that life sure had a way of making things turn out okay sometimes, Ozzie returned Elmer to the bowl, ensuring that the cardboard and the carton of soldiers were firmly in place, and got ready for bed.

The following morning, Ozzie felt like he hadn't been to bed at all. It was only the prospect of the forthcoming adventure with his father that finally woke him up sufficiently to have some breakfast. And even then, he almost forgot to take Elmer. He finally remembered only when Tom Nelson's car's headlights washed across the still-drawn kitchen curtains, when he made a big thing out of going to the bathroom before they set off. Amidst the confusion of Ben and Eleanor shaking their heads in frustration while they greeted Tom, Ozzie snuck out of the kitchen with one of his mother's carefully washed screw-cap jars from the cupboard beneath the sink. Minutes later, the jar safely tucked into his jacket pocket with its passenger intact and apparently healthy and happy, Ozzie climbed into the back of Tom Nelson's Pontiac and they set off for Moline.

The trip down was fine.

Ozzie sat quietly, hunched up on the back seat, watching the landscape drift by and listening to his father trade stories with Tom Nelson about guys at the depot and workloads and how summer couldn't come soon enough. They'd had their fill of the winter, which in 1945/46 had seemed to go on forever. Hauling the big rigs around on roads slick with rain and sometimes sleet took an awful lot of concentration, Tom explained over his shoulder to Ozzie. Ozzie's father seemed to agree wholeheartedly, but Ozzie saw him give some kind of shake of the head to Tom, after which Tom went to great lengths to say just how great a job this was and how he wouldn't be caught dead doing anything else. Ozzie's father said it was amen to that, whatever that meant.

Having left the house at a little after four-thirty in the morning, the trio hit the outskirts of Moline just after eight o'clock, after stopping for coffee and donuts at Bohlman's Cafe, one of the PIE drivers' favorite stopovers, in Sterling. The place was little more than a shack at the side of the road, but the parking area was filled with eighteen and twenty-four wheelers, sitting ticking and clicking in the early-morning gloom. Ozzie sniffed in the smell of hot metal and diesel fumes and the scent made him feel as though he could fly.

Inside the cafe all you could see was peaked caps, smiling faces, and steam from the back room. The place smelled of cigarette smoke, frying bacon, and hot coffee. Ozzie couldn't decide whether he liked this smell better than the parking lot or the other way around.

Waving bye to Tom Nelson made Ozzie feel a little wistful suddenly and his father must have sensed it. "Okay, trusty navigator," he said to Ozzie in a loud voice, wrapping his arm around the boy's shoulders. "Let's go get ourselves a rig."

And that's exactly what they did. Eventually.

Delays crossing the Rockies through bad weather had put hours onto the schedule and the rig that Ozzie's father was due to drive to Chicago didn't arrive until almost one o'clock. It was another hour after that before they finally set out from the depot, Ozzie loaded up with candy bars and comic books bought for him by different men in the depot, all of whom had treated him like he was the President or something. But when they pulled out onto US6, Ozzie's father muttered darkly.

When Ozzie asked what the matter was, Ben Masylik pointed to the sky. One side was almost pitch-black and the other was sunny. Ozzie guessed straightaway that they weren't heading for the sunshine and, sure enough, the road wound round to the right and all that was ahead of them was darkness.

The rain started almost immediately, a drizzle at first but soon building up to a full-scale downpour.

With the windshield wipers going, making a squeaky sound like chalk on a blackboard (which Ozzie didn't much care for), reading his *Action* Comic was pretty much out of the question concentration-wise, even though the story about Superman and two magicians called Hocus and Pocus looked like being a doozy. So he chewed on a Tootie Frootie bar and took out the jar containing Elmer.

"What you got there?" Ozzie's father asked.

At that point, they were about six miles from a place called Atkinson, which Ozzie thought was a strange name for a town . . . until he thought about Pecatonica. Ozzie had seen the signpost.

There were to be lots of occasions down the years when he would wonder whether what happened next was a direct result of his pulling the jar out into the open, momentarily distracting his father's attention from the road ahead. But each time he was to think that, he would discount it.

The road wound sharply to the right, almost a hairpin bend, and the rain was hitting the rig's windshield like someone had a hose trained on it.

Before Ozzie could think of how to answer that question without having to tell his father about the meteor and the way the little amoeba-things had repaired all the grassland, the road was going off one way and they were heading on another.

Rocks added to the situation, or detracted from it, rocks freshly loosened by the rain and fallen down onto the road.

Ozzie watched his father holding onto the steering wheel and shifting down the gears; he felt a sudden lurch and then another, and his father said, as calm as could be, "Blowouts."

He looked across at exactly the same instant as Ben Masylik looked down at him, just a brief look—couldn't have been more than a second or two—but it contained a lifetime of sadness, regret, and guilt. Then he looked back at the road and gritted his teeth.

As Ozzie's father slammed a foot down hard on the brake pedal, he reached out with his right hand and pulled the boy close to him, folding his face into his jacket. Ozzie could smell the sweet aroma of perspiration and soap, of cigarette smoke and body-warmed material. The last thing that Ozzie saw before he nuzzled into his father's jacket was the edge of the road, approaching fast, and a steep drop behind a two-rail fence. Right in the middle of that fence—and right in the middle of the windshield—Ozzie also saw a tall pole with some kind of sign on it.

His face in the jacket, Ozzie felt the rig jerk once, heard the sound of breaking glass, heard—and felt—his father grunt, felt the back of the rig jackknifing around behind them, turning the cab over to the right, and then there was a sudden weightlessness, just for a few seconds, and then he was pulled by some unseen and unimaginable force from his father's arm against something solid, just for another second, and then he fell back against the seat and down onto what had to be the floor—he had his eyes closed, but, jerking out his hand, he felt his father's foot pressed down on a pedal.

There was a lot of crashing sounds all around, and Ozzie was buffeted up beneath the front shelf, and then everything went quiet. Just the sound of rain hitting the cab and the distant hiss of water on hot metal.

Then just one more sound.

Ozzie listened, hardly daring to open his eyes in case they were still falling through space and were about to hit some valley bottom a hundred miles down at the other side of the fence. He could feel the coldness of outside.

The sound he could hear was coming from his father.

Now Ozzie opened his eyes.

He was still lying on the floor, the bench seat behind his back and his face pressed against the rubber mat. All he could see were his father's feet, still pressed down on the pedals and trapped beneath a thin sheet of flooring that had peeled back.

The feet were not moving.

Ozzie wanted to say, *Hey, it's okay, Dad. You can take your feet off the pedals now: we've stopped,* but something deep down inside told him that it wouldn't do any good.

He struggled to his knees. Parts of his body groaned at the movement and he felt a couple of sharp jabs in his back, but it didn't feel much different from when he crashed his soapbox into a tree over by the creek last year. And he was still around to tell the tale of *that* one.

Ben Masylik was lying back on the seat, his head slumped forward onto his chest. Ozzie saw straight away that there was blood. In fact, there was a lot of blood, and it seemed to be increasing as he watched.

His father must have sensed him reaching forward because his father's head moved. It was a slow and precise movement, and, when Ben Masylik's head was in a position where he could actually see his son, he let his eyes do the rest. They looked sleepy.

"Dad, you okay?"

Ozzie shuffled forward and took hold of his father's hand.

The eyes closed, slowly, and then opened again just as slowly. "Go get help," he said. The voice sounded like a cross between a whisper and the hoarse croak you got after a bad head cold. Ozzie noticed that the flow of blood seemed to increase with the words.

"You're hurt, Dad." Ozzie realized how ridiculous that must sound. His father had probably worked that fact out all by himself.

The eyes closed and opened again, this time more slowly . . . like they didn't really want to open at all: they just wanted to close up for good and take Ozzie's father off into a nice deep sleep where the pain wasn't there any more.

Ozzie reached across and lifted his father's head.

The piece of windshield fell out of Ben Masylik's throat and slid down his chest. As it moved, a thin spout of blood sprayed up into the air. It was only then that Ozzie realized the windshield had gone and they were covered in pieces of glass, some of them large but most of them tiny shards that crunched under his knees.

"Dad!"

Ben looked at his son with a profound sadness. His mouth started to move. *Get out,* the mouth said without any sound, the eyes drooping closed again. He lifted a shaking hand and moved it to his neck. Just before the hand covered the wound, Ozzie saw just how bad things really were.

Ben Masylik's neck looked like someone had taken a saw to it. There was blood everywhere, some of it spurting—even now, around his hand—and some of it just seeping out, in tiny waves.

Ozzie clenched his eyes tight and then opened them again.

He's dying, a tiny voice said in the back of his mind. *He's dying like they die in the western movies and in the* Mr. District Attorney *comic books, only this time it's your dad who's doing the dying . . . and my, isn't there a lot of blood.*

Ozzie took hold of his father's free hand and almost gasped at the coldness of it. It felt clammy and frozen, already dead. Even at seven years old, and without so much as a First Aid certificate to his name, he knew that his father would not last until Ozzie could get out and bring help. He patted the hand and said, "You'll be okay, Dad." His father's slow and gentle smile made him turn away.

Then he saw the jar.

It had rolled up against his father's door. He must have

dropped it in the crash. Ozzie leaned across his father's knees and picked it up.

Ozzie let go of his father's hand and ignored the way it simply flopped down onto the seat. He quickly unscrewed the cap and tipped the amoeba thing into the palm of his hand.

"Got a job for you, Elmer," Ozzie whispered. Was it his imagination or did the thing actually seem to be listening? Certainly, it wasn't moving, which it usually did when it was given a brief moment of freedom.

"You got to fix up my dad," he said.

Then, being careful not to drop the creature, he leaned over his father. As he pressed on his father's legs, reaching around to the neck wound, Ben Masylik whispered, "Eleanor."

Very carefully, holding the amoeba thing tightly in his right hand, Ozzie lifted his father's hand from the wound. It was no consolation that the spray of blood seemed weaker now.

Ozzie placed Elmer on the gaping gash and moved his hand away.

For a few seconds nothing seemed to be happening at all—in fact, Elmer seemed not to know what to do, but just sat there or stood there . . . or whatever it was it did. But then the creature seemed to ebb and flow, to contract and expand. Ozzie leaned down closer so he could see what was happening.

It seemed that Elmer's underbelly was being pushed into the wound like clay into a mold. The process lasted only a few seconds, and then the amoeba-thing stretched itself out thinly across the neck like a membrane, its edges continuing that same fluid rippling movement. Soon even that stopped and there was no movement at all. In fact, as he looked so closely that his nose was almost touching his father's neck, Ozzie could see no trace of the creature at all. But best of all, there was no sign of the wound.

Ozzie moved back on his haunches and took hold of his father's hand again. It didn't seem to feel as cold.

Ben Masylik raised his other hand and lifted it to his neck where he rested it on the spot where, just a few seconds ago, Elmer had worked its wonders. He opened his eyes.

"Ozzie?"

"I'm here, Dad."

"Are you . . . are you okay?" Ben moved his head around and looked straight at his son. The eyes seemed brighter now, seemed to contain life.

"I'm fine," Ozzie said. "A little bruised is all."

Ben smiled and closed his eyes. "Good," he said. Then he slept.

Ozzie considered lighting one of the emergency flares he found in the compartment beneath the dashboard but decided it wasn't necessary—after all, it wasn't completely dark yet and the road up above the ravine was well traveled. And anyway, he didn't know how to light them.

He got out of the cab and crawled back up the ravine to the road, the rain still lashing down on him, waving his arms when he got to the top like he was trying to take off. The first car he saw also saw him, swerved a little and pulled in at the side of the road a few yards ahead.

The events which filled rest of that afternoon kind of got watered down over the years.

Ozzie's father said that he was traumatized, which was probably right.

The truth of the matter was that the man—a Mr. Ward Henshaw from Princeton—drove Ozzie into Atkinson where the sheriff called an ambulance and everyone went back out to the scene of the wreck. By five in the afternoon, Ben Masylik was sitting up in bed in Geneseo District Hospital looking for all the world as though he could climb a mountain, although two thick plaster dressings on his forehead and newly shaved scalp suggested that wouldn't be a great idea.

Eleanor arrived at a little after eight o'clock, given a lift by one of the men from PIE who seemed almost as concerned for Ozzie's father's condition as anyone else. Turned out that the rig wasn't too badly damaged. PIE had an empty rig out at the site before midnight and the load was on its way again by six A.M. Nothing damaged and all present and correct.

In the hustle and bustle, the people at the hospital had removed Ben's clothing and it had been thrown into the trash. While it had caused a few raised eyebrows on the part of the doctor and nurse attending Ben's wounds, the sheer amount of blood on the shirt had been ignored. And why not? There were just two gashes on Ben's head and both of them had been sutured. There didn't seem to be any other injuries to speak of . . . although, while he was drifting under the anesthetic, Ben had rambled on about his neck being sawn almost completely through. This did cause a couple of smiles. But not from Ben's son, who was quickly shooed out into a large waiting area containing a big table littered with copies of *Life* and *The Saturday Evening Post.*

Flicking through the bright pages of a *Post* and keeping one eye on the door behind which his father slept, Ozzie decided to keep quiet about the amoeba-thing. Telling everyone seemed like it would cause more problems than it would solve.

And he maintained that silence all through his father's life.

Ben Masylik had a good life and a long one. In fact, there were times when Ozzie, for one, thought it was maybe just a little too good and too long. Nothing ever seemed to ail Ben . . . although, inexplicably, he took to sitting outside a lot after the accident, simply staring into the night sky, watching the occasional comet or shooting star hurtle through the gloom.

Eleanor died quietly in her sleep in 1996, by which

time Ozzie was long gone from Pecatonica, having moved away to Forest Plains in 1959 where he was now happily living the life he had made for himself. Ozzie's mom had fought the cancer that ravaged her body but in the end it simply overpowered her. Ozzie's father said to him, quietly, that maybe if cancers could think, this one might just recognize that Eleanor Masylik had been a worthy opponent. Ozzie thought that was a nice thought.

Ben had seemed to be okay. Ozzie stayed for a few days after the funeral, quiet days during which—overlooked by the ornate urn containing Eleanor's cremated remains—Ben spent long hours going through drawers and wardrobes, marveling at each new or just forgotten discovery of his wife, sniffing (when he thought his son couldn't see him) at notes she had left or clothes she had neatly folded . . . all in an effort to recapture, albeit briefly, the scent of her fingertips or the lingering perfume of her warmth. But the time came that Ozzie had to go back to his own home, though he asked his father to come back with him . . . even if it were only for a visit.

But, no, Ben wouldn't think of leaving Pecatonica.

Then, less than a week later, Ozzie answered the doorbell to discover his father standing on the other side of the screen door, looking more frail than he had ever looked in his life.

Beside him on the floor stood a small valise.

In the crook of his left arm he held the urn containing Eleanor's ashes.

Ben nodded and, seeming to draw breath in from every corner of his body, announced, "I'm going now, Ozzie. I just came to say good-bye."

"Going?" Ozzie said, pushing open the screen door. "Going where?"

Ben drew breath in, head shaking slightly, and for a second Ozzie thought the old man was just going to fall down right where he stood.

Ozzie helped his father into the house, hoisting the old battered valise carefully only to discover it was so light it might well have been blown inside by a stray gust of wind.

Minutes later, lying on the sofa in his son's lounge, Ben Masylik was fading fast. "Take it easy, Dad," Ozzie told him. "Just get your breath."

"No time," Ben Masylik said. "I know what you did, son."

"What I did? What I did when?"

"The thing—" he patted the side of his neck, "—it told me."

Ozzie felt a shudder build up around the back of his shoulders.

"Sit down, son."

Ozzie sat.

"Everything makes sense now," Ben Masylik said, his voice little more than a whisper. He gave out a little chuckle. "All those evenings I'd sit out there on the porch, staring up into space." Ben shook his head. "I was looking for some sign . . . some sign from out there."

"Out there?" Ozzie leaned forward and rested his hand on his father's knee. "What are you talking about, Dad?"

Ben put a finger to his mouth. "No time for questions," he said softly. "Just let me speak."

Ozzie nodded and settled back in the chair.

And so Ben Masylik explained about the endless blackness and the swirling planets, whispered of the cold journey on the meteor. Then he told of how the meteor grazed a large colorful planet, and how the thing that his son had placed on his neck all those years ago had been tumbled off onto the ruined ground. There were many of them, Ben explained, but only it had been unable to find something to repair . . . something to put right.

"Thanks to you," Ben said, interrupting his own story, "and thanks to a couple of blown tires on a hairpin bend and a careless driver too intent on looking after his passenger, it didn't have too long to wait."

"And so it's been repairing ever since," Ben continued, "putting right anything that happened to go wrong or even looked like it might go wrong. Kind of like shoring up weak beams in an old mineshaft.

"It fixed cells and blood flows, straightened and strengthened brittle bones, massaged strained muscles." He rubbed his head briefly and let his arm flop down to his side. "Even looked after my follicles," he added, with just a trace of a smile. "My father was bald as a coot, and his father before him." Ben pointed at Ozzie. "And if you didn't see fit to grow the half-dozen hairs you still got near on down to your waist before swirling them around your ears, folks'd see that you, too, was pretty much shiny up top."

Ben shook his head and chuckled, and then his face took on an expression altogether more serious. "But there are some things that get broke that *nobody* can fix. Not even the little doodad you put on my neck."

"Elmer," Ozzie said.

His father frowned.

"I called it 'Elmer.' "

Ben licked his lips tiredly. "Well, the time came when your mother died that . . . that I just didn't want to carry on. It wasn't so much a case of breaking a leg or pulling a muscle or a few cells splitting every which way . . . it was a case of me simply wanting to close up the shop and go home."

"But you *are* home," Ozzie said, pointing down at the floor. "This is your home, or it could be."

"No, your mom is my home," Ben said, though Ozzie had to lean a little further forward to catch the words. "She was my easy chair; my cool breeze in the summer and my fireside in the winter. Fact is," he added, a single tear brimming from each eye, "I can't go on. Don't want to go on.

"And that's something your doodad *can't* fix: a broken heart."

Ozzie knelt down beside the sofa and took hold of his father's hand between his own.

"I guess that was when it spoke to me . . . in here." Ben

tapped his head with his free hand. "Asked what was happening . . . though it didn't do it in those words, of course. It did it . . ." He paused and frowned. "Heh, I don't know how in tarnation it did do it, but it did. Pictures, sounds . . ." He shook his head.

"And then it told me all about what happened. And how it, too, wanted to go home."

Ozzie started in amazement. "Back into space?"

"No, home is where the heart is, son, and the heart is where your loved ones are and where your friends are. Applies to every living thing. Now, we don't have a lot of time left to us," he said, struggling into a sitting position. "Here's what you have to do."

Ozzie listened.

At first he was astonished.

At first he refused.

Then refusal became reluctance; and reluctance became "maybe." And that's when he knew he was going to do it. No matter how strange the request might seem, he was going to go through with it. He was going to go through with it because he had just said "maybe" to his father . . . the way his father and his mother used to say "maybe" to him, back when, all those years ago, he had asked if he could stay up to listen a show on the radio or have an extra dime's allowance to buy a new comic book. He knew—and he remembered—"maybe" was just a delayed-action version of "yes."

Ben Masylik died sometime between 10:45 that same day and 5 A.M. the next.

He died someplace between Bloomington—where Ozzie had pulled in at an all-night diner because his father had seen the trucks parked out in the lot—and Rockford, where they stopped for gas with the first rays of autumn sunlight bathing the pumps in the filling station. The way Ozzie had it figured, his father had died soon after the truckstop, just upped and drifted away—the urn containing the last remains of his beloved Eleanor nes-

tled beneath his arm—with the familiar smells of the old
rigs calling him home stronger than ever.

Although the final few miles out on Highway 20 to
Pecatonica were driven in silence, it seemed to Ozzie
that the inside of the car was awash with the sounds and
smells of his youth.

The old turnoff down to his parents' house looked the
same as ever, but somehow, on this morning, it looked
extra-special. Standing there on the early-morning road-
side beside his car, Ozzie couldn't help but feel that if he
ran down that left-hand fork, he'd see his father and
mother standing waiting for him. Couldn't help but feel
that, if he turned around real quick, he'd see a seven-
year-old Will Jenner creeping up behind him, breath
held, arms and clawed hands at the ready to squeeze his
sides. But Ozzie knew that Will wouldn't be there if he
looked . . . but maybe he would be if he didn't. So he didn't
look. He left him be, creeping forever in his memory.

Ben Masylik's neck looked as though a mountain cat
had got hold of him and been interrupted. The only good
thing was that there was no blood. The amoeba-thing had
waited until Ben was gone before it detached itself.
Ozzie pulled the old man clear of the door and laid him
gently on the ground. He stood the urn right next to his
father's arm, actually considering wrapping it around the
urn before deciding that was maybe just a little ghoulish.
Then he took the rock-hammer out of the trunk.

Elmer was sitting—or standing: Ozzie still couldn't
figure out which—on his father's checked shirt pocket,
looking just as sprightly and fit as it did all those years
ago. He placed the creature gently into a small plastic
bag and placed that in his jacket pocket. Then he lifted
his father onto his shoulder, placed the urn beneath his
arm, grabbed hold of the rock hammer, and set off for the
edge of the ravine.

The way down was a little difficult and Ozzie half expected to hear a car pull up and someone shout down to
him *Hey, you need a hand with that dead body, mister?*

but no cars appeared and no voices called. Only the wind and the insects and the birds made a chorus of sound that seemed somehow wholly appropriate.

The whole job took around about an hour.

Scattering his mother's ashes over the body took less than a minute.

The hardest part was breaking up the rock and pulling enough stones out of place to expose a suitable area to conceal the old man; putting them back seemed a whole lot easier. He watched his father's body grow smaller as the rocks were carefully placed to ensure maximum coverage.

Then he removed the plastic bag from his pocket.

He took Elmer out of the bag and nestled it in his hand. "Hey, wittle wascal," he said, "how you doing?" He hadn't expected an answer.

But there had been an open blister on the palm of his hand, caused by wielding the hammer, and the amoeba-thing immediately folded itself across it.

Then the world opened up wide inside Ozzie Masy-lik's head.

He saw/felt/heard/smelled the vastness of space.

He understood—as if he'd ever doubted it—the power of friendship and the security of belonging.

And he learned the power and wonder of watching the future unfold before him in a swirl of color and sound and texture and aroma and taste.

He looked down at his hand and saw Elmer detach itself from the blister. Reaching out, he placed the creature on the freshly split rocks and watched it scurry along a seam amidst the dust.

Then it disappeared.

Then, out of the crack between that rock and the one alongside it, thin shoots of mossy grass appeared, tentatively testing the wind and the air, folding in on themselves and curling out again, spreading each way until they had reached the end.

Then the moss spread to the other cracks between all the other rocks.

As he watched, Ozzie saw the construction of haphazardly-placed rocks heal over and knit together with a lush green, forming a kind of rock garden of tiny swaying fronds and smooth granite.

All the way up to the top of the ravine the rocks were being welded together with the moss.

Ozzie got to his feet, hefted the hammer, and started scrambling back up to the top of the ravine.

By the time he had reached the car the first flowers were already appearing, a myriad colored tiny petals sprouting out of thin stalks, spreading all the way along the bowed path of that long-ago visitor from outer space.

As he started the car he realized what it seemed like: It seemed like jubilation. It seemed like coming home.

WATCHCAT

John DeChancie

John DeChancie has written more than seventeen novels in the science fiction, fantasy, and horror fields, including the acclaimed *Castle* series, the most recent of which, *Bride of the Castle*, was published in 1994. He has also written dozens of short stories and nonfiction articles, appearing in such magazines as *The Magazine of Fantasy & Science Fiction*, *Penthouse*, and many anthologies, including *First Contact*, and *Wizard Fantastic*. In addition to his writing, John enjoys traveling and composing and playing classical music.

MERCER,

This is the first note you will retrieve. If you are reading this, you found it in the exact place I told you it would be: taped to a support strut under the warm-fusion generator in the subbasement of the house. Don't worry about radioactivity. It's the latest unit and bleeds only about .01 rad, about the dose you'd get from a one-ton block of Alabama marble, if you slept on top of it for a night. Walk three paces away, and the dosage halves.

I remember the first one I bought for the place, thirty

years ago. It was an act of defiance that flew in the face of the then-prevalent hysteria about nuclear energy. It bled like a kosher chicken, but Eleanor and I weren't afraid. I'll have to give her that. The girl has, and had, guts. But now she must die, and you must kill her, if you are to collect the one million New Euro price I will pay to have her killed. NE1,000,000 is a lot to pay, even in inflated currency, but the old harridan must go. Her voting stock alone will give me the leverage I need to carry out my plan for domination of the solar system's energy industry. I have been thwarted long enough. Jupiter Hydrogen will be mine, despite what the news services said last week about the Commerce Ministry's censure and threatened consent decree.

I digress. Sorry. If you're reading this, of course you've gained entry to the subbasement and have locked the secret escape door by which you entered. I hope you turned the light off in the tunnel. Actually, I hope you had no need to turn the lights on down there. It would have registered on the energy-management system's records—but the police would never think of looking in those records. No matter. In any event, the lights would have turned themselves off in three minutes.

You are a professional, and I assume you came prepared. Before you entered the basement, you should have scanned it with your instruments for any signs of life. And aside from a roach or a mouse, the only life that would have registered was The Beast. That monstrous alien thing my wife calls a cat. Oh, it looks like one. It looks more like a cat than the common terrestrial variety, an actual cat. Bother, I suppose the damned beast is an actual cat, for all that it was spawned on another world. It purrs, it mews, it hisses and spits. God, does it do those two last! At me, at any rate. It hates me. I sense its evil, and it senses my sensing. My wife says it senses evil in me, of course, and I tell her to go to the devil and take that devilspawn with her.

So sorry. Again, I go off the trail. What is important is

that the cat, though an alien species of same, is just as harmless (unless you try to touch the damnable thing) as the terrestrial type—with one exception, for our purposes. It must have at one time in its evolution been kin to the equivalent of a watchdog, for unlike an Earthly kitty, on sensing an intruder it will not merely run and hide; it will send up an appropriately unearthly howling the likes of which you have never heard. The hairs on my neck rise at the very thought. Its scream will wake Eleanor, she will alert the estate's private security forces, and that will be the end of your little adventure, and our little conspiracy.

So, if you are still in the basement reading this missive, and the security people are not now bursting through the basement door, you are safe. The Hellcat was not prowling the nether regions of the house as it sometimes does. It is somewhere upstairs, either skulking through the mansion's many rooms, or eating, or—the likeliest scenario—sleeping, for the critter apes its terrestrial kin in its predilection for constant napping. When it isn't hissing and spitting at me like a psychotic carpet remnant come alive, it is either sleeping or eating its costly special food, for which I have to pay through the nose. Against my will, I keep the bloody thing alive. Specially modified protein with altered DNA, and all that. And other delicacies, which we will get to shortly. The cost of one meal would feed ten families in Baja Mexico for a year.

Again, I wander. Now, my dear Mercer, listen closely to what you must do. You must make your way upstairs, quietly, oh so quietly, and there find The Beast and outfox it. I gave you instructions on how to neutralize every intruder detection system in the house. Now I must advise you that unless you neutralize the biological burglar alarm that I unwillingly harbor in my own domicile, you will fail in your mission, and we will fail to pull off our cute little caper.

You must now ascend to the first level, the finished

basement, where you'll find the game room, bar, bowling alley, squash court, gym, and sauna room. The critter might be lurking there, and you will have to be mighty careful not to alert it. Before you go up, you will, of course, go back to the master security box on this level and disarm the movement detectors on the level above. But as you know, you must go directly to the control box on the next level to reactivate the detectors, lest their inoperativeness draw suspicion at the security guard-house, outside. You must reprogram the detectors to ignore the large moving object which is you. The detectors will then scan you, learn to recognize you, and ignore you thereafter. We have covered this in a previous communication.

Now, as with all past messages from me to you, eat this note. Yes, go ahead, and don't be worried. As I've told you, the paper is rice-based, and is quite tasty. The ink is mere food coloring. Fully digestible, it will dissolve in your stomach, and with it all verbal record of our conspiracy. Hurry up now, chew it thoroughly, and let us proceed. You will find the next note taped to the underside of the bar in the fully equipped barroom. You have seen the schematic for the house. You know where it is. See you there presently. By the way, watch yourself as you move through the basement. There are any number of low pipes and dozens of varieties of high-tech house machinery—there is even a small plutonium-run static reactor for the auxiliary lighting system. The plutonium, a small amount, is encased inside a half-ton of shielding, so don't fret. Just watch your step.

Yours,
Rappaport

Mercer

Congratulations on reaching the basement level. Nice, isn't it? It cost a fortune, and I rarely use it. Some of Eleanor's friends and guests use it, not very often. Thus the entire place sits and . . . well, it doesn't gather dust.

The dombots keep it squeaky clean and honor-bright. It depresses me, sometimes, to visit those plush purlieus, to see all those high-tech exercise gizmos hulking there like paralyzed robots. And the empty barroom. I had it designed to resemble a club Eleanor and I frequented, back when she and I were young, and the moon was bright. . . .

Ah, again I am off on footpaths lost in the undergrowth. Back to the main agenda, which is the imminent death of my once-lovely helpmate, Eleanor. You have scanned for the Hellbeast and found it . . . him? . . . I never did get it straight . . . found it not to be around. Good. So far, so good, to coin a phrase.

Check and make sure that the Hellkitten is not about— pro forma, because the beast would be wailing now if it had seen you—then proceed to the first level of the mansion. Upstairs is a maze of rooms—drawing rooms and sitting rooms and dining rooms, a big ballroom, library, Eleanor's private office, my private office, main kitchen, dombot stations, and on and on and on. And I haven't even mentioned the conservatory and music room. As I say, a maze, and one in which you could easily go astray. I hope your visual memory is as good as you say it is, because if you go stumbling around up there, the Devilcat is sure to hear you, and you are sunk.

Therefore, you must thoroughly, and I mean thoroughly, check out that level before you enter, using that marvelous gear of yours. You must send your detection beams well ahead of you. I have given you samples of Hellbeast's biological detritus, and your instruments can recognize those molecules to the point that if one single molecule of pheromone registers kinetic energy, your silent alarms will go off. The movement of the molecules will mean that the cat is about, prowling. If you detect no movement of these biological telltales, then this means that the cat is elsewhere, upstairs, on the next level, perhaps.

If you detect the beast on the level above, you must

wait until it leaves, goes upstairs, before you enter. And I hope it will eventually. For on this next level lies the means of outfoxing the cat. I will explain in the next note. For now, *bon appetit,* and good work so far. The next note is in the kitchen, in a jar marked *Fines Herbes.* The jar is in a rack of about five hundred different herbs and spices. Oh, maybe not that many, but you'll see it immediately. It's set up against the wall on the counter between the refrigerator and the Turkish coffee machine.

Oh, almost forgot. On the next level you might meet a dombot going about some nighttime mission on its schedule, for instance the dusting of areas that see heavy daytime use. The dombots are not security devices. They are not programmed to squawk if they detect unknown visitors. Too much of a chance of flustering a guest in the house. If you encounter one, it will approach and politely ask if it can help you. You will then utter the code word "Parmenides," and it will clam up and go clanking about its business. Thereafter, pay it no mind. It will not deter you in any way.

Later, upstairs.

Yours in crime,

Rappaport

Mercer,

Again, kudos accrue to you and your resourcefulness in getting this far. You have scanned the coast, and it was clear. Any meddling 'bots have been dispatched on their appointed rounds. Huzzah. The Feline That Ate Cleveland is upstairs sleeping, as I had hoped. Now comes the tricky part. You must bait, lure, and entrap the Hellcat.

Here's how you do that thing. You must go to the larder, which is just off the kitchen. Open the enormous freezer. You will see a large box labeled "Alien Rodentoids." That's right, rodentoids. Frozen. In cryogenic suspension, really. No, it doesn't take liquid nitrogen or anything so exotic to freeze the buggers into suspended animation. Almost any temperature below freezing will send them into a cross between suspended animation and hibernation. You must open the box, select one of the critters, and then go out to the kitchen sink and run warm water—quietly, gently—over it until it comes alive again. I warned that you might not believe it, but it is true. The thing is from the same planet that orbits the godforsaken star—I always forget what it's called—Beta Something—that the fiendline hails from. Why the hell those astronauts took the risk of hauling them back. . . . Maybe it wasn't a risk, and they breed magnificently in captivity—and all the world's ailurophiles want one of the bloody beasts. You would not believe what I had to pay, and who I had to bribe, to get one for Eleanor, who absolutely, positively had to have one, or she'd die of a broken heart. They're so cute, so cuddly, so beautiful, oh, and they look just like our cats, only more so. So what, I say. I think they're ugly. Shaggier than a Persian, obscenely plump, with a mouth cast into a perpetually conceited sneer. And those extra-long whiskers. We don't even know what whiskers on a conventional cat are for. Beautiful my eye. Looks to me like a cross between a walrus and an animated shag carpet. But you know all this, and again I meander.

All right, let's get down to it. Do the thing with the rodentoid—ugly aren't they? Elongated bodies. They look like ferrets. Pink ferrets. And here's what you do with it. First, don't worry, it's harmless. Take the revivified furry thing and push it through the tiny door to the monster cat's playroom. Yes, our Terwilliger—didn't I tell you the thing had a name?—has his . . . its . . . own playroom, a plush haven filled with cat jungle gyms, playhouses, multilevel platforms, high perches, furry boxes, straw baskets, and canvas bags. These are all of Terwilliger's favorite things. Shove the animal through the door. It will run and try to hide somewhere in the room.

And there's the curious thing. Terwilliger will eventually awaken. The ferret animal makes hypersonic cries that only the Fiendcat can hear. It will hear the thing mewling away inside the strange playroom.

Hide in the closet just across the hall from the play-room door. Wait until Terwhosis appears—and you will realize that he's not much to look at, really. Just a damned cat, a little bigger than our variety, and a little strange looking. A simple cat. Oh, how looks deceive. For in this beast is pent up all the furies of Hades. Any-way, wait till it appears. Don't let it see you. Wait until it slips through the door to the playroom. And then, quickly, before it realizes what it's hearing outside, slide the big Federal highboy, sitting just to the right of the tiny swinging door, over the entrance and block it. There is another door to the playroom, of course, for the dom-bots and we humans, but it is always locked.

The beast will be trapped. There is no way out. It is an intelligent beast, to be sure, but it is not up to deducing that there is an intruder in the house, much less what the intruder is up to. Besides, he will be a while stalking, killing, and eating the rodentoid. Takes his time. Good that you will not see the process, either, for it distresses even my unsqueamish sensibilities, and may yours. These star cats outshine their earthly brethren in the ferocity of their sadistic hunting habits. They stalk, they pounce, they tease, they torture; cruelly they play felinoid-and-rodentoid. Then, while the poor prey is still alive and kicking, they eat, slowly, methodically, deli-cately. It is exquisite torment of a kind even humans are incapable of. I've watched the whole game, and it sick-ens me to realize that the cat is doing it deliberately, in-telligently, relishing every twitch and scream. For the prey screams hideously the while. As my boy used to say when he was a teen, of anything that disquieted him, "Grosses me out, Dad!" It grosses one out, to be sure.

Oh, hell, I shouldn't have mentioned Stanton. He's in Los Angeles, and God knows what he's doing there. Los Angeles hasn't been habitable for half a century. Who knows what cult, what motley gang, what gaggle of degenerate subhumans he's hanging with. Who knows what chemicals he's ingesting. And who cares. I ceased to long ago. He's long since cut off, disinherited, disowned. He is not my son. But once he was. I loved him. I miss those blond curls, those happy times. I miss the way he used to . . .

Enough. We have work to do. Mind that you move the highboy gently. If any of that antique china comes crashing down, not only will I be out thousands of euros in useless old plates (thousands, ye flipping gods!—for what, for what?), you and I will have failed utterly, because for all that Eleanor saws logs like a British Columbian lumberjack, she will surely hear that, and so will the sound detectors. And the jig will be up, my covert friend.

Barring any accidents, the highboy will block egress, and Hellbeast will be trapped until morning. I've researched the question, and the best authority I could consult has it that these critters do not possess a keen sense of smell. So, there isn't much chance that Devilcat will sense your presence. And your various devices and garments and such which neutralize your biological exudations should do their job and take care of any residue of probability.

Now to the main event. The killing of Eleanor. First, though, you should know a few things about the upstairs. I will cover this in yet another billet-doux, which you will find tucked under the carpet at the top of the main staircase, second step down, to the right, against the base of the banister. Sit on the stairs quietly and read it. And then we will be ready for the climax of the evening.

Your pal,

Rappaport

P.S.—By the way, don't forget to make a snack of this message. Mustn't leave incriminating evidence for the gendarmes.

* * *

My dear Mercer,

I think we can now speak as friends. As you sit on the steps, I want to take this opportunity to thank you for doing this my way. The read-instructions-as-you-go method has saved a lot of prior meeting and planning as well as limiting interceptible communication. All our written communication has been read-and-eat, and we spoke briefly face-to-face once in a dark bar in Tangier, thereby drastically reducing the chances that the two of us can be linked. The mechanics of getting into the house and doing the deed would be, as I predicted, very complex and a mite difficult to understand. That is why I insisted on doing it this way, step-by-step, ploddingly, carefully, with written instructions to give you time to study them and obey them to the letter. You see now why I insisted on this method. We are very near success. Hellbeast has been dealt with, security has not been triggered, and all is well for the moment.

However, the floor above presents more problems. The hallways are constantly being scanned by beam after beam, and any shape they don't recognize, they pile up on and howl. All hell breaks loose. These are semi-intelligent systems, and they know me and Eleanor, they know Terwilliger and the dombots, but they do not know you. You will be an anomaly. You will be tagged as an intruder.

How you will negotiate this trap is beyond me, but I have every confidence in your skills, which come highly recommended to me. This is your specialty, I am told, and you told me yourself. Foxing intelligent security devices. How you will do the thing, I do not know, and you would likely be loath to reveal your trade secrets. Still, I'm tantalized. Will you fool the things into thinking that you are me? Eleanor? Terwilliger, perhaps? Horrors! Or some other way? Whichever way, you will do it, and you will enter Eleanor's bedroom and fire a silenced bullet into her cranium. And she will be dead, my long lost darling.

Oh, where is that seventeen-year-old girl I married? There is a picture of her. God, you should see her. You should have seen her then. She was still a girl, lovely as a spring morning, face radiantly girlish and beautiful, and in this picture the sunlight catches her hair and sets it afire into a yellow-white halo. She is demurely wrapping her arms about a silver maple sapling just abud and looking at the camera and smiling a smile of innocence and youth and sex and romance, all at once. We were young lovers, and the days were warm and long and the nights were cool and soft.

Oh, God, there I go again. Indulge me, Mercer. You are the trenchantly silent type, muted emotions, all business. I am supposed to be a heartless capitalist, but most people would be surprised at the poignancy with which the tenderer emotions assail me. I grieve for Eleanor even now, a full night before she leaves me forever. We hate each other now . . . God have mercy . . . how can things change so radically? How can a bright, burning golden love be transmuted into a lead-dead thing over the span of a few years? Was it money? Was it me? Oh, it was me, it was my money, it was a hundred regrettable words and retorts and recriminations. It was the stress of big business. It was my fault. But I have no choice. She threatens, with her lawyers, to throw not a monkey wrench into the machinery of my ambitions, but to take that machine apart nut by bolt. I can't let it happen. I have obligations! People's livelihoods depend on me! Oh, sure, you can say that I never gave a fig for other people or their livelihoods before, but most people don't realize that I work for the benefit of the public! I create wealth, vast amounts of it, not only for myself but for the world and its billion-footed masses! You must believe me, you must. . . .

What's the use. Why am I going on like this? Why am I telling you this? You, of all people, who mustn't be distracted from your demanding task. Eat this note, chew it up, let it be gone forever, just like my darling seventeen-year-old love. (Egad, am I in my dotage lusting for the Eternal Nymphet? Is that what's bothering me? Just a yen to screw once again a woman who has not yet reached majority? It may be true that men get kinkier as they grow old. "Dirty old man" is an unkindness, but it may be based on an irrepressible observation.)

Enough. Go ahead and work your high-tech wiles. Thread your way to her room and do the deed, and be done. Afterward, break into the safe in her room—behind the original early Van Gogh—the painting of peasants eating a humble dinner—you know Van Gogh's style if not the actual painting, being a man of culture as well as stealth. (How I wish we had had time to talk in that darkened den in Tangier! I enjoyed our time together. You are an amazing man.) Crack the safe and steal the jewels. They are yours, as an added bonus.

Then repair to my private office and library. Make yourself a drink at the little bar. Relax. You will have nothing but time then, afterward. The house will be quiet, you will have defeated all its intelligences, alien and machine, and your mission will be accomplished. See you there, then, where, taped under the third left-hand door in my desk, which you surely can open (no alarms or anything on it), you will find a final missive, this one just a chatty note to wrap things up. There's a good chap. Go now, and make the world safe for monopoly capitalism.

Your client and friend,
Rappaport

My dear, dear Mercer,

First an apology. That drink is probably going down hard on a sour stomach. As you may have deduced by now, the notepaper was poisoned. You have ingested quite enough toxin to kill you. It will take a few more minutes, and in the meantime be comforted with this apology.

Don't worry, it will be swift. You will die of a massive

coronary occlusion, engineered not by poison, per se, but by a potent molecular nanotechnology weapon. It is, in principle, untraceable, not because your average forensic pathologist would be unfamiliar with it (which is quite true), but because after it does the job of sabotaging your coronary arteries, it will break apart into its component elements, all of them common to the body. There will be no trace of the device left, and unless the coroner in question is also a nanotech engineer, an unlikely eventuality, he or she will suspect nothing. Not a blessed thing.

This murder will be our secret. You see, I could not take the chance that an old spook like you is not working for one of any number of hostile corporations. I checked you out over and over, I screened you, I investigated you. And then investigated the investigators. But this is a world in which a certain degree of paranoia is completely justified. I know for a fact that there are vast conspiracies out there arrayed against me. God, I've been informed of the fact! People have threatened me for years, some to my face. I could not take a chance on you. You see that, don't you, Mercer?

So now, you will be a dead body in my house. A body I will discover on going into my office. Not only did I need an ironclad alibi for this evening, I needed to be expunged of all suspicion. You will be not an assassin, but a high-tech jewel thief, and your death will be strange but not uncommon. Forty-eight-year-old men die of sudden heart attacks every day. The stresses of this difficult caper were too much for you. You had a heart attack, and you died, your pockets stuffed with my wife's jewels. My wife, whom you murdered in her sleep. Unusual, but not unheard of.

So, sorry, old man. Eleanor must die, and so must her killer. I would have had you go after Fiendline as well, but that beast, I think, is unkillable. I didn't want to take the chance. I once bumped into him and found him to be as hard as steel under all that fur. My wife says that he's all muscle under there. He weighs three times what you'd expect. Not that I ever picked that Hellbeast up. Eleanor told me.

Well. I'll cease to natter, and leave you to do your dying. I will be home soon. I will come into the office to put away some papers, and I will feign surprise, to no one. Oh, who is this? Why, my God, it's an intruder, and I will rush upstairs to see about Eleanor. I'll react, even though no cameras will record my reaction. I'll do it just in case there are cameras that I don't know about. Eleanor's cameras. Corporate cameras, police cameras, whatever. Just in case.

No, this note is not poisoned. Any human touch triggers a reaction that will cause it to disintegrate to dust in about three minutes. I won't have to dispose of it. It will be gone. House dust. No traces, no witnesses, no worries.

Good-bye Mercer. You are a man of the world, and you know how these games are played. Still, I'm sorry. Rest easy. You did a brilliant job. Truly. You have unique talents. I don't know of any other covert operator who could have defeated the security measures of this house. For what it's worth, you have my admiration and my hearty congratulations. That's something, isn't it?
With regret,
Rappaport

Dear Mr. Rappaport,

You will come home, enter your private office, and see no body. You will rush to your desk and retrieve this note, which you did not write. I wrote it, on your voicewriter, on ordinary paper. Oh, I can speak. Perfectly, Mr. Rappaport. And I have read every one of your messages to Mercer. I observed you stashing every one.

Mercer is dead, all right, but I caught him as he entered the subbasement. And dealt with him there. I killed him quickly, then ate him just as quickly, every scrap of him. To do this, to accommodate his considerable bulk, I had to revert temporarily to my natural form, which is much bigger than the creature that you call "Terwilliger." We are a shape-shifting race, Mr. Rappaport, something you could not know. No one on Earth knows it. Now.

We originally planned to take over your world in a straightforward way. Infiltrate—I am the vanguard of that invasion—and conquer. But those plans may change.

I like being a cat. I like the way cats are treated here. They are kings. They control their owners. They own their owners. We took the form of cats . . . well, let's not go into that. Like you, I have tendency to digress. I'll stick to the issue at hand.

Mercer. Oh, yes. I ate him, ballooning up to my regular size, which is about that of a Kodiak bear (though we look nothing like that Earth creature). And just as ferocious. Ten times as ferocious. I went to the kitchen and regurgitated him, then stuffed him into a dozen plastic bags, packed him into the freezer and labeled the parcels "Hamburger," though "Manburger" would be more appropriate. I did this all quietly (I have fully prehensile forepaws and walk upright in my natural form), as your mate slept her usual deep sleep. So much for Mercer. Then, I waited. For you. I am still waiting . . . for you to finish reading this. I am right behind you. Compact and catlike again, I am sitting just behind the curtains on the bay window. The moment you finish, I will do a quick metamorphosis and spring up to my fighting size, and I will then deal with you. But not the quick way. I will proceed to dispatch you in the method we reserve for the foodcreature, the "rodentoid." I will eat you very slowly. I assure you, Eleanor will not wake up, for I have drugged her for this very reason. I have been wanting to eat you for a long while, Mr. Rappaport. For a very long while. For I detect in you all that is nasty about humans. But you understand why I like to indulge in this kind of play, sir. You are a predator yourself.

As I said, we originally planned on taking over your world with a combination of stealth and force. But soon Eleanor will virtually control the entire world by herself, and as I control Eleanor, it seems senseless to do anything other than to go along with our good fortune. More "cats" will be imported from our home system. More will be bred here. Colonists they will be. In time, I suppose, we will tire of being pampered pets, and will take over de jure as well as de facto. But maybe not. We share with Earth cats a lazy streak. Perhaps we will do the pampered pet thing for a couple of centuries before we tire of it. Who knows?

That's about it, Mr Rappaport. Now, turn around, and behold the race called the Yuzloon in all our ferocious and warlike glory. Behold the race of "pets" that has come to master you! Turn around, and be afraid. Be very afraid. I like that so much.

Cordially,

"Terwilliger"

a.k.a. Mrrwoluu the Fierce and Terrible, High Operative of the Council of War and the Subjugation of Inferior Beings

THEY'RE COMING TO GET YOU. . . .
ANTHOLOGIES FOR NERVOUS TIMES

☐ **FIRST CONTACT**   UE2757—$5.99
Martin H. Greenberg and Larry Segriff, editors

In the tradition of the hit television show "The X-Files" comes a fascinating collection of original stories by some of the premier writers of the genre, such as Jody Lynn Nye, Kristine Kathryn Rusch, and Jack Haldeman.

☐ **THE UFO FILES**   UE2772—$5.99
Martin H. Greenberg, editor

Explore close encounters of a thrilling kind in these stories by Gregory Benford, Ed Gorman, Peter Crowther, Alan Dean Foster, and Kristine Kathryn Rusch.

☐ **THE CONSPIRACY FILES**   UE2797—$5.99
Martin H. Greenberg and Scott Urban, editors

We all know that we never hear the whole truth behind the headlines—let Douglas Clegg, Tom Monteleone, Ed Gorman, Norman Partridge and Yvonne Navarro unmask the conspirators and their plots—if the government lets them. . . .

☐ **BLACK CATS AND BROKEN MIRRORS**   UE2788—$5.99
Martin H. Greenberg and John Helfers, editors

From the consequences of dark felines crossing your path to the results of carlessly smashed mirrors, authors such as Jane Yolen, Michelle West, Charles de Lint, Nancy Springer and Esther Friesner dare to answer the question, "What happens if some of those long-treasured superstitions are actually true?"

Prices slightly higher in Canada.   **DAW 215X**

Don't Miss These Exciting DAW Anthologies

SWORD AND SORCERESS
Marion Zimmer Bradley, editor
☐ Book XV   UE2741—$5.99

OTHER ORIGINAL ANTHOLOGIES
Mercedes Lackey, editor
☐ SWORD OF ICE: And Other Tales of Valdemar   UE2720—$5.99

Martin H. Greenberg & Brian Thompsen, editors
☐ THE REEL STUFF   UE2817—$5.99

Martin H. Greenberg, editor
☐ ELF MAGIC   UE2761—$5.99
☐ ELF FANTASTIC   UE2736—$5.99
☐ WIZARD FANTASTIC   UE2756—$5.99
☐ THE UFO FILES   UE2772—$5.99

Martin H. Greenberg & Lawrence Schimel, editors
☐ TAROT FANTASTIC   UE2729—$5.99
☐ THE FORTUNE TELLER   UE2748—$5.99

Martin H. Greenberg & Bruce Arthurs, editors
☐ OLYMPUS   UE2775—$5.99

Elizabeth Ann Scarborough & Martin H. Greenberg, editors
☐ WARRIOR PRINCESSES   UE2680—$5.99

Prices slightly higher in Canada.   **DAW 105X**

A feline lovers' fantasy come true . . .

CATFANTASTIC